brütt, or The Sighing Gardens

AGM COLLECTION

AVANT-GARDE & MODERNISM

brütt, or The Sighing Gardens

FRIEDERIKE MAYRÖCKER

Translated from the German by Roslyn Theobald

Northwestern

University Press

Evanston

Illinois

Northwestern University Press
www.nupress.northwestern.edu

Printed in the United States of America

10 9 8 7 6 5 4 3 2 1

Library of Congress Cataloging-in-Publication Data

Mayröcker, Friederike, 1924–
[Brütt. English]
Brutt, or, The sighing gardens / Friederike Mayröcker ; translated from the German by Roslyn Theobald.
p. cm. — (Avant-garde and modernism collection)
"Originally published in German in 1998 under the title Brutt oder Die seufzenden Garten [...] by Suhrkamp Verlag."
ISBN-13: 978-0-8101-1966-6 (pbk. : alk. paper)
ISBN-10: 0-8101-1966-8 (pbk. : alk. paper)
I. Theobald, Roslyn. II. Title. III. Title: Brutt. IV. Title: Sighing gardens. V. Series: AGM collection.
PT2625.A95B7813 20078
833.914—dc22

2007026907

∞ The paper used in this publication meets the minimum requirements of the American National Standard for Information Sciences—Permanence of Paper for Printed Library Materials, ANSI Z39.48-1992.

When I washed my steps with butter, and the rock poured me out rivers of oil . . .

—Job 29:6

in a letter from X (or William or Ferdinand): "I think I should write to you now while I can still hear your unexpected voice resonating and chiming through the day.

"If this is still going to appear at the beginning of the prose you have borrowed from me, then please, by all means, leave out the 'probably,' even if I did—wrongly—write it that way. '*I am now living a love story : my last*' is how it must read.

"The joy I wrote about to you is of course not all that happened, there is also a sense of dismay at how happy and unhappy I can be at one and the same time—that I am again as callow and naive as I have ever been, and to a degree I never imagined possible. But, be that as it may, you will find a way to your language without the BACKGROUND COLORATION of what I have experienced, and it will be a language not all that much in need of mine . ."

9/13

"and doughy voice / my Papa departed and Mama"

step-by-step one foot and then the other leaving the house less and less often walking more and more slowly as if A HOBBLE, A WEIR, A DAM had been built into you, down there, and less and less interested in going out because now seeing less well—put glasses on take glasses off : both equally bothersome / distracting, everything somewhat displaced blurred, right, not in the proper perspective, taking every thing in the street for another thing . . *strange and misperceived* (Beckett), and the annoyance at not recognizing people you know quickly enough, not until the very last moment, sketch out the contours of someone close to me, like allusion on paper, etc., greetings mostly from people I don't know, return the greeting, almost always too late when friends colleagues passing me, always going the same way, familiar surroundings preferred, every house every park bench familiar, falling leaves / already autumn, soon the beginning of October, and when you are among a circle of friends acquaintances : at first not really being able to make out who is there, head and build, simply replying when greeted, kisses on both cheeks then withdrawing to one place and observing events as they proceed, registering every word, taking down a few notes, most undecipherable once back at home, because written in too much haste, then sitting down at my typewriter again, and when sunlight infiltrates in the afternoon reluctantly closing the curtains—growing more and more estranged from the outside world, more and more apprehensive about events in the outside world, avoiding every possible danger, every kind of RISK, etc., scenting complications everywhere, and then over the course of my day, no longer even adept enough at crossing the street, sometimes the fluttering hem of a coat by a car, I mean already TRAPPED, already BEING DRAGGED ALONG by a car turning into the street, and looking back out of the corner of one eye to see if maybe run over, imagination still in good working order, so EXAGGERATED, almost everything EXAGGERATED, or raced across the tracks right in front of an oncoming streetcar, etc., always in a panic, breaking out in a sweat back and chest forehead and neck, always furious at all the noise, and the appearance of all those characters scattered around : visor of baseball cap turned to the back, afraid, they might attack you, avoid eye contact! afraid of bicycle riders, who come from all directions at breathtaking speed DARTING : SHOOTING : at the very last moment giving way / braking / roaring past, and skateboarders, in-line skaters on sidewalks, cobblestone streets, paved playgrounds etc. and finally wanting to withdraw *totally,* but not wanting to show it in any way, always acting as if you still belonged, as if you were still keeping up, with entrancing attributes : backpack, windbreaker beret set at angle over your right ear . . laughing and joking when someone who recognizes you stops in the street and asks HOW ARE YOU?—(perhaps thinking : THE OLD LADY'S STILL KICKING AROUND!). Oh appearances I mean appearances : appearances can be kept up for a long time, after all, appearances are helpful, and laughing and joking and hoping, the encounter, the meeting soon over, nothing between me and getting home, where still equilibrium and sanctuary, after all, then finally alone and secluded and no one there to disturb you and no longer necessary to worry about showing any kind of consideration or kindness, right, alone with yourself, *at last,* quiet, and doing whatever you feel like doing or not doing anything at all, stretched out on that broken old bed for hours, telephone next to your pillow and hoping that no one will call and just being there for yourself and just starting to let thoughts, observations surface, and think about a way out of this mess again, etc. and then suddenly, from one moment to the next, a distinct sense of well-being and solace, and the wish that everything would just stay as it is, fervently hoping no changes, no deterioration, and wanting only to write and be undisturbed and yearning for lots of letters, especially from Joseph, and looking out of the window more and more often and reading in a book—not necessarily from the first to the last page, most of all reading around in books that have an attractive typeface, and making excerpts so you won't forget, of things that have pleased you, right, but soon forgetting, actually forgetting, because scrap of paper or notepad misplaced, *writing on the wane,* writing (basically) : in vain, etc. and paging back : what was that word that sentence that train of thought, and then thinking about how, just a few years ago, you still could race up every slope, every steep rise in every street, the stairway, and how clear your vision was, how little harm everyday affronts seemed to cause, in any case everything still tolerable then, everything surmountable, and, again and again, always thinking about developments, changes, difficulties, always aware of how time passes, how quickly weeks months years, how quickly spring and fall and again / winter and summer, and wardrobe changing : fur coat, swimming suit, beret, wool turban, rain boots, fisherman sandals—and time simply disappearing, and the way it simply disappears, expires—where to? like one wave in a stream which we can follow for a long while, then gone—and so is this day this hour this breath, a plunge into time . . and it never gave out this time this hour this half day this week, this month, the favorite season, the year, the recurrence of private celebrations, right, the encounters the lovers the rain the enchanting tones the exhilarating word the beloved voice, *the eyes the eyes connecting and in flames . .*

9/15

oh these days are making me happy again, cascading geraniums, and *I'm raking out what there is to be raked out,* I tell Blum, this old manuscript, once half-gone, I say, now seems to have found new life, I say, I run around all day in a white smock and my hair tied back, because I have so much to do, so much to write, suddenly everything is multiplying in front of my inner eye, everything seems to have CAUGHT FIRE again, a late-blooming stand of wild roses, chestnut trees in blossom for a second time, in pink and white, I can feel how all this is lifting my spirits, on one slip of paper I find a note : "a little flirt, nothing serious : a few little sheep among the clouds . . ," and all of a sudden I feel I'm happy that I can't open either my dresser or my closet, yes, it almost amuses me, my closets are blocked off, I say, with overnight bags, suitcases, work materials, piles of paper, books, notebooks, cloth napkins painted and scribbled on (with a felt-tip pen), wayward bird stuff, etc., it's been a long time since I've been able to take a bath, I say, I enjoy seeing the bathtub stuffed full of junk and pages of manuscript, *there is also the experience of direct entry into a piano,* I write to X (or William or Ferdinand), I mean no tone, no music out of it at all, because stuffed all the way out to the sides with mummified objects, dog bodies (?DALÍ?), etc., CLUBBING OF A DIFFERENT SORT, I tell Blum, half-filled with water, the broken cooking pot under the footstool, to pour over my head ("head rinse"), when brain begins to boil, for dunking head, the way I used to those summers as a child, dunked my head and hair into a large rain barrel on hot August days, and embraced the sun and sweet winds, etc.

Am an *uneven* person, I say to Blum, yet shaken by a blissful ecstasy, oh these happy days, in which EVERYTHING appears to me in a state of melting enchantment, uncommon days, I tell Blum, I see rooftop antennae

pulling microbes down out of the sky, we are probably all going to get ill from the astral excreta infiltrating our houses through satellite dishes, I catch myself talking to my dead mother, I say to her, Blum always has a clean handkerchief with him, good manners, and when he is thanking someone for something over the telephone, he makes a slight bow, as if the person he is speaking to were standing right in front him, *threadbare old stuff, worn-out goods,* Blum says, I am not sure whether he only means the old pots, cracked plates or my notes too, why don't you just throw everything out?, Blum says, PIETY, I say, everything PIETY, forbearance, patience, successful attempt to identify with living creatures, things (apparent) fidelity, taking yourself back, nothing but piety, I say, actually untenable, actually inappropriate, actually out of tune with the times, *not popular,* still you keep at it, etc.
As far as X (or William or Ferdinand) is concerned, I might add : that he writes, *all he can really think about is ocean ecstasy nothing but ocean ecstasy, he's going to experience the transformation of all things on his own body,* and then I dream that I'm telling Blum : LET ME BE YOUR ECKERMANN!, and to this he replies in my dream : a collapse of the connectedness of the senses is responsible for the general insanity and the ascendancy of brutality . . LAMBNESS, pleasantness, I say, cannot be equated with beauty : animals lack an aesthetic component, in front of the windows, the verandas the *eternal pond,* no not frond, *my platter my telephone running by.* Oh, this Odeon throat, oh these days dripping like honey, I shout, as far as X (or William or Ferdinand) is concerned, he is a big and independent spirit not easily understood, I tell Blum, he should have taken me by the hand and led me into the labyrinth of his soul, then perhaps I might have understood, I believe they've rolled some huge water masses (—melons) into the greengrocer's display and in the depths of the shop window there was a figure operating a lawnmower, in a green garden smock and hat, etc., and during the night I sipped at my entire collection of pain medications because the tension in my shoulders almost unbearable, the METEOROLOGICAL GENIUS and the silk scarf wrapped around my neck, it has suddenly turned cold and wet, I tell Blum, through cracks around the windows a draft sweeping across to the table where I sit, I say, not a bad idea to put on something like a wool cap, hood, beret and muff, right, what does my RABBIT CLOCK say, Blum says, for one reason or another I don't hear his question, although I immediately register the term RABBIT CLOCK, I mean I don't need him to tell me what or whom he is referring to, and me, *for weeks on end,* face over machine, I say, banner of stars in my window because I'm working

at night now, too, everything mysterious in its grounding, I tell Blum, I think that's the catch, often don't really want to know myself what's happening, how all of this is working (playing) out, right, and when people ask me about it, how this all came about, I don't really have an answer or I say something inconsequential, etc., AN ALPINE PLEASURE, I say, as if I were trying to pluck one very specific thread out of a dappled mat, writing is AN ALPINE PLEASURE, and *that's all there is to it!,* I say, but the questions keep coming, no, I don't get any ideas when I write, I say, you have to be taking risks when you're working, I say, there has to be something at stake, your life actually, your health, you have to dare everything, I believe rabidly, I say, without any regard for anyone, least of all for yourself, ignore every rule of good taste, yes : scorn good taste, cross over every and any boundary. When I produce my drawings : amateurish play, when I write : heart ravaging; nothing will work without PERSPECTIVE, I say, and sometimes I believe that I have never really *couraged* enough, this entire attitude toward my writing all too temperate, all too carefully scored, you see, *the kitchen is fluttering.* The stimulating the boundless prayer wheels of language, I say, thighs open scissors slide into the bathwater, then your postcard was lying in my lap, I tell Joseph, Kirk Douglas shows up on television, aging, but in no way aged, I say, A SPECTACLE OF A FACE, I tell Joseph, we are spooning down *instant soup,* we are sharing the soft inside of a roll, crust too hard, I tell Joseph, infantile phase of aging, no escape, I say, nervous leaf top, etc. I was sitting in front of my tent and dozing in the sun, I was sitting at the stove, I was sitting in the laundry room and thinking about Joseph while talking to Blum. Joseph and I, I tell Blum, strangely enough, avoid referring to this my emerging book as "my writing" or "the manuscript" or "the new prose work," instead, if at all, we talk about the PROJECT.

I open one of my favorite books and find the following sentence, which shoots right through me : ". . in the journal you discover that now and then what she wanted was something completely capricious, e.g., *a kiss,* nothing more under any circumstance, because with this particular person it was the most beautiful thing . ."

9/16

in his most recent letter X (or William or Ferdinand) wrote to me from Spain and *he was thinking about ocean ecstasy nothing but ocean ecstasy,* and I wonder, is an ocean ecstasy in Spain different from an ocean ecstasy along the coast of Greece, how do these 2 ocean ecstasies differ, how does 1 ocean ecstasy really differ from another ocean ecstasy, how do skies in different countries differ from 1 another, how do mountain peaks differ . . X (or William or Ferdinand) writes to me that he is thinking about ocean ecstasy nothing but ocean ecstasy, he is writing to me from Spain, on his way to the Greek island we, Blum and I, cannot visit now—all of these things are going through my mind when I think about X (or William or Ferdinand), when I try to make out his inner contours : his contours and mine, perhaps determining 1 another, a kind of CORRELATION, right, I say to Blum, but I don't actually know anything about him, I hardly know him, I hardly recognize him, although we have met so often, written to each other so often, I tell Blum, maybe I'm not really even all that interested in understanding his inner contours, I tell myself, but when he wrote, he was *so sad* that he was having to make the trip to Siphnos alone and that his head was as gloomy as these skies, I felt I was beginning to get some sense of him, and again I recalled our mutual connection with Joseph, that is, the letters that had been flying back and forth between them, and suddenly this circumstance took precedence over everything else, appeared to be more worthy of consideration than anything else. My gaze up to the opened window : dangling from the window latch a paper-thin Chinese doll, in a bluish green silk caftan, red sash, *on wandering feet,* I say, it's on a journey, apparently being drawn along by silk threads—where to? suddenly tears well up in my eyes, when I look at it this way, wandering off into a distance neither he nor I can know anything about, how long has it been living here in my room, I say to Blum, on my window, sometimes it turns its strange somewhat contorted face (contorted in anguish) to me and looks at me, charming in its fine pain, then my throat ties itself up in knots . . *misery of speech?* I wonder, switch my desk lamp on in full daylight, because surrounded by stacks of paper blocking off light and air, etc., the same old song, I say to Blum: *language history,* I say, everything is language history, we just don't want to admit it. Where options are left open to us, I say, where options are left open to us in a work of art, we start searching in vain for some kind of rules to follow, I misread the address of the sender, instead of Schillerplatz : Achillesplatz, I wonder if there is any kind of connection here?, I couldn't tell, was that car in the dark coming toward me or headed away, instead of writing the address "München" most of the time "Mündchen," it occurred to me early this morning that I'm trying for a kind of NOVELNESS in my most recent work, I am striving for NOVELNESS, whatever that means, I say to Blum, what do you think about the *transitions in your work,* a journalist wants to know, but I don't know what to think, I tell him : this constant, I believe *impassioned* attitude of fantasy (and so not actual fantasy) is still an overarching influence, and saw tears on the amputated tree, glittering gold-colored tears of resin, I say, saw roses on tall stems, wilting robinias along the boulevards, the shrimp on my plate, that is the entire secret, or as Botho Strauß says : SUDDENLY THE END RIGHT IN THE MIDDLE OF THE DRESSING ROOM . . but sometimes, I tell Blum, when I take stock of everything, in these miserable, barren hours, it happens that I find myself having to say : I have done everything wrong, I have lost everything, wasted, missed, I headed off in the wrong direction, maybe the AESTHETICS OF LANGUAGE, which has been at the heart of my work since the beginning, was simply the wrong goal in these earthshakingly monstrous times, oh, the composites did it to me, the composers, the strolling, as Elisabeth von Samsonow writes, in her mind she sees me the way I was *strolling,* in her ocher-colored handwriting, an ocher-colored woman's hand with red border around the wrist, offering me a small bouquet of spring flowers, now in the middle of autumn, I tell Blum, stars in bright colors, plump green stems cut in uneven lengths, bundled together with a doubled cord, long-legged out of water (climbing) . .

by date, sorted somewhere, supposed to have noted down, "early, pearly," *The large meadow marigold,* or as it's known here *blood drops,* Angelika Kaufmann writes to me, now in meadows everywhere. For five days, Angelika Kaufmann writes, I have been alone in woodlands and am astounded to see how well I am doing, 6 months after Harry's death—I walk in his tracks, pick up his things, things he had held in his hands, and I do work that he once did. And this is both : sometimes very satisfying and sometimes very sad, so sad that my throat is tied up in knots.

For weeks on end I have had problems with my circulatory system, dream.

A swallow's feet, *a swallow's face,* never seen, I tell Blum, surprising, because the many summers of my childhood spent in their proximity, only beaks, wide-open beaks, when they flew low, almost grazing the village streets, which meant rain, people believed, never heard a nightingale, but recollection of pheasants flapping up into the air, back then, above the bared fields, in this accursed countryside which I will never forget, I tell Blum, oh the source of breath, flames, blackmailing of heads in those midsummer months, the astonished eye, sometimes, even then, tears welled up in my eyes at the sight of abundant wonders, now, after so many decades, I live in agony, in lumberjack's clothing, uprooted-lost, when writing falls to me, I say, I stagger between ottoman and table, catch sight of a bright sky on an early morning, and now rain is forecast, the dear cheek. And keep asking myself, in the middle of all this, engrossed in writing : what is going to come of this, what is the point of this work, after a few years everything will be forgotten, lost, every book I have written, long out of print, everything, everything scattered to the winds, everything in vain, every wave, every breath of air, every lightning bolt of thought as if it had never existed, my books junked, pushed off the market, I believe, there has never been me at all.

And as far as aging is concerned : meaning that this face has been reached inside, into this face of my old age, I believe time has reached inside and left its track inside this face, the dark niches of sunken eyes, the limp cheeks : senile jowl : dimples of a young child but settled down into the lower half of my face, aged and ugly, clownesque, unruly neural pathways, marled feet, body laced with wrinkles.

St. Mark's Square, I tell Joseph, who is visiting me again, a square full of elders, I mean SO BLACK, not the way I had remembered it, I fell into a panic, fled back to the stalls I had just forced my way through, I believe it was a caricature of St. Mark's Square, not unlike a combat arena.

And now I am making a cursory flight through my first draft, I am *overflying* my first draft, it has escaped me, but maybe in this superficial way (of reading?) there are still a few *glowing ravages,* or something like that, which can be brought into final, into the final, I mean into a usable form, etc.

9/19

she has no GRADE *only a raincoat : this fly . .*

she has no GRADE only a raincoat : this fly, instead of into the cup coffee poured onto the floor, imprint of an ISLE, by the wet soles of my feet, when startled I, out of the bathwater without drying off : when I splash, wet, drip, trip and drops (coffee rinse) run off my thigh . . would like to have kept right on slurping, but everything rolled onto the floor, while the telephone meaning that one of the GENERATION'S NIECES called to make arrangements for an afternoon meeting, etc., while as flagellant the print (now mistakenly called "poster," what is poster supposed to mean, something like pollster, upholster, at least there you've got something soft and upholstered, upholstered bench, mountains of upholstery to shut yourself off from the world, etc., might be, don't you think, I say to Blum), and I keep showing my weakness (dementia) *my soaking wet hide,* etc., it is like a pretext every morning, I say, first of all NOT DOING A THING, NOT HAVING TO DO ANYTHING except submersing my feet in boiling hot water until as red as a lobster, etc., and write, carefully gently : deliberately, while feet down below in their hot pulses and the first fly of autumn appears I mean the first housefly, maybe only a trompe l'oeil, the fly that is : *standing in corners and gathering* (hushed) the thousands and thousands of dust particles in my room, like me, exactly like me, we appear to be surprisingly alike, thoughtful, contemplative, maybe even a little sad, what do I know, in any case it doesn't have any tears, that distinguishes us one from the other, in any case no evidence, no evidence yet found, not yet established, fly with tears would be a sensation, I tell Blum, but it is flying and sitting and lying on a *sofa of dust,* it is probably feeling the way I do when I cower on my dusty mat, my eyes closed, humbled, fearful, in a panic even, both of us it and me we live in a state of panic, that is absolutely clear isn't it, sometimes I am overly enthusiastic, I tell Blum, I go head over heels (in my affection for Joseph, e.g.), I say, *I meditate every day,* I tell Blum, but the typewriter carriage, which bumps up against I mean abuts piles of paper on both sides, jolts me out of it and I see the words END GETTING DUSTY sprayed on the side of a building . .

and when I have contact with other people, am forced, to have contact with other people, I get this awful sense of being ENSNARED, and my throat constricts, my polite smile freezes, and I ask myself WHAT IS ELUDING MY EYE MY EAR?

but back to the fly, I say, I meditate a little every day, as soon as I am soaking my feet, while I observe IT, the first housefly, even the way it sits and strokes its head with its front feet, perhaps a gesture of introspection, what do I know, but I am sure of one thing and that is it will meet an early death; staying in this room will mean an early death, in this room death will overtake it, it as well as me, 1 day, tomorrow perhaps, maybe it will outlive me, it has no choice, etc. *oh! stomping language!,* you can never let your lover read what you write, Marguerite Duras writes, no man can endure that, but for the present I lie more than sit, and like my housefly I hang around a little, lie around, my feet immersed in water, I tell Joseph, I stand and sit very still, waiting for that day in 2 months when we will see each other again, anyway all time so expanded and slow, like those figures outside on a Sunday, holiday, like syrup, they are hardly moving at all, it seems, it is an image that touches me, Sundays, holidays have a stifling effect, it seems. But the year has gone by so quickly, Joseph says, sitting and lying too brief, Joseph says, how does this all fit together, I ask myself. Oh, why didn't I just throw my arms around him last night when he left, simply embrace him, my arms around his neck and kiss him, the way I have wanted to do for so long, the way I have imagined doing for so long. Anything can be imagined, I tell Joseph, but very few of these things can actually be realized, as soon as what has been imagined gets to the point where it is about to be realized, it collapses in on itself, yes, it is a real collapse, you hide behind an embarrassed laugh, a painfully distorted smile, you wave to the one who is leaving, wave from the window, and the one who left and then returns asks : did you watch? did you wave to me as I left? did you stand at the window? an interrogation, it seems. And for the first time, I believe, on your face, in your eyes, a small ironic smile, but also a futile attempt to conceal it, and it is saying, you have seen through me, all of my hopes, all of my high-flown ways. My hand touches your hand, your arm, as if I had inadvertently bumped into it and had hurt you, and say : excuse me!

and again touch hand and arm, as if I could make up for what I had done wrong, etc.
And all of this, I tell Joseph, not so much memory as the shadow of a memory, or : since this morning : the feeling, I am not living a dream but the shadow of a dream. (A rigid Zeppelin in the sky is trailing an advertising banner in its wake, without moving, the meadow is rasping, the yellow feet : *small naked yellow bags* of a seated person in a bathroom . . Elisabeth von Samsonow writes to me, in any case your German is the only natural language, and : I see you *strolling*!)

9/21

"an orange, an ocean wilderness in her body and during an afternoon nap"

again and again afraid to have mislaid lost the old notes, cut up torn up drowned in beautiful waves of blackberry and poppy juice, spilled glasses, pitchers, cups or surge of India ink, ink, what do I know, submerged in streams of oblivion, in rushing rivers of tears, like thundering waterfalls plunging down from the peak of a mountain, constant snow-white torrent, etc., just this water poem and everything, this source gurgles into a broken old pot sending water right onto the floorboards plummeting spraying, see a puddle in the shelter, cigarette butts swimming around in it, tiny swim fins, a puddle in the subway station I'm frightened, from a distance like small boats on a lake, papers when they flutter down from the oval table, and every morning this *throat attraction* : clematis blue larynx declination because no longer able to swallow etc., these huge tablets, I'm going to choke on them, I tell Blum, blue-dizzying me in the haze of a kindling (inflaming) morning light, crises, Kirghiz cap on a woman (thick velvet), climbing, still summerlike temperatures, I say, wet fur, cap pulled down over my face, enveloped life, enveloped life development, I tell Blum, everything carefully considered and put into its respective drawer, no longer anything spontaneous, nothing extraordinary, everything locked up, LETTERED, right, only in the back of my head : in a dungeon of longing, this bursting this rotating VAGABOND LANGUAGE, LANGUAGE OF MENDICANTS, dialect of the LANGUAGE OF LIFE, *love's funeral* every morning, I tell Blum, can you imagine that, every morning carrying this yearning for Joseph's embrace to its grave, I mean, his arms wind around my neck and we look each other in the eye, actually a very simple thing, right, but won't happen, I say, MODERATED LOVE IS MUZZLED LOVE!, says Blum.
Oh, I dry my hands with sandpaper onionskin paper typewriter paper, sink

my BEAK into a large mug full of coffee, see milky skin on the surface of my hot coffee, clap my hands together, cross my arms behind me, and notice, suddenly in the window things are sprouting and jumping the way they do in spring and salvation, and me bending over the edge of the tub and smelling the greenery : peach leaves in a bowl, i.e. leaves throughout the whole room and their fragrance—inhaled from their body. And no urge to eat them, to consume them, only suck in their fragrance and the greenery, and the green slopes of forest and wind and wilderness of wild roses.
In my room piles of wildest word stuff I mean *a glimmering up* a glimmering up a flaming up, a moon gleaming and a sun glowing, oh, I say to Blum, I've let go of what I wrote 2 years ago, *this inspiration is new,* I say, or I believe I'm writing everything with a new intensity, you see, dreamed this and that, told myself I'd be able to keep hold of it until morning, but now it's all in fragments, no significance, somehow I was sitting completely naked at a gathering and saw S. sitting there with one of the great philosophers of our time—probably Bloch—deep in conversation, she accompanied him everywhere, etc.—What was all of this thought about walking, marching forward, getting myself going, I say to Blum, I don't believe I can remember anything anymore, I don't remember anything, the places I went to give readings, I don't remember the people I met there, I don't know who came and spoke to me after the reading, looked longingly into my eyes, pressed my hand, gave me flowers, a souvenir, *a paintbrush bouquet,* etc. Apparently, in all of these places I can no longer remember, I just played my role, I had learned it by rote, and everything proceeded automatically, and my feet walked along all on their own, and there was the shuffling of my feet, 1 foot pulling the other along, 1 foot set down in front of the other, a belching gait I believe, foot belching, a shuffling, isn't that right, a declination of the feet, legs, a bow, right, bowing step-by-step, FOOTWORK, I say to Blum, no not BOOKWORK : FOOTWORK, I say, meaning walking around shuffling and *praying for indulgence* (hubris instead of selfless rapture : the true sin!), flowing following pilgrimaging crawling, and dozing while walking, my feet know their way, like faithful dogs who can find their way home from even the most distant of places . . I will be given a wilderness in my afternoon nap etc.
Landscape, craggy peak, green brook, I tell Blum, maybe those are the only memories that will stay with me, oh, in this my *endless abyss,* or this single drop of blood that remains after the shaggy little dog snapped at me, didn't leave, just stayed put under the skin of my middle finger like a tiny, ruby-red pearl.

9/22

once I was a boy, I have also been a girl, bush and bird and fish that leapt up warm out of the water . .

—Empedocles

have gotten involved with this feather, feathery instrument (*sounding out clothes, etc.*), *read Mallarmé!,* and even though I knew I wouldn't have to wait long in doctor's waiting room, I equipped myself with a rucksack full of books so that I would have something to read until it was my turn, I tell Blum, everything is simply getting wilder, yes, extraordinarily wild and impenetrable, even the most perfunctory of events or endeavors had become puzzling, incomprehensible, unfathomable, making me feel like withdrawing into a corner so as not to add to the turmoil, the gentle *earthquake : heaving,* because a tiny fly swallowed (swallowed down) with a full glass of water, in the mirror my MIDDLE EYE : broken white, alien eye, stranger's face, I say, had better not look in the mirror until late in the afternoon, written on the arm of the chair, I tell Blum, all these letters and cards written on the arm of my chair or in the palm of my left hand, standing, written, on the run, in just a few seconds, the same old STRUGGLE every morning, when I'm looking for clean underwear, shirts and skirts, not finding them, might just as well work at my machine in my pajamas until evening, same STRUGGLE with the outer layer, socks, sandals scattered around somewhere in this housing of mine, pot with cold overcooked milk (fish) on the carpet next to the honey table, and some one of the cast whimpered these words to me in my dream, GO GET MY CLEAN CLOTHES, GO TO THE LAUNDRY ON PILGRIM STREET AND PICK UP MY CLEAN CLOTHES, but I didn't know whose voice it was, and I asked myself in my dream, who is that speaking? but no one answered, actually the only thing I saw pass by was her shopping bag (woven straw) and when I woke up, I still had tears on my face, I tell Blum, because my dream had really frightened me, and actually during our sleep we should be confirming ourselves in the world of our emotions and our thoughts, I say, and I wake up, I mean again and again this feeling of JUST HAVING WOKEN UP, so I wake up and pull my hair away and back, and wake up with the words *one-eyed washcloth mitten,* but other than that rather sterile, I tell Blum, can't make much of it, at least nothing very SUBSTANTIAL, and when the telephone rings, it seems to me less and less likely that : it will be Joseph . . whispering paper and perennial plants, I write to Joseph, a thread of blood on 1 lens of my glasses, o lift me up out of this heavy ink, etc., in the Odeon, that time, I said to Oskar Werner, I write to Joseph, that I wished he would read my work, but it didn't happen, the same with Francis Bacon, I could always trust him, I could always *trust in him,* I mean I could trust in the ugliness and the stench of his paintings . . we rush around, that's how we get through life and we end up standing at 1 open grave or another again and again and even there we can't manage to focus our thoughts on the person who is being removed, you see, but what is the solution, what are we looking for, what keeps pushing us spurring us on, and so very hard, we drag ourselves around with this heavy and black ink on our body and our soul, and are overflowing . . there is after all this miserable, because penetrating right to the marrow, little parade bell with its thread-thin ring, a frail breath, and it's all over, *please very express 1 distress taxi, e.g.,* SOMEONE ELSE HAS WRITTEN MY BOOKS. Then an awakening and telling yourself : now I am at home, in my nutshell, now rather sad : no letter from Joseph, and now I know everything, the way rain on cheek and head raps and slaps and tufts and hair, and all along the street I push myself up against the walls of buildings, because no umbrella, and fumble around with the LITTLE BOX, LITTLE BAG, LITTLE SACK with the mail, the many letters I wrote today, deep down inside me, BELOVED LETTER PAGES, I whisper to myself to protect them from the rain, and deep into the inside of my coat, in the street brooms, horse ceiling, then back at home some sort of porcelain shifting : teapot clinking up against teacup, some sort of porcelain shifting : that's what it sounded like, I tell Blum, as I was shifting my head back and forth on my pillow, i.e. as if a piece of porcelain had clinked, *some sort of carelessness (with the heart), etc.*

I curse my way down the street, and Blum is a companion, our devotion as commanding as it is obsolete, strangely enough, I tell Lily, I mean you see a large flower in his wide-open eye when he says something or asks a question, *almost a record reading what he thinks when I look at him—*

and how everything can change completely from 1 moment to the next, I tell Lily, because now the fact that he doesn't write, that Joseph doesn't write, has almost become something *well-meaning,* like the warmth that envelops me when I come into the room, making the first fire in the green fireplace, or stoking embers in the fireplace, a tender log or Joseph's arms tender arms, and wake up from afternoon nap with the words LAND-SCAPE OF A KISS, and glowing in front of me green lanceolate web of leaves, etc.

9/29 *late afternoon*

so *pastoso,* viscous this music, I tell Blum, makes me uncomfortable, as if someone were painting on my bare skin, etc., Elisabeth von Samsonow sends me a photograph of her garden, the longer I look into it, the more astonished I grow, I say, in the background *the bust of a woman drenched in orange hues, flower of a woman,* on a pedestal, or someone whose arms you can't see, hidden behind a stand of laurel, female most likely, but maybe the green arms maybe they can be seen as green arms laurel arms, right, and in the foreground a small workbench, picnic table with a teapot, cup, small black dog, notebook, pen, mobile telephone, and, like an endless black fence, a chair with a seat made of wooden slats, steel construction, black too, but how everything is in bloom, everywhere, green bunches of wonderfully wild weeds, leaving open earth, sand, winding paths, and at the foot of the table a bush full of roses, very pale, *spare,* which is actually a contradiction, etc. To get back to the WANDERING POET, I write to Elisabeth von Samsonow, he has settled down instead of wandering, I mean he has settled down and settled into my *soul's berth,* and this to my displeasure, a giant grape, dark violet is hanging in the sky, I can see it from my window, I feel its ample physicality, something that has to do with the having written a book, or the breast flung away, the breast gulped down, the breast channeled away, *i.e. vaults* and leaping flames, it almost tears my heart apart, etc.

already parental bread, etc., parental breast, etc. or fissured tears, fissured mountain massive tears, you see.

Have completely liberated myself from the data of 2 years ago, I write to Elisabeth von Samsonow, how can it possibly be that you hear everything

so differently, I mean, an entirely different rhythm has imposed itself and damned everything previous to this in its entirety, but perhaps in another 2 years I still will not have finished this book, maybe just damn everything again, and write something new and think : "this tattered idiom, just pieced together out of extraneous parts, thieving behavior . ."(oh, the first draft doesn't recognize the manuscript anymore, and vice versa!) And when you are entirely absorbed in your work, I tell Blum, you become perfectly content, isn't that so, working on thought wings, and the silver watch fallen onto the kitchen floor : no, a piece of tin foil in a crack in the linoleum, you don't even notice how quickly the days pass by, it was just summer and now the end of September is taking its leave, and the filthy loft the dark leather band of the silver watch, the way I had imagined it, tricolor in the sky. And picked up from the floor again next to the sink : blood-saturated scrap, with a red pen, blood pen, trembled : "until the fever lining" . . and you are entirely focused on only one thing, day after day, and year after year focused on this writing, this writing work, this drumming and celebrating and howling, i.e. to this one sole center, *as if the fate of the world depended on it, you see, yes, as if the fate of the world depended on it!*
And in the meantime more note scraps landing in water, because in the basin for my feet, cooled down, no longer of any use, still under my desk, I tell Blum, and I don't know what to do with my feet, my legs, and trample around on the notes that are still dry, here and there pick one up as if it were a treasure uncherished, or I decipher : "heaven away, tiger-striped trickery, word rocket 5 o'clock in the morning after eye opening," and on another : "and made up cheeks more and more often, because I was wearing this three-quarter length coat ('paletot') with cheap fur collar," etc.
3 birds have pecked holes in the window, don't cry! Joseph writes in his most recent letter, which I had been awaiting with all my heart, and what has become my favorite occupation, I say to Blum, waiting for letters from Joseph, and might it be possible, I say to Blum, that Joseph is irritated by this favorite occupation of mine and feels self-conscious, perhaps having learned via telepathic means or even his own observation (of my behavior) of the state of things . .
but early today cried a lot for my mother, wondered where she might be, and if she found herself able to keep her promise to be with me everywhere I go, I tell Blum, then to comfort myself my feet immersed in hot water, under the table, I say, and then observed for a period of seconds the creations of my brain reporting in to me, but everything immediately ex-

tinguished because I had not written them down as they occurred, haven't yet looked in the mirror today to see if perhaps I haven't sprouted horns or some other sort of grisliness, at which point someone in hiking boots : while following too closely behind as he was getting off the train he stepped on my left foot, which is weaker than the right in any case, etc. (*"my only good foot in this language Volière / violin . ."*)
As he walked by I heard a young man say to his companion FOR A SMILING DECADE, etc.
Blum says, when it's dark he sees almost nothing in the street, he feels the need to take his eyes in his hand and illuminate the way, I have peeled off my tunic. While reading Roland Barthes I come across a quote from Robert Musil—comparing his with my own stylistic means I see myself lagging far behind, an abashed loser : if I compare the soundness as well as the transparency of Musil's language with my own, mine seems vague, frail, superficial, and incapable of *casting real shadows,* one of the prerequisites for good literature : as we are dealing with living objects of art, *they have a shadow,* but this must be proven in the practice of language, I say, the most difficult thing, I say, is the use of verbs. If for example I note : "in a dream I *betrayed*" ("a young person") as I have so many times before. I pause—NOT THE RIGHT VERB! it must read : "rejected (maligned?)" often, I say, not having the appropriate verb at hand, early signs of dementia, mentally underequipped, or there are these tiny PARASITES in my body (head), etc., probably *monkey business.*
Leaving the inner windows open does me good, it offers evidence of the infiltration of bluish gray world, in this way not ENTIRELY walled in, right, I write to X (or William or Ferdinand), am shocked : the *naked* : unmade-up eye of the landlady, almost indecently out of her white powdered much too flat face (no promontories, no bays!), when I look up from my machine, I see the head of a friend across the way on the front side of a factory annex, quite strange, I write to X (or William or Ferdinand), the way it is imposing itself : the sloping tin roof on the annex corresponding to the way she wears her short hair, gray tiger-striped, the melancholy windows (eyes) underneath the roof . . to which X (or William or Ferdinand) replies—no, our letters crossed : "when, where, shall I now tell you about my last love, since we will not be seeing each other for such a long time."
A moth startled up out of the bath towel, the refrigerator is snoring, or seems to be imitating a turboprop plane (in flight), I pack my bag made

of artificial leather, as many pairs of underpants as there are nights, so 9, 1 toothbrush, the collected works of Jean Paul, bits of hair on the tile floor, everything swirling greenishly.
Has so much of my VIEW really changed, I say to Blum, I mean, since I began writing this book, that seems basically inconceivable to me.

9/29 early

it is almost all ARRANGEMENT, I answer Blum, who calls me up with his questions : what does this mean, what does that mean, in your text, it is almost all colors, thoughts, feelings exploding, right, I say, an *exhaustion,* can't be determined, an *exaltation* of head and body and memory—

but today, I say to Blum, I had quite an experience : as I was waking up, still very DOCKED ONTO my dreams, 1 dream, which then escaped me, but whose taste I can still sense on my tongue, this sentence came to me "IMAGINED UDINE DIFFERENTLY," and at the same time it seemed to me that I had already heard seen this sentence somewhere before, shortly after 1 episode of waking up as well, the same feeling, the thought I mean (as sentence) : "IMAGINED UDINE DIFFERENTLY, WITH A WAREHOUSE DEPOT I MEAN," while at the same time asking myself what a warehouse DEPOT was, that is : "IMAGINED UDINE DIFFERENTLY"—with a very compact city visor, I say, yes : VISOR! : the green wooden casings over the windows which stood open during the night, the way they once had back then in the village intimacy of D., and when we opened them up in the morning summer flooded in, and the delightful fragrance of wet grasses, glittering from the dew, the fragrance of billowing trees in the wind, the fragrance of tall white straight standing lilies in the front garden, wafting fragrance of freshly mown grass, etc. So, I woke up with the thoughts, actually with the sentence "IMAGINED UDINE DIFFERENTLY, HAD IMAGINED UDINE DIFFERENTLY," upon which followed a kind of correction this time : it could not possibly have been UDINE, it can only have been Venice, looked it up again just a short time ago, and so the sentence as I was waking up must have been something like "IMAGINED VENICE DIFFERENTLY"—I lay there and clung to "IMAGINED UDINE VERY DIFFERENTLY" or

"IMAGINED VENICE VERY DIFFERENTLY . . WITH A WAREHOUSE DEPOT . ."— so it was this word concept, this sentence, detached from any sort of memory bits, "IMAGINED UDINE DIFFERENTLY" including the nightmarish "WITH WAREHOUSE DEPOT" . . in a half-conscious state, I say to Blum, scribbled down on small folded mauve-colored napkins, my little finger gliding like a ribbon of syrup across the empty page, *a pinch or a trick or a drink,* I am walking down the middle of the street at night lost in thought, my black billowing mother by the hand, my ring finger as a ribbon of syrup, I tell my mother, she is wearing a long black dress and a pair of thick-soled shoes, the kind that are now in fashion, I tell Blum, my ring finger wrapped in a piece of string I took from a small package, I am crying into my black cloth coat, I always feel cold, even on warm summer days I leave both gas burners on in the kitchen, *daisy flames,* I say to my mother, that you have agreed to it, that it is your wish to be burned after your death is a source of everlasting pain for me, I mean when I think about your hands, your eyes, your lips, your hair, everything going up 1 single flame, even your bones, I cried into my black cloth coat I cried, then pulled the sleeve over my nose and mouth, over my eyes, this entire *parade dress,* my parade dress, this invalid's coat of mine, flea-bitten bike tarp, shawl, decorated with long carpet fringes, this is all so trivial, I say to my mother, she wants to talk to me about getting a CHEST OF DRAWERS, she wants to discuss how she might *pack up* all those things wildly scattered throughout her apartment, etc., everything furniture and objects acquired without the slightest bit of forethought, they are not really *utensils,* they are impossible to use because they are always in the way and provide nothing but an excuse to trip over them, right, I tell my mother, actually to curse them when they are (finally!) lying shattered on the tiled floor, etc., I cross the street, am careless, the driver of a small car (Alfa Romeo?), who is *driving lying flat back,* just caught the hem of my coat, I say to Blum, instead of a full water glass to my mouth I put a receiver to my ear, I'm that distracted, rhythm of the world and Stifter's heaven of stars (until the fevered membrane), I say to Blum, because you are still only speaking inward, Blum says, communicating is too much of a strain for you, you basically go out of your way to avoid every instance of communication, Blum says, you say you're not at home when someone wants to talk to you, you act as if you're at death's door when someone is trying to look you up, even a conversation with friends : you do violence to yourself when you're with your friends, your inward conversation is being interrupted and this leads to SOUL GRIDLOCK, probably BLOOD GRIDLOCK, and all you want to do is run off and hide, isn't that right, that even I, that both of us, friends from week to week and month to month put off everything, the last time in July, Blum says, before we took that trip and promised them, BUT THEN! : IN SEPTEMBER! . . and now : September has passed and we haven't even seen one single person, isn't that so, *now in such a way that the other was magically coated, or wavered;* the new morning came very gently, I tell Blum, after too little sleep, but all of the *indispositions* of the past many days had been forgotten, it was as if they had never been, I say, these *indispositions*: this our NOT FITTING IN ANYWHERE, NOT FITTING IN ANYWHERE, everything odd and unhappy as if wiped away, blown away everything that had inflicted terrible pain on us, isn't that right, anguish, fears, foreboding, etc. and against which we had tried to defend ourselves with curses, fits of crying, moving to the attack, which of course had led, would have to lead, to our total exhaustion . . at such times I usually just let myself fall back onto dirty bed sheets I had not changed for weeks because it would have been too much of an effort, just as I avoided taking a bath in the morning, it was just too much trouble, it also seemed impossible for me to coordinate anything, get things under control, make decisions, I was leading almost all of my life within my own body, and in any case it was from there that almost everything could be determined, organized, read, unraveled . .

oh, jacket and pants pockets bulging and bumping into everything everywhere getting all tangled up in my cramped quarters, I say to Blum, always knocking everything off the table whenever I made my way to the only unobstructed window, then *trampling around* in rubbish, rags / bandages at the feet of the rickety old art-deco table : blood-smeared scraps of paper, blurred red felt-tip scrawl, no longer legible, UNTIL THE FEVERED MEMBRANE, UNTIL THE URINE AND BLOOD PINCER, UNTIL THE ANUS HOWLS AND ROARS, etc.

My contorted face in the shiny teaspoon : mirror cabinet : image in utmost miniature.

Clean out the head!, mend the wash!, no juice no jump!, Blum cheers me on over the phone the next morning, *let's get to work!,* and I second him : *until our pigtails fly!*

9/30

"regarding fallen angels"

delightful snow flaking, no snow dandruff floating across my housecoat, I tell Blum, *dipped* in white powder countless powder bristles shaken out over this red housecoat of mine, I say, how do you suppose that looks, sifted and silvered and puffed white powdery, what do I know, in any case *bizarre, this German language, and how!,* or AN ALPINELY DRAMATIC SPACE : STORY, isn't it. My feet are about to run out of the room of their own accord, Elisabeth von Samsonow writes, and I have to hold them back to keep them from leaving the lecture hall, and I keep trying to exhibit an intelligent an interested face that is, so that no one will notice how bored I am, etc. It occurred to me, I tell Blum, that the head of a dog was protruding out of the wastepaper basket, the head of a giant wolfhound I believe, with large cropped ears that were constantly changing color, and then it seemed to me that the cello, I mean the small cellophane sack with the CANDIED GINGER is simply smacking along on its own, *or in the rot of Nina's Roses,* this morning's messages were of a varied nature, I believe that someone was *rattling* my sidecar cycle into the shade I believe I WAS MY FATHER, I HAD TRANSFORMED MYSELF INTO MY FATHER, he unwillingly allowed the motorbike as if of its own accord to keep going back into the shade, but the sun kept shifting so manically that we (now there were two of us : father AND me) could not keep up with it and pull it out of the shade, it was an unending struggle, or it was the time when mother had to crank the *Talbot* by hand until the engine started up, I mean she had to crank with all of her might at the Talbot's snout until it finally roared to life, a complex noise, right, the rhapsodic nature of things, I tell Blum, or, as Markus Lüpertz calls it, *the dithyrambic nature of things,* and so enthusiastic admiration, etc.

The old stationery shop across the street, THE GREEN HUNTER, I say to Blum, do you remember, seemed to have suddenly opened up again after decades, where I used to buy school supplies, paper, pencils, folders, two old paper-thin women, their hair pulled up and back, treated their customers with exceptional courtesy, but one day one of them was no longer there, I say, no one asked what had happened to her and no information was offered, but in last night's dream that store became a *sandal shop* and I run into, demand sandals, yes, brown, I say, size 44, *on the sale counter,* I am told, there are still some left, but only the right sandal from each pair was on display and of course I wanted to try on both shoes before making my selection, I mean it probably was not only a motorcycle with sidecar which my father drove so wantonly tearing it in and out of the shadows, but it may also have been a German sheepdog, and it wasn't like him, I almost never saw him angry when I was a child, instead he was much more likely to be taciturn when someone, when something bothered him, his mouth seemed to be sealed.

I wash my hair before going to bed, and then I lie there on my wet hair, which is not very comfortable, in the hallway it smells of shampoo, the large white pores of the shirtfront, I say, are of permeable reminiscence . . I mean when he, the way X (or William or Ferdinand) threw himself down on the grass or *up into* the hayloft next to the house, after he had driven us, Blum and me, for hours over passes and mountain roads, I tell Alma, and we had finally arrived at this house, and he fell asleep there lying on his back, in the meadow in front of the house, his arms spread wide, a strange sight, I say, but his sleep did not last very long, then he leapt up embraced us all and said : how beautiful! back here again! made it back here again!, etc., and then said, we're going to go hunting for mushrooms now!, but retreated to his garret room anyway, and I then climbed a small hill some distance from the house which gave me a good view into his room and I was able to see how he quickly undressed and threw himself down on the bed, completely naked, without having closed the curtains, and I then picked some flowers, I loved him so much then, and put the wildflowers on his pillow, once everyone had left the house, etc., and I say to Alma, then, in this summer I said to him, LET'S LIE DOWN TOGETHER because I loved him so much and simply laying flowers on his pillow could not satisfy my desire for him, he said quietly, without looking at me, *I cannot tell a lie!* and when I said I SIMPLY WANT TO LIE DOWN NEXT TO YOU FOR A WHILE : FEEL YOU CLOSE TO ME, he said just as quietly, then we can just sleep together. But he got sick because he had drunk too much warm

Coke with rum and he threw up, and I helped him clean himself off and to change, and then he fell asleep and I lay down beside him and we slept, fully clothed, until morning, his glasses were lying on top of the bedspread when we woke up, and apart from that nothing happened, and nothing more, and then *these blue cards of the ocean* came again, year after year, the Aegean, he wrote, the hanging gardens, the gray olive orchards, I feel so strongly attracted to them, and : we might have come here, this is a place we might want to go, and from the steep cliffs along the coast, here we might have been standing watch.

And for the past few days *the proverb spirits* have been pursuing me, and they bear me ill will, or maybe it is me bearing ill will inside them, toward myself and the actual events and turns of events, because I said to myself, I kept saying, or the proverb spirits kept saying it to me, grimly and full of rancor : I AM A DEAD MAN!, that is what they were saying, or I was saying it, I could see that I was a dead man, I admitted that all of my energies had been drained, and that I was as good as dead, I simply lay there on my mattress, sunken in long ago, so completely that I could have crawled down inside its deep hollows, and the only thing I could do was sleep, constantly, nights and afternoons, and I thought to myself while I lay rolled up on my plank bed, maybe I want to write like Beckett *and* Jean Paul, like Hölderlin *and* Brecht, etc., or I formulated it another way, maybe I wanted equally to be a Beckett and a Jean Paul, a Hölderlin and a Brecht, but those were only fantasies and I sank back down into a half-sleeping state, entirely without plans and obligations, unprepared and without any hopes, without *whispers and passions,* I felt almost as if I had no consciousness at all, and at times it seemed to me that I was disintegrating into formlessness and namelessness, I was someone, I was some sort of almost lifeless piece of meat, indifferent, bereft of thought and feeling. Something had driven me into a state of BRAIN CONTRACTION, I confused times and places, and when I woke up from an afternoon nap I didn't know whether it was 4 o'clock in the morning or the afternoon, oh, I hardly even knew where I was, the way we sometimes feel having spent a night in an anonymous hotel room, days and weeks and months passed this way, and when I thought about sojourns in summer freshness, I confused the names of places and the impressions I had stored of them, the two places I confused most of all : Saint-Espang and P., in my memory they had collapsed into one place, indeed, they had become interchangeable, that is to say, it seemed to me that the events and observations I had retained of one place were transformed into aspects of the other, and I thought to myself, maybe 1 of these places wants to imitate the other, you see, and so the memories and experiences ground into one another and at times entered into a turbulent even erotic relationship to one another, they melded into one another, and I observed everything from a certain distance, and not without some amount of pleasure, and one morning, after having slept for hours, on a scrap of paper I saw the words : *magnifying glass, lupin up-and-coming,* but I didn't know who could possibly have written them down and what it might mean.

As far as this NATURE BUSINESS is concerned, I tell Joseph, there is an enormous hat on the windowsill, the way I see it, white hat, or maybe even a sack, set over a plate of garbage, a hood, hull, birds are pecking holes in this hood, the banana tastes like a half-cooked potato, I tell Joseph, a *complaint,* I believe. Reinhold Posch says, showing up here in his INDIAN SHIRT, everything at home is one big chaotic mess, can't find a thing, my clothes all crumpled up rolled up somewhere probably on a pile of books, but then in the evening I at least have to get something together for the next day, etc., just as I was, he suffered from a growing confusion and bewilderment regarding all circumstances and sheltering of things, right, I tell Joseph, the blinds like jackals, I say, it was such *an excess of sleep,* and there was this stag-beetle corpse lying on the floor, I tell Joseph, flat and blackish, I believe the dummy of a stag-beetle corpse on the parquet floor, then I go to the cosmetics shop and say to the salesclerk, I bought this BEAUTIFUL BAR OF SOAP from you, but there were these tiny rats the size of ants inside the wrapper, and the rose color of the soap had also faded and it made me sick, it appeared to be the color of vomit, *so I washed the soap off,* without even producing the tiniest hint of a lather, just imagine, it lay there like a rock in my hands, did not even slide out of my hands in that almost amorous way a wet bar of soap usually does, but what concern is it of yours, when I tell you that its ghastly color spread over other of my things,—I mean when I came back from one of my most recent reading tours, I found that the banana skins had turned color and become slippery in the side pockets of my suitcase, I believe A MEAN THOUGHT, I tell Joseph, a nervous head heat, probably, let's say : ART WENCH.

(Into the décolleté of the envelope, before I sealed it, in tiny : antlike letters scribbled : say hello to Mario—because I had forgotten to write a salutation at the end of my letter.)

10/1

"March comes in like a lion, and leaves like a lamb"

in my room : matches (Fidibus Kien Lohe Firebrand Docht) nothing but aggravation, I tell Alma, in my everyday street, somewhere I read off the heat on my body, and Joseph says, his (his friend's) ignition point cannot be determined, cannot be discovered, and he (Joseph's friend) could not remember having once made love to H. although he had lived with her for 3 years, etc. Just let the following *glimmer* its way to you, I write to Lily, which quite possibly is just another expression for dispatch, fax, transmit by some sort of telepathic means, get me as quickly as possible 3 PILOT ballpoint pens in black and blue, and if you pass by WOLFRUM'S, a reproduction of this Matisse painting, and I'm also looking for a GLASS DROP ("GLASS TEARS") for my damaged collage, so that I can remount it (the way they are used in chandeliers), and also : fire-red crepe paper, a package . . the birds are pecking holes in the window this morning, *Paramount* is lying on the bathroom sink or I am Hildegard von Bingen—a HOOD : a white sack, the birds are pecking holes in the window, pecking holes in my HOOD, A BAD LOAF out of the oven, *furnace,* as my mother used to say, or lateral wooden piece of a completely rotten cutting board, I tell Blum, claw marks clearly in evidence, the space between the toes, it is singing and singing the PAW, the wagtail, the siskin, the Turkish dove, the Alpine jackdaw, Alpine glow, in an OCHER SPRING, I believe an ocher-colored spring, which of course represents the obverse of autumn, right,—oh, these *pneumatic scraps language* of mine, how I love it, I tell Blum, or as Alberto Sánchez writes : "may my rapture hurl me down off these cliffs; may my body turn into mud from so much standing up and falling down; I would gladly foresee myself asphyxiated deep in this ooze and meet the reptile of my dreams on his field . . " oh, I tell Joseph, wanted to turn a page in one of my favorite books, in a dream, a heavy book lying on my chest, but then when I woke up I saw that all I had done was take my hands off my chest, they had been resting there while I slept, I believe these words came to me in my dream : *reckless to love the love in you!,* and such were the unbroken conversations between me and myself, you and me, Blum and me, Alma and me, and so on. I find it stimulating to think that you, dear Joseph, I say to Joseph, could imagine a conversation among the characters in my book, of course, they can't really speak, have never been able to, they had memorized a text and had to rid themselves of it in this book of mine, but now they don't have much of a part any longer, they are not, they would not even be allowed to perform a little improvisation. Furious furious with the coloration : discoloration : with dying? away of the light, this an observation made by Markus Steffen, an unknown reader, his card completely faded, a number of years old it seems, encrusted in dust, on the upper left still the dark head of a thumbtack in the Styrofoam board where the card had been tacked up, a remnant of the outline of one of my earlier books, I say, obsessive WATERNESS, etc. New page inserted, because after so many tumbling rumbling hours no longer any connection with things previously noted . . sparrows dog shit air tearing open and daylight probably sunlight, am not sure because table lamp still on, all of this, I tell Blum, actually a FOREST VENTURE everything, what do you mean by that, Blum says, I don't answer; helplessness, no answers, beyond the agility of thoughts, garlands of words, linguistic beauties : I believe it was in this kind of zigzag that my cogitations progressed, while Blum continued to speak, but I didn't hear what he was saying, THE DELUSION DOCTOR THE DELUSION DOCTOR, is what kept running through my head, and I thought about the dishes in the cutlery box, and how it had gotten so messed up during the accident on the train, on the way from Passau to Vienna, isn't that right, I write to X (or William or Ferdinand)—and I had to smile to myself as I recalled that is how he now referred to himself and signed his letters to me—so : chipped all of the dishes, I mean PLATES and KNIVES and spoons, jingling, when I carelessly, and the protruding plastic shelf in the lavatory bumped into my forehead, or I bumped into it, pain and tension and MEGASCENE, because in the mirror mounted above this shelf I was immediately able to view my distorted features with so much revulsion in my heart that I said to myself, it had served me right, whatever had struck me on the *awning of my head* I mean the foundation of my skull that I howled, *have commonplaces scattered from my head . .* (on my mind), something like community, and now I have bruised myself actually misbruised myself into my head and it swelled up into a real bump, after this breathtaking blow, etc., I became 1 big bump on the head, with all of my hysterias and hypochondrias and prenatal anxieties and subspirits, and I understood how my mother this gentle and delicate creature must have suffered the most atrocious anxieties throughout her life and had thus passed on to me awful and for the most part unfounded anxieties, that they might accompany me on my life's journey, which appears to be without doubt one of the most complex of any in my generation, within my view in any case, but I love her, my mother, with her flashing indeed : glistening ideas, nimble insights, intuitive intelligence *no less* for having given me such an inheritance, I mean having passed such a burden on to me, my love will never be diminished and all the more so since she is now gone, etc.

The loss, Blum says, the loss of such a close friend, of a HAND and HEART COMPANION, is a shock through and through, but basically you have to tell yourself, perhaps you are able to tell yourself basically (thus NOW, from the very onset giving yourself words of comfort), that you will continue, continue speaking with this LIFE and LOVE and HEART COMPANION, i.e. that you will be able to continue your conversations, and also expect responses from this person who has preceded us into an unknown and unintelligible realm. *Slid* into the COIN ROSE, I mean staggered, reeled, sailed, my full page of text sliding into a bowl of milk, *lapping* now as if lapped up, drenched and dipped and sheltered, teared, and everything washed away, wasted . . and if perhaps, if my work, in this LAY or that (in the sense of melody) hadn't resonated / wasn't resonating with the voice of one of my already dead colleagues, H.M. supposes, when I met him again recently, the watermark on the left instead of on the lower margin of the page. I think, might that have been the answer?

Emotional canapé, something had stuck in my throat, that is how I felt this morning, I dial Blum's number, but someone from the provinces answers the phone, someone I had known quite well years ago, and I think, maybe a sign from my mother, I should have gotten in touch a long time ago, they may well have been waiting for years for my call, etc., and during the night someone rang my doorbell, I believe 3 o'clock and full moon, stuck in my throat : a hand not shaken, an insight lost, a word reaching someone close to us too late, etc., all sorts of misgivings, I tell Blum, maybe even my own fear of BRAIN MOVEMENT, as we can read in Psychrembel, cerebral devastation, shock to the system, and that wouldn't surprise me at all, I tell Blum, when all around me I see the devastation of what was *once such a delicate aura,* you see. But now, and for quite some time this place has been a kind of battleground, and at the same time *enclosed* plane, which may be understood as either a kind of tree or a geometric structure, I say, *common white willow, common scenes day and night,* and only sometimes, for some hours, the awakening of apathy, a kind of RELUCTANCE to continue living and writing, then immediately erased, sat up, 4 o'clock in the morning, punched my pillows and scribbled my notebook full, then, at the threatening *window sky* fled to my machine, stammered, *heavened,* and worldwide. Your colloquial style, says Blum, not always pleasurable, says Blum, jagged, cramped, also, hysterical, concocted (cooked up!) with STREET TALK, and so on. And both of us have, Blum says with a laugh in his voice, *pages begun on our graph paper notepads,* and then standstill there in the middle of a sentence, get no further, gaze into a sky already growing bright again and wait until things finally inch forward, etc., or drafted long lists of thought flashes, a bunch of Talmi stuff more or less strung together, *cheerfulness of your fontanelle,* e.g., and peasant's shoe : athletic shoe : zippered high-heeled shoe : actually oversized foot cover, a kind of *arte provera,* on the tabletop, black felt-tip scrawl sideways, probably the sketch of a plan for a wholesale warehouse (for women's clothing), somewhat broken : broken off the line between the base and the top of the small art-deco table, pseudo-Jugendstil apparently, what do I know, arcaded DARKENING of the BRAIN PÂTÉ, I say, right, if you know, if you can remember, how splendid even glaringly brilliant this first was, I say to Blum, usually footprint on the rim of a mountain range, or a small oval table, would love to slip into a *solid* hand-rubbed climbing boot and scale the Großglockner, but all I have is the left boot, for the left foot only, perhaps interchangeable, and also for the right, well I mean *all of these perils of foot and head,* so arduous, painful, but also comical, full of misunderstanding, irony, isn't that right. Hysterias, hypochondrias, and *wagging,* no : not : waving—*wagging* curtains and DESCENDANT DAUGHTER—*because we love your work so much,* Alexander von Bormann writes, while a fluttering in the adjacent room : while me scribbling in bed, 5 o'clock in the morning, and a flake of gusting outside, fluff, so that the open window in the adjacent room, only slightly veiled, with a honey-yellow material, and *literally* the green SWEAT PANTS hanging from the doorknob fill out with the curvature of Joseph's right calf, that's how it looked, viewed from my bed, and something vaguely swaying inside this pants leg, but only in the right pants leg, and somehow I tell Blum, this SQUINTING with its excessive line : dislocated figures : was something like THE PREENACTMENT of a manic Bacon-like painting.

10/2

pulled on my threadbare old bathrobe, switched on PERGOLESI, PINE TREE HORIZON in my window, no, a dark cloud formation, watery cellophane on the floor, and once more : saw the dark edge of a forest as I woke up, something like a low range of mountains, in the window, from my bed, as one fragilely sees, I say to Blum, or, my fragile seas, as Elke Erb always says, I say, the elongated bank of clouds, as if I were in some strange place, and there the astounded view from the window, after waking up, that is how moved, enthused I was, maybe even carried aloft on wings of some sort, you see, these phantasms soon disintegrated and left behind a half-shredded early morning storm, a frayed sun, my imaginary island sea . . which, after its colors had been growing brighter and brighter, began from one moment to the next to fade and was now presenting itself to me as a well-kneaded doughy mass, almost a little repulsive, unappetizing, bulging and in a desolate sky, my god, and this is how I began to get hold of myself and my eye inventions, I found myself at home again in my housing, hotel days survived and could take up my work again, I say to Blum, then, went back to sleep, swirling letters, words, half sentences, I couldn't recall, only remembered the end, it read : "*more likely a kind of forest machine* . ."—a storm swept through the house, angels with parachutes fell from my desk lamp, these parachutes so tiny, like the bright-colored Japanese umbrellas that are stuck onto overfilled ice-cream cones as ornamentation, I say, well, it was something quite beyond imagination, but I could see it, do you understand, I say to Blum, it was raining from my desk lamp, it was raining tiny angels, and they all landed on my white sheet of paper, I believe they are getting it dirty somehow, but when I look more closely I see they turn into black letters, words, sentences and enchanting blocks of fusca language, oh, a storm swept through the house and when I woke up again I tried in vain to decipher a table with numbered sentences that seemed to be full of secrets, I did not succeed, perhaps a TABLE OF LAWS, but the *paella* I had been served the previous day, after my reading, there had been just enough left for 1 serving, that the staff of the institute had not eaten it, and I wolfed it down in a fit of hunger, shoveled in that is, did not sit well, the *paella* was sitting in my stomach like a stone and I would like to have regurgitated it, if I had been able to, but it just sat there in my stomach and tormented me until morning, *am employed in the field of anxiety,* I say to Blum, a specialist in the field of anxiety, or something like that, intense states of anxiety, you see, I say to Blum, the patter of a gentle rain begun, and you notice it on the cars flying past, the way they spray out their innards, I say, the rain is pattering, and the angels are pattering down, out of my desk lamp, and Monika Böhmert writes, I must thank you for your poem about the LITTLE BLOUSE : the rain skin, and when I was a child, Monika Böhmert writes, I was alone : ours was an attic apartment, fearfully and I stood at the window, on the sidewalk, under the song of the rain, the boys from our building, and holding rain ponchos over themselves, in the driving rain, the dark trees, and there was a severe storm, I was about 9 or 10 back then, etc. *and hand-trembling thanks for everything, etc.* Joseph writes, Thomas Pynchon no longer allows himself to be photographed, makes no more appearances, perhaps worth emulating, etc., and in the small plastic bag that feels like silk, really as soft and as light as a breath of silk, I tell Joseph, and was now empty, but before this contained several days' worth of notes, all in complete disarray and most of them sticking together, because often with wet fingers, I mean, scrawled down while doing heavy housework, and with a translucent body, right, and desire, every thought of desire suddenly seemed to have become translucent, disembodied, actually *languishing,* that is my longing for the desired object, *you,* overcome, sometimes desiccated insects with wings like that, transparent wings, with parched, dehydrated, yes, faded wings, you see, and they don't move anymore either, and then they take up residence instead of winging around, they take up residence and shelter in the curtains, next to the inner window panes, they are like A WINTER VAGABOND, who must somehow to an emergency shelter, I mean before he is devoured by the cold, etc., utter despair, I tell Joseph, utter despair between us, *a cooing naturally,* simply like that, because there is nothing that can heal me anymore, the wounds hardly close, for days, for weeks I run around with open wounds, especially my fingertips, I tell Joseph, who said I am exhausted from my work, and

the nighttime feathers I tear out every morning in order to write my poems haven't grown back in by afternoon, etc., the only comfort I have found, I tell Joseph, is in my almost pathological FORGETTING, so I forget everything that hurt, I forget my wounds, the millions of nerve cells in my brain have forgotten everything, and this way I can begin each morning anew, as if everything that caused me pain had been swept away, you see.
Dear Sabine, I write to Sabine H., I am in great pain, because it seems to me that you are following in footsteps I set down 2 or 3 decades ago, why must all of this be repeated, almost a copy of my own life's course, what you are showing me, what is happening to you, and all I can do is cry over it. Back then, I was also enchanted with this scarlet red cape cascading down over my left shoulder onto a *gory* table, I mean I showered everyone and everything with my passion, and it became nothing but 1 single bloodbath, this in the context of James Lee Byars's Performances, i.e. this intoxication with scarlet red productions, this arm and sleeve this blood-red robe, pouring off the right shoulder down over table and floor and stairs and door, a bloody train, and I wonder, isn't there some small piece of Matisse in this, something like his *Still Life with Oranges,* but it will shock you when you see it, I'll send you this piece of paper, and I think, not necessarily in this context, everything, every single thing, and whatever you have to say about it will be a work of art, although already expressed by Duchamp, etc.

(*oh, lift me up out of this heavy ink . .*)

10/3

In the candlelight there appeared to be rodents hanging from both of her cheeks, hanging by their teeth.

—Peter Handke

these catastrophes, castanets, noodle napkin in mauve is lying in my lap, on a *party plate,* what a disgusting word, immediately feel like throwing up, I tell Blum, on top of the napkin, on the paper plate, a piece of fruit cut into bite-size sections, peeled apple, right, noonday delicacy, leaned over it in order to be able to eat on my small chair, all of the tables occupied, no more trays available, these damned swellings : paper swellings all the way out to the kitchen, the entryway, the hall, all the way up to the chests, essays, built-in ruins, hanging gardens up to the ceiling, no more escape—entered a loser, I tell Blum, beginning in childhood, loser, last row, failure, stutterer, unable to articulate a single thing, mute puppet, unable to react appropriately, wrong gestures, wrong movements, started a loser, I say, a matter of upbringing, I say, my mother meant so well, but I developed in other dimensions, nothing to be done, *once a loser : always a loser,* I say, in spite of every concerted effort, exercise of will, dedication, the glowing fire of enthusiasm—in a *trenchcoat* that was too long : transitional coat, as a child, or in a fur coat I *dragged along* behind me, always expecting I would grow into it, and everyone smiled this particular sympathetic smile when they saw me this way, in this GETUP, right, S. on the other hand, my little childhood enemy, she started out as a winner, the eternal winner, she was self-assured, had thick chestnut-brown hair, carried her shoulders straight and was always at the top of the class, and later on as well. Once a winner : always a winner! and she was only the first in a series of this type under whom I suffered, feeling myself to be their subject all the way into the misery of my old age, you see.

In tender notebook of 10/18 written out longhand, I say, these pages went off to Karla Woisnitza yesterday evening, oh, the aesthetic of abbreviation, a kind of coloration or seduction, I say, as if I were trying to type in stenographic shorthand on a machine not yet invented—4:30 a.m. catapulted out of a contrapuntal daybreak by a ringing (telephone?), then back to sleep, dreaming : saw musical keys in my dreams : audio frequencies, I mean Karla Woisnitza's tomato-red foot, and the way it stomped against a *chimney of grass!* : shimmering green!, a tracing of her foot that is in a fine pen stroke rotted into those WOODLANDS, I say, the way they look to us when an extremely intense pain announces itself, isn't that so, WOODLANDS can't get rid of them, I say, hammered into our ether and our heart's stuff, never to be expunged, and when this evil rises up, we fall, come crashing down sideways, nothing to hold on to anymore, nowhere, and our consciousness slips away and we say to ourselves : I KNEW IT! SENSED IT! JUST THE WAY I FORESAW IT!, etc., IT HAS PRECEDED ME!, oh, I say, aired out the bedding and found all sorts of things, plane ticket to Bremen, scrap of paper with possible titles for the book I'm working on now, "father / mother playing ninepins, 1926," and "Stroll through a world broken apart : breaking apart and characterized by gyrating phenomena," etc., yesterday's blood pressure reading on the back of a page scrawled full and torn out of my notebook.

When I was reading around in one of my favorite books, I tell Blum, when I began to read, when I continued reading—only a few pages every morning—it seemed to me that the poet was enriching me with his language, with the constellations of his thought : this language of his was not restricted, dried up, chiseled in stone, it didn't revolve around certain themes and verbal rarities (mannerisms), the way mine did, instead it informed me—something which both shamed me and gave me great joy—how expansive and high and deep the dimensions of a *living* poetic language can be, even must be, laid out in order to be able to attract readers these days, right. In order to create the kind of appeal which makes *all kinds of people truly want to read*—actually transports them into a READING STATE, something that is hardly possible at all these days. This language had nothing crude, no contortions, no quirkiness about it, rather it was fresh, expansive, full of color, supple, renewing, delicate, concise. Not stilted like mine, I tell Blum, oh, how I had held myself at such a great distance from LANGUAGE CORNUCOPIA, my own language seemed so old, laborious, yes, ossified, nothing but a dressed-up : decked-out skeleton, nothing behind it. And I read and read, through my tears, what I had lost, what I had sacrificed, in all these years, decades of my untiring work, and how miserable, and with empty hands I stood there, still only circling around myself, with my well-practiced vocabulary, stereotypical expressions, odd phrases, how impoverished I had become, how self-satisfied too, although, I was still consumed by ambition, I say, but nothing comes of it, I say, I mean the result always appalling, sparse—I might just as well have stopped writing 20 years ago, I tell Blum, and no one would have been any the poorer for it, no one would have missed a thing, isn't that right, my DAYS OF FAME, which I never really had, were coming to an end, but I didn't want to believe it, didn't want to admit it, kept right on jogging : trotting : stumbling along : an old man deceiving himself, trying to make his way around his room, while in his mind still over hill and dale, the way he once did, right, self-deceit this writing coming to an end, I say, a hopeless attempt to fool yourself into thinking you can simply keep on writing, *lethal experiment,* etc. Am now neglecting my work, I tell Blum, because my publisher *faxed me that he has great hope for the newest generation of German writers*—I can clearly recall the small black bed, with black pillows and sheets in Meersburg, how I love your letter, Elisabeth von Samsonow writes, *the one about the footbath,* when I read it a feeling of intimacy comes over me, the way such a feeling comes to someone who, let us say, *goes swimming* with her friend, etc. And so, from the affront (irritation), see above, I made something watery : shimmering blue, you see, I say to Blum, and once in a while it seems that it is actually given to us to soar over mountaintops in the rosy fever of a drinkable May, breathing fresh and open air. And then mercifully the sensation of raindrops tenderly moistening brow and cheek, and once again viewing the world from on high we see a large and beautifully haloed eye, and the cherry blossoming long since past when like milky pearls we, mankind's children, still danced over the earth . . bushes immediately sprouted out of my body, Elisabeth von Samsonow writes, and as an answer I am writing to you a KIND OF SPRING : VER SACRUM you have made me in my last SNOW YEARS, I write back, I don't love the sun as much as I used to, I write to Elisabeth von Samsonow, a budding twig in my throat, cherry blossom twig, or it was a blossoming piece of crepe paper, a green butterfly or a geranium leaf on the stone tiles in the hallway, flattened, and when I went back to P. after many years, when I saw this place again, I felt that I would have to make a very hushed entrance, the memories of nostalgia and joy were so overpowering . . the transistor radio on my knees at first, while I was writing, then spread out on a tailor's scissors, and then it sounded as if the telephone were constantly ringing, *I had to piss like a guard at the gates of heaven,* and this is how I snapped this sentence down on the blank back of a brochure from the

LOST KEYS COUNTER, smooth snow-white paper *like an ice rink,* and my pen danced and flew across it, pirouetted and raced in a way it had not done for such a long time, the outermost earth, the outermost corner edge, at the outermost edge of the room 2 scissor-cut portraits, one of Franz Schubert, one of my mother, I was able to extract that from here where I am sitting at my writing desk, with everything on my knees while I write, very *rigorously,* I tell Blum, the tip of my left thumb wounded, for example, right under my fingernail, hasn't closed for days, I say, that's simply the way it is, because the wound keeps opening up again, and I have been running around for days, even weeks, with an open wound, hopeless I mean, I say, birds scratching, or a motor turning over, isn't that right.
I switched on the fluorescent lamp over the bathroom mirror, and it's been on all day even in broad daylight, the arabesque of a strand of hair on a paper plate, which is bordered with an arabesque of flowers, both repulsive, I tell Blum, when I wake up from my afternoon nap I have the sensation of being in a WETLAND, finding myself in a WETLAND, although, my mouth dry and sore, Ingrid Fichtner writes to me about a heaven of a relationship, in connection with the sculptor Karl Prantl; when I, while I, even all day long, lie on my plank bed and from which position I do not see the small alarm clock on the easy chair next to my plank bed, i.e. when it is somewhere else in my housing, I mean because I, lost in thought, simply set it down *somewhere,* I mean left it, or, in preparation for a trip, have already packed it, this situation sends me into a state of great unrest and insecurity, and after a short afternoon nap I ask myself where I might be, whether it is day or night, especially as twilight commences, and feel forsaken, or, as Wendelin writes a card to me from Braunschweig, this *lightning visit* had been very welcome, but with a constant change of place, always waking up in a strange hotel room, he never knew where he actually was, etc., and because, since early morning, both of the GEWISTA workers had been remounting old posters onto new billboards with an oversized stapler, actually stapled them up, or *sewed them on,* the noise was almost unbearable, I turned the radio up as loud as possible and was almost able to annul the aggravating noises from downstairs, this *bodily transparency,* I tell Blum, and on top of that *the inner dissolves,* it's exhausting me.

10/4

am reading in great leaps and bounds, I tell Blum, while standing read 2 pages of Novalis prose, then inserted a BOOKMARK, at the point where I stopped reading, the shorn suits : with horns musical horns suits decorated with musical horns, I say, by the first rays of dawn, what a sight, I say, it's the lake, Blum says, LAKE CONSTANCE, Blum says, it has worked its way into your heart like this, the whirlwind, I say, I blew the whirlwind out, it had been swelling up blowing up in the early morning, right, my brain was already a little MY GOD or something like that, do you think I'm crazy? I think it just seems that way when you have been touched by a wonder, I mean by an extraordinary sight, you see, sometimes I find myself grazing on the thought that I am crazy, which is of course playing with fire, I say, frivolousness, because in reality it is a pure horror, and I wouldn't ever want to experience what it really means, something you shouldn't be playing around with, I believe, even introspection is far too advanced, and I should be keeping things a little more under control, right—it's ringing inside my shoe : I believe the most immense of circumstances, my left pants leg has been caught under the spray of the shower, etc. Oh, I love to eat RED FRUIT PUDDING and am gradually developing a taste for the WISDOM ROSE as well, I say to Blum, we were sitting on the cold terrace of the Literaturhaus in Berlin, it was in June, my two friends and I, and I was freezing all the way down to my knife, I mean my teeth were chattering, was exhausted after having survived my reading and I wanted to go back to my hotel, but the questions, the differences, I mean between the sentences, and in these moments I hated the city I otherwise love so very much, because the cold weather keeps intruding deep into the summer, etc., what will come of all the wonderful books spread out over my blankets, right after getting up, I tell Blum, *I count : 17 most excellent literatures,* and lying completely crumpled up on top of one of the books was my right hand and my left hand was all numb because so many books had been piled up on it during the night, etc., what is the significance of those many wonderful letters at my breast if I have to leave them all unanswered, how it almost makes me hurt, such loving voices in these letters and I cannot tell them how grateful I am, and : do you really love me? and : just have a little patience with me, *because the migrating baptismal angel,* I mean, this other obligation, *this obligation to write,* this writing pluck plan has laid claim to my being, etc. I have to keep climbing the ladder and plucking the fruit that is almost growing into my mouth, isn't that right, you can all understand that can't you, you can all forgive me, I believe, you can all picture for yourselves what I am feeling, with so much sweetness just hanging there in the tree, I simply *must* make my daily climb, climb up the ladder and pick, piece by piece and often don't know how much more there is still hidden among the dark foliage, I stick my head deep into the foliage and let out cries of joy, the foliage smells so good, almost like fresh white lilies or mimosa, a smell of profound promise, right, I knew it even as a child, sitting there in my reveries, as I was sitting there on the hot stone steps in D., something hovered over me like a wing perhaps of my angel, my GUARDIAN ANGEL, as my mother used to say, and my angel whispered a promise to me, then I didn't yet know what it was, what form this promise would take, but now I know and have known for a long time, and it is making me the happiest of all people, you see, the great leaps and bounds in my text, I tell Blum, and there are also times I must pray (beseech)—then it rings it chimes in my shoe, because the spoon fell into it, the spoon in the running shoe, while the hooded lark flutters overhead, so hobbled, I say, the disappearing swans in P., the fleeing swans, I didn't like the way they ran off in the grass when they left the water, they showed themselves to be awkward and grotesque, they had relinquished all of their *swanliness,* you see, and perhaps, perhaps falling was even an obsession, sometimes it looked that way to me, they seemed to fall over as soon as they stepped out onto the lawn, they fell into the grass, they rolled around in the grass and were laughed at by the children romping all around them—

this is one aspect of HIGH POETRY, Blum says, don't you think, isn't it true that poetry occasionally reaches a point where it seems laughable, *the forest divide,* I say, as a pad to write on, or something like that.

Yesterday I bought this mauve-colored *crepe napkin* and a new typewriter *with pearl keys,* and I was taking them home but on the way I left the typewriter in a store, I simply set it down under the counter, out of my sight, while I was paying, when I left the store, it was incomprehensible to me that I could simply forget this typewriter, the acquisition of which had made me so happy, I had in fact forgotten it that is I had forgotten its existence, I say to Blum, it was simply incomprehensible to me, I ran back and someone had already taken it into custody, I believe the clerk in this store, she said I THOUGHT THE CHILDREN (HAD FORGOTTEN IT) . . which also seemed incomprehensible to me, it seemed incomprehensible that she had assumed the two children who were paying for their purchases at the same time I was had forgotten this wonderful new typewriter, what could they possibly have done with it other than drop it to the floor right then and there or mistreat it by banging around on the keys until it finally gave up the ghost, etc., I mean I was so agitated while I was panting down the street to get to the store before closing time in order to retrieve this new typewriter of mine, in these few minutes it had captured my heart and my pulse began to race, it was as if I had reached the summit of a mountain, that's how it felt, and I thought about my hypertonia, and how I was going to survive all this, I had the mauve-colored napkin, I had everything twilight, the ephemera of a dream, the sequence of life seconds and life phenomena, and I embraced it, my typewriter, and carried it home with me very slowly, this time I took the elevator because I had so much to carry, and when it came to a stop and I stepped out into the hallway, the words BASKET LIFT came to mind, they had bubbled up several times before, at the very moment when I stepped out of the elevator, you see, before it stopped it shuddered, swung a little like a basket in your hand, etc.

There was quite a bit of PUDGY PAPER : or pudgy-cheeked paper that had landed in the bowl of water, soaking full of water, and I took it out, the ones I had scribbled my notes on, I mean the dripping hair of someone drowning, that's how I felt, and I laid it out on the dusty carpet to dry, this kept happening to me and at one point I was even afraid that every page of my final draft was going to land in the washbasin, and for me, I mean, it would be an irreplaceable loss, wouldn't it. I set one of the clocks for 10, I tell Blum, ("call my internist!"), and set the other clock for 12 ("Dr. Kellein is coming from Bielefeld!"), felt some pain in my eyes again, I say, the pain of revenge, yes, I say, I tore off the dress, gargled revenge, and heard things murmuring, singing, rustling, gurgling somewhere, like dripping, trickling water, rain perhaps on the windows, now it is trickling, is it coming from outside? is it in the radiator? in the water heater? my soaring flight may well have lasted for no more than 3 minutes, I tell Blum, that is this wonderful feeling of being able to sweep everything away and in a storm wind over the earth, and soaring, over the entire globe; then, like a pricked balloon, down to earth, sail back down onto the earth, there were sounds in this morning, I tell Blum, telephone ringing, probably, and in a very ungentle way it brought me down out of the heavenly writing realm I had just managed to enter after some number of days, entered again—

and I had to think about the lake again, I tell Blum, as I had seen it from the small terrace, on its shores the hotel where I had spent a few days, I had an expansive view of the lake, I will remember the ripples on the water for a very long time, like shimmering layers of hair in tones of bluish gray and deep black, I say, and I thought about a close relative who had recently passed away, she had kept her bluish black hair all the way into her old age, only at the end were there a few scattered strands of white, a water legend, I say, now, the rest of the water in the teakettle was still warm this morning, from this past night, it was a very unusual but soothing event, these small, inconspicuous things, these small, almost imperceivable breaths of things, isn't that so, there is such a wonderful sense of well-being in these small, inconspicuous things, I believe, raising my shoulders, *aping* (!)—what a word—my own posture, like the upper part of a silk dress draped over a hanger, in this *well-practiced* posture of mine, right, and it means : am entirely withdrawn, completely unassuming, don't want to attract attention, go to the end of the line, the way I did even as a child, practiced, exercised, because that's the way I was trained when I was a child, trained in this discipline, I say, instead of the discipline of assertiveness, self-assurance, etc. Not that I blame my mother for this, not at all, I say, actually something she practiced herself, even though a rebel, I say, extraordinary, isn't it, this mixture of subservience and rebelliousness, split heroic character, infinitely deep, and boundless depths of her being, bottomless, the abyss. We were walking through an enormous park, I tell Alma, last night we walked all the way through this enormous park, Joseph and I, and this walking together, this free and easy movement led me to a MONOCHROME bouquet of touching and embracing, *darlings and buds of moss or May, etc.,* and while walking along the street noted, I noted : subdate and : blossom showers and : thought's spring and : supernature and : superbreathing and : mistaking; I remember while walking getting things wrong and misreadings, and that we are unnerved when someone calls us on the phone : 1 moment, please!, because instead of that we hear : 1 accident, please!, and it is because of this perhaps I should call my book, the book I am working on now, "or a Forest Misery" but this was not the end point of my thought meanderings, which

had begun to spread themselves out so expansively before my inner eye, because I wanted to remark that while we were wandering or flowing through this large park, Joseph was talking about the songbirds again, the ones which were lamenting, seemed to be lamenting, their WILDNESS, while they sang, a point in his discourse, I said to him, that I did not really understand, I mean it wasn't really clear to me what he was trying to say about a bird's paradise (on the one hand)—in this part of the AUGARTEN—and these laments, birds' laments (on the other hand), and he could not explain it to me, I mean at the edge of the park *a hairy hand or a dog's paw* reached out of a phone booth, out from the bottom of the booth and we were both distracted, I thought it was a human hand or a bare foot, but the perspective was misleading apparently, in the restaurant, at one of the tables the face of a girlish double smiled at me, flowers bunched together in a flat vase : flowers bunched together on the restaurant table reminded me of girlish heads bunched together when they whispered, twittered, traded secrets, isn't that right, I say to Alma, actually pastel-colored faces of young girls, and Joseph and I, while meandering, flowing under the foliage and I thought, this is the way it was in the ELECTIVE AFFINITIES, meandering metamorphosing flowing, and full of birdsong this—*head scaffolding,* that is, this head scaffolding of mine, and the way it handles its *note treasure,* all too carelessly, that is, scattering, misplacing bits and slips of paper throughout my housing, and Elisabeth von Samsonow is asking if in its diligence this magic wand or pen of mine is bringing wondrous things to light, etc.
This is where everything falls apart, I write to Joseph, I am writing under the most unimaginable, yes, even hair-raising of circumstances or conditions, just think, my entire natural treasure I mean word treasure is in a process of decline, this is especially clear to me when I am reading in one of my favorite books and taking notes, I mean, I find a few good sentences in a dream or I create them and without fail the telephone rings and tears those bold whispers : implants I've heard, to shreds, you see, and it's not raining as much as it used to, the best of circumstances for work, *absurdly enough* it keeps clearing up and more and more often this treacherous sun keeps me from my work, it lands directly, *claps that is—that is, thrashes around—* on the stacks of notes covering my desk. And I can't do anything about it, you see, I have to keep this view out of the window to the outside free, an open view of the sky, and the mountains in the west. And this is the point where everything finally breaks downs, I say to Blum, I am already writing on the whitish backs of my favorite books, this really is the final stage, I say, sleeping on the pages of open books, and when I crawled out of bed this morn-

ing, I was forced to suffer this inane, yes, even obscene music ("Wedding March") by Felix Mendelssohn Bartholdy because I didn't want to miss the world news report which followed, etc. The messenger / Alhambra : dream, I say to Joseph, want so much to write provocative books, but on a slip of paper the words SOMEONE ELSE HAS WRITTEN MY BOOKS, NOT ME!, because, you see, the finest thoughts, the most beautiful wordings have been rendered meaningless, and also unable to find most of my sketches, wildly scribbled notes in this housing, I mean somewhere they had been fired like projectiles into a landscape of absurdities and that is how they had been lost to me, the bold and daring phrasings / tropes of a semi-anonymous authorship, etc.

10/19

I often wake up with the feeling that there are 2 or 3 people *I want to put my arms around,* a kind of dissipation of self, isn't it, I say to Blum, on other days I feel myself utterly lost among other humans, or I come to feel that having met one person or another I have lost something of my own substance, or I have been enriched, as the case may be . . all kinds of thin objects stretched thin in the stairwell, in the hallway, don't know what it means, *I believe obscene;* Pergolesi disc has fulfilled its role, I say, at least for a few days, I know the music by heart now, then pigeons flew up and down and then a piece of laundry, gray laundry or cloth ripped up and down, and then pigeons again, from the top floor of one of the neighboring buildings, bitterly cold today, stiff breeze, underneath a parked car : pigeon torn to pieces, it's already time to get out our warm gloves, I say, I believe the traffic sign was bandaged and pasted up with strips of paper like someone with a head injury, here at the window the red peony is in full bloom, walking is thinking!, Alma calls me on the phone, you should get out more and walk, infernal, I say to Alma, 1 more button torn off my *fall coat,* I say, shoelaces keep breaking, ready to come apart at the seams!, *could be straight from the fields,* I tell Blum, after having pissed, I say, it's so green!, probably a reflection of the green plaid curtains, Blum says, my excrement has taken on the repulsive form of a slug, I say, trumpet blast / John Lennon Aria / poisonous brotherhood, etc., not even my mother could contain her joy over a successful bowel movement, *then with her hands indicated the approximate length of her product,* I am going to the supermarket, not to shop for anything, I'm just going to the supermarket to walk around for a while, I tell Alma, in the APPAREL department I see a POLO SWEATSHIRT, *a pound of slogans, an inch of sausage,* etc.

The beautiful middle eye, came to me in my dreams, the castle invention, came to me in my dreams, I tell Blum, I've got a new paperweight, actually a giant pair of tailor's scissors, looks very ambitious, and some tacks with big heads for tacking up notes on those dusty old Styrofoam boards, strangely enough, I say, I've got some books back, tools, ones I lent someone, don't seem to fit into the previous order of things anymore, I mean they don't have their old *angles of inclination* anymore, they've become foreign bodies, are going to be put away *somewhere* where I won't find them anymore, "a heart of red moon drunk," a word from Koulish Kedez, strangely enough these days I keep coming across this name in my reading (in various books) and I can't seem to figure out what it means, I tell Blum, *ah landscapes of kisses,* I shout, verbal states of delirium . . sometimes I start reading a book simply because I am attracted by the title, and then I reach for a BOOKMARK and place it between the pages, which really means : I won't be able to continue reading, or : I will never be able to finish this book. I already knew that, once a BOOKMARK is placed between the pages of a book, it has always been the KISS OF DEATH the BLOW for that book no matter how worthy it may be, it has always meant that I would *set it down* among the other 100s of books which stand and lie covered in dust in boxes and baskets and on shelves, and thus would it be condemned to the same fate as those other 100s of books to which I had already administered the blow the kiss of death with my BOOKMARK, I would probably never again or only after many years ever even pick them up again and they would be covered in dust and grown musty and tattered in their baskets and cages, wouldn't they, I say, maybe upon the rediscovery of these treasures I might open one or the other of them again, to the page with the BOOKMARK, read around in it for a while and then set it back down for good.

Woven in among the straw flowers, I say, actually old sketches that had to be refreshed, there will have to be a few bunches of fresh flowers, I mean a few fresh bolts of thought from this day on which the final draft is to be completed, and so a beautiful and brightly arranged bouquet came into being, old *and* new, but it was the composition : arrangement : combination or MÉLANGE, actually the fresh blossoms should dominate, they should overgrow the old blooms and bunches, so that you might only vaguely imagine how it once must have looked, you see, *and what might have been going on, where it might have roamed,* before it was bundled together into its final, complete perfect form—anything is possible and everything is allowed, Blum said, and gazed out through a fiery eye.

Writing paper fell off the machine, clothespins hopped from the table, everything seemed to be in energized motion, the black EMBROIDERED JACKET lay on the oval table, next to it 2 darning needles and black wool, as if waiting for someone who would do the mending in my absence, I tell Joseph, I don't wait for letters from you anymore, I tell Joseph, sometimes it takes all of the energy I have simply to stand up and go to the door or the window, and on soft knees I walk around in my housing hunched over, as if I were supporting myself with a cane, and I don't understand what's happening—a fainting spell—but what had caused it? exhaustion, I wondered, brain function closed down to a minimum, I say to Joseph, before long I'll be just as ossified as most of the other old ladies around here, the multiples on the billboards, in every color, depicting a huge semi truck, directly under my window, but it's not really bothering me because it's quiet now, today currents in the air like currents of water, temperate / cold, temperate / cold over and over again, the air with its various currents the way you feel it when you go swimming in the ocean, where the temperature of the water is constantly changing, right, strange weather, I say, an hour ago raw air, now warm currents, similar to signs of a mild season . . bread rolls and flowers running a zigzag pattern through the city streets, palms wild blossoms, all because of this spell of dizziness—probably an empty stomach, I stumbled, tripped over any number of uneven surfaces : suitcases and chests, bags and luggage, in the bathroom, that's where my mother caught me, I mean I let myself fall into her arms, the only thing I tore was a fingernail. But early this morning I was already telling myself YOU'RE NOT GOING TO BE ABLE TO WORK AT ALL TODAY! because if you do you're going to get stomach cramps, on the windowsill, in miniature, there was a copy of the German translation of HORACE'S LETTERS I, I tell Joseph, the edition high school students use, I mean *for my dizziness,* I paged around in it, found the letter "to my book," something I found very interesting, but the tiny print strained my eyes, I saw *curls in the heavens* the way Hopkins once saw and recorded them, and in my mind I saw the dark waves of Lake Constance *toss and crash up* against the far shore—it was a stunning sight : it was an excruciating sight, forcing tears into my eyes, my own body curled up into a huge wave crashing onto the shore in perpetual repetition of the same motion, I was this surge of dark water, I believe I was wounded crashing onto the far shore, the spray seemed to be taking on the color of drops of blood, I responded with a flood of tears, I had never seen a SURGE OF WATER before, it was a changing water, you couldn't tell what color it was, probably gray or blue gray or greenish, and there where I stood in the meadow and gazed at the phenomenon of this WALL OF WATER I could see delicate stars of blossoms on a green square, and I thought : daisies or marigolds, white eyes wide open, right, and in front of me the cherry tree bore pea-sized pea-green fruit and a sparrow was sitting in its branches, right in front of my eyes, singing—

is this little SWINDLE BOOK OF HORACE a piece of burlap, a book of Horace, a hairpin, a sewing needle, a redheaded tack? I wondered, I say to Joseph, that's what was going through my head as I went lunging into a soft woolly wall of vests, curtains, hats, fur capes, all hung as they were on a rod that was mounted straight across the bathroom, and that's how my head ended up sunk deep into a profusion of suits, jackets, wigs, wool slippers, leather jeans, etc. Alma sends me a notepad with black snowflakes, they run down the pages like black tears, I tell Joseph, you have to see this.

If possible, I say, I would like to simply keep on writing once I have finished this woolen script, just keep writing, I think I'll just keep on writing in my head, I say, I think some burden will be lifted once I finish this book, I say, and then I'll just keep on writing in my head, I won't write anything down, it will be a torment, and I will curse everything and everyone and banish all from my presence so that I can be left alone with my adversities . . and while I was falling into the woolen curtain of dresses and skirts and coats, a Latin verb came to mind, how could that be. Today so weak, I tell Joseph, that even brief moments writing, my stenography, are exhausting, the soup bowl next to the notepad, the cooled soup, the *soup strings and bread, etc.* in a magazine in color and glossy print the insipid photo of an infant chewing away on a broad maternal nose, apparently because it is so hungry for her breast.

Someone asks : what is this actually all about, and I say : it's not about anything, these are nothing but shadow plays, imitations of a mania being recorded here, or how else could these things be made concrete, these things which are driving me, constantly spurring me on, giving me no peace, no sleep, *buffeting* me, slinging, propelling, leading me to sudden collapse in the early evening, just lying there, eyes shut, fleeting dreams. A photographer who comes to visit me says : come over here, the light is so natural over here, I ask him, a man who comes from northernmost Germany, what are you doing in the Waldviertel, he answers : MAKING MYSELF DELIRIOUS! : I like that, I think I'll walk right up to him, right into his lens, and put my arms around him, a muffled thud in one corner of my study, one sort of conglomeration or other, I say, some study entity *dropping in on us* (as my mother used to say!), close relatives long dead were always *dropping in on us,* I tell Joseph, I think I am quite given to this superstition, etc.

An earthen gallery, what is that, I say, the wad of paper in my hand in my coat pocket, and prickly in the stars of my eyes, *finis.*

evening, again 10/19
"we are not real at all!"

butterflies are fluttering around in my room, and my thoughts are fluttering, a crackling like crystals of ice from my eye, I say, and all this rage is going to be the end of me, I say, and I survey the chaos in and around me as if it had nothing to do with me at all, I tell Blum, I sit there and observe what is happening, from what I can remember I believe I was standing in a grove of cherry trees and staring at the far shore, and as a SURGE OF THUNDERING WATER I hurled myself up against the far shore, I stood by the lake and metamorphosed into a SURGE OF WATER, and I could feel everything in and of me becoming water and in this transformed state I raged, I hurled myself up against the far shore of Lake Constance, right, that's how it was, inside my skull I felt the glittering breaker making me half-crazy and smashing my skull open on the rocky shore across the lake, I was outside myself and I was able to stand back and observe me, and what I saw was a terror, I tell Blum, I was no longer in me in my body in my head, instead a huge surge a raging wall of water I crashed across the far shore of the lake, etc., and in the most frightful tones it blinded my eye and took my breath away, looming so close, I say, that I cannot recall where I first got first felt the impulse, the FORGING, the SWELLING, the SCIROCCO, when and where, and even whether or not it had actually happened or simply arose from my imagination, hysteria, in such a way that I no longer discern the constant chirping and quivering of the atmospheres, I tell Blum, over the lake, I mean came up. Cooing, of course, I say, with a furious *brio* : the water gardens, came to me in my dreams, and : the ballad of the boat, and : the midnight beret . . ah this image, I say, *translucence,* back then on that green quarter by the lake, *the fingery blossoms,* tiger shapes, *the feathered instrument* in the branches, so close to my eye, close enough to touch, so close to my ear that I felt as if I could read the notes of its song in the air, they were there in front of me in perfect notation, exhilarating notation, partitur, breathless states of delirium, right, comparable to this provocative act of SPATTERING BLACK (DRIPPING) LETTERS, I mean this completely mad element in the *metamorphosis of reality into poetry,* etc., a delicate : rose gone wild, for example, 1/8 Paganini and Paraguay, or the apotheosis of SHOWERS OF FLOWERS, if I may, not to be too sweet sounding.

At about half past 4 awakened out of a contrapuntal dawn by a ringing telephone, I tell Blum, actually catapulted out of my bed, right, I tell Blum, but no one was on the line, climbed back into bed and kept on dreaming : "anxiety as anxiety or garden in a landscape of anxiety and gardens . . a little red cheek and a reflection in the mirror, dark . ."

I would like to have a typewriter I could use to write down my shorthand scribbles, words in my shorthand are always poised to leap out of my head onto a piece of paper, sometimes I catch myself writing in stenographic script, words becoming symbols as I write them down before they are typed out on my typewriter, I mean the abbreviation for "people," for "not yet," for "again," for "landscape"—

I noticed, I tell Blum, that you were wearing leather soles yesterday, more precisely sandals with leather soles, I was afraid you were going to slip and fall on the freshly waxed parquet, fringed outcroppings of clothes like segments of a feather, down toward the hem, I say, the "translation library, volume 267, *Horace's Letters I*" slipped down among the other large books, in any case, one thing covers another, isn't that so, when I woke up for the second time ANDALUSIA came to mind, the word, and a desired destination, I tell Blum, let's go to Andalusia, in my imagination I see all of Andalusia covered and veiled in wisteria like blue silk curtains billowing out over an endless horizon, I saw how luxuriant they grow, I smelled their sweet fragrance so many times when I was in Rome, emaciated cats roamed among the vines, actually they were feral cats, they belong to no one . . the small spoon landed in a laced shoe, it fell off the edge of the credenza, all of this brings tears to my eyes, I speak another language, no one can or wants to understand me, it is very likely a beautiful language but it has never found any resonance, I tell Blum, I tell Blum, you want to be a MENDICANT POET, I say, like Bashō, that's what I understood when you declared what course your future life would take, isn't that right, when I saw you in your leather sandals, I was afraid you might slip, trip, fall and hurt yourself, and you were surprised that I had even noticed your leather soles, I mean, in general, I mean, in general I understand EVERYTHING that is said, what is said to me, no matter how distant it is from the realm of my soul, how far it is from the *true* realm of my soul, because I can listen very carefully, right, *put myself in someone else's shoes*—what a thought!—and I can envision everything that is said to me, I can picture, yes, actually that's the right word : I can picture, picture everything, even the most far-fetched, unusual, extraordinary, the most absurd, most mad, atrocious, bitterest, etc., these days we sometimes speak a kind of ROBOT LANGUAGE, I tell Alma, it's such a pleasure, it's a delight, we are like two children again, we speak a truncated language, like primitive first-GENERATION robots, and we enjoy ourselves, especially when we talk this way on the telephone to each other . .

Maria Callas / the sun / on 1 black folding chair, the *embroidered jacket,* and with a needle and black yarn, I tell Alma, and while I'm looking at these stores, the word RECHAUD finds its way into my consciousness, I hadn't thought of it for years for decades, hadn't spoken it, then it caught up with me from an early childhood experience, in our robot language, Blum says, our occasionally raging emotions are somewhat restrained, don't you think, on the floor under my writing space, I tell Blum, I telephone to Blum, just think, still on the floor the basin from this morning's footbath, a steaming bowl of soup already sitting on the oval kitchen table, that's how quickly the day passes, I'll soon be bedding down, the fundamental structures of the substance of our two bodies/souls could not be any more different than they are, I say, there can hardly be 2 other people who are so fundamentally unalike in their actuality (their natures) while being so tenderly devoted to each other, isn't that so, just forget the AMORPHIC, I cry into the phone to Joseph, the waterfall, the sunset, the mountain range on the horizon only *rented,* don't let this word bother you, don't think it's too much of a stretch, and the heavens the way they are overcast with the first snow-filled clouds, etc.

10/21

there is an unending stream of talk, talking in dialogue, talking to myself, Blum says, when I am alone, all day, at night too, the banana tastes watery, I went to the stationer *and flew like an Oslo,* I say. I cannot see my way through the thicket of this first draft, I tell Blum, a galloping rendition, it's all taking up an enormous amount of space, I mean, those things I could have finished off in a few brief moments 1 or 2 years ago now take twice as long, doing the least little chore, the simplest bit of housework, putting a new ribbon in my typewriter, for example, is almost impossible, at best it happens on paper, I write lists of things to do, things that urgently need doing, but I can't do them, there is something very leathery and sticky in me and about me, and most of all I would love to lie down and stretch out on the couch all day long and watch time pass, or I would love to be on the trail of a wonderful book whose author I do not know, and I would let myself be enchanted, bewitched by this book whose title I do not know and whose author I do not know. The ethereal paths, I tell Blum, I know exactly how far I dare to go, I never enter a realm where I might feel out of control, I circle around treacherous terrain like that, but I never set foot inside it, etc. Sometimes it is nothing more than a piece of an overripe banana that makes me sick, even when the first few bites have done me good, usually it's the end of a meal that makes me sick, the boundary between pleasure and disgust is thin and permeable, *an incessant ticking* coming in through the closed window, from the street, I can't bring myself to clean my glasses, polish my shoes, to sort dirty laundry from the clean everything is just lying there in one big pile; we can never escape our flaws, we are continually being drawn into them, a path we enter on in childhood, *the rut we settle into,* isn't that so.

I was embarrassed, I tell Blum, at not being able to finish the meal I had in front of me, I had ordered *a half portion,* knowing that my stomach could only tolerate a minimal amount of food, I say, still, it takes an enormous amount of effort to force down *these 2 asparagus tips, with garnish,* no matter how good the first few bites tasted, each succeeding bite became more difficult. While I was sitting across from the doctor and reciting my infirmities, the less interested I became in that part of me which was suffering from some undefined ailment, instead I was applying my full powers of concentration to my writing, which I had interrupted because of this visit to the doctor, and which was waiting for me at home, I felt as if someone close to me were waiting there counting the moments while I was away. Basically, I tell Blum, I didn't really care what was happening *to this other person of mine,* I almost felt as if I were being imposed upon by my doctor's compassionate interest in my condition—

these trees, these trees in the restaurant garden whose name I'd forgotten but which I then remembered as I was rushing down the street, typewriter under my arm, these trees, these oleander trees, it came back to me, and walking in front of me there was an old man who resembled my dead father in both his appearance and his posture, his white hair, his light-colored jacket, his deliberate gait, and I passed him, my typewriter under my arm, in order to get a good look at him, his face did not look like my father's face, *that is, the appearance of likeness, or aspect.*

My fingers had picked up the unpleasant scent of this bundle of keys, my study was filled with a noxious odor, it smelled of Tipp-Ex, I say, my coffee spoon had been soaking in dirty dishwater too long, I could smell it, even at a distance. There was a kind of jubilation in me I had not felt for a long time, I ran down the street, my typewriter under my arm, and it began to rain, someone opened the doors to my building for me, held the doors open for me, and I could see a few rays of sunshine seeping through the rain. It came back to me again, it was oleander, this plant in big containers or pots in the restaurant garden, smelled like ham and roasted meat . .

when I went back to work on my notes after a few days, I no longer understood the mood that was speaking out of the preceding few lines, I tell Blum, rather I sensed a kind of melancholy settling in and it had me repeating the following sentence over and over again : LIKE 1 DAY MY LIFE HAS FLOWN BY LIKE 1 DAY EVEN LIKE 1 SINGLE HOUR, etc., a galloping rendition, I say, the galloping gardens in that village, I say, vineyards, and it was burning inside the sense of my skull or my stars, or there was a source of light scraping my powers of imagination raw, I say, as I was climbing

through the vineyards in that small town on the shores of Lake Constance, in May, as evening began to break and I saw light glowing through an enormous larch, it may have been a light in the window of a house, but I couldn't help thinking of paintings by Magritte as this light came breaking through the airy middle of the tree like a full moon, *a coming of lungs* and bushes like locks of hair : locks of grapevines, right, little by little this first draft has become unreadable, I tell Blum, a fact that may just spare me the necessity of making a clean copy of the rest of my first draft—
the approach of the pine forest was fervent, I say, in the morning, for myself, I concoct the most impassioned things imaginable, complete calculation, and over and over again this gulf between vision and realization, and this applied to every single breath of my life, not only to my writing, I say, I had sticky feet, I mean those little feet in the fairy tales of the Brothers Grimm, somewhat forgotten, sticky little feet, then I wandered around in my housing, it was I mean it had the taste, or the smell of REMNANTS. Actually, I was about to put a sock on my left foot, I tell Blum, the way we are all supposed to do, but at that moment I found myself pulling it on over my hand like a mitten, so awful, I say, actually, at this point, all of these lines should be set in italics because that would provide an accurate representation of my elegiac mood, wouldn't it, I say, you come into you fall into a moment of sleep, I had simply lain down in the early evening, exhausted, fully clothed, my hat still on my head, and when I woke up it was past midnight, I didn't know where I was or whether it was night or day, I was overcome with fright, the storm shocks in my body scared me, I appeared to myself as a *washed-out* little bloodhound, entirely stalked out, I have no idea what I'm doing, what I'm concocting when I sit down at my typewriter, I say, there's a whip cracking over my skull, I duck and scratch my way into a desolate corner, or something like that, but Joseph is talking about SELF-WILL, he's writing an essay on SELF-WILL, I like that, that is something believable, something that dissipates, I tell Blum, because the older you get the less WILLFUL you become, I have always been stubborn, I tell Blum, but SELF-WILL is something different, isn't it, and I am no longer able to vent my feelings either, just let things out, I am very afraid of *expression,* I lie all rolled up in a ball, as silent as I can possibly be, somewhere in the room, and explain the connotations of "cabinet notes," *about to appear!,* I yell, it's this catchphrase about to appear, I say, sesame seeds scattered across the floor, the young schoolboy at the airport : Botticelli curls, entrancingly pale and open face, says, YOU LOOK LIKE PATTI SMITH, he says to me, that's almost like being a solitaire, he says,

I can't stop looking at him, and while I am looking at his face, something in me is speaking, it's saying : maybe I'll use a quote from Harold Brodkey as the motto for my book: "in my book there is not a single sentence that is not sexual" or from Koulish Kedez: "a finger burned from the angels in my neck," and, by the way, this would make a very good title for a book—what do you think. A provocative aspect, I say, : SOMEONE ELSE HAS WRITTEN MY BOOKS! and while putting on my makeup I notice that my left eye has grown (is sitting) somewhat askew, I say, *an iron climate,* Joseph says, we can extend this somewhat imprecise, uncommon concept to cover various aspects and life and writing, I add more hot water, my footbath having cooled down, I believe the contours of my hands are crouching in 1 corner of the room, the county fair, or the book fair, how should I know, at the BOOK FAIR I saw a man, I saw myself facing a face I had never seen before, I think I knew his name and his rank, but I began to reel as I was looking at him, I was truly caught up in his eyes and this state persisted over a matter of seconds, I say, we didn't speak to each other, we simply held one another in our gaze, but he disappeared, I'm not certain but I think I saw him again, probably a high-percentage hypochondria, I say, an excess that doesn't cry out, that makes it a PRIVATE HORROR, what a thorny orb, stylized system of observation, etc., Sartorius, a friend of Goethe's (also), a small wad of paper in my hand, my right hand crumpling up a small wad of paper, at some point it will begin its transformation into a rosary, such a green VEIL OF NERVES over my tearing eye, will you really hang the two drawings I made for you on the wall of your study, I ask Joseph, take a picture of them for me so that I can get an idea of how you live, I tell Joseph, I mean in a SNOW OF NERVES and at any time, I tell Blum, this transition from an exchange of glances into a conversation and regard, I say, we also laugh a lot, but actually I'm on the verge of tears, I say, because of his, Joseph's, reticence, I roll the wad of paper between my fingers in my coat pocket, and something : a FRESH BLANKET OF SNOW or ECSTASY is quivering inside me, while the man high : ticklishly drenched pant's length in the vicinity of my right knee or eye I don't believe we can possibly see everything in a work of art, I tell Joseph, in one way or another there will always be an insuperable disparity, isn't that right, you want it, you struggle for it, but something about it will always be indeterminate, a painting can pierce you with arrows, the viewer is always exposed, willingly or not, to an awful wound, but we writers, we are always trying to catch up, we keep trying to achieve what painters achieve, we hurl glowing word matter through space, I believe we even offend our faithful readers, we are supposed to be creating well-defined states, using well-defined means of expressions, but our hearts belong to the painter's arrow-slinging realms, you see, but maybe there is another way out of this predicament, maybe even we, we writers, maybe even we can sling fiery arrows, or in an approach to Marguerite Duras, when she says I HAD ALWAYS BELIEVED A BEDROOM WAS SUBJECT TO CONVENTION, I sit at the window and contemplate *novel spirit,* or the Hebrew : *Sinning means that we should have taken better aim.*

At this point I cannot imagine putting myself in the company of other people, I believe my introspection has become entirely too expansive, and I've started taking that wonder drug ASCETICISM, I tell Blum, but it isn't always particularly palatable, it's supposed to have *a narrowing effect*—

can't seem to focus on anything today, attentive when it comes to my work, I tell Blum, but somehow distracted, maybe because I'm secretly waiting for a phone call from Joseph, because I'm secretly hoping for a phone call from Joseph, maybe that's it, looks like a fishhook, this capital J, I tell myself, I lie on my right ear, I tell Blum, I write while lying on my right ear, from my right ear, I write down what it says, what it prompts me to write, you see, I turn over onto my left side when I sleep, I lie on my left ear, I write down what it says, Joseph says, each of your books has its own distinctive tempo, the slowness of language is always giving way to breathlessness, or vice versa, everything has to be daring : guarded at the same time, actually language submits itself to everything, I say, most likely it is the image of a society, but the negative image of this photography, or distorted or out of phase or used as a fishhook for the treasures we have stored at the bottom or our consciousness, as if on the ocean floor, isn't that right, our unraised treasures . . sometimes *the hot cracks in the text* : passionate fantasies as if they had been extinguished : never there, *quivering language* vanished, forgotten, lost—

a frond of fern on house doors, I say, an Alpine horn without a musician to play it, leaning up against the restaurant arbor (still green), or maybe it was 2 crutches, a handicapped man, a distorted young creature who shot past me, cursed at me HAG!, probably because I was all dressed up in black again, etc., back then, I tell Blum, in this virtuous state, in my childhood summers in D., the red tongues : elongated droplets of blood scattered across the streets, a celebration of Corpus Christi, I remember as we, Joseph and I, proceeded down the valley I couldn't help but think of CASTANEDA, of a very specific place in one of his books, though I was not prepared to say anything about it, we snaked our way down into the valley, below us the roofs of the town jumbled up against one another, and in front of me I saw this place in CASTANEDA's book, but I don't believe I would have been able to retell it, or talk about it, even now I can feel my own footsteps, I can hear their muffled resonance in my head and feel the resilience with which my body seemed to gather them up, as if each step were landing on a rubber mattress, you see, sun-scribbled white.

10/25

I have owed you this segment for a long time, it seems so anecdotal to me, and it fits, I don't believe it really fits in here, I tell Blum, I can receive *extreme unction* any time I choose, even if I am not about to die, I say, while I'm still running around in the best of health, right, I'm too attuned to this PERGOLESI record, I say, I know the whole thing by heart, the music just isn't really a STIMULUS anymore the way I need it to be, it isn't a scalpel anymore, it can't cut my heart open and let all my blood all my bloody language come spurting and gushing out in murderous chaos, I let the record play through to the end, and I felt as if I had been delivered, the record went silent, I don't want to do anything but sit here at the typewriter all day long and half the night, I tell Blum, even though every fiber in my body is being *dragged absolutely and irrefutably out into the open,* you see. The big heavy sacks filled with plastic, laundry and junk, shoes that need repairing and empty bottles, *drained and slaughtered,* in the entryway bags filled with garbage and bread crumbs, so many that you have to leap over them, etc., for months, before she died, my mother's false teeth lay grinning on an old *country table* that stood next to the BATHROOM, it hit me so hard and I couldn't even look that way without breaking into tears, I think I was in the grips of something like evanescence, or rapture, or my teeth were starting to chatter, a faint aroma of honey wafted through the room, *the stuff of my Sunday,* I tell Blum, and while she slept, while my mother slept in the afternoon, I sat at her bedside and paged through letters from Elisabeth von Samsonow, I remember the last lines of her most recent letter : "summer is a wonderful season for me, but awful too, because everything in me is contracting, when I think how I would dearly love to fly around in this BLUE and I cannot . ."

such a PILE OF ART, I say to Blum, I woke up with these words early this morning, I think *it was being stitched into the sky,* what I was seeing through the aperture of my window, I say, something stitched into the heavens, in crosshatched letters, while I was watching my whole life passed before my eyes over the period of a very few minutes, I mean, I was asking myself WAS IT A POOR LIFE WAS IT A BRILLIANT : GLITTERING LIFE, and I was also trying to determine my current location, how I was doing and where I was, etc., hadn't I felt shut out at every moment along the way? even as a schoolgirl, I say, I was an outsider from the very beginning, for almost all of my life I felt shut out of what was going on around me, *a life magnet or nerve,* I say, for example, when I get into a conversation with intelligent people, I immediately know, I cannot break through my own limitations, the ones I've inhabited for years even decades, at best I can nod my head in agreement, even though I am unable to follow the opinions, views and learning of this highly intelligent person, and I'm not really even interested in getting involved in these opinions, views and learning, it's probably beyond me, I tell Blum, in that it forces me to leave my DOMAIN, so dear and familiar to me, and in which FLORA : what a word, I am interrupting myself!, how pretentious, still : in which flora, no matter the season, arch over me in lush abundance, and leaving, what would that do to my work, etc.

WORD SLEEP : and there was something else on it, on the slip of paper, a disparate mood, *blood horizon,* the two carriage horses both spotted black and white like dalmatians, I think the way in spring individual linden leaves sprout directly out of the trunk of the tree, quivering in the wind, you could hear water rippling in the canals, it was so quiet on that weekend day in the city, I tell Blum, you might even imagine mountain brooks, waterfalls, geysers under the asphalt everywhere in the streets all over the city, and that would be so relaxing, wouldn't it, the sign on a tour bus read see the FIGHTS (instead of SIGHTS), it is plausible, after all, hysteria savagery, I say, all dressed in leather, a wild man on a motorcycle sped right through a bed of pansies in the parkway bordering the main street, an old man sitting on a low concrete wall, wearing a dark cap shaving himself on this weekend morning, looked up, startled as I approached, pulled a hair out of his nostrils with a tweezers, probably a grandson dancing around him there, etc.

On the same day : power machine, and ragged belly, I tell Blum, *how bitterness races on,* wrote everything down while I was still half-asleep, I say, actually it has nothing to do with me, does it, I tell Blum, in a variety of colors so that I can keep everything straight in the morning, I'm up to my neck in alligators, that's what people say when things start getting complicated, desperate, even treacherous, *with blond hyenas,* I'm going around as if I were surrounded by a pack of blond hyenas, I don't dare take even one bold step, am more silent than silence, don't have enough courage to raise my voice even though I am raging inside, tormented and screaming and howling, no one will hear my raging and ranting, or acknowledge it, my face motionless, one single torment playing itself out inside my brain and my heart, I can feel myself breaking apart, disintegrating into my component fibers, shavings, reels, something like the tiny wood shavings of this brittle book I am touching, whose pages I am turning, and tiny wood strands kept crumbling away from its insides and lay scattered across the bedspread making me sick, a defense mechanism, and seeing how it completely *fell to pieces* under my touch, disintegrated, I believe it simply dropped into the pillows and hollows of the bed—I rolled around in its paper parts, unpleasant sensation, at the same time an intense desire to wash my hands, disgusted by its raggedness, fraying, infirmities, woundedness, and while I'm turning the pages I keep wondering about whose hands may have touched them before me, what kind of hands—limp, sick and wrinkled—may have put them to use, was I exposing myself to an infection simply by associating with it, *with bare hands,* maybe I should wear gloves while I'm reading, I tell Blum, so ESPECIALLY ALMOST WONDROUS, and I am reading Butor at the same time, I say, so especially almost wondrous, I tell Blum, I've had a very close relationship, I say, with one of the books Joseph lent me, that goes both for Joseph and for Butor, it seemed to me that I had begun to project my constantly rekindling desire for Joseph onto this book, its margins scribbled full of notes, as if by reading Butor I might be able to unravel the mystery Joseph represented for me, and while working my way through the mysteries of Butor's writing I might also come closer to understanding the mysteries in Joseph himself, etc., and I am also too timid, I am also tattered and frayed, an unscrupulous dreamer, *a mass image* : *a painting in splotches,* shed tears by the bucket, *ah sun scribbled away.*

X (or William or Ferdinand) writes to me that he's not happy about being referred to as X in the book I am now writing, would you like me, I write back to X, to call you William or Ferdinand? William is a beautiful name, but it's hard for me to simply stop referring to you as X—perforated again and again, pierced through, I write back to X (or William or Ferdinand), *stood on my head,* I'm so bewildered, run down the 4 flights of stairs, walk around the block a couple of times, I go shopping, I go for a walk, I'm that schoolgirl again, the one who punched holes in those hand-painted paper plates, the paper patterns, *sewed my waistband shut with the embroidery needle, etc., immense and stringent,* I'm troubled, race down the 4 flights of stairs, rip through the streets, my notepad, my leaking green felt pen always in my pocket, and everything is flowing green, into the greenery, flowing green overflowing everything, even my notes flooded with green, back to my typewriter again and again, tentatively write down a few words, type a few sentences, actually embossed, I tell Blum, piece by piece, jerkily, an awful domination, day and night, and all I think about is how I'm going to finish this damned book, this *blessed book,* I'm probably not impassioned enough, I feel as if I've been unplugged, that'll have to change, won't it, I tell Blum, words, expressions, pyramids, I say, heartfluttering, textfluttering, platefluttering, all very festive, fluttery, which has other meanings, etc.

I am looking for something in your letter, I continue writing to X (or William or Ferdinand), that would help me along, can't find it, it's hidden somewhere, it's hidden and at the same time it's not hidden at all, how am I supposed to understand that—how can something, something you've been looking for, it's right in front of your eyes but you didn't see it, somehow you looked right past it, I don't like it, I write to X (or William or Ferdinand) when someone says YOU CAN READ IT BETWEEN THE LINES, *there is nothing* between the lines of a letter, that's such a damned overused expression, close to setting me off, the fact is : there is NOTHING between the lines, 1 space, 1 void—which must be filled in by your imagination, I'm not interested, I hate having to fill things in with my imagination, everything should be said right out, a kiss is a kiss, a scream is a scream, and when I am waiting, e.g., my eyes closed, for this first good-bye kiss of Joseph's to be followed by a second, I have already been put at a disadvantage, isn't that so, a second kiss that was, it seemed to me, long overdue, and then was simply given away, CONCEDED to me, that's it, that's what it was, and I felt rage, shame and hurt, I think I collapsed into sleep, while half sentences on my knees, scribbled down on strips of shredded paper, the lunatic sketches for the next morning, for the work I would continue the next morning, I mean : the bird festive in his antenna garb, I believe it was 3 hours the bird stranded on the back of my hand, over here or there and next to me, etc., that is, 1 PALM OF 1 HAND : 1 HANDYMAN for the night on my bed, and that is how I came to my misreading. And during the night the storm flung open the shutters, shook, or I believe the storm lashed my heartbeats and drove all sleep out of me, and my body sinking into misery during its sojourn in the gardens or other diversions as pink foot towels or terry cloth sheets, etc., but then in my dreams everything in me turning completely green and in between dreams I wrote down everything that came dancing my way, words, sentences, blessings, anesthetics, in accordion folds : my parents' last utterances delivered in an almost comatose state, numerous SMACKS, *thus striding both and in forests deep.* In INCOMPREHENSION I write to Joseph, now I am finally able to return the two books you lent me this past spring, but I am not able to bring myself to discuss how all of it is connected with which things, especially the BUTOR, which I kept with me every moment of every day and everywhere, even when I traveled, it was in my lap, and at night it was in my bed, and it was wrapped up in my afghan on those evenings when I lay down still fully clothed to read, it is so very much a part of you, I believe he is one of your favorite poets, *and he especially so wondrous,* the voice of the bird chasing me, and a housefly is sucking warm milk from the pot on the stove, *it has been drinking* I mean the fly has been drinking HEADFIRST out of a pot of warm milk, and while I watched it drink I was thinking, it's drinking some of the warm milk, it's drinking my breakfast milk and I'm going to have to throw the milk away, *so that I won't be drinking what it has left for me in the pot,* and something, probably a combination of disgust and affection, brought tears to my eyes, something *attack or annexation,* and then I thought to myself, actually I should chase it away or kill it, I could see it was completely absorbed in the warm milk and it would have been so simple to sneak up on it and swat it dead, don't you see, I could have MUGGED it, but I didn't, I acknowledged the trust this creature was showing, it licked its lips : a dizzying concept, I seem to lose all sense of proportion at every turn, I tell Blum, this may be a genetic predisposition, don't you think, I am talking to Blum, but I am thinking of Joseph, I am talking to Blum, but at the same time, in my head, I am carrying on conversations with Joseph, etc., *he is spending the winter in my thinking,* or something like that, maybe all of this is nothing but a rhetorical blunder, I tell Blum, talking about an inside of language, or believing that under certain favorable constellations the inside of things and processes might be transformed into an inside of language, and therefore all we really need to do is arrive at a state of perceiving the inside of things and processes—not something we can control—to perceive the inside of language in order to take possession of the inside of language. There is a constant growling, in my ears, a HEART THUNDERING, and you begin to believe you can see how everything around you is reaching a climax, and then everything slashes you cuts you open, and, you surrender to some damned sense of salvation, and this utterly vast glow reveals itself to you, finally this the inside of language makes itself known, or I suddenly have a kind of glimmer : the hint of a word, an expression and I start looking around in dictionaries and encyclopedias hoping that they will put me on the right track and that something which had until now seemed hidden will start to twinkle and then glow, it is something like a paraphrase of a feeling, I think, a feeling that manifests itself both visually and acoustically. While I slip off, have been slipping off : *my head's jersey,* and right under my writing space, between my feet : the washbasin full of steaming hot water—"from the periphery," Joseph would say, but that is another matter.

10/26

"Torch Along the Tramway"

it really is / simply / a FOREST ENDEAVOR, I tell Blum, and these words are going to stay with me for a very long time, it occurred to me, I am attached to them, they ignite a fire in my heart, I must pour, I think red grape juice over my toes, or must have poured, then I could work more fervently, I tell Blum, the rug, the beautiful fleece, wet and a reddish purple discoloration, I am gulping down my criminal soup, don't know what that's supposed to mean, maybe I am committing crimes in my head, maybe the body of my thoughts, the blood of my thoughts is committing crimes nonstop, it's one criminal act after another, I tell Blum, the only reason I am so careful about my health is so that I can keep on writing, completely self-centered process or progression, if you like, the soul I believe, a writer's soul must be virginal in order for a writer to write, it is a piece of silk paper, must not be sullied, a telephone conversation early in the morning can sully the soul, I tell Blum, I often think to myself, I can't fight my FLAWS, I mean, even if I know they're going to destroy me, it's as if you're just rolling down a set of rails, and any attempt to leave is useless, you are too old, you are a little too comfortable, *day in and day out an orchard like this went past.*

I need the books that I buy almost every second day, I tell Blum, I need all these books so I can suck a little out of each one of them, I mean I can't finish reading any of them, but it is a delight, here and there, to hear things whispered in your ear, isn't that so, oh, this constant repetition of words, half sentences and I'm not even really aware of it, I say, I mumble along, a sand dune if possible, 1 that is constantly shifting : a new contour every day, and as if it were wandering along with me. 3 large green drops, I tell Blum, leaves of a rose on the dirty tiles of the bathroom floor, and suddenly a gaping void opened up inside me, when I came across the word

MENAGERIE, while reading the newspaper : MENAGERIE . . suddenly, I no longer knew what it meant, I said it out loud a couple of times, trying to find the meaning again, but it was useless, later I could hear the lions roaring inside my skull, the trumpets, the elephants, the cry of the lynx, *as if tears* . . here in the orangery, Marcel Beyer writes from Wiepersdorf, it smells like a CAMEL, and apparently there really were CAMELS here up until a few years ago, in the park!—well yes or my god, lame-winged anecdote, I say, I loathe anecdotes, but now I'm taking refuge in them myself, ignoble act, maybe what follows is an anecdote, and I am finding this profoundly disconcerting, I tell Blum, actually I spend entire afternoons doing nothing but lying on my OLD BED, don't feel like doing anything except reading around in the newspaper, the Mongolian dwarf dangling from the window latch again, Alma says that as we grow older we grow more and more quiet, that we are simply somewhere else, that something like *a fulfillment of apathy* takes over, in this state you are brought to tears over something which causes you pain, but then you simply forget, after 2 or 3 days you forget the pain, or it doesn't get to you anymore, even if it had been the cause of some very considerable anguish, sparrows, dog shit : the vehicle scoops up everything, I mean the 1 that is making such a spectacular racket, I kept wondering what it could be, I knew I had heard this unnerving sound before somewhere, the evidence suggested construction equipment, laying asphalt, excavators, but none of this quite matched up with my acoustical recollection, then I leaned out of the window and saw that despite the generally frosty conditions there was a garden mower accomplishing its hellish chore among the greenery on the roof of the parking garage across the street, I would never have imagined this, but somehow, even though I found the noise unsettling, I was relieved to see that it was a mower, in the middle of fall, etc. So obsessed with feeding, I say to Blum, this shearing, this vehicle ingesting every bit of refuse in its path, I say, it was ringing right in my ear, I write to Joseph, the ringing wakes me up, AND WITH THE BOUQUET OF FLOWERS I WAS . . at this point I lose the image, I write to Joseph, I guess it just slips my mind, what was there about this bouquet of flowers, what was it really, what were the circumstances, what was the whole context, so, I am unable to finish the sentence, because when the image, when the context vanishes, when my consciousness deserts me, there is nothing which *grates or provokes* me to write, I believe that for 1 moment there was an image, and I could have translated it into something wondrous, into a language, but because the image, the image I had in my mind escaped me, from 1 second to the next,

I am unable to pursue even this most enchanting and beautiful impulse, it would be an act of betrayal, an artifice, almost a crime, isn't that right, so everything is going to have to remain a fragment . .
such a fine dog, I say to Blum, I report to Blum, in front of the mirror in the supermarket doors, staring into it, where his caregiver, his protector, his true love, his food provider, etc. has gone, my transit body is exhausted, I lie down on a sleeping mat, a lark is *shooting salvos* around inside my skull, no I don't mean salve : I mean salvo. By afternoon I had already forgotten what I had written in the morning, I say to Blum, you are a concept, a finely tailored concept in my life, I say, you are the only constant in my life, now that my mother is dead, you *give me speech,* you guide my spirit, stern, watchful, understanding of my weaknesses, as if tears. As I was leaving the bar, 2 youngsters grumbled at me: BITCH (or WITCH), very mean and menacing, I tell Blum, I had tripped on the step as I was leaving and almost fell right into their raw beings, it was a real shock and I was deeply embarrassed, I say. Where is the anecdote, Blum says, where is this anecdotal material of yours, Blum says, have you let it get away from you, did you trip over it, stumble the way you did when you were coming out of the wine cellar—ah, what was once a plastic bag larger than life has *crashed* into the bare crown of a tree, I mean on the storms of my night it flew up into the branches and was ensnared, there is something very strange about it, even bizarre, a kind of grimy veil, with a ghostly temper, and it's flapping, fluttering in the uppermost branches, actually it's disgusting, nauseating, a frayed plastic skin, caricature of a banner, flag, dirty pennant, or something like that, it is still a mystery but above all it is, I feel it is unappealing, no one wants to have anything to do with it, just seeing it is enough to make you throw up, isn't it—for days on end this webbing on one of the bald robinias, strangely enough, I say, but completely unobserved, no one looks up into the crown of the tree in which tattered and frayed vileness, etc.
Readingly poodle, I say, readingly used as an adverb, telefeed, text feed, I say, my stranded skull, written on the arm of my chair, I tell Blum, just think, all of these letters scribbled out on the arm of my chair, using the palm of my left hand as a pad, hurriedly, eerily, in a matter of seconds, pasting the stamps and the return address sticker onto the envelope takes up most of the time, this is what I do with my time, I say, and the entire afternoon will have to *put up* with my aimless dozing and muted daydreams, tracking down sensations or simply letting myself be deluged by them so that by evening I can write again, an *amusing illness,* isn't it, being able to write : not being able to write, idiotic to ponder around until you find just the

right word, to let yourself be inundated with an overabundance of words and sentences, sometimes this, sometimes that, never taking control, I say, but surrendering yourself unconditionally to this functioning or nonfunctioning COPULATION MACHINE, you see, with silk paper, onionskin paper, with delicate carbon paper I dry my hands, dip my *beak* into a large mug full of coffee, with my shortsighted eye regard the unappealing milky skin across the surface of my hot drink, clap my hands together, cross my arms behind my back, forget to play PERGOLESI, forget to put the vegetable casserole on the stove, forget to buy milk, bread, apples, wave to Alma when we part, and while doing so think about the new : trendy practice, instead of waving a raised hand, your hand only half-raised, you actually *flap* your fingers open and shut, as if you were reluctant to let the departing person go, a haptic phenomenon, isn't it, I tell Blum, especially popular among the young, etc. As far as all my books are concerned, I tell Blum, I have gotten into the habit of spreading my *current* favorites all across my bed, opening them up one after the other, and reading around in them for some time, for an entire afternoon, let's say, and then the next day I might switch to another book, and this is how the voices of the poets changed, that was a great pleasure, a congenial amusement, and I couldn't stand any interruption, especially of an acoustic sort. I couldn't stand any music, not even Pergolesi, not even Bach, it would be nothing but a distraction, I couldn't stand anyone near me, I was deep in conversation with my favorite poets : in a physical sense a completely relaxed state—I lay stretched out flat on my mattress—in opposition to the psychic, I believe I was reading in these books with my mouth wide open, my nerves as taut as they could possibly be, sensation and perception open, and no one, nothing, other than my own writing, could possibly surpass this joy . . the next morning I slipped a bookmark into the books where I had stopped reading, and turning to another of my favorite poets, maybe that's the way it was, more than anything else I wanted to avoid succumbing to 1 style of writing, and I read around like this so that I won't become infected, etc. Wasn't that so, I say to Blum, I also related to my FAVORITE PEOPLE in a similar way, I say, I approach 1 of my FAVORITE PEOPLE, something comes glowing through to me, I approach this person in the most intense possible way only to leave him after some time in search of new inspiration, I keep exchanging FAVORITE PEOPLE, there is permanence in change, you are the only exception, you are the CONSTANT in the play of my love attacks, isn't that so, among my changing cast of friends Joseph is something of a high point, I am addicted to him to a truly cruel degree, you might describe it

that way, but even in Joseph's case I sometimes feel that my obsession is no longer as unconditional as it was at the beginning—sometimes I have this sneaking suspicion that my obsession, my addiction to Joseph is actually nothing but an obsession, an addiction to the nature of love itself, given my abject grandiose and theatrical qualities, etc. And incidentally, I tell Blum, these days Joseph seems to be showing me a certain fine contempt, no : an ironic reserve, once he sensed how completely taken I was with him.
This athlete, I tell Joseph, you must have noticed him, you gaze into this picture, into this photograph, and the first thing you notice is this athlete, isn't that right, how extremely attractive, I say, the tiny creases in his neck, the bushy panicles at his feet, *day in and day out such an orchard passed by,* pleasing and soft, against a white background, the windlass racing in the wind, it envelops me the way a hull does a seed, I mean this my writing, this my GATHERING of secret messages, etc. When I read Blum's most recent poem, some of his expressions were unclear to me, I said, I don't understand that, he replied, MAYBE A SECRET, a SECRET MESSAGE . .
sometimes I simply don't bother, I tell Joseph, sometimes, in my text I simply don't bother with all of that miserable choreography, putting experiences, observations, feelings, opinions into the mouth of 1 character or another, the choice of words : *access to words* can also be a measure of the closeness or the distance in a relationship between characters, I choose a very specific language in very specific situations, you see, as piety dictates, although I don't know if this has anything to do with feelings of piety when I'm talking to Blum, when I'm talking to you, I speak GENTLY, intending to show consideration, and also masquerading. Even this *layman's* talk, I say to Joseph, unknowing talk, *bird's antenna shirt,* e.g., *or a bird in a shirt of anemones,* etc.
jackboot steps on a bird's foot, I hobble away howling, a PRESLEEPER, i.e. I can sleep at any hour of the day because writing fills me with such an abundance of joy and awe, I feel quarried out and exploited and powered out and raked over, raked over with a poker and scraped out, right, nothing but ashes falling out through the grill, you see, still, the only joy I know is my writing, I tell Joseph, do you understand what I am saying, of course you understand, it's just a part of this constant jargon going on between us and between me and Blum, and between me and the other CARDBOARD COMRADES in this book, it's all cardboard, isn't it, papier-mâché or something like that, don't anyone believe that these are real people dancing around in here, not all at all, NULL JOY, I tell Joseph, all that's left in my life is NULL JOY, except when I can write or take a walk among the trees,

I believe that trees and animals touch me most closely, I believe, branches in the crown of a tree, whether bald or full of leaves, looking into a dog's eyes can bring me to tears, it's true, I tell Joseph, I called the insurance office, got put on hold, a melody I knew loved kept being interrupted by a voice asking me to PLEASE WAIT, I was happy to wait, the melody I knew, but did not know who had composed it, touched me, and that is how I felt being put on hold by the INSURANCE AGENCY for the SOUL, of course this is an outrageous expression, I tell Joseph, but it forced its way out, *millefleurs on the street.* By the way, dear Joseph, I write to Joseph, you are beginning to show a touch of remoteness, or what kind of expression is this, what do you think about an expression as idiotic as this, *I am a simple rhyme between a footstool and a washbasin,* most of the time I hold your letters, let them sit around in an unsealed envelope so that I can reread them, make corrections, lying around on the ottoman, my heart beating wildly etc., and I keep coming up with things to add, I note them down so that I will be able to include them or add them on as a postscript, as a footnote or a postscript, that is, *off track,* you see, I'm dumbfounded, my washed-out face, all of this water, oh, my dear old study, *topology as nudity,* etc. an eternal ADORATION, dear Joseph, the drift : monstrosity of my deluded behavior, and on top of that the whole of my UNKNOWING, I write, how miserable, humiliating for me, this past summer the first swallows appeared on the 14th of May, I noted that down in my calendar.

As far as anecdotes, an anecdotal aspect is concerned, I tell Blum, for the time being I still owe you an accounting, maybe I can come up with a footnote in the not too distant future . .

10/27

"in such a Roentgen Press, Dream"

I knew it would attract flies, the leftovers would attract flies, the window was open; my room, right, full of nothing but aggravation, I tell Blum, the earth's axis is cutting through my body, I can feel it, I am prone to panic attacks, I tell Blum, when my stomach is empty I am prone to attacks of hypertonia, I slumbered, I cried, the lantern in my mother's eyes, I hear the buzz of the first fly, it's buzzing on a zigzag path through the room, the lantern on my mother's cheek, I am sitting down to a meal across from my dead mother, she really does have rosy cheeks, and that embarrassed expression around her mouth that I knew so well, and that always came over her face whenever anyone wanted to take a picture of her, whenever she was photographed, I say, this appearance : this *translucence,* these fingery blossoms next to the red armchair where she was sitting, her billowy gown her thin body underneath, etc., when I opened the smooth shiny piece of paper that lay on the table, and which I had been using to take down notes, I was stunned : it was the obituary of a very dear friend of mine, apparently, because of its slippery surface, this sheet of paper had simply slid in among my notes, I had slept, cried, I don't even have so much as 1 corner of a table where I can eat my soup, I tell Joseph, Joseph had let cold tap water run over his face after eating, then dried his hands in a white hand towel full of holes, it was a remarkable day, I tell him, a woman in bare feet got on, in one arm she was carrying a very alert-looking white dog with pointed ears, and I kept looking at it, because I liked it, *I had transformed myself into a dog again,* the metamorphosis took place over a matter of minutes as I had crawled into this dog and was now inside looking out, looking at myself, sitting across from myself and admiring me, and inside my skull this sentence was taking form : *that was some trick!,* before she got off, the

barefooted woman handed me a garishly green straw hat and said, FROM VIETNAM!, I attempted to thank her by saying : *You have a beautiful dog!,* to which she replied : *And now you have a beautiful hat, too!,* apparently, instead of understanding me to say DOG : HAT was what she heard . .
TRISTANO, Lily says on the telephone, Easter is called TRISTANO, it means the eye of a needle, I am sewing on a RAG in the living room, dark, it's a prayer, I think dark blue, how can we create reality, *I would go into the forest to the wolves, the ruins with honking color, dream,* with these words Lily ended her conversation, I tell Joseph, these moist glistening leaves, I see May, but it's October, what can I possibly do with this old stuff, with these old notes, I tell Joseph, it is so difficult to make anything beautiful out of stale old notes, a poorly tailored suit, a bungled plan, can anything be salvaged, I ask myself, etc., I'm going to go see Artaud, I say to Joseph, don't know what that means, maybe anemone hand or skin, for example, it sounds like a dream word, doesn't it, nightgowns have wings, I say, I mean they're full of static electricity, just like my hair, A FEAR CONSTRUCT, when days are at their coldest I start perspiring all over my body, because I am afraid, indeterminate states of anxiety, awful malperceptions, devastation : extermination of my self, I am afraid of people, afraid of their brutality, cunning and lying, then my keyboard begins to blur in front of my eyes, I say, *and flew like an Oslo.*
Oddly enough, mounted there on the kiosk, a reproduction of the painting of a woman in a red armchair by Emil Orlik replicating the image of my mother that I had stored away in my memory a few months before her death, I tell Joseph, this picture on a kiosk that I discovered after more than 2 years reproduced everything I had locked away, closed inside me only a few months before she died, she was sitting there in her woolen things, feigning physical presence, but underneath her billowing robe she had completely withered away, she was holding a cup of soup in her trembling hands, raised it to her mouth, smiled, said THAT TASTES SO GOOD, etc.
I had to wait until the sun went down, switched on the lamp at my writing desk, then *birds being stranded in the palm* of my hand, nothing but fluttering faces.
Flapping waves of doves in the low-ceilinged hall of the train station—a place to which birds are always mistakenly attracted, and then somehow manage to find their way out—but it wasn't the flapping wings of the doves, it was the crackling paper bags of the old ladies in head scarves, they were carrying such large sacks around with them, set them up on the

benches, and whenever anyone else came looking for a place to sit, they rummaged around in their paper bags and crumpled them shut at the top if they could, things hummed and whirred and beat with wings, and while I was waiting for my train, seated on one of those ugly plastic benches with their "ergonomically correct" seats, I couldn't really tell whether the sound was the flapping of wings or the crumpling, rustling of paper bags—
on the first day only cried, I say to Alma, *I believe only cried,* all evening, all night, in the morning dry and irritated eyes, when Blum left, and I had gone with him to the train station and he kissed me good-bye, and in the doorway of the train car he turned around to me full face, stood up straight as if to say, now, look at me once more, this 1 last time completely, and then I cried and cried the entire evening the entire night, and held my hands over my face as if this were a final good-bye, I say, or he once said, lend me your favorite books, 1 of those books you like so much, a so-called difficult book, he said, I think he was smiling as he said these things, by one of your noble poets, exalted poets, outside the last leaves were rustling in the red oak, falling, *porridgely,* he said, I tell Alma, before he left, England is a huge OAK SURPRISE, then he said NIL, that is so much more expressive than "Nile," and for a moment all I could think of was HIPPOPOTAMUS, this morning began with extreme hunger despite the flood of tears, I tell Alma, in tears I choked down my black bread, a hole in the middle of my body : cavern apparently, I tell Alma, *have a heavy heart or pericardium,* to what extent, I ask myself, is the caustic in art *a reveling* in what is caustic, a caustic ecstasy, or an admonishment, a criticism?
I believe that if a sense of ecstasy does not emerge prior to / during the writing process, I tell Alma, the resulting text will be bad, somehow disjointed, misshapen, contemptible, isn't that right.
When, out of the corner of my eye, I caught sight of Rühm walking through the underpass, I tell Alma, the impulse to call out, call after him, call him back, was not strong enough, I believe I shouted : HELLO GERHARD, but only inside my head, in no way did my shout cross the threshold of an actual : acoustical outcry, so I found myself having to watch as he hurried off, disappeared into the milling crowd, and until late into the night I could not escape the sense of having LOST something, this unarticulated HELLO GERHARD!, I was, I believe I was too slow, I was unable to coordinate the wish to greet him with the discharge of HELLO GERHARD, might have cost too much energy, that might have been, there was definitely something in play here, I say to Alma, observing me, more particularly, the way I failed, and he ran off, but I was still able to sense his bright, surprised

voice / mood, inside my skull, so maybe I hadn't done everything wrong, after all, because I was replaying the entire scene in my mind, yes, evidently I was seeing my poet friend surface out of the crowd over and over again, nonstop, I was able to replicate everything hundreds of times, even my hesitation, and his disappearance, too, his greeting, his good-bye wave, his laugh, which means nothing other than the fact that IT, more precisely, HE had sucked himself firmly into my consciousness, in a way that he would not have if I had actually greeted him, and now it would take days and days for his sudden surfacing, his being greeted by me, his re-disappearance to be replayed, replayed and disassembled . .
excrement drifts up against the spur of the heel, milk coal forgetfulness, the glockenspiel of bus doors closing under my window, I am a drinker and I start drinking early in the morning, I / he : the drinker we don't really want to, no it's not our intention, on the contrary : when we wake up, circa 4 o'clock in the morning, we are full of resolve to do right things, clean and straighten up, bathe and cream, change into fresh clothes, do the shopping, get flowers, and getting melancholy things out of the way—but we tend to relapse : between brushing teeth and breakfast already two tablets scribbled full of notes!, I believe TRISTANO (purple notes, etc.). The yellow hair I mean *dipped,* cacophonous clamor everywhere, at 5 o'clock *time for handiwork,* I catch up on my hammering, that is, my heartbeats catch up on their hammering, hardly able to heave myself up out of the bathtub, I say, marled resignation of ligaments and bone, what do I know, looked through *the entire Brothers Grimm, etc., corral* my winter clothes, can hardly get through to my closets, not much use to me, mountains of writing paper, *murmuring literature,* in bright-colored binders block the way to the doors, with my tongue the laundry, with the JUNK the dirty laundry, with the junk the tongue the dirty laundry licked off, right, I mean all of a sudden I have so many friends, I say to Alma, it was never like this before, I say, all of MY OLD LOVERS ARE, like a butterfly emerging from its cocoon, now new friends slipped—if that isn't a gift!, why everything so discreetly veiled, Lily says, WE STINK AND WE ARE CAVERNS, Lily says, a dove greeted me in the window, with wings as black as coal, milk coal forgetfulness, I say, then I dribbled, right into the middle of what I was writing, my rough drafts, original notes, letters, because, I believe it is because after brushing my teeth I get an undeniable urge *to spit out into the space around me,* the PARK NOTES, alternate between calm and excess, as if collaging Kleist notes : the sights of my heart—NO! too precious : will have to be crossed out : ridiculous hyperbole!

10/29

directing (distress / distressing) the dear little book, I tell Joseph, or the tome I'm working on now, from tune, dance tune, dance to the tune, dancing now, dancing around in my poor old bed, etc., the ART OF STIRRING THE SOUL, as Novalis writes, I say, THIS ENVELOPE STIRRING THE SOUL, the one I'm holding in my hand, containing your most recent letter, to be more precise your literary experiments on your own very breathing brain and heart, instead of "breathing" : "cleaving," what a getup, what cynicism, right, what a tirade, how sophomoric, how *soft-soled,* I was going to write : and here I want the reader's entire attention directed to the theme of *soft soles, loaded,* aimed, trained, leveled, pointed, etc., will he then allow himself to be lured, allured, I ask myself, will he surrender himself, I think it is his innermost wish, his innermost desire to be seduced by what he is reading, dragged here dragged there, led, accompanied, ripped up into the heights and back down : into the heaven of language : into the hell of language, until breathless he lets the book fall from his hand because he has reached the end of his powers his emotional capacity, I believe at the end of his nerves, isn't that right, it is an issue of the spirit, it is *a social issue,* impelling the reader up to the turning point : heaven / hell, cracking the whip in one / another direction, chasing, hunting him down—this must be society's 1 true concern, and all other social issues must bow down before it, diminish, disappear, it will be a *book of screams,* I tell Joseph, yes, you heard correctly : a little book of screams, not a little book of dreams, and the reader will scream, though not of his own volition, scream, lose his senses, go mad, etc.

What remains of an ALPINE TOOL, I say, here what remains of an Alpine tool, text moth, text feed, what do I know, my whole housing stuffed full of useless objects I can't get rid of, because they belong to me, I say to Joseph, as you can see, there is hardly enough room to sit down, hardly enough open space to get to the window, although when the two of us are standing so close to one another, probably because of the cramped space—right? so when the two of us are standing at the window pressed up so close to one another and looking at the mountains in the distant west, the veiled mountains, fog or fine haze, a delicate tender wall almost nothing but intimation on the horizon, and I hear your heart beating, because we are standing so close to one another, and I sense your *body majesty*—or am I being too lyrical? and I am overcome by a most profound attenuation of nervous sensation, and all I want to do is throw my arms around you, simply needing you to give me hold, but you turn away, the deepest burial of ecstasy, the deepest, the most typing, the most typed burial of ecstasy, don't you see, a sinking drop in sensation, right, it takes my voice away and all I have left is a whisper, and even the world the world of mountain folds to be seen out of my window has grown more and more somber, dark, a storm is brewing, the scar, the steel trap, the May-like weather in fall, *and how could I forget all of this,* I write to Joseph the next morning, with each evocation the touches we shared develop a different shading, a different shadow, there are both bright and dark shadows, isn't that so, I believe a different nuance, and in the meantime both shadow and light have flitted over the original image any number of times, *undergrowth and sense of hearing,* I say, a dark wavy horse hair on my body, I look down at my body as I write, I wonder if I have washed, taken a bath, gotten dressed, milk, coal, forgetfulness, *secondary date* etc.

a sea of forgetfulness, I write to Heidrun Loeper, so many lips and hearts but never enough, too short this life and tough and limited, and how is your arm, when I think about your infirm arm it always makes me think about EMBRACING . . maybe there is a correlation between a love affair and a betrayal : inflicted on ourselves, I mean, by a part of our body, you see, when I am very happy I get hypertonic, I believe, oh, we can turn illness into health, Heidrun Loeper writes back to me, if I have understood her correctly, right, Heidrun Loeper writes, I don't write anything but letters these days, and my right arm is lame BECAUSE I OFFENDED IT?—I don't know, or maybe you know, do you know how all of this happened, Heidrun Loeper writes, all I have to do is close my eyes and I see you, translucent : enveloped in glowing light, as light as a feather, ah the galloping illnesses, Heidrun Loeper writes, do illnesses gallop after us or do we seek them out, do we gallop right into them? my great aunt, I write back

to Heidrun Loeper, always said, he (her brother) HAD THE GALLOPS, something my childish mind was unable to comprehend, she meant TUBERCULOSIS, the bleeding malady, isn't that right.
You have to read Flaubert, Blum says, like shoes on a doormat, I say, drying a *silvery* foot on the pink terry cloth towel, then tossing the towel away, the shit in the terry cloth—such *stalking weather,* I say, dream or storm clouds, or I believe I got a whiff of it from the enervating stench of sweat on the streetcar, a sudden rain splashing through the radiators, the puddle of water between bare feet, in a panic, afraid all my notes will tumble down into it, the basin full of water under my writing table, *the dark flowers from Lisianthus* are swimming around in the tub in order to be refreshed, I say, so, I won't be able to take a bath today, either, I like projecting myself into everyday objects in my house, the physicality of a mineral water bottle, e.g., : its harmonious figure, its slender neck, its closed cap or mouth, when someone tilts it or me, the way we start to fizz, release water, camouflage weighs so heavily upon my soul, the way the cross of Christendom *flies* above a sky full of cumulus clouds, or it's the clouds flying while the cyclist with the gypsy scarf (not tied under his chin but tightly wrapped / wound around his forehead) races past almost knocking me down, while a ship capsizes inside a gold frame in a nearby antique shop, *Assorted Viennese Art Grill or something like that.*
("*The wind outside is writing this book,*" George Bataille.)
Flickered out me : burned out, this brain talk is raging inside me, am I afflicted with escapism, I wonder, I say to Blum, color of the room, color of cinnamon; penis, lacquered; passages with occasional puddles of rain, and in every puddle a monstrous face *en face,* in profile, and pictures of animals too : hunchbacked dogs and fish, little pouting mouths, eyes wide open, grimacing countenance, am channeled into the eye slit of a giant cat, subdate, enervation, etc., held my breath when I came upon the word MENAGERIE in my reading, suddenly no longer knew what it meant, who had where, while I was writing this sequence down in my notebook with the STAGHORN BUTTONS, out loud the phrase STAGHORN BUTTONS, so loudly that everyone around me—where did I hear this? from whom?—stopped and looked up, isn't that so, or did I just make it all up, was it pure fantasy, invention, I say to Blum, and maybe my relationship with Joseph, too, is something I have only imagined, maybe I had simply talked myself into it, apparently invented everything myself, exists only in my fantasy in my desire that it be.

10/31

"und Liebling Knospe v. Mai . ." / "rough winds do shake the darling buds of May . ."

—William Shakespeare

E as in Elisabeth, I am writing to Elisabeth von Samsonow, packing for my next trip, have nothing but small gold disks in my right hand, am *peeled,* right out of the egg, freshly hatched, it all depends on your perspective, I write to Elisabeth von Samsonow, the perspective from which you view the world, from which you judge it, isn't that right, in the morning a view of the world that is different from your view in the evening, morning a piece of gold, evening a foretaste of the end of life, etc., in the morning just hatched, freshly hatched, hatched right out of the egg, preening my feathers, full of energy and mischief ready for any madness, any daredevil leap, for any grinningly EXTREME SPIRIT!, etc., the taxi driver is wearing a very provocative fragrance : disgusting like PITRALON, a *pants revival,* isn't it, right here in Vienna, I am writing to you, completely *wilted,* because it's already evening, writing is a matter of devotion, and of grace, too, and above all, later, dear Elisabeth, when I am finished with this book, you will read yourself in my book, and I already have a title, actually several titles, in the early morning, 3 o'clock, woke up, turned on the lamp next to my bed, wrote down : "to be alive, pure, with an ambitious (also elegiac) heart . . what a gift, etc."

you are now in Rome, dear Elisabeth, I write to Elisabeth von Samsonow, last year on November 7, I read in Rome, 12 days later my mother died, the monstrosity of death, the outrage, the scandal death, I will never be able to grasp it, accept it, apparently I am not mature enough for this life, and not yet ripe enough for my own death, sometimes I think that I am standing at the beginning, at the beginning of my life, of my writing, *as if I still had everything before me,* an intimation that I still have a few years' time and can perfect myself—

when I look at my first draft, I say to Blum, when I check through my first draft in order to prepare the final version of my manuscript, I say, I suffer, I am standing in front of a broken mirror, individual pieces, all falling apart, no longer have anything to do with me, with my current view of things, there is something dull, I am confronted with something dull and threadbare and I hardly know what to do with it anymore, a kind of purism has overtaken me in the meantime, etc., such coincidences, I say, this morning the radio announcer kept swallowing the final consonants of every word he spoke, so that it sounded as if every word ended with an "e" instead of an "r," and then the voice of a friend on the telephone, and she was also dropping final consonants, why, I asked myself, and I was about to *help her out,* to correct her and provide the final "r," but I didn't interrupt her after all, the arts of color intersect with one another merge with one another, and right now I am in the middle of a color conflict, am being nailed to the cross, find myself achingly involved in the orgasm of a picture, everything is raining down over me, each fluid color in all its ferocity : boundless unstaunchable flood of tears in all the colors of the rainbow, a weeping icon, etc., liquefaction of motive.

Tear-filled morning, I tell Blum, I am polishing my soles my soul, passed judgment last night : last judgment, I mean most recent chapter, passed judgment on my most recent chapter, it can't go on like this, I tell myself, my most recent chapter : weak chapter, I tell myself, most recent chapter, *bedeviled* chapter, has to be firmed up, has to be skinned, right down to the bones. In a taxi on the way to a friend's house I saw TEGETHOFF rowing his way through the fog with his arms, etc., a heart of red poppy seed drank, or you might also say, a heart of red moon drunk, some quote or other, probably Bashō, have cultivated something of a pained capacity for imagination over the past 2 years, punches and blows from all sides I mean the GOOD BEATING with which our fate is allocated to us, blow for blow and you start getting sore, and more and more so, and again and again, etc., then look through a gauze curtain behind which the events of the world of human beings appear to be comprehensible, no matter how thoroughly concealed they may be, I say, HEART CLOACA, I say, then I see right through it : right through everything, I say, and it shakes me, until I break down in tears, the thumbtacks are called PHALANX, out of stiff cardboard cut out a 3-piece breast form : or, put another way : 3 pieces of petal from a paper flower, colored up, passed through a crack around the doorframe to a friend on her birthday, etc., while the fumes or ecstasy (snow blotches) and ran down I mean into my underclothes, into the whole lower part of my body, in my lower body, in my underclothes, getting caught there, in the folds, borders and ribbons, and everything steamed up the way things do in a hot wash, the way my damned Poetry Production is 1 big hot wash, right, where all everything does is rumble and bubble and boil and babble, where everything is getting brewed up together and mixed and stirred and incorporated pitifully, the tiniest bits of language garbage, and blended and used and *reinvented,* and the wind blew so hard, and rattled, until everything was swept from its place, I say, even the tiny leaves of Venus, the Piano Sonata no. 2 in C Minor, by Domenico Donizetti, so full of soulless virtuosity that it makes me want to howl out loud, *snow lingerie / splinter clothing,* I am standing here *stark naked,* bared of every last piece of my soul's raiment, do you see.

Thought flowers, paper flowers : and grew so obliquely, Elisabeth von Samsonow says, we should not forget that machines have a desperate poetry, this changeable dove sky, I say, so imploding, such a writing storm, isn't it, or I am entirely generalized, wasting my time, or one morning is like every other : while I am putting on eye makeup I am reminded of the marketplace in S., I mean the way I am roaming through the little town with Blum, finding a rolled-up geranium leaf on the sidewalk, probably torn loose by the wind from a window garden on one of the upper floors, dried-up, raked-up foliage on the skin of the carpet, the season's official seal, I shout, birds of paradise painted on a black tray glided toward me, grazed my eye, my forehead . .

it was a stormy phenomenon, I tell Blum, an enormous mass of energy came gushing out between the horns, of my skull, directly onto the sheet I had fed into the machine, there is a chase going on inside me, there is a machine loose, some kind of machine is loose inside me, I say, last night water was running all night, I mean I had forgotten to turn off the water before I went to bed, in the morning a sliver of fingernail on my blanket, probably fell off while I was sleeping . . in any case, a lot of things are moving inside me, and am AS IF a waitress in a bar, I tell Blum, magnet, or something like that, when I slip on this *motley* smock, the one with staghorn buttons and the buttons hanging by a single thread and me not capable of sewing them down tight, simply not seeing a STEP AND A WAY, can you understand that, there are some household chores I can just do, but faced with sewing, mending, patching, something brings me to a full stop, something INTESTINALLY WEARING, I believe, I don't understand it myself, and during all of this NEEDLEWORK I find myself having to throw up any number of times, my sewing needle in my hand, just imagine that, shoulders contracting (just an aside to the reader : I am trying for a truly absurd effect here! something despicably calculating, you see?), as a MAGNET or something like that, the simple old coat the hand-worked coat with the ridiculous staghorn buttons, god knows the person who came up with these staghorn buttons must have had a really overgrown mind, an honest work jacket it is : proper work jacket which I hardly dare to button up, *because at any given moment the buttons might fall off,* and then me with my wings wide open I mean all there is underneath is this UNDERWEAR, right, and the shore is opening wider, I say to Blum, my feet in the washbasin under my writing table, the basin is overflowing, *all my papers,* I yell, my battle jacket wrap shawl cape, this is how I protect myself from a ringing telephone, I have learned by heart the stereotypical script to be used in response to every inquiry : YES, YES I'M FINE, EVERYTHING'S FINE, DAMNED GOOD!, etc., I'm cleaning myself up, I'm cleaning up with my sense of justice, and what I get from this is something like an obsession with injustice, I carry it around in the world with me day in and day out, but no one notices no one has got the slightest inkling, you see, because what I am showing the whole world is *lunatic good behavior,* so that everyone will get the impression that *I am a completely normal person, through and through,* and while I am typing something or someone some sort of clientele is sitting on my shoulder, or is resting up against me as I saw it do yesterday, a hunchbacked old man who DID NOT FEED, the way many old people do, because they are so lonely, I mean he did not FEED THE PIGEONS, he simply stood there against 1 wall of the kiosk, but I couldn't tell whether he was putting something in his mouth or writing something down, then a plump pigeon came and landed on his shoulder, a second one landed on his deformed back, and as my streetcar made off with me I was still able to see how he angrily raised his arms and chased the 2 birds away, so I can feel something at my back, behind me, haven't been able to get at it, but there is something *crouching* there, I say, some kind of sinister remark, or the like, something ominous, I don't know, maybe I don't even want to know, but as long as this unknown : this indeterminate thing is present over my shoulder, at the back of my head, brushing up against the nape of my neck, almost anything can happen, maybe it will even overexcite my heart, the stammering on the machine, the trace of a tear or promiscuity etc. What is it really? a bird, a stinking fish, predatory cat CROUCHING ON BRANCH AND NECK, etc., a little Cerberus-like with neither manners nor bars, I say, the handle is lying straight up on the notebook like the pointed-pencil skyscraper in F., the one I took my hat off to, I think, 2 heated-up YOUNGSTERS behind me on the bus, aiming their aggressions at me from the vantage of their hideout, but I was wearing my storm hat so nothing much could happen, they were shorn or they were wearing baseball caps : visor to the back, they were loud and irate, probably tanked up, etc., giant bottle of Cola, bottom up, on a billboard : used as an exclamation point following the command TAKE THAT, also allusion to a pop group of that name, I say, SPLINTER WEAR of a moss-colored bottle spinning around over the tabletop, I say to Blum, sesame seeds on the wood floor, a trough full of garbage, crumbs of consciousness and a flagon of mind, and whatever else was whirling around me, I say, *my only language* beloved language scrapped, right, and a hailstone came crashing down on my skull, everything smashed, AND EVERYTHING BEGAN TO GO BLURRY, etc., all these clichés, all of a sudden it seemed to me that I had simply gotten used to them, or reeled in, right, NOTHING ACTUALLY IN EXISTENCE, simply learned everything by rote, borrowed things, right, tattered brain, doesn't hold anything anymore, *leaving everything sit,* like a slobbering old man, right, an execution maneuver, enthused over everything hawked it all, so I could apply it, use it, display it, show, launch it into the dark night sky like a rocket of nerves, so that everyone will see, extol it, all these bits of audacity, craziness, arrogance, this feeling myself to be the center of an exulted state of writing, attuned to the vibrating soul of writing everywhere, this hubris, this unfolding of self, expounding, displaying, etc. *Have just hawked my own brood of children,* I tell Lily, who truly applauds these expressions of my mind's desolation, she is a dedicated feminist!, and then I break down in tears, I tell Lily, in view of this FIERY DISPLAY (Hermes's Baby), and how her tiny teeth form such a dainty bite, isn't that right, I say, temperatures in the morning low, cold as the day begins, but my body burning, my brain is broadcasting radio announcements, I keep writing them down, nonstop, I say, and the stench already perceptible through conduits and schemata, I tell Lily, you know this phenomenon, the belt dragging along the kitchen floor, the belt buckle crushed, the joint of the right-hand thumb showing traces of eye makeup, and I meet up with all of the mad people in my sleepless nights, early morning hours, while they are ROCKING MILLING AROUND inside my brain, they have gotten used to it, I mean they seem to feel they have a right to wander around inside my skull whispering things to me that I don't understand but must write down, etc.

He sat among the blooms / so that among the blooms he sat, and was blonded through (appeared), Lo Duca writes about Bataille at the end of his life, and thus on the onionskin paper of my daily writings, I tell Blum, is it so, I mean stimulation of the nerves, I ask Blum, and then I see her old hand again, my mother's old monochrome hand, or the capricious *swallows* (billowing cirrus) of music, a minor deviation from Derrida's wonderful tatters, I tell Blum, *a cooing, naturally,* I say, CULTURE'S CORNFLOWERS, or : I am utterly enervated from all my work / in this region of the forest, I say, and in the end I cannot make out things written down, in shorthand with a fine-tipped pen, etc., then mirror images of correlations I hadn't intended to make, creating new platforms in the midst of this my night, haze, navel societies, right, I say, had to feed a fresh sheet of paper into the machine because the end of the transcription I had fixed in the previous week did not harmonize with today's feather robes, mind's feather robes or something like that, more likely a paper dress, a feeling of satisfaction that came with emptying the contents of the teapot into my cup, down to the last drop, with crumpling up a cigarette pack I had smoked my way through, with PEERING INTO an empty box of pills, every last one swallowed, empty stuff pitched into the paper corner, housecoat dropped and slips of paper, family colors, bouquet of barberry on whose stems the wilted, I mean it is disastrous, all too disastrous, I mean this exalted language, if, e.g., I were to say, on the bouquet of barberry . . , it is bedecked with paper flowers, word flowers, this is too precious : overwrought, ornate, not something we ever really wanted, just as we cannot tie into an *old tone,* the notes we took down a week ago emanated from an entirely different set of emotional circumstances, and they cannot be reproduced, isn't that right, art fragment, but all in all a matter of DEVOTION, I say, *a forest greeting, a textile embrace,* all pieces collected by a paranoid soul, your voice on the answering machine is like a dear, familiar photograph of you, I tell Blum, "when you get back from STRAWANZEN, etc." Only after the fact do we carry on our true : pertinent conversations, in our heads, I tell Blum, 2, 3 days after one of Joseph's visits, I suddenly know the correct : the right responses, questions, inserts, additions, or where in course of which discussion I should have kept quiet rather than *letting loose,* do you see.

11/2

it wasn't the fliers / he loved the damsel too dearly
—*King Kong*

all of those Japanese houses huts are oppressive, as alike as they can possibly be, if you put the paper in the wrong way, I say to Blum, the watermark is on the upper edge of the paper upside down, that's not the way it's supposed to be, had I really cut my bangs yesterday in front of the bathroom mirror or was it only a dream, breaking out, teeth coming loose, teeth falling out in your dream is supposed to mean bad luck, they say, the forest and the wind were both of red chalk as I looked out of a window on one of the upper floors of the hotel, and Joseph in the background of the room said, more to himself than to me, *I don't know who God is.*
I still have remnants some slight nausea from the previous landscape : word landscape which is giving me heartburn, making me belch, I say to Joseph, I can hardly keep it down, *a string of mountains the edge of a forest, such glaciers, volcanoes, ridges, mountain peaks, craters all framed in that window and rotating,* and I knew, I say to Joseph, there was a voice, an old dust-covered notebook, and the voice reminded me of another voice I knew very well, then the *snow wear,* too, and then I turned around and no one was there, everything in negative and positive connotation, all depending on the tenor of the day, I say, and I observe how the tablet *quivered* slightly inside its FOIL GARMENTS, ever so slightly, barely discernible, and I couldn't help but think of encapsulated creature, or something like that, gulp down a feathery swallow, to swallow, *my work visor, etc.*
You are leading a double life, Joseph says, you don't ask enough questions, you are afraid to ask questions, you are still embarrassed, the way you were when you were a schoolgirl, right, you find it unsettling, you are ashamed the way you were then, and still are now, to admit your ignorance in almost every field of knowledge, or you ask questions when you don't know what

else to do, even when you already know the answer, it gives you space to pursue your own thoughts, you don't even have to listen for a reply, because you aren't even really interested in it, isn't that so.

Am confused / perturbed, forgotten of soul, it was a desperate hunger, the onslaught breathtaking, notes only to be taken on the diagonal, simply flung down, flung out, and absolutely uninhibited, language released into open space, I say, I remember, it was a brass bed, and one of us, father, mother or me, one of us slept in this brass bed, cold to the touch, ice cold, had to be cleaned, scrubbed until it gleamed, gold-colored, I did it or was made to do it, though I did not care for the task, there were doorknobs too, the many doorknobs, doors to each room, door into the entryway, door trim, all brass, and long ago, very long ago, I say, the stove, it had to be polished with sandpaper, I had to polish, and I disliked doing it, disliked it very much, turned myself around, outside sunshine, summer images floating before my eyes, WHAT ALREADY PAST!, the seasons keep changing, the years, the decades, HE HAS ENTERED UPON HIS 70TH SPRING—can't really say that, why can't we say that, I say, well, no one says that, why not, images, films in my brain, I say, you know what I mean, images of my childhood, most of the film torn, torn somewhere right in the middle, you see, at some point the strip of film comes to an end, at some point the scene fades out, heaps of landscape, brunette dreams, cropped photographs, sand-colored, beige, like the soft-hued domain of red deer, etc., or the picture the way it's projected, intensely luminous, as it was when it was first seen, strangely enough, in the midst of a state of loss, in a loss of thought, in the midst of a family setting : images flashing into view, torn strips of film, 1 SOLITAIRE (only 1 in existence outside the standing tree of the *woodland ass,* e.g.), still have my finger in the Dictionary of Foreign Words, it was a few days ago, when I was looking up that very word : SOLITAIRE, beautiful word, differentiating word, illuminating expression, right, I say, see myself scaling a mountain, walking along the *railbed* with mother, flat stretch, storm clouds gathering, mother's horrible fear of thunderstorms, her fear of the wild horse on the forest path, her waving both umbrella and hat as I stood at the window of my compartment and waved back, most of the time she carried an umbrella rather than a cane, didn't want to acknowledge, admit to herself that she needed the support, she held onto the straps of her shoulder bag as tightly as she could, I'm keeping hold of my bag, she said then, you don't have to support me, she waved to me, probably couldn't see me, but she knew *I* would see her waving, she waved to me from the top of a small slope, a gentle rise, so I would be able to see her, I didn't look, somehow this was also a feeling of liberation, I was able to leave for home, *ah, language is a tumult—this forest of honey*—I say, she is waving with both hat and forest and I am crying : she is waving with both hat and forest and wilting, ah, this futility, I say, this momentariness . . snow wear snow slope, *I wash I rumble I spit,* my spit inside my left cheek, I say to Blum, dirty laundry in my bent fingers, and Panama hats, this is how I try to get them clean, body shirts, dark-colored things that show every spot, etc., and then I stand here all washed and dressed again, here I am again all cleaned up, here with my shriveled-up old CONFIDENCE TALK, who is going to understand it, I say, don't even understand it myself. I never write anything down, says Blum in a rather distant tone of voice, before I have thought it through completely and understand it, Blum says, *language is a tumult,* I say, *like the senses,* like ecstasy, clearly our libidos are controlled by our brains, isn't that so, I say, last night's housefly has gone back into action, a page full of scribbles is covering the dirty empty champagne glass on the floor, the soul's stencil, what's that, POPPY CREATURE in the entryway, a bleeding foot, I had jumped into the sewer ditch, cut the sole of my foot on a splinter of glass, lazily inhabiting a chaise longue, a hammock, the blackbirds flew up and away from my plate, I've lost my sense of song because I'm in pain, pain in my foot, in my knee, next to the lamp on my desk 2 typed pages from my lover, pages embracing one another, had he actually arrived the night before last, had I really met Joseph at the airport the night before last, or am I just imagining things, everything mingling with everything else, I feel unbounded, feel like a hysterical poet, since I've been reading Bataille I am also an obscene poet, I am going over his, the line of Joseph's buttocks, somewhere on the bookshelf there is a line, I say to Blum, it is essential to what I am now writing, I rummage around in my bookshelf looking for the line, I excerpt what I find, I lose the page, scattered traces, of bird feet, I say to Blum, our entire life scattered traces of bird tracks, isn't that so, something has appeared on the floor, I don't recognize it, what is it, a piece of string, a fly, a trompe l'oeil? *a treat from a most rigorous lip?* : early every morning prompting, whispering, a soufflé, actually the INFLATED THINGS, as if I were my own prompter : *inflater, whisperer,* my own plagiarizer, right.

The elevator smelled of fresh hair, in the elevator the air smelled of fresh hair, I mean hair that has been caressed by a cold wind washed clean by the rain, it smelled of fresh air, the way a person smells who has been out in the cold and involved in strenuous movement and then comes into a warm room, and everything comes streaming out of him, everything the wind and the cold in the air have blown into him, into his hair, into his skin, in the folds of clothing, too, I love smells like that, I say to Joseph, smells that are so close to the scent of grasses in spring or the promise of fragrance in the simple delicate flowers along the edge of the sidewalk, in belts of grass along the road, you know.

When I came out of Molière's MISANTHROPE, the fly was buzzing around my room, and although I found it disgusting, I felt sorry for it, it was weak and appeared to be nearing its end, and I could have swatted it dead without expending an effort at all, then I opened Joseph's letters, 2 letters had arrived on the same day, clouds of smoke rose, tears rose, etc., when I am with Joseph I start to vibrate, I say to Blum, I lose all sense of perspective, control, when I am with you, I say to Blum, I feel myself at the center of circumstances and connections, I say to Blum, this means I am capable of clear judgment, etc., *I have a sure eye,* and without seeing a reflection of myself.

In the morning you have to be very quiet, keep quiet, I say to Blum, lying in wait for this voice which is constantly whispering to you, I mean there is something whispering inside my chest and I have to listen to it, no interruptions! no talking, please! we don't talk while we're walking, we're out of breath, from time to time we just trudge off, pound on the table, *directing without a baton, with both hands,* when the right formulation fails to show up, we go searching for it, lure it out, with our own hands, right, a kind of *birth art,* you throw things, rip out pages of the dictionary, when you can't get any further, when everything begins to drag, is at loggerheads, your vocabulary coagulates, etc. A most dubious declaration of love for literature casting its pall, I say, poetry's fetuses, I say, preserved in tall thin jars, repulsive, language is CONSUMING, that's the way it should be, I say, full of all sorts of sparks, with energies that do not come from us, appear to come from us, right, even this obedient pen, this furious little machine!, this flat rubber cap, at one time a white cap, was sitting on my head at an angle and I was thinking about Joseph when I caught sight of my revolting reflection in the mirror. Looked through the rest of the mail, I say to Blum, bright red car in greenish air in the courtyard stormy green white willow as well, almost Indian summer, *a trough and undulating tiger in gray-green next to it,* a profusion of ferns and wings, wool-clothed beings in frost, etc., and in the same way that clouds *enthuse* us into believing they are mountaintops, forest glades and snow-covered peaks, even volcanoes, and that's how it is with us and words, too, we have the gift of being able to INSTRUCT them in relating to us in ways that are full of fantasy, we can simply TRAIN them to *come to us swarming,* and sailing ("come under my roof") and to inhabit our thinking and our feeling—Amen.

11/3

"cutlet of businesses"

a little moist this eye dream, in my eye sockets, in the hollows of my eyes I feel remnants of tears, I say to Blum, splendid electrifying EXTRAVAGANCE this writing work, excited in the extreme, intent, explosive, *my heart is on fire,* as in : I have exploded am exploding am as explosive as TNT, etc.

My room in Bielefeld what was it like, I say to Blum, crazy, can't remember anymore, it has literally *fallen out* of my memory, can't find it anywhere, but I can, strangely enough, remember the time before I moved into that room, I mean I can remember what I *imagined* the room would be like, before I had actually seen it, and I can remember this image very clearly, as concrete as it was unsettling, in my mind I saw a small room stuffed full of furniture, 2 skylights instead of windows, the walls, the floor, the ceiling all radiating a horrible chill, probably musty and damp—in the entry, on the first morning, viewed from bed : little black dog crouching : shoulder bag sunken in, *like a dog act / yap,* etc.

Oh, dear Reinhold, I write to Reinhold Posch, and because my eyes aren't really any good anymore, I saw you coming toward me, but it was this nice philologist from K. I thought it was you, with a thin flowing reddish beard, gentle eyes, you recognize things without actually recognizing them, right, you can never uncover the sensation completely, you don't know any longer who is who, etc. And because I have made a typo here, actually had forgotten to type 1 letter, it makes me think of that old-fashioned practice, that custom, of using IDLE LITTLE DASHES instead of writing out double consonants, as I've said before, all of the women in my family were afflicted with this WOUND, I say to Blum, even my mother, who from childhood on was adamantly opposed to all things old-fashioned, used this mode of abbreviation, distortion and crumpling of words—

it all depends on the body's state of health, attitude, the doctor said, if you, e.g., were my mother, the doctor says (at this I winced, with an acute contraction of my shoulders) : I would have to advise you against having this surgery done on your right leg, and it occurred to me, I say to Blum, that I knew what had made me wince, the source of my alarm, in my relationship with this doctor I had assumed the role of a child seeking protection and help and refuge in her motherly warmth, oh, my mother used to say in her last years, I say to Blum, I would rather die than have this eye operated, she possessed a lively, the most lively sense of fantasy, and I read Bataille to her, he writes DEATH IS THE MOST TERRIBLE THING THAT CAN BEFALL US, and she said, I don't want to die because then I won't be able to see you anymore. She had INHALED THE SPIRIT, that's what it was, she was filled with A SPIRIT, she possessed a powerful imagination, given the most gossamer and obscure indications she was always capable of drawing conclusions based on a profound sense of everything that was happening around her, long before anyone else understood, I often feel her close to me, I say to Blum, she may even tell me things from time to time, *but how will she ever be able to materialize herself (given her imprisonment)?*

I am now wearing her dirty sand-colored gloves, see her bony hands in them, the open wound on the side / napkin, it tears open my sooted breast, I say to Blum, bloody mesh pelican breast getting closer to pain, etc.

a rush into your fantasy, I say to Joseph, we are sitting on plush upholstered seats in a café, and I with my tongue counting the little homeopathic pellets—that's 4—in my mouth, they are supposed to calm me down, I wanted them to calm me down, I mean the turbulence in my body or soul what do I know, I wanted to *soothe* it I mean the way you try to soothe a wild angry howling child, it was the deep kisses we had exchanged 4 × that afternoon, I say to Blum, and I told myself, this is going to be the end of me, it's crushing me, or I'm going mad, *a bursting boy pink boy,* gulping down a swallow to swallow, but also the evening hunger for writing made me feel I was about to burst, from 1 day to the next, I say to Blum, it seems, I may be *allowing myself to be converted to writing in a classical style,* very on fire, in flames, I say to Blum, *I panted and puffed and became my own Fury, isn't that so.* STOPPED shoe soles on the street in the middle of the thoroughfare, suddenly can go no further, almost forward, onto my hands, fall, or I stumble, trip over an obstacle on the sidewalk, right, a pebble, a paving stone protruding, a slender crack in the asphalt coating the bicycle path, just as I begin to cross, with underwear open on an open street isn't that right, writing an exaltation, exhibition, I say to Blum, now you are dead, Blum says, when I called him and told him about my fright, that is, I imagined I had gotten an electrical shock when I reached into the telephone answering machine to change the tape, and in utter terror every flower from the table, and drenched everything, tablecloth, clothes, floor, hopelessness and despair every little bouquet, Matisse bouquet swept from the table, anyway and drenched the blanket, paint box, father's things, etc., apprehension, fatigue, and the opposing impulses of this day, I say to Blum, as if, from 1 hour to the next, I had let myself be converted to writing in a classical style, and I didn't want it to, I say to Blum, and on top of all that moments of being humiliated and sullied, I say to Blum, the way Joseph looked at me, turned his eyes away from me, could not rest his eyes in mine, and I asked him, I suddenly asked him, after we had both been silent for some time, WERE YOU EVER A CHOIR BOY? DID YOU SING PERGOLESI?, but he let my question go right past him, and *from Rötel the wind,* as we walked out onto the street, after he had helped me on with my coat, I say it is the 1 × you have helped me on with my coat, as if he had helped me on with my childhood coat of 60 years ago, that fur coat I had, it seemed to me, always been wearing, and had already grown out of, but somehow it had not grown along with me, and I never understood why, he is holding my coat at shoulder level, and his face had a forbearing-condescending expression, as if I were his unruly little daughter, as if he were comforting protecting me helping me with this coat from my childhood, I mean as we were leaving the café, and as I was buttoning the bottom button of my coat I said to him, BEEN READING BATAILLE, THAT OBSCENE WORK, what had made me think of this at this particular moment, he asked, he is miles away from me, I think, the response was a purely associative phenomenon, I say, my colossal body, I say, when Helmut W. photographed it, back then in '52, I believe, leaning up against a fence, in just this coat, charcoal eyes eye makeup, blurred face, he called me "Russian soul" I mean he gave the photo the title "Russian soul," you see, I say to Joseph, before he and his Porsche drove off a bridge in France in the early morning haze and he was killed, an obsessed man, narrow forehead well supplied with blood, while he drank Spanish wine he chewed on the edge of the glass, bit it to pieces, had an incestuous relationship with his eldest daughter, a true beauty who accepted him as her lover, I say, though a THUNDERSTORM OATH, a certain melancholy in her eyes might have been interpreted as a sign of contrary feelings, etc., he kept inviting me to come and visit him at his house in Madeira, but because of the colony of spiders he kept I didn't want to go . . *with a bare cheek I mean crocodile shield, etc.*

Oh, this 1 drunken set of notes, I say to Joseph, have to modify everything now, spent the entire fall reading in your books, and was able to keep them here for so long, I say to Joseph, was actually able to WATCH OVER them, I mean the several books I had borrowed from you, that they were allowed to spend time with me, *as close to me as my own skin,* I say, on my bedspread, pressed to my cheek, on my breakfast table, next to my jar of honey, in my suitcase, in my backpack because I always because they always had to be at hand, because I was no longer able to separate myself from them, because they had become a part of me, because they are a part of you, I say, the penciled notes in the margin, almost illegible, concealed passion, I say, traces of a concealed passion, etc., like this scrawl, *standing,* strangely tilted forward while writing, standing while writing, isn't that right, careless element, at the oval table, as if touching the keys while standing, to hear how it sounds this morning, the tone and the song of the piano, not even out of tune, I say, standing, as I once was pressed into the waist of the piano, noting things down, hardly 14, still a child, my only refuge within the narrow confines of the family house, tapering : recessed writing desk, I say, the indentation in the middle the way it is on wasps, indentation, Derrida says, makes the chest stand out, *and the way I was so wound up about the housefly,* and hair, eyelid and neck, while Dalí placed the lamb chop on top of Gala's head, etc., sideburns, hair on both sides of his face next to his ears, I mean Joseph.

on or about 11/4 night

tore the spine off the book (*DUDEN Dictionary of Foreign Words*) on the floor, book all read up, straw basket on the kitchen floor, my *everyday shoes* inside, burned up, beat up, whitish from the dust on the street, I can, when I am with you, sit with you, look into your eyes, have conversations with you, I say to Blum, completely forget myself, I mean I can forget myself forget my squalid self at least for a time, and *attune* myself entirely to you, and then everything is the way it should be, I believe I can tune myself the way an instrument can be tuned to a fixed reference tone, right, and that is why I always feel the need, I always feel such contentment when I can spend a few hours of the day with you—but when I'm with Joseph, it's different, I am tuned in another way, in another way *outside myself,* uncertain, vain, pretentious, I talk too much, or I'm too quiet, and everything is somehow out of balance, you see. I cannot surrender to him, I cannot surrender, I mean with arms and hands and white flag, etc.

My awkward little cap is sitting at an angle over my ear, my awkward hand, my awkward foot : my weak joints, I say, I resolve not to answer the phone, I promise myself I will stay at my typewriter when the telephone rings, or the doorbell rings, but I can't do it, I race to the little table, I rush to the door, I hear the curtains falling, with their embroidered bouquets, tiny embroidered bouquets, which headfirst I believe I have never seen anything like it before, this *Still Life with Oranges,* by Henri Matisse in which the dark-red dahlias, bundled together into small bushes, exerting an unsettling charm over the tablecloth : a sweet compulsion to plunge into the depths, these bouquets on the tablecloth *actually do fall out and onto the floor,* they fall out of the texture, out of the text and onto the floor, you see, and I can look at them every morning and once again they will bring me to

tears every morning, I do not believe that any other painter with any other painting moves me this way, and I cannot explain it.
It may be, I say to Alma, Blum asks me, ARE YOU HIS LOVER? (referring to Joseph), and that would mean something entirely different than it would if he had asked, IS HE YOUR LOVER?—it is something else entirely, something entirely different, isn't that right, I say to Alma, and when we talk about writing, it may be possible that he will say MAYBE YOU THINK YOU ARE TOO GOOD TO TELL A STORY!, and in truth I would not know how to respond to those words, I mean I would not be able to present anything in my defense, etc., all the more so, because I would be refuting what he says about his view of his own writing, basically I WRITE THINGS WHICH ARE VERY MUCH LIKE OPERETTAS, I WRITE OPERETTA LITERATURE, etc. *while the body needle . . the language sounds . .* etc.
This paper is the shirt chest on which I may write my notes, Blum says, slowness is life extending, in old age slowness is life extending, Blum says, you are always so impetuous, you just sweep past things, you sweep past everything, because you are trying to think feel and say any number of things all at the same time, Blum says. In the morning, while I am washing my face with a hot cloth, I say, soul for soul, eye for eye, remembered images rise into my consciousness next to one another, after one another overlapping one another, it is like a film that tears after a few scenes, keeps tearing and finally tears apart, snapshots, shockingly sharp and shredded to pieces by the most glaring bolts of light, you see—I have been working on this sentence for more than an hour, I say to Blum, and I am still not completely happy with it—I have this draft, I have these notes, written 2 years ago, and I've grown out of them, that's what it is, how can I fit myself into these first sketches, take possession of them, without having to surrender myself, without slipping into a rage, I ask myself, I say to Blum, at the door a small plastic bag with my neighbor's new telephone number, and a silver spoon, unwashed, it had fallen into the toilet, etc., at the herbalist's inside the store, while outside a swirl of flakes, for 1 long second a FLUIDUM, I mean I clearly sensed the presence of something unknown to me, no, I say to Blum, not in the room, not wafting through the shop, no, but something both inside me and outside me that was functioning, was present, broke out, radiating beneficence, etc., I felt MY HEART GROW WARM, as they say, in this very second I had all the intensity of a very young person with all of the passionate drives, desires, hopes, yearning, I couldn't grasp it, I tried to attach myself to this extraordinary sensation, but it dissipated, didn't come back, I quickly left the store, picked up my mail rushed to my

apartment with its lights left burning the whole day, a cosy sensation in the entry, in my study, sat down at my machine, next to me, *at my feet,* the paper bag with its fresh letters, cards, and book packets, I was in no hurry, I practiced patience, everything was lying there, at my feet, a familiarity almost a feeling of warmth, I say to Blum, my tranquil writing space with ceiling light and burning table lamp, inner window blown open during the past night's storm was still ajar and offering me the paper-thin Mongolian doll, green silk costume, red sash, white face, blood-red lips, upward gazed fixed in its laces, gold cap. In my breast language sounds, vibration in my head, actually in my ears, which, pressed tightly to my head, I could feel it, told me it was an animal head, I had grown an animal head with ears pressed up tightly against my skull, and lying in wait, it whirred, glittered, blinked : a burst of flakes against dark-colored clothing. Spray somewhere around the heart, accelerated pulse, bouquets of dahlias, I say to Blum, next to my bag of mail, and how one thing devours another and intertwines, as if being UNWRAPPED out of one's clothes late at night, before we *crawling into bed, etc.*

And when I pull all of that paper stuff off the wrong way, pull it off over my head, I say to Blum, I also pull it off the wrong way the next morning, you see, but the next evening, when I pull it off the wrong way, and pull it off the wrong way again, *then I will have it right side on!* and I will be able to take it right side off the following morning, and so on, I say, strangely enough, I say, you ask *what is this all about?* IT ISN'T ABOUT ANYTHING, I say to Blum, it's a FAVORITE FOOD, actually a FAVORED FOOD, isn't that right, I say, while the morning drips ice-blue / beautiful : *ice-flower blue,* etc., a sequence which may well cause literary critics to dismiss my writing as "lyrical prose," the way they have already done so many times, etc. To friends who have been waiting for years for me to answer their letters, I confess on the phone that I HAVE FORGOTTEN EVERYTHING, I mean I MUST FORGET EVERYTHING in order to finish this work, you have to get yourself in *harness, no enmeshed,* once you get involved in a writing project a writing diktat, there is no going back, or everything will be ruined, isn't that right, maybe it's getting your claw hooked into the robe of language, you attach yourself, you get snared, you get snagged in language in the MATERIAL in the TEXTURE, etc., and in the same way language seems to get hooked, attached, it hooks its claws into us the moment we acquiesce, so, we lead we guide each other, in equal measure, you see, and while we are writing we are also constantly thinking about the future reception of what is written, I believe it is so, I say, so smart and precise, not only in the roar of the elements, while waters from the cavern of our body drift and thrash, etc., on the other hand it is possible to imagine, I say to Blum, writing should drop of its own accord, fall, without exertion or force, don't you think, like fruit from a tree, and then the entire meadow covered with plums—(they fell! the child yells, yes, they're lying in the grass, all we have to do is pick them up and put them in our basket, etc.)

Strangely enough, I say to Joseph, what I remember most clearly is what happened along the way, *in the landscapes,* in forests of fern, thickets, at the edge of the paddock, in the zigzag bends of the cornfields, as tall as a man they blocked the sun for hours, and how did it happen, how did it happen again and again, I ask Joseph, why is it that while we were walking along the road I started feeling as if I were going to faint, so many times, so unsettling, like a fleeting memory that grazes our consciousness and leaves something like a strange taste in our mouth cavity, and it makes us think, makes us fearful, makes us uncertain, etc. while sputum collects in my left cheek . .

and always almost Easter, always almost Easter again and always almost Christmas again and always almost spring and the lake and the mountains and the summer rain and roaming through moss and grasses and always almost autumn, the first autumn color, and snow and turning back, going back, PORTENT OF END.

Like a hanged man the Mongolian puppet dangling from the window lock, I say to Joseph, in the traces of a wind which through the closed window, right, paper-thin marionette with a snow-white face, timid eyes, cherry-red mouth, green caftan, laced socks, pantaloons, I believe blackened eyes, but I can't remember who gave it to me anymore, *or the way I was so engrossed in the housefly,* right, I haven't been turning any pages for quite a while, I say to Joseph, I haven't been turning the pages of my desk calendar, lots of empty pages in my desk calendar, on the 12th of September, that's when you're coming, I wrote it down, in the afternoon at quarter to 5, and in the meantime we have hardly seen each other at all, *the angle the angel of the book,* I say to Joseph, I mean the STREAMING OF LINES DRAWN between you and me, and so on.

11/5

bellhop, thin milky weather, I say to Blum, so much splintering on my papers, I say, secrets in gestures, head turning always back toward the dusty armchair, with indented WHORLS of cheeks, with each brush past, the same thought, "needs a good dusting off," the *guy* with the black face mask, blue stocking cap heading right for me, in my everyday street, young black man at the very last moment sighted a young black man, my everyday street like Artaud's, etc., the way Artaud has mastered it, feelings secret winding turns in whose secret winding turns, overturned, actually tipped pot of hot milk over the rug, had poured down on the rug, catch sight of, as I am slurping down the last drops at the bottom of my teacup my deformed face, I had been thinking whining wool scarf I mean wine red scarf which had been thrown over seat back : much-cherished terry cloth towel to dry off my feet, am standing in hot water, the barberry batteries the barberry bouquet on paper plate trivet tray folded over, have lost PERSPECTIVE, am only crawling around on the floor of my consciousness, eyes only for the most wormly of small things, beefsteak in the vicinity of the trees in the park, ecstasy in the palm of a hand, fallen out of my state, out of my standing up, *transported out of my skin,* being outside of myself, out of *façon,* etc., I say to Blum, every time I go to see this doctor he seems to be throwing some kind of net over me, maybe it's hypnosis, mentions one thing and another, smiles and laughs, jokes and talks, I take the needle, he offers me a pair of opera glasses, games he has played hundreds even thousands of times with great success among all his patients, and when the appointment is over nothing remains, not a single recollection of a diagnosis, a prescription, advice, and while I am making my way down the steep and narrow street, this constant throbbing inside my head : A PERSON WITH MIND

SO BROAD, BARONIAL, BARITONE, etc., and am afraid, beard stubble in the gardens, the many gardens along the steep narrow street on the way to the bus stop, Hans Arp writes, I say to Blum, "birds after a storm are messengers from the realm of the dead, they land at your feet and look up at you out of fathomless eyes . ."—it has been shown that for most people the date of death will fall on a day close to the date of their birth, I say to Blum, actually a secret science, Blum says, what you write a secret science, the way you deal with language, Blum says, decipherable to no one, accessible only to you, without intent : intentional your prose rhythm, your consecrated work, as you call it, your writing work, as you call it, an absolutely exclusive discipline, don't you think, the *serenity of the moon or mouth,* the moon patch that is your language, impetuous and provocative, ah, that's the way it is, I say, *that's the way it was with the birdcall* : my father's cheerful whistles in the spring, right, my good-natured father, today, e.g., on this stormy day I believe, this will be a day for long conversations, *for long illuminating conversations,* just talked to Alma on the telephone, after having thought of her every day in 1 breath (corner) or another, dialed her number and she says, I was just going to call you, so many auspicious loving conjunctions, folds, intertwining voices, of our two voices, thoughts, words, strangely enough, concurrence, flashes of fresh insight, layers of pigment exposed, etc., the one EYE TUTOR, I say to Blum, and the washcloth (dishcloth) under my pillow, it won't stop haunting me, am bewildered, gone wild, earlier this morning, I say, a young black man I believed a *man with a mask,* spit the seeds out onto the floor, and the peel of a shriveled section of orange, make haste, I tell myself, when in the morning a great urge to keep myself laid out flat, lots of scribbling on back of bundled-up printed paper, suddenly an image in memory me walking ambling along the road in a small summer resort town, along the side of the road, a little ambling gamboling through the grass scar, dust, and noticing my slip-on sandals, my feet in my worn-out sandals, which (LOOSE STUFF) are almost dangling, dangling from heel and toe, sometimes my feet slide out a little, stepping on the heel leather, very soft, soft as a feather, weightless, these encasings, a little *baggy* as if you were sitting in a large room and all you had was a writing desk, etc.

I am translating PR : public relations connection, in the stairwell it smells of garbage, asphalt, feces, *bone-blond* I say to Blum, never heard of it before, don't know the meaning, out of the corner of my eye the box of laundry detergent flung itself out of the vertical and into the horizontal, I was not able to see what had happened, but from 1 moment to the next the carton that was standing up was lying flat, but a few seconds later when I looked that way again the thing was standing there the way it always had been, thrashed, the dream, dreaming during the night had somehow CRUSHED me, I mean I woke up and felt banged up and chopped to pieces, a thing that had been badly beaten up, I was nothing but a thing, battered thing, etc., in the RING AS THE UNDERDOG IN FREESTYLE WRESTLING . .

as far as *flight of breath* is concerned, I say to Blum, just think of Artaud's crap, raven (everyman's ecstasy), the glowing color BLACK : feces, everyday gas, the solipsist and how he stomps on the housecoat in his hand, slung over his arm, with each step, and shuffling, stumbling over the hem of the coat dragging along the floor, in the dirt, and the dishwater, and rolling in the mud in the morass in the muck in the manure in the ordure in the dust—

beard stubble in the autumn gardens I am racing past, I say to Blum, little language gardens : this whole part of the city is blanketed with frost-stiffened parcels like this, most miniaturized forests, unfoliated wilderness, or little GARDENS OF WRITINGS, Socrates, because I am running back and forth, noting, writing cards, left hand as writing pad, cards, letters to X (or William or Ferdinand), with a little flaming text (style) : like : "your sea over there lies on a glowing tabletop on which a boiling hot teakettle I mean heated up the whole situation, and given your descriptions of the landscape one might ask, dear X (William or Ferdinand) which of us is really *the biggest con that is the consummate poet,* etc."

A person, I write to X (or William or Ferdinand) with mind balcony or *balloon,* that is, rising and floating up into heaven's clouds, what a delight, I write to X (or William or Ferdinand), you that is, and I am being sent up in flames, *flickering away* into the heights of tenderness and delight by what you have written, you see, looking for glass of water just poured / spilled, second glass filled, first glass found at my feet, I write to X (or William or Ferdinand), have an idea : first notes done, won't fit into the current body of text, have gotten myself into a dilemma, alien complex, can't fit it into the most recent construct, etc., as I thought light burning, but it was the reflection of a sun which settled onto the end wall of the entry, I say to Blum, everyday street, I say, the most everyday of things, acts, the most everyday love for my things, envelops me, god-fearing fixation on this 1 thing, this writing thing, this attitude most dear, art embrace, used the notes I brought in as a place mat for my soup bowl, I mean I didn't push my work notes aside but used them as a tablecloth, pad, bib, instead, what do I know, they, the pages of notes were so densely packed, made up of numerous (textiles?) individual existences, table mat upon which a full bowl of soup, spoon, napkin were I mean *resplendent,* what a word, highly unusual, I say to Blum, these days Lily says : you are quite possibly a charlatan, yes, she said that to me, I was chagrined, as if someone had caught me committing some awful deed, I write to Joseph, you won't believe it, but we're already installing the EASTER OFFICE, been cultivating all sorts of window thoughts and I have no idea what they might mean, have been fighting my way through a web of communication problems, truly am painfully inhibited in my relationships with things and people, you know what I'm talking about, don't even know which eye to close in order to get my eye makeup on without putting myself in danger of being injured, every time you kiss me, when you hold me, Blum says, you must know that you are kissing you are putting your arms around an old man who is about to *go away,* your fingerprints on the leather binding of the book I gave you, and suddenly in the morning, I say to Blum, still lying flat, after a substantial sleep *the impulse* the need to be embraced, held close, *to be devoured* by some LOVING BODY . . and into the WHIRLPOOL : moist wind, my mother said so many times over, *I don't want to talk about it,* not even with you, she said, I say to Blum, I will take it with me, to my grave, she said, I will take all of that with me, she said, it will be buried with me, no one will ever hear a thing about it, she said, not even you, she said, whom I trust completely, to whom I have given all of my trust, she said, and I knew exactly what she was referring to, but I didn't tell her that I knew what she meant, and then she soon went to bed in her clothes, etc.

Joseph used the word ARDOR in a conversation, I say to Blum, to which I have always had a broken connection, I was simply not capable of using this word, I say, yes, I would have been embarrassed to use this word, whenever I heard it or read it—which was less and less often—I always choked on it a little. But once Joseph uttered this word, IT WAS LIBERATED, it had transformed itself, it had acquired an intellectual aura, I say—

the apple background / eyeball background, shoulder blades shrugged, always makes me think of a pair of wings, I say to Blum, *and this is the way the morning heavened to me,* up in flames and forest udder, and as everything blurred, etc., the rubber band in front of me on my nightstand in the shape of a violin scroll or a violet.

11/10

really, it's going to be a state of DELIRIUM, Elisabeth von Samsonow writes, when you're not looking at the world through your own eyes anymore, rather it unclearly, that is ensnared in UNSLEEP, prepared for, and WHAT THINKS? and I begin to love so much what we speak and *write,* and you inspire me to do it when you put your writing on the line in such an extraordinary way, with all those expressions lined up in a row, etc., ah, I write back, feel it in my body and as if nothing but bushes were about to sprout out of it, and then a foot a shoe *etched* into the pavement, as if someone had set up a barrier, and this perception blends together with emerging points of memory, or comes bursting out of wild awareness, there is always something *hovering around* in my mind, something which I believe I can see, but perhaps only the intimation of an entire thought or feeling, right, some point of yearning, an open book, tiniest typeface, on my writing table with the big rough stone flattening 2 open pages, and my suitcase, the trip *complet* (the old dress, do you remember), hand towels patched, killed, cut to shreds like WOMEN'S SILK AND WOMEN'S SIDE, threadbare from decades of use, etc., crowns of trees, foreign coins, brought back from travels to so many different places, kept in saucers, glasses, boxes and small tins, as prompts for my memory and brushwood, from travels, junket and junk or sprout or allusion, there are places, I write, which have a radiance that comes streaming out of the earth, e.g., Heiligenkreuz, such sites of ancient cults . .

this paperback book lying open on my writing table, I say to Blum, it is so touching (and avenging) that it makes me cry, the open pages weighed down by a large stone, under that a notebook, midday sun with crossed blades over my skull, on a slip of paper : PALERMO AND ARROW, and handwritten prescriptions handwritten notes, and is it like that for you, I ask Blum, you *put off* everything, slightly pushing things away from you, for the time it takes you to inhale you postpone, simply forgetting this one moment of acting, simply closing yourself off from this acting, etc., and go on like this from day to day and week to week, and so on, so on like this, the watermark on the lower margin of the page, I say, and these our conclaves, as if you could simply set them aside simply by putting them on a list, only somewhat, this obligation and that, and write down on your list what you will do today, only for this while, while everything is at rest, I mean now while you do not yet have to begin to get involved, take steps, only these few seconds of idyll, could you call it that? I mean, LOCOMOTION postponed for a very brief while, just this while, sit for hours almost in front of the window, look out and up into the sky, and the color and the bitterness—

ah, I say to Blum, and composing letters in my head, but not writing them, never writing, not now, and not later, and weeks later not even remembering if you had actually written them or not or had you simply *stalled in a state of devotion,* in which you see the recipient of the letter right before your eyes for that 1 second or 1 hour, recalling this and that, things which had long been submerged, letting this memory and that come to the surface, in an illuminated hour, daylilies, what do I hear, the elevator ringing in the corridor, I say to Blum, strangely enough, an airplane overhead and the purring sounds of the elevator, a double swim . .

Roland Barthes : "I have not succeeded in getting to know you means that I will never know what you think of me," I write to Joseph, this upcoming trip with you, I had been so looking forward to it, and now it disheartened, I am afraid of this trip, afraid of myself, afraid of you, everything is exceeding everything else, a sleeve saturated with tears and I saw you have been wearing your plaid work shirt 3 days in a row, etc., feeling feverish as the clock advances, these 9 or 13 hours until our departure, I tell myself, I feel awful, overcome by dizziness by nausea, feel as if I'm going to throw up, lethargic Smetana composition blaring out of the radio, I have been sitting at my machine for what seems like hours, until the last moment, until my taxi comes, we still owe each other : I AM LOOKING FORWARD TO THIS TRIP, or IT'S GOING TO BE A REALLY GOOD TIME, etc., do you know how I unfold my hand, I write to Joseph, how I open my hands, standing, scribbling into the flat of my hand PALM OF MY HAND, onto a scrap of writing paper, already illegible by the next morning, settings and numbers, letters with my left hand, a thermometer, feel feverish, scribbling, note taking, in large letters, taking excerpts from Roland Barthes up until 10 minutes before I leave, indecipherable by the time I get back, soft morning light in the left-hand window, etc., this color tears bitterness, *this stagnation,* etc., Gerda Halik calls and asks about the NAPOLEON HAT, while she, Gerda Halik is speaking into the phone, yes, and I have caught my own shadow with my camera, beyond the garden fence, she relates, oh, you should come and have a look at all this, there are some pictures here, I say, in which I appear in just that kind of NAPOLEON HAT, that is, a snow hood, or a winter hood, off to 1 side, I mean with earmuffs protruding from each side, I mean 1 of those Russian fur caps, fur hats, etc., unmistakable, a shadow like that, I say, long shadow cast along the snow-covered ground, I say, long winter shadow, isn't that right, photographed from behind, a few of these pictures were even taken during the war, even the dog has been *fenced in,* I say, the little dog in the photo, even his earmuffs are protruding from both sides, *dog sash,* actually a gauze bandage around his skull, shaggy little dog, his gaze fixed on me for a long while, almost human eyes, isn't that right, I say, and I back at him with TRUE EYES : DOG EYES SASH EYES, etc., and me taking the collar and leash off the dog's neck and putting it around my own, wrapping it around my body, this is how love weaves its way in and out, and UNEQUALED . .

oh, Joseph, I write to Joseph, I am now reading your letter 4 × 12 hours, and though I have read it in all its variations, I mean, in all loud and quiet variations, and screaming variations and in any case already installed them all, loud quiet screaming silent etc., anyway I have read it and still I feel as if I haven't read it, read it again, word for word, sentence for sentence, try to memorize it, but here and there pieces are missing, and I am not yet able to detach myself from your letter, my breast in shreds, read Peter Weiss and Wolfgang Koeppen, a slender volume *and now know that I have done everything wrong,* dear Joseph, including my feelings for you, all I ever have is this feeling of imminent collapse, right, can you understand what I'm saying, and these days I cannot defend myself any longer I mean these INSTRUMENTATIONS OF PAPER are suffocating me over and over again, mental trash inversions, etc. The icebox is humming, *a few real records* on my small oval table, wrote down some notes, played piano, dear Joseph, shadows of the restaurant signs are clapping up against the walls of a building, never seen before, honey spoon completes 1 full somersault on my breakfast table, took out my HOLBEIN HAT again, dear Joseph, everything 1 big green dabbled cant, right, downright nonsense writing it down, hearing the voice of slender silence, a drop of spit breaking loose from my brain

and dripping down into my trachea a wild scream of convulsive coughing fills the hollow in my pillow, the recesses in my blanket : dog puke, at which point I sit up, scream, tremble in cascading coughs, while twisting and stumbling my breath drives through glottis, gums, pharynx—
all measured in beats of my heart.
a field jacket, what's that, I ask Blum, *a book poncho* you can pull over yourself and hide inside, over your face and your experiences, because today is the day my trip begins, I say to Blum, and I wasn't able to sleep, strangely enough, for days and weeks the 1 thing I have been longing for, *my trip with Joseph,* and now, now it's about to begin, I am full of uncertainty and fear and I am making myself ridiculous and embarrassed, I worry that during the trip, no, even before, I'm going to faint on the platform, and later in the dining car I'm going to get sick and have to throw up, and Joseph is going to feel just as awful and come down with a migraine and shortness of breath, he'll be smoking nonstop and he'll simply sink down into the upholstered seat in our compartment, while I am trying to immerse myself in one of my favorite books, something I would not be able to do because I would not be able to stop thinking about Joseph and how he would be sitting across from me looking out at the scenery from time to time, hardly saying a word to me, etc.

11/13

"got lost, in the fire in your eyes . ."

thrown out into this landscape we are, to this place, I say to Blum, to this other place, I say, where we *dash through* forests in our loosely laced shoes that is shoveling in sand the fine grains of sand, a short way up into the forest I mean, to every bush glade to every stand of oak, on the scent of something like droplets of secretion, seeing smelling, remarkable enough, I say, this region of the forest in the hues of urine drops urine dripping from leaves bushes branches, into my throat, as if into my throat, I say, but it was shimmering yellow, dark yellow color of bells, we can see, hear, pealing, trickling slightly, isn't that so, and me going up the mountainside with my friends, again and again with one of them falling back, disappearing behind ridges, waves of mountain meadows, bushes and underbrush, etc., such a fluid morning, while the others went on ahead, *1 nota bene, 1 bamboo, and so forth.*

Heard lots of small humming noises, objects, thoughts, breaths, but they were all entwined and I was not able to distinguish one from the other, I mean the impossibility of *writing them,* you see. They lay there in front of me all intertwined or stretching across the horizon like the footprints of a bird . . oh! still rushing past *the inkwell,* very anachronistic image, well everything has already become anachronistic, there is hardly anything that isn't *outmoded* or appears to be, a flight setting what is that, sound waves are endless, they never stop, that means, dear Joseph, I write to Joseph, your voice will never fade away, even if I am no longer able to hear it, I was almost at the point of giving myself away when I waved to you from the window, the next time you came for a visit you asked DID YOU WATCH ME GO, that was the first time you had ever shown the slightest sign of concern, but I didn't take this as a warning, I write to Joseph, when

I squint I see a painting by Degas hanging on the wall, *Les élèves en pointes,* tutus in white, I say to Blum, it is a picture of you at the age of 4 running through a meadow, but the tutus are open skies, the plantations on your shoulder, I say to Blum, plantations a rose seller's shoulder, from 1 café to the next, he is carrying the bundled white bunches on his right shoulder, he *is shouldering* the roses, at night, while the female customers are carrying their bouquets on their left arm like a nursing child, carrying bouquets of flowers like a burden and seek to free themselves of it as quickly as possible, they hold the bouquet head down like an extinguished torch or let it drag slightly behind them, broom. Paper bush.
It is all about the 1 significant moment, Alexander Kluge writes, I say to Blum, that's why we close our eyes, we close our eyes when we kiss we close our eyes when we think try to concentrate, I close my eyes when I am brushing my teeth, when I am talking on the telephone; each time I proofread something I use a different colored pen, no system, I say to Blum, I don't have any systems at all! oh tell me what you think, would CONVULSION be a good title for this book, you know, I have always had too little time in my life and now that it is nearing the end, I see that I will never be able to make up for the things I have missed, which it seems all has its roots in the *indulgent nature* which has dominated my life from the time I was a child, and extravagant as I am I will probably end in extravagance, without having the slightest idea of how things really will be, the way a hare bounds off in 1 direction and then the other when it's hunted, that's the way literature has to be today, I say to Blum, *you have to bound off in 1 direction and then another,* the *cut-up* method as fluttering eyelashes : a twitching of lids like jump cuts pass by—*a re-inspiration* . . throwing whip cream in your face, at night pulling on a REVERSIBLE SHIRT the wrong way, and sleeping saturated in perspiration, waking up, a tin bucket in the middle of the room and rough meals at twilight, in Galtür, 2 cars collide in the street, but very softly as if shadows had crossed paths, etc. In the morning the swelling over my right eye, after a long sleep, I say to Blum, who or what has encircled my days, my nights, crying grass or crying glass, I say, a bright stripe under the hotel door from an illuminated hallway, but the room dark and cold, as I am crossing the square a comparison comes to mind, the second part of which immediately slips my mind, this so very important second part, without which a comparison cannot be formed, had in fact escaped me, not 1 moment after it had made its appearance, in a very devilish, even insidious way it was evading me, reveling in such signs of my advancing dementia it had begun to giggle and rage, still, I had

managed to hold on to the first part, it went like this: "the way we all fall into a panic, when a train, a car suddenly comes to a stop in a tunnel and we imagine that we are not going to be able to get enough air to breathe and we would certainly suffocate unless help arrived in time . ."
Greek to me, I am in the middle of a flood of thought my eyes are so tired, glittering down an entire river, *forest hour* (Celan), and so on, all of my objects given terminology, I say to Joseph, then swallowed the terminology, morning and evening this is how I grapple with the unruly objects in my room, etc., paper bush, planted it, I say, the milk pot on the grounds of grimy bedsheets so that it will find its way back to the phenomena of designation and redesignation within language, ginkgo leaf visualized as brain energy, plowshare as relic of masculine sexuality, etc., give me some sign of where you now are, I write to Joseph, and how you are doing, and NOW wish me an amply filled breakfast table and the beat of a wing (intuition), writing a text in a straight-line progression, I write to Joseph, is probably a suspect procedure, here and there you have to work in a speck of exuberance, willfulness, lunacy, leave the road well traveled, it will be the best thing that has happened to you, even if everyone persecutes scorns beats you. *Chomping into the countryside,* my mother says, with concern in her voice, AFTER THIS SLEEPLESS NIGHT EXHAUSTION'S GOING TO OVERTAKE YOU LIKE A THIEF!, I MEAN ALL OF THAT WANDERING AROUND, SIMPLY ALL THAT WANDERING ITSELF, etc., I say to Blum, the wanderings of a bird around my room while I'm on the phone, I say to Blum, while I was talking to Joseph on the phone a bird with widespread wings was drifting around in the sky as well as living room, I didn't know if it was only a reflection, or disorientation, that's because I go crazy each telephone call with Joseph, and then abruptly from the left edge of the window a soft morning light that from minute to minute opened wider and glowed.

11/18

in a dream Giordano Bruno speaks about the WONDER OF LOVE, no, not WOUND : WONDER, and it is truly a wonder, I say to Joseph, when in my writing you I mean that you come and go and appear and disappear and speak and call, as if you were in fact a living being, but you are of course simply something in writing, something written, a figure on a slip of paper, a cardboard comrade, what do I know, what kind of encounter can I possibly have with you, where you put in question, in that you embody yourself in my writing, whether or not you physically exist, that is exchanging looks and words, touches, signs . . maybe we might imagine that the figures in this book of mine also form relationships among themselves, amusing themselves, separating, without the person doing the writing, the person doing the reading ever knowing anything about it, etc., dragging myself through the *alphabet region,* I say to Blum, among my *oracle figures,* I say, dragging around this bandage, gauze bandage on my left foot, somehow been drawn : *misdrawn,* someone just flung me down on this piece of paper as a distorted figure, someone says to me, someone said something about a TULIP to me, but I can't put it all together, it was in a telephone conversation, I say to Blum, how can it happen that you can't put these things together, don't remember what someone said, in which context words were said and exchanged, someone said something about a TULIP to me, it was in a telephone conversation, but I couldn't follow it, someone was thanking me for something that had something to do with a TULIP I had drawn, someone was thanking me for the TULIP without my being able to reconstruct the events that had led up to it, sometimes I would like to memorize, I say to Blum, sometimes I feel like memorizing what Joseph writes to me in his letters, but I can't, I read Joseph's letters over and over again without being able to commit them to memory, OR ACQUIESCENT IN MUSIC, I am neither able to memorize Joseph's letters nor render favorite musical passages, my favorite musical passages, what I mean is warble along, I hear something like a series of tones intertwined with one another, embracing one another, one determined by the other and they move around inside my head in a very graceful and magical way, but it is *an inner melody* which will never be able to find its way to the outside, etc., Joseph's letters are a treasure, I keep them in a folder, I say to Blum, I reseal the letters, sometimes I feel like burning them so that no one else will ever be able to read them, maybe that's the only reason I keep trying (in vain) to memorize Joseph's letters, the way people learn poems by heart in order to be able to *recite* them at any time and any place, isn't that right, a fetish perhaps, I say to Joseph, our leechy weather today, the grimy stairwell, we sit down on a grassy slope, Joseph says, a kiss as the boundary of passion : an absurd claim, an absurd image, a reflex full of fantasy from somewhere or other, etc.

Everything is earringing, I say to Blum, and sometimes I don't know if I have actually LIVED a thing or had I only imagined it, had I only experienced it in my imagination, an endless letting yourself be deceived, not unlike many trompe l'oeil, I say, that confound us with such an enduring intensity; well okay that's *a brash washbasin* and I think, we can never proceed realistically = radically enough or we can never write realistically = absurdly enough, which also means that we can never be crazy enough about 1 thing or another, this thing or that, person or thing, it doesn't matter which. Such *digital people,* from *digitus* : finger / toe, toe through what I write, with arm extended, hand, finger etc., saw figure in the street, I say to Blum, running to catch an arriving train, not catching it, then *reaching for it with extended index finger* : demanding, almost ghost, strangely attired, red cap, blue vest, black basket-weave skirt, maybe a few of the figures in my book are also reaching for a departing train with pointed fingers, having missed the train, having come too late, not having their say, etc.

It is crackling with the disposal of the body, is the dream that came to me, dear Joseph, don't know who we're talking about here, certainly not you, dashing through the weather housing that is, actually cloud housing, probably the first flakes, and you in your armchair sitting over your books, that's how I see you, while the letter housing, the letter heaven, the buffalo alphabet is darting around inside my head, etc., just think, I received a card with a segment of a painting by Ambrogio Lorenzetti (*Hand of Saint Dorothea*), I find it very moving, red lace border around the wrist, a woman's ocher-colored hand is offering : giving : a small bouquet of spring flowers : stars in blue, yellow and red, the plump green stems cut in uneven lengths held together by a double band of green cord, the background a bright carmine red, cloth with decorative border. The inside of the hand slightly indented at the point where the fingers join the palm, *the small flour cloth.*

somewhere around 11/19
"on a bloodied branch . ."

wet apron, calipers on my desk, dear Joseph, I write to Joseph, caught up in a writing fever again, or something like that, feet in basin, Pergolesi on endless replay, feeling like a stone pedestal, no, like a cement figure somewhere up in the heights, exposed to the winds, sleeping fitfully, because you called me, late at night, and wished me good night, I write to Joseph, restless night, because you tell me : a large meteor has escaped its orbit and in one calamitous explosion it is going to annihilate all life on earth, extinguishing the sun, o earthshaking prophecy, from time to time this is asking too much of me, I am all too locked up in my everyday comings and goings, instead of a normal greeting at the end of her letter Lily writes (on 14 eau de cologne) THE FOX IS LAUGHING, my skin has gotten extremely thin, dear Joseph, or I am stumbling over any and every crisis in the news, lose my sense of balance, feel everything with my skinned body, maybe everything affects me all too directly, short-circuited, causing a corresponding amount of pain, I see SIGNS of everything everywhere; everything I hear, everything I see is a sign of everything that's happening everywhere, but would otherwise remain hidden, the greatest catastrophes are transmitted to me by the most unlikely signs, it's like prophecy, right, you hardly dare to open your eyes anymore, to let yourself look around, you feel like covering your ears with your hands so that you won't have to hear all of this awful news at once, the total panorama of this revelation is hardly to be endured, things that force themselves upon you minute by minute are as devastating as they are inescapable, the most unlikely signs in this life can only be decoded as both private and collective devastation : collective and private fate, collective and private collapse, isn't that right, the TEST VULTURE, isn't that right, every morning the TEST VULTURE circling around my skull, all of which leads to an *attenuation of nervous sensation* I mean a total nervous crisis, etc.

As I took his letter out of the mailbox, I say to Blum, it seemed to me that it contained something I had been waiting for for days, something I had been fearing that is, the contents foreseen days ago, in fact I had predicted the devastating effect this letter would have on my emotional system, overwhelmed by a collapse unequaled by anything I had ever known, as I read and reread the letter—before I tore open the envelope I felt the pain to be inflicted on me as I read and reread the letter, while unfolding the two densely filled pages of letter paper I was assaulted by something not unlike total annihilation of my powers of reason as well as my soul, etc. *it blew me across the water* it was the Rhine, I say to Blum, we were proceeding very cautiously so that the train would not be lifted off the tracks by the continually rising water, it was a deluge or it was the words in his letter, or the flood, and that I was about to start staggering, it was the delicacy of his writing style, I say to Blum, such that I was always starting over I mean over and over again, again and again I had to read his letter from beginning to end and then once more, it blew us across the water, we were on a train crossing a platform or trestle over the river, you see the river had risen so high that it was overflowing its banks, we were gliding over one *bank of the river,* me gasping for breath as I read his letter, from time to time the train got stuck among branches torn loose from the shore by the high water, and now spinning around in the middle of the river, etc., *feelings plundered,* I believe, in view of this constant tendency to overflow, I remember, I stood on the tips of my toes in order to grow lighter, with my hair torn apart, only zebra sky : black wavy lines across the white paper of his letter, and on the slipper, in the slipper : rip threads of water droplets, I mean the *liquefaction of motive,* etc. : rain, storm high speeds. When I *grew blurry* the bouquets fell to the floor, I mean when I grew blurry the bouquets fell right into my lap, I was standing in front of Matisse's *Still Life with Oranges,* 1912, oil, linen, 94 × 83 cm, they fell from the edge of the tablecloth directly onto the floor, at my feet, these bouquets of flowers they keep falling directly onto the floor, I say to Joseph, at our feet, just look, they plunge headfirst down onto the floor, at our feet, isn't that right, I believe they plunge down headfirst, bunches of violet dahlias, marigolds, roses, turtle doves, pleated curtains, etc., when things began to blur, they came plunging toward me, the table fossil purplish red and stone gray, would like to *pluck* : tug the tablecloth, straighten it, and then it suddenly winds away from the pink cloth, winds, collapses, whistles, sighs away with all of the local deities, isn't that right, the small apples almost crushed by the fruit bowl, carafe, wineglass, *or you smell the ODALISK,* I had used my notes as a place mat for my soup bowl, I believe I had not pushed my notes aside but instead used them as a kind of tablecloth, right, they were all piled up on top of one another, it was a not a multilayered place mat made of fragile individual pieces upon which the full bowl, the spoon, the paper napkin created well-situated feelings, or the wind piercing through a closed window, had pushed everything from its place, I mean blown away, objects from the lost and found collected by a paranoid soul, it seems to me, Blum says, but I have a feeling, I say, that everything fits together and works out, like wet sash, the eyes of a fenced-in dog, the small black boxer shorts (brochure), insect on the lower edge of 1 lens of a pair of glasses falls onto a flowered piece of underclothing, plunges onto the brightly colored ornament, onto the small cutting board sticky with drops of honey, onto the saturated notes, the SASHED EYES, etc.

11/20

"the warmest of bird wisdom . ."

sitting in a telephone bunker, time is growing short, been sitting here very ILL all day and half the night in a telephone bunker, thinking about the *shower* (shivering) life, and how it might possibly bring me into bloom, beyond the term of life given to me that is, the way grasses and flora are sprinkled and watered, drizzled, inspired, misted, etc., as bounteously as possible I mean : 1 shower life and then another, and another, and each 1 would be reserved for a very specific purpose : 1 for reading wondrous works of poetry, 1 for hiking, traveling, roller skating, looking at paintings, for the vista of the bellowing stag with white meadows stars and sword-leaf trees (Matisse), for a view of the sea, for a ride through the desert, for the FIGURE IN THE ROOM, etc., but before long, I say to Blum, not very long at all everything would simply *fizzle out,* the way it always happens with me, right, I mean before long everything would be the way it had always been, leveled off, normalized, in the sense of : happy to be able to stretch out on my bed, to page through a few books, my favorite books next to my pillow, my flecked coat in the window, perfectly quiet, inside / outside . . harmony, I say to Blum, like Henri Matisse's *Harmony in Red,* a painting in which the wallpaper merges into the tablecloth, while the FIGURE IN THE ROOM or the AMATEUR IN THE ROOM is burying her left hand, dipping her hand into the construct of fruit, while her right hand is gripping the neck of the glass bowl, next to the oil implements of bread rolls, pine saplings, horns of fishes . . and gathered up off the floor slip after slip of paper because there is air streaming through the room, air bubbles, brothers : air streaming through my study, air streaming and wafting, the moment I gently *air out* the blanket spread over my feet, and falls : everything falls out of my hand, the empty plastic bowl crashes onto the

floor, I see the generously blanketed Van Gogh bed, I say to Blum, when I visited my friend for the first time, my eyes immediately turned to the tall bed in a very long room with high vaulted ceilings, like a hall, leather goods factory that is, once had been a leather goods factory, someone said, someone explained, an austere room, I told him, austere : well kept, I told him, that's it, and blue crystal vases (chalices) like the ones in fashion in the 30s on various pieces of furniture, then I lost the scissors, I say to Blum, then the floor flooded, then the water in my footbath spilled out across the carpet, smell : wet dog, etc.
oh, the casualties, I call Blum, oh neck armor neck transplant : just the way we misread / mishear, so much is there, I call Blum, so much is there when / I mean : so much *washbasin or Bechstein* (even in the former leather goods factory beneath the vaulted arches, next to the Van Gogh bed, a black Bechstein with an open book of sheet music, I say to Blum, you should have seen it), when the water faucet is on under my desk I mean simply forgotten : everything left under my desk EVERYTHING ST. MARK'S SQUARE! : underwater and the house dove, the white-haired terrier, the young weasel . . only *zebra heavens* : the black wavy lines on white paper, and on the house slippers : slip into the slippers : the rip threads of water droplets. What's going on, Blum says, please tell me what is all of this : water, portions being washed away, footbaths, enigmas reflected in water, ferryboats in your study, what has all that got to do with your production, what is *machining* you on?, appears to be subjectivity of the most extreme sort, I shout, get the ponds laid out, at home, the house ponds, and let myself be smuggled off in faraway *nymph mail, etc.*
Soaking-wet pillows of moss scattered across the floor, and how the floor uneven so that a foot stumbles, I say to Blum, liquefaction of motive that is, an amoeba, mollusks at the table covered with tin cans and the way I just sat, there, slouched, not saying a word, lamb on my tongue . . my friends served leg of lamb, nettle salad and mutton testicles . . the preparation of this sentence took me 3 hours, and looking back over it the idea of eating mutton testicles disgusts me. I spent these 3 hours in the supermarket, I say to Blum : more precisely : on the premises, on the expansive premises of the supermarket on the corner, there I can push my shopping cart around, once having transferred all of the baggage I normally carry around with me into the interior of my barred cart I can make my rounds unhindered, it's like being in an amusement park, today I actually wanted to get into the little red coin-operated car, but I managed to repress my desires, I say to Blum, anyway I only go to the supermarket to get a little exercise, and

maybe to pick up a little inspiration, what I mean is, I don't go to the supermarket to buy anything, I never NEED anything, on the contrary, I'm always giving my leftovers to the neighbor, or I buy things knowing that I am never going to be able to use them, I say, a pigeon and a little dog were racing around, on the sidewalk . .

when I left the supermarket *in a daze,* having noted down everything I've written here, I recognized Joseph's handwriting on a postcard among the mail I took out of my box, oh Joseph, I say to Joseph, who is not there, it was a happy shock, I only read your message and left the rest of my letters and cards lying on the floor.

You shouldn't be surprised, Blum says, when you try to force yourself to write, nothing comes of it, Blum says, it's like having your picture taken, if you pose you're going to get a bad picture, the moment you assume a working posture everything's going to go wrong, isn't that so. The recent sense I've had, I say to Blum, of having distanced myself from Joseph somewhat was contradicted by the joy I felt today when I read his card from G., good god, it shot straight through my heart, had I forgotten my love, had I, half-relieved, let myself feel that he was no longer my heart's desire?

as soon as I grind the *knackerbrot* between my teeth there is a crackling noise in my deaf ear, we had agreed to meet at the MAXIMILIAN, I say to Blum, then, and we were talking about writing and promiscuity, he seemed very thoughtful and I saw fire in his eyes again, a dark fire, flared blazed in his pale face . . it was quiet in the café and I kept ordering hot chocolate to calm myself down, I kept getting up and going out because his intelligence kept pressing me, etc., and while we were having our discussion over the top of the table, I was thinking about the part of his body under the table, wondering what it looked like, his soul and his body both attracted me in equal measure, and I had the feeling I wanted time to stop, can you imagine, I ask Blum, how I was feeling, the mineral water bottle on our table was casting a green shadow, the sight of the half-empty bottle the way its green shadow I mean meadow shadow I mean it flowed it glistened it shimmered over the tablecloth, or its green glow seemed spun out across the cloth, this lucid glowing FOREST GREEN took hold of me in the innermost reaches of my being, and it was an aching sensation it was also an elation, I don't know, I say to Blum, because I'd never seen a green shadow before, this forest-green shadow touched me in my most tender place, and I covered my face with my hands in order to hide my tears, etc. These light-green fringes, too, no, beautiful deep-black fringes : Joseph's wreath of eyelashes,

I say to Blum, now between deep green and deep black, the sight of this green light had transported me into a state of profound ecstasy, etc.
Then, that afternoon in the café I suddenly understood that Joseph, in the *manner of Scardanelli* had had to refuse me a visit, however brief, in his housing, ANY GUEST WOULD BE INTRUDING—how often have I repeated this sentence myself so that I could work undisturbed stay at a constant temperature, now I understand that Joseph's claim was legitimate, I say to Blum, *1 moment of the lily, tearing the soul apart,* etc.
We have to always be ready to accept this cloud full of fragrance (rendezvous brushes), I say to Joseph, who isn't here, I mean everything was in such a spontaneous state of great anticipation, that something like a corporeality (truth?) of art could have been achieved through this momentary fixing, I mean when we harvested potatoes, then, in P., and held the ungainly roots in our fists, glistening clumps of earth hung from the tubers, *they quivered, the clumps of earth quivered and I brandished,* etc. I held the tubers over my head and waved them around at the end of my outstretched arms and the tiny potato plot lay in the shade, and the morning and morning storms raged through closed windows and the storm even lifted the blanket I was lying under, and that is how the storm rumbled, I mean : back and forth language must be shaken : 1 PHEW and 1 HOT, well-formed sentences alongside shattered sentences, language burst apart and language compleat, the rejected and the true, the recollection of a word, or better the echo of a word, of a half sentence which, which rests in us, encapsuled, so many years, but suddenly arisen, it looks, it looks at us, it calls us to us, etc. an imploring force : you must write it down, you must write everything down, you must let it rise, maybe you picked it up, read it, heard it, experienced it, invented it years ago, decades ago, it was immersed in you, but now it is back! what an inexplicable phenomenon, it's stayed with you in such a wondrous way, preserved in you, what kinds of beautiful things had you stored away inside you? you probably forgot it inside you, you had probably forgotten about it, you had slept many sleeps over it, but now it awoke in you and sprung forth : a magnificent moistly smooth reptile shimmering in every tone : in your childhood it had sat in your hand like a salamander and the sight of it moved you to tears. And now you can't stop it, you can't stop it anymore, toward evening I called him on the phone, I say to Blum, because I was in need of his voice, and when I asked him if he had been asleep, he quietly said, I WAS JUST READING, and I was distressed because this kind of interruption is inexcusable, because reading like writing (praying) is a sacred activity, because we are seldom thus

consecrated, etc., and then I experienced various eye phenomena again, I saw the *open* (piled high with bedding) wooden bed in my friends' vaulted hall, couriers of light on the ceiling, etc., saw myself sitting next to my mother in my *prisoner's uniform,* in a meadow, but sometimes she crossed her ear lobes with some sort of costume jewelry or other, and after a few hours she took the clips off, oh, they hurt so much!, I look into the mirror and see the Murillo boy, I say to Blum, the plum pits spit out onto the floor, I say, stepped on the Piatnik playing cards, in front on the house, in the sleet and snow, the way they lay scattered around, 6 or 7, among the parked cars, a gray Beuys hat in the cloakroom next to the eye doctor's waiting room, I say, *and he never had more than 20 heads, etc.,* I must have been suffering some kind of DELIRIUM, probably an overdose of some medicine, stretched my home being (myself) out, felt good, under my right eyelid I catch sight of a glistening light, glaring light source ("peroxide blond"), I mean I (daydreaming) began TO HOP through the pathways and peacocks of an enormous park, yes : HOP, as it seemed as it was, and the peacocks strode through the park ahead of me or sat in the trees and screamed, like small children, and the sky *shone* peacock glorious, a peacock glorious sun that is, so that light-green sheaths of leaves on trees and bushes trembled and I was able to imitate this trembling, my body trembled and even my teeth were chattering, and I knew I was hopping, that I was hopping away, having to hop away in this state, and that this was the only word I had with which I could describe my condition, I mean the particular way in which I moved and I spread my arms, somehow it was exhibitionistic, and now they were marching past me in formation, those peacock pairs that had colored the heavens, and I performed this HOPPING of mine for my friends who were standing around and talking or walking, and I knew that it must have been a ridiculous sight, and I was suddenly ashamed of the way I was moving and for the introduction of the word HOPPING, I listened for the cry of the peacocks and twirled myself into and through their show, my arms spread wide, actually swinging, as IF FICTION AND REALITY WERE NOT SEPARATED BY A BOUNDARY BUT CONTAINED WITHIN IT, but while I was lying there and writing by twilight, a lush bouquet of gray roses / in the bud appeared on the piano . . ("*and then this light baboon . .*")

11/22

"Yearning for the woodlands" : Schumann, I say to Joseph, very eye-catching, I say, the apple in the background, eyeball background, etc., and in the RESTAURANT, I say, as Blum suddenly gets up and shouts : WALTER PICHLER! and before that asks me to guess who has just come into the place, and me, sitting with my back to the one who has just entered, I immediately say his name ("got eyes in the back of your head?" etc.), and he then, at our table, and says, what is 1 day, or a whole string of days for that matter, you have to have weeks, months in front of you, without limits, without interruption, esplanade of trees, chain of mail, cordon, etc., and me telling him, what for you studio artists *the crafting work,* reading is for us writers, right, eyeball region, blood thought, and the forest of conifers on the tabletop, isn't that right, I mean you have to be *attuned : in shape* in just the right way, to brave the lunacy (luminescence) of writing, I say, in order to achieve a WRITERLINESS you have to feel this *jumping and running,* this *through forest and field,* this putting yourself above and beyond, this being above and beyond, light-footed prancing, in the most fervent of states, etc., young dogs play this way!, no obstacle too great, no moderation with your own energies, with your own time, *in a state of lunacy, me the monster woman* or *the no one,* what do I know, while my heart is beating away with its fist, *it's hammering!* against the wall of my chest, grain, ink, banana dress, a process of tearing apart, etc., omnipresent demand of myself : REACTIVATE REASON AND CONSCIENCE!

the upward and downward images, the raging films in our head, I say to Blum, with this cloth or rag on my left foot I dust my way through my household chores, actually it's an ingenious kind of sewerage system, I say to Blum, and I am the vermin inhabiting it, the rat scurrying off, a fugitive monster not knowing which way to turn, darting back and forth, acting only on reflex, raining down on me from somewhere, deaf ears, cannons of PANIC trained on me, the cups the pot held under *a stream* of cold running water, instead of being thoroughly *washed, rinsed,* the way my father used to do when he wanted to reuse the pan from the previous day, simply held them under running water, over and over again the same utensils every day, and left right on the stove, the pans, the pots, the cups, the spoons to be reused, *eggs every day!, very Orphic,* I say, *these Orphic things on the kitchen floor,* you know.

Liquefaction of motives, I say to Joseph, and the way the floor is so uneven that your foot trips, soaked, I say of the geysers bubbling up there, sitting there every morning in the spray of the geysers springing up out of the floor, my feet in a footstool bath, and you get this OKAY NOW and this WATER URGENCY on the floor and stacked-up photos sliding down onto the floor, sliding directly into the bathwater and blistering, documentary blisters, should be wearing life jackets, should have worn life jackets, should have been wearing life jackets, outflanking that is.

Eruption of light / concealed shadows / Nirvana of storm—where did I pick this up, I ask myself, an art sleeve, I say to Joseph (but he isn't there!), an art sleeve : you slip into it in reality and come out the other end in fiction, that's it, that's all there is, the entire definition of art, this is the entire canon, you see, this is the recipe!, we take a point of view and then we take it all back—emphasize, expose : immediately cover back up, retract!

when you express the formulation, FICTION AND REALITY ARE NOT SEPARATED BY A BOUNDARY BUT ARE ASSOCIATED WITHIN A BOUNDARY—you might also say the same thing about our relationship, *the animated envelope,* I say to Joseph (who isn't there!), I mean the animated handwriting on the envelope, the apprehensive rashness of the characters, and before I had even broken the letter open, had read it, I knew, I knew in advance what would be in it, lost my head over it, dear Joseph, this perfect letter-writing style, the trepidation in your message, my writing is unclear because it has become unsteady, when I began writing to you in response to your letter, you can't accept love, no : you won't accept *the fantasy of my love,* that's a better way to put it, I need something to put over my head, some kind of bag or pack, I say to Blum, so that no one can see me, still people are constantly ringing me out, out of my writing, above all, but this time it's devastation, this time it's feelings of devastation, and I want to keep them to myself, I want to hide them from the world, preserve them, press the pain into my heart LIKE A REAL CROWN OF

THORNS, do you understand what I'm saying, I ask Blum, just two slits for my eyes, and an *urgent writing vow,* LAPTOP = hot water bottle, that I can hold on to in bed, tap around on it, how would you translate LAPTOP, I ask Blum, without waiting for his answer, we shout in unison that is : lap dog, etc.—

The other day I thought to myself, how uncomfortable, when I saw them, a group of young people along the edge of the street, on the steps leading into the Academy of Fine Art, they were sitting in a crouch and conversing in hushed tones, they appeared to be sitting on stools or low chairs, but they were actually sitting on their haunches they were in a crouch and gave the impression that there was no other more comfortable (more unconventional) posture.

Now I am sitting here, dear Joseph, I say to Joseph, who is not present, now I am sitting here and sparks are leaping out of my eyes, I was lying there writing, and a luxuriant bouquet of roses, still in the bud, appeared on top of the piano, I couldn't see what color they were, they appeared to be gray, probably made of wool, a dull gray, AND ITS EMINENCE . . everything appeared to be illuminated, the whole house and the pond, I imagined a wreath of roses, brackish water, the element of a sticky spoon on the bedcovers, and what springs over our tongues, I say to Joseph, is it ROCK-SOLID NATURE?

11/24

trembling, yes, my knees are wobbling, a very unusual time of the day for me to be sitting at my typewriter, I say to Blum, how would you explain it, *and always right into the church when I flew,* I say, mother always in church when I was traveling by plane, and back at home world news on the radio, television in order to reassure herself that there had been no plane crash, no bus accident, etc., and her shoulders hunched as she walked along the street, brisk, choppy steps, but I loved to watch her walk, brown *trotteurs,* beige stockings, old well-preserved coat, you see, she would say to me, I wear my clothes, underclothes, coats, hats and shoes : for decades, I don't have to buy anything for decades, it usually is a matter of years, decades before a handbag, a scarf, a pair of shoes has to be replaced, but everything you have *wears out* in such a short time, 2 coats every season, and everything gone to rags and threadbare because you don't take care of your dresses, clothing, caps and shoes, etc., and then we both laughed when she started in on me, I especially loved her then when she TOOK ME UNDER HER WING LIKE THAT, and a *Bisamberg for the children,* I would say then, and we would laugh again, and then she would usually say, *you keep functioning everything around,* what's going to come of that, the doubled person on the lawn, it seems, I say and the steely blue sky, and the fire wheel in my chest, I say to Blum, at this unusual time of the day, what was it that had thrown me off balance like this, I say, do you mean paddling or pedaling or crawling, I say to Blum, do you mean *childhood checkered, childhood coloration, and megarage,* when you are alluding to my UPSIDE-DOWN NATURE, or something like that, oh my verses and adversaries, I shout, oh what has been rattling me this way : and lifting me up as if I were flying through the air, oh a human and his *clone,* will they both have the same soul, you animate me, I write to Elisabeth von Samsonow, you animate me to continue with my writing because you write me such wonderfully beautiful letters, and when I read these letters it seems I feel as if I am hearing your voice, as if you were *reading* the letters you have written to me, *to me,* a rather unusual circumstance that someone who has written a letter and sent it then *reads it to the recipient,* it might seem that it was not even necessary to write it in the first place, isn't that so—what do you think of that, I say to Blum, and mother always going to church while I flew and at home studying the itinerary I wrote for her in large block letters, and said, departure now, transfer, arrival, now bus to the hotel, now sound test, reading, now telephone call . . experiencing every station of my journey—and THE ART OF BREATHING and speaking *on the valley,* no not : in the valley, *on the valley,* this speaking on the telephone : one of the most subtle forms of communication between us, I say, not that way with Joseph, *not at all,* because with Joseph always self-conscious, or blue jay, not even that way with you. 3 moths bagged this morning, after being on the lookout for cockroaches in the kitchen, they favor certain parts of the city, the papers report, met Lily entirely by chance, I say to Blum, and walked uphill and down the steep street in front of our buildings that is, up and down the way we once had as children . . and talked and laughed the way we once had as children on our afternoon and evening walks, expeditions through gardens, playgrounds and parks in the surrounding neighborhood, and why, I ask Blum, still / over and over again this swearing cursing where everything seems to be working out I mean working out according to some mysterious plan, etc., year of the monkey.

A few of us become nothing but ardent businessmen, I say to Blum, who are trading on *the goods of their souls* they created 2 or 3 decades ago, because there is nothing new coming out of their heads, isn't that right, all they care about is making a profit on the products of their minds which they created 3, 4 or more decades ago, the venerable powers of the soul : fruits of the soul presented to man and to woman as fresh produce right, I say to Blum, but a soul won't allow itself to be sold without exacting a price it's not like a cow on the hoof, a herd of sheep, a barrel full of live fish . . . . (*or deep into the nether realms of the Chinese empire, etc.*)

And even when the sun is shining switch on the light because the mountain of notes in front of me is growing higher and higher preventing me from seeing clearly enough what I have written and have yet to write, always the time before a trip, I say to Blum, is the most dilatory, on the one hand, I always allow myself much too much time to pack my bags, make travel preparations, on the other hand it is the most refreshing, invigorating because in a sly, even cunning way the repressed flow of writing breaks free only minutes before the drive to the airport, to the train station, forcing me to sit down at my typewriter and peck away, as if this were the last time, the last opportunity to get everything out of me, right, just this *styling*, etc., 1 school : 1 shoe of fish, 1 side of hill, 1 mass of pines in the garden, or whatever happens to leap across our tongues, Blum says, or whatever is all worked up in your writing, Blum says, this completely bunched BLOSSOM TRAFFIC, WORD BLOSSOM TRAFFIC, and *banner box,* leaves behind indelible tracks, *nerve tracks,* isn't that so, and telephone conversations are like that too, I say, you have said what you have to say, said good-bye, and you start all over again, it is almost compulsory, *say something (approximately) in through the door,* the voice on the other end : CANDY!, and although in retreat, I have to start talking to her again, to him, this and that, and licking her (his) voice because it is so sweet, more questions and suggestions, agreement, splendor and joy, and laughter, chortling laughter—

with the weight of my own body sitting on the armchair, shifting around, I mean the armchair the leg of the armchair almost punched me a hole through my ankle, without a doubt and various other unfortunate events in the morning hours of this day, always have the *food bag* with me, I say to Blum, food bag buckled on, a kind of *bird prayer station* as fanny pack, right, and the moldy old bread, leftover pieces of bread thrown into bags, but never found time to scatter them over fallow lawns, *and blown away the hen or the hound,* I say to Blum, everything allusion, nothing more, realized inside your head inside your imagination, not having the energy actually never had the energy to carry out these expansive plans, concepts, *just gave my breasts a shove,* Lily says : shoved them inside my blouse or someplace like that, Lily says, went to bed fully dressed, had forgotten to get my blanket, woke up around midnight because shivering, interest in new relationships keeps dwindling, I say to Lily, often think about head or dog burial, and food service during the flight very generous, I say to Lily, effective : less afraid, in the cabin and then during the flight, the lox rolled rotated : down my throat, I say to Lily, and after the second dose of psychopharmaceutical, after washing down the second dose of psychopharmaceutical I feel animated, energized, liberated and winged, all of my despair and pains seemed to disappear I mean, prevailing SPERBER SPIRIT, etc.

Today, after my guest had taken leave, I say to Blum, I felt disoriented, had to make an effort to find myself again, was I still this and this person?, my limbs, joints, hands, feet, my head felt strange, I had no center, no sights, etc., an endeavor : all this EYE FOREST, I say to Blum, but then Sibylle Heusser came up to me, gave me a banana-shaped lighter, and she said to me : have you ever seen palms, have you ever heard palms?, it is a glassy sound sharp as a knife, actually cutting, have you ever seen palms, Sibylle Heusser says, have you ever heard, have you ever heard palms when the wind when storms blow, roar through their crowns . . yes, I say, in Nice, once in Nice, it was in November, I say, like glass, and cutting, on the coast, I fantasize my way to this place whenever people start talking about Nice, I fantasize a figure from Samuel Beckett's books in a sandpit, Malone is dying, probably, but I fantasize that the old men there in much too baggy swim trunks and withered arm musculature, I mean their way into the water so carefully, step-by-step and then let themselves glide, many years ago, 1 November, meanwhile the ancient swimmers exhausted and spent and hidden their bones in the sand and soil, I say, bleeding butcher hands, I say to Blum, when my guest took leave, and he said, a pool of blood on the ground floor, maybe someone with a cut-up hand or something like that, butcher's hands early in the morning, butcher's cap, I say to Blum, I mean I was wearing a butcher's cap when I got up, raised myself out of bed, dried my hands in the finest the thinnest onionskin = carbon copy paper, and I forgot to begin the morning with a curse the way I usually do, I had forgotten to curse, strangely enough, I forgot to curse, as all of the robes and pajamas fell off the hanger to the floor, while the cloned moon : whole world of my eye : that is, several half-moons next to and over one another glowed, *that's my astigmatism,* you see.

11/25

read Peter Weiss, read Koeppen, I say to Blum, a thin book, I know now that what I've been doing is all wrong, I say to Blum, a younger-looking father comes my way, I am dreaming of my father, in a light-colored suit, I walk up to him, want to give him a kiss, he rejects, he lets out a scream, ah! my tooth!, strangely younger-looking father, we go by car to visit my mother in the hospital, see her only for a moment, dying, and beneath her—the last take in an old overexposed film—in intertwining letters THE END . .

in the early-morning light I see the mineral water bottle that I finished during the night is covered with dust, everything here covered with dust, the books the tables the spoons the houseplants : nothing can be done : I circle over these my appalling circumstances and say to myself, you can't really change any of this, this state, nothing of this my pitiful situation can be touched, it's an ironclad law, I say to Blum, and maybe I don't really even want to change it, I say, I've often wondered whether or not I would be comfortable, find my way around a clean and uncluttered room with bookshelves and books all lined up in order, could I write in a place like that, and then I think 1 way and another, I say to Alma, and I answer this and that without thinking about what I am saying, and when Blum gives me his advice, and I express my appreciation and agree with his suggestions for the improvement of my situation, take another look at it and come, as before, to the conclusion that everything will just have to continue as it is, unchanging, irreversible, etc.

On a serving tray the note, *fodderly fluttering,* day and night, I say to Blum, the Strauß of Bethlehem, this mountain of notes my 1 and only chapter, I say, who will understand it, I get a call from Fabienne V., and she says

YOU UNDERSTAND ME SO WELL, YOU REALLY UNDERSTAND EVERYTHING, somewhat chagrined I demur, it all depends on my STOMACH CONDITION, I say, I mean whether or not I have stomach cramps, when I am well, I understand everything, at least I feel I can BE UNDERSTANDING, even of the darkest signs and caves, eye cavities, abysses and systems, as they say, or as they say "you'll have to learn to live with it," as they say, and then that afternoon I was talking to the elderly saleswoman in a perfume shop, and she says I CAN'T MOVE MY FINGER ANYMORE, and reaches out toward me with the index finger of her left hand, I ask if it's rheumatism, or maybe gout, she says yes, one of those two things, you just have to learn to live with it, etc., you'll have to learn to live with it as they say, I say to Blum, I have never uttered this sentence, I don't like it, rubber band in front of me on my night table, has taken on the form of a violin scroll, or a violet, and what actually happened last night, I say to Blum, I was supposed to meet Th. P., but my consciousness was revolving around the certainty that I had arranged to meet Franz K. at 8, that lasted several hours, I couldn't get away, and when I thought about my meeting with Th. P., I kept thinking *wrong scene?*, I had to meet Franz K., *or then suddenly a sun arose,* etc.

The color of DEPLETED, Blum says, now that your mother is no longer alive, Blum says, over and over again, since your mother is no longer alive, Blum says again, he says it again and again, he keeps starting this sentence : since your mother is no longer alive, but never finishes this sentence, I ask myself why, since your mother is dead, and again, since your mother is no longer alive . . I say, when I was in Rome 2 weeks before my mother died, to give a reading, I called her and told her that I was in Rome, in a most reverent voice she said ROME!—YOU'RE IN ROME! MY GOD YOU'RE IN ROME!, her voice trembled and I had to cry.

Remembering those incensed scented images, I say to Blum, which have been with me since the days of my childhood, I say, it is a kind of HEAD HOLINESS, isn't it, bouquet of barberry on a folded cardboard mat, the tray with densely packed pages of notes, pages of notes everywhere, narcissus, tobacco leaves, mignonette, in a *false twilight,* I say, on a tea bag in *false coloring* an appetizing apricot, overcolored that is, zipper on the cheek of the actor over the bed, I say to Blum, the floor so uneven that your foot catches, everything in the household so worn out!, I say, you come in your Batmobile, I say to Joseph, when he comes in the door carrying his crash helmet, pine forest on the table, no a 50 zloty coin from my most recent trip to Poland, I say to Blum, contrails in the window, I say to Blum, I'm just getting sidetracked here from what really happened, he avoided looking into my eyes, I say to Blum, when he came in, carrying his crash helmet under his arm, he avoided looking into my eyes, on the one hand the kiss he gave me on the right cheek and the left might be understood as a soothing gesture, or as a final garland (the kind you find at chapter endings in old books) or coda on the other hand (the end or addendum to a musical movement), which then might well mean: OKAY, THIS IS ALL THERE IS! or I EXPLAINED EVERYTHING IN MY LAST LETTER, AND YOU STILL DON'T GET IT?, these rising and falling images, but it is a *mind desire,* I say to Joseph, it is only a mind desire, you have to understand that, *and I tread carefully on the needles,* blood thought!, I say, barefoot, the entire floor covered with pine needles, because that way everything sparkles and glitters on the parquet when rays of sunshine, I mean, I wonder, I ask Joseph, which psychic line of demarcation—in front of each other—are we going to withdraw behind, etc., . . write to Alma, dear Alma, I write to Alma, the 2 cocoon dolls from Japan arrived in good condition, Blum chose the red doll, he hung the red cocoon doll on his left, that reminds me of my cherry garden childhood, the way we all did it as children, hung pairs of cherries over our ears, etc., I chose the black doll, will hang it from my desk lamp, came to me in my dreams today WE HAVE ALREADY BEGUN TO INSTALL THE EASTER OFFICE, but don't know what that means, I was reading Wolfgang Koeppen, while reading Wolfgang Koeppen's book "once upon a time in Masuren" I broke out in tears, now I know that everything I have done, I have done wrong, how is it possible for me to work at all after reading this, I wonder, how is it possible for me to . . dropped everything, all of my outlines, will have to begin all over again, and in the end the book I am now working on will be an entirely different book, I am very restless, breathlessly take my blood pressure, everything inside me churning, pages of manuscript on my desk, rolled up into a tiara, it seems, when I view the array of papers around my typewriter from some distance, I keep thinking my way through my work over and over again, here I am buried here all alone and writing down things as they occur to me, I am so curious about the *intonation,* I mean the way my work will speak, etc., have my favorite music, the music I find most stimulating right now, Bach's cantata : *ich habe genug,* set on REPEAT, singularly jubilant like the song of the white *Amalfi blossoms.*

11/26

shoveling down those pills like candy, Blum says, I keep getting better at these *passions*: writing passions, getting heart palpitations racing pulse, etc., just take it easy step-by-step, Blum says, not so many aerial leaps, Blum says, that brain rush early in the morning, I say, when the sky outside is gray and it's raining, OF RELATED *TÜREL / TÜRL :* came to me in my dreams, I say, and then with my bare hand squashed a pale moth on the fringes of the carpet and such life juices I mean such a disgusting wetness on the tips of my fingers . . it has to be pulsing with life, none of these mind acrobatics, cutlet on top of GALA's head, right, the way Dalí painted it, accomplished it, Camembert cheese *wiped* across the bare garden bushes flung down and dripping like dough it collapsed, poetic heart palpitation every step of the way, then the silly cuckoo clock calls out the bird in my heart, announcing the hour, the time, it's wound up, I'm wound up, but don't want to be wound up, want to have a free hand with my passions right, I say to Blum, with my writing passions and other desires, the Star of Morocco, the Strauß of Bethlehem, its shadow is fluttering across the kitchen wall, so *fodderful* every day, the lady-in-waiting day the lady-in-waiting night, and all of this VENUS AFFAIR, the baptismal church once on the water, I say to Blum, and now torn down, destroyed, etc., but as far as Dalí's time is concerned, I say to Blum, we used to have a different concept of time, I mean a week had 7 days, but now only 4, no 3 : on Thursdays people are already saying have a good weekend!, and *right down to the last spoonful!*

remember, try to remember, rewind your time, I say to Joseph, my eyes locked onto your eyes, like a contact lens my eye floated on yours, we sat across from each other at Tomasselli's, do you remember, our glances touched so intimately so close, the innermost skin of vessels / feelings,

while we sat across from each other at Tomasselli's, do you remember, and *glowed* : yes, my cheek glowed I believe like pink hollyhocks : wild roses, and everything so *featherly contained* because I was immediately writing down what pleased me what you said, I don't remember, Joseph says, if I can't remember, I can't have been there, Joseph says, or I have only done those things I can remember, etc. Halo or hot air balloons, I say, am doing everything mechanically as if underwater, I say, we were sitting at Tomasselli's, do you remember, and I was *tripping over myself,* I was tripping over myself or I had plummeted down into my emotions and was submerged in torrential waters, without having been able to foresee the consequences for even one moment, in the meantime I had come back, had been thrown back onto the raw, *onto the raw object,* etc.
"merciless / merciless," a swab : swabbed face, Dalí places the cutlet the delectable cutlet on top of GALA's head, he has 5 great men of letters (their likenesses) pose on top of a wall with his feces on their heads, my swabbed face, face darkly covered with tears or traces of the black felt-tip pens I am constantly using to correct what I have written, you see, the potential for tears unimaginably large, as is the potential for lies, I say to Blum, I store lies under my tongue, am occasionally astounded at how fluently I speak lies, they glide right off my tongue, and my mother also enjoyed lying, she confessed this to me a very few months before she died, strangely enough, I say, that something like this found a place in her memories, so shortly before her passing, I mean *morning is my time for Holy Mass,* you know what I mean by that, I don't have to explain, or morning is a holy time, that is what I might say to the uninitiated, right, or an affinity of the senses because Arno Schmidt came walking toward me on the street, in any case people long since deceased cross my path, more and more often, a few months after his death my father came walking up to me again, I saw him from behind, his cloth coat with its broad shoulders, the gray hat, his upright carriage, and the way he walked so that only a knowing eye could tell how difficult it was for him, then back at home, hat removed, tossed onto the shelf, hair underneath soaking wet : *shoved* to the middle of his forehead, walked up to the mirror, studied his profile, his hair stroked to the side back over his ear . .
gather slips of paper up off the floor, pick up notes from the understory, I say to Blum, on 1 slip of paper I see ORIENT, SCARECROW on another, I say to Blum, perhaps the instinctual hunting down of an intellectual taste (on the tongue), probably a scent, honeyed tongue of a REPAST, etc., the chirping of whelps and thrushes I believe, I believe the *soul of pansies*

by Horst Jannsen, "I am all eyes," he wrote, placed pansies over his eyes, blanketed his eyes with pansies, terrible his open and laughing mouth, maybe he also knew what it was to be afraid of going crazy, like the rest of us, too, like my mother when she felt compelled to watch THE EYE OF LAKE GOSAU, I am afraid I'm going crazy, she would say, because I have to watch THE EYE OF LAKE GOSAU all day long, nothing but that, always THE EYE OF LAKE GOSAU, and wait for the moment when I go mad, because no one even talks to me, I am forgetting how to talk, I'm so miserable, don't even have any ink, always have to spit into the ink jar, and that's why my handwriting keeps growing paler—a little mad and head sanctity, I say to Blum, I take the day planner out of its cellophane sheath, anyway it shouldn't be *tasteful,* it can't be! I mean thinking and writing simply don't have anything to do with the concept of tastefulness, honey spoon doing gymnastics on the breakfast table, I say to Blum, 1 somersault after another, paper cutlets in house slippers, *and everything so completely uncorresponded.* And to think that it's the rain teaching me how to write, etc.

Maybe I can tear up with tap water I mean I can intoxicate myself, boost my brain, or something like that, and I will be struck by a blessing like a lightning bolt, I say to Blum, in my dreams I saw a GARRET RIBBON, actually a SCARF, it was strange, high spirits, outdoor stairs, summer residence, and it was *belling,* in my dream something was belling, lots of bells, they weren't ringing, that wouldn't be quite the right word, it was more like a belling, and that's it, the end.

11/27

and everything falling into the water, bathwater, no : *stage water,* sliding, drowning, I mean everything made of cellophane every paper ribbon every armband, white armband, strangely enough, I say, not all of my manuscript sliding down, have to be careful, and cards from artists, photographers, related, friends, photo cards, Menjou moustache, tableaux to remember, someone with a name something like Robert Frost calls up and tells me that all of the fruit trees in Sarajevo have been cut down, I remove the washbasin in order to avert any further paper drownings, did I say drowning, drowning in tears, drowning myself in tears, a photograph, father took it with the Boxtengor, during the war, I say to Blum, do you remember, I was supposed to be reaching for an imaginary ball that was dropping down out of the air toward me, bathing suit, DOUGHNUT FOREST POOL, food scarcity, can of food, 3 reheated rolls and 2 slices of sausage each day, *hard-breathing dialogue,* etc., did I mention cellophane, cellophane skins over the glass jars full of marmalade my mother made, emergency rations, *deathly stifling,* the Vienna Woods entirely cut down, no heating fuel, this morning woke up with the sentence STORED IN MY WARDROBE JAW, I say to Blum, and immediately started crying, then turned on the music of my hopes, Bachwerkeverzeichnis 82, *ich habe genug,* of CLAWING DIRT, I say to Blum, fingernails all worn down, breaking, what am I saying, about CLAWING DIRT ABOUT APPAREL : clean up sticky spots, fingernails already ruined, thumbnails, peeling off layer by layer, coming loose, nothing left but ragged edges and cracks, from CLAWING DIRT away thumbnails ruined, I say to Blum, in any case everything here in a state of disintegration not only fingernails; papers, letters, backs of books dissolving in bathwater, irretrievable loss, etc., and as far as that lover is concerned, who waves to his parting visitor from the *car team balcony,* I say to Joseph, as you described it to me in one of your most recent letters, under a stormy violet-colored sky, or, as you called it, in the clean air after a thunderstorm, I can see the whole scene right here in front of my eyes, as if I had drawn painted it myself, or as you described it, under a clear night sky cleaned by a thunderstorm, including the cellophane layer, pull the cellophane sheath out of the bathwater, drips, pouring out over a bristly carpet in its own way, bristling fur, fur of a wild animal, the company is called Charles Dickens, on the inside of a wool shirt recently produced, the label, why, I wonder, Charles Dickens, not really read much anymore, required reading, once, I say, indication that this piece is of English manufacture, Blum says, and cellophane wrapping here too, as I roam through my housing, I write to Joseph, I mean through my *cellophane casing,* I pull all the clothes hangers down, which with every step, I mean damp laundry hung everywhere, sunny day, I say to Blum, still morning, I console myself, more than half of the day left for walking, feet in bathwater, on a white cloth napkin "from the abyss that is," stamps scattered out across the bed, absinthe on the stool, or had I squandered *the spontaneous moment* early this morning, or had I *almost squandered the spontaneous moment* early this morning, scared it off, given it away, dawdled it away, knowing that everything depends on it, I say to Blum, where we after all, where it after all, I mean, it robs us of our entire day, life, compelled by it we transform ourselves into a breathing / what do I mean breathing : PANTING GASPING : key machine, our furious fingers have become furious keys, a *forest rush between head and hand,* etc.

Such wordly lubrication I mean when will I find time to commit Droste's poems to memory and her life history, required reading once again, I say to Blum, and the Swiss feuilletons, etc., eyesight in the battery of the head getting increasingly weaker, both of the two previously blue WATERWAYS, winter light penetrating into the interior of the eye, the optician's window display "in progress" : coated azure blue, impulses blinking on and off : first designer frames, then monocle, a nun comes walking toward me, *balcony in profile* on the top floor of an art nouveau building against a blood-red evening sky on the main street, at least the UNITY OF THE SEASON should be maintained in this book, I say to Blum, I mean attributes of winter, for example, should be maintained, if the first draft is written in winter, and the final draft is finished in spring, then I should take care to avoid attributes of spring if they try to work their way in, seeking entirely random inclusion, if they were so to speak to *lose their way* into my deep-winter work, or something like that, then I should retain the winter regions, if I complete the manuscript in spring, I am already imagining trees coming into leaf, I say to Blum, maybe I already heard the first blackbird of spring this evening, this stuff, scraps of paper stick to my body, it really is already the end of February, an imposter of a spring day, I am wearing my dark fur coat, too heavy if you're walking at a fast pace taking notes while you're walking, suddenly incense wafting up from one of the hallways . .

how will I conceal myself from the world, I ask myself, I say to Blum, how will I conceal my cellophane face from the world, this citrus face, no : armored face, etc., fished out of the bathwater, cellophane sheath which had contained a packet of envelopes, cellophane paper boats, *flashback techniques,* I mean.

Right into winter and then right back out of winter again, right into summer and then right back out of summer, right into my winter wardrobe into the lambs and right back out of my winter wardrobe, into my fluttering coats, light jackets and out of my fluttering coats, light jackets, spectrum of vibrating colors projected onto the wall as if onto a movie screen, over my desk lamp, and from the right, and taking an afternoon break on my worn ragged bed, arrows of sunlight directly into my eyes, that is the eye incinerating rays of the winter sun, and seasons changing so swiftly that you hardly have any time at all to put away the clothes you've just taken off, so you simply hang them up, as if you had put them there in order to be able to exchange them for the attire of another season, summer/winter, spring/fall, there simply wasn't any reason to put away clothing appropriate to a given season, *everything was right there at hand all the time,* shocking repetition, isn't it, I say to Blum, not until much later did I notice that my bathwater had grown cold, I hadn't paid any attention to it while I was writing in the early hours of the morning, my feet had gotten cold, the most varied of inks I mean bathwater discolored, reddish 1 moment and black the next, cuttlefish in my bathwater, very sadly I am distancing myself from the original draft of this work, I say to Blum, what do you think that means, what kind of consequences will this have, I say to Blum, the direction has changed, current ideas, word impressions, light impressions are completely different from those of my first draft, and only a few short months have passed since I began, I feel as if I'm running amok in the underbrush of my own words, where am I going to land, I am my own mad and milling or mendicant poet, race through the streets with my notepad and pen, hide behind the facades of buildings, pillars, kiosks in order to be able to take down my notes uninterrupted, not long ago I got a letter whose

writer, unknown to me, addressed me with the familiar form of you, I say to Blum, he explained that he was writing to me because friends had told him *I was still alive*—
last night so many letters, this morning, wrote so many letters in bed, my pen with a very fine tip, scribbled a white paper plate full for Joseph ("here anguish, shapeless, everything a betrayal, an assault, am in the abyss, etc., cry half the day, rest of the time in bed utterly exhausted, baffled spoon in the honey jar, what's *blaring* out of the damned music box in the early morning, writhing, what gets *eliminated* so early in the morning, damn it all, I could howl, this ICE RINK MUSIC, or tricks young children can dance right through, etc., not GETTING OVER anything anymore, what an expression, how can any language admit an expression like that, I ask myself, am so washed out from writing and crying that I spend half of the day sleeping, found a disk in the book I'm now reading, I could send you a disk : paper plate like that, disk, discourse. I live from one day to the next, my life is going crazy and rotting, and I am living in a dialectic of circumstances, after reading Alexander Kluge for a few days, I am drawn to Bashō, but it also works the other way around, after reading Bashō for an extended period of time, I need Barthes or Butor, *suppressed in exercises, etc.*"), dear God, how did I ever come up with that, I say to Blum, a collage of nerves or something of the sort, fingertips of my left hand mysteriously tattooed : felt-tip pen gone leaky, steaming footbath under my desk is putting me in something of a panic as it penetrates into the lower reaches of my body with its rising heat, AND THAT'S HOW PICTURES TELL STORIES.
(Wasn't there a crutch lying across the sidewalk? wasn't there a double rivulet flowing across the sidewalk? or was it dog piss running off in 2 parallel tracks? I could have stood there for minutes on end in an attempt to work out what it was, but the winter sun was so blinding that I raised my hands to my face and rushed off and I kept holding my palms to my eyes even after the street was in the shade)—
am unsettled from writing, the little Mongolian man (marionette), covered in dust, dug out from behind some old books, is now dangling from the window latch, his kimono-like suit is made of blue-green silk and has a red sash, his face appears to be powdered white, his red mouth is smiling in a very mysterious way, when I found him I shed tears of joy over our reunion!, he had been hiding for a long time, actually I had forgotten about him, I felt as if I had been given this gift again this morning, and I didn't even know whom I had to thank for it . .

I imagine *a white tiger cub* in his company, like the 1 I noticed in Bozen in Walther von der Vogelweide Square, because it was just running around loose as if it were looking for its keeper or looking for someone to feed it, I could see that the cub belonged to no one, so I bought 2 sausage sandwiches at a nearby kiosk and stuffed them into the cub's mouth, it greedily gobbled them down, then crawled away under a half-built grandstand. *Start, or food in the country, etc.* Swirling cellophane in my dreams, something (approximately) coming in through the door, I say to Blum, upward and downward images all essence of paper : essence of paper devices, may my writing fervor be flung down onto paper unceasingly, I understand my bloodstream now, I say, the icebox is humming, a discarded crutch is lying in the road, I remember, some days ago I experienced similar sense events, you see, writing is a consuming passion, why a red sky like a thread is running through the book I am now writing is unclear to me, if the books piled up on my bed can take the weight of one more book, I say to Blum, that is a matter of INERTIA, isn't it, actually underbrush, and I keep tripping over it, over everything actually, I say to Blum, haven't read any further in this old crumbling book that Hans-Jürgen Hereth gave me, it has had to make way for other books, and in turn they have made way for others : half-read books, literally crumbling in my hands this rotting old book had dug itself into my skin, though, sometimes I am gripped by a feeling like nausea, when I page around, read, I can smell the dust that has collected in its pages and I register a smell peculiar to old men and women, but Joseph had also nested himself in my skin, in my bloodstream, I tow him around with me, he is my BACTERIA, he is my fever, source of my material, my eardrum / fur instrument, etc.

They had gotten *tied up* in the computer, the saleswoman in the flower shop protests, the delivery order for my flowers had gotten tied up in the computer, of course the flowers really had gotten tied up, the order had been sent 2 weeks before, flowers from Texas, oh they had simply gotten tied up, somehow the flowers had gotten tied up there, the saleswoman in the flower shop regrets to say, she would like to deliver the flowers now though late, oh these *Venus affairs,* nothing is right in my soul, I say to Blum, I'm on the dog trail, dogs pissing on me : angels raining down on me, on the trail of honey, because my consciousness is revolving solely around being able to write, right, constantly taking notes, firmly stuck, I say, YOU HAVE MY BLESSING!, Blum says, the songbirds waiting in line.

12/5

the way we go about living our life is nothing but a balancing act, I say to Blum, these days the sharp morning light as threat in the window, because spending my afternoons with the curtains closed is a torment, welcome however cloudy skies, rain, snow, veiled days, welcome the waters inundating coats (chicks), I say, or tears welling up . . *3 gaping jackets* in a tumult of pillows, I say to Blum, building little towers on the kitchen counter, and pile up for example supplies of Nescafé glasses 1 on top of the other, because these towers I mean because everything stuffed full BURSTING, I took particular care in my movements so as not to cause any sudden jolt that might bring it all down, etc., *flood of chicks,* the monkey outside over the clothes hanger, with long black fringed black hair, the décolleté of the envelope : in the décolleté of the envelope before I sealed it tiny antlike letters heralded GIVE MY BEST TO MARIO : had forgotten to include this *ornament* at the end of my letter (CODA!),* today don't really seem to have quite enough time, I mean everything cut just a little too short, can't really let my emotions spread out, the line of my horizon otherwise so rippling is confined today, forced into a framework, or something like that, numerous overcoats, shawls, capes thrown over my shoulders while writing, and got up with the intention of putting on the Bach record, momentarily forgot, simply into the kitchen, torn from the hook, I say, *drastic suits,* dressing gown, *transparency of apparel,* scarf, hood, terry cloth pantaloons, and don't even know whether Joseph called in the morning, this morning or was it yesterday, etc.

* the décolleté exposed my scribbling, greetings to Mario, or my scribbling peeked out of the décolleté my greetings to Mario, etc.

As far as Joseph is concerned, I am happy to imagine him sitting across from me in his Bordeaux-red running pants or confetti pants or in his lantern-colored dress suit, while he is speaking *untenable* languages to me, which I don't understand, what happened, I say to Blum, what was going on, I am feeling as light as a feather, along the station platform, on flying soles, my knapsack on my back and while I am thinking of Joseph, while I am reading a book on the run, I read this phrase "in the three-sided forest, after dark," in Breton's "l'amour fou," a quote from Jarry, I say to Blum, and then I felt this sheet lightning go off inside me again and was transported into a state of delight, and I was astounded that while I was running along the platform my head immediately came up with another version of that phrase, "in the three-sided forest with dark roses," Joseph was running along with me, as I imagine it, he didn't want to go on this trip with me, he was wearing a rain poncho and under that his frigate pants, or frittata pants, Bordeaux-red *transparency of apparel,* and which allowed a view of the gentle erection of his sex while he was sitting there in front of me, as I imagine it, I say to Blum, so he was running at my side along the platform, as I imagine it, but he was also sitting across from me during the trip, in my mind, right, I say to Blum, the rose snails, and I turn on all the lights, I say to Blum, even by daylight, and at the same time I'd like to be out running around these buildings, in the streets and sitting, here in front of my typewriter, all at the same time, I say, or in the mirror in my compact, while doing my eyes, I hold my mirror in such a way that the face on the wall, the beautiful face on the poster over my bed, with the barbed wire lip, appears, reminding me of Joseph somewhat, but it is the handsome head of the lead actor in *Jenůfa,* by Leoš Janáček, Frankfurt Opera, maybe exists only in my imagination, maybe this too only exists in my imagination, something that my overworked brain is leading me to believe, I am so fully fledged, my brain is fully fledged, a pleasant fluttering and flitting and circling and hovering of my mind, and I am dancing around my own shadow, in the middle of my room, and I don't know what has happened, but it is a thrilling day, as if I had just come directly out of the sky and back down to earth, I say to Blum, this well-known euphoria after a flight, you know, and Joseph's letter, too, Joseph's letter was part of it, this chirping *well-put* rapture, on the other hand reeling in my bones, in my brain, Joseph writes, the wind had scattered his name, as it was being called out from the balcony of his lover's house, but some of the letters were lost, maybe only the first letter of his name, it had disappeared in the gusts, in the glow of an approaching storm, *a mind mission,* Blum speculates, might that be it, yes, I say, but the key correlations the key sense the key points are not clear, Lily writes, I shudder in bewilderment, but when I ride my bicycle through the moors, Lily writes, AS IF FOR THE VERY FIRST TIME I look into the open blue calyx of the wildflowers growing rampant on the horizon, you see, and then my heart quivered and I wondered, is this all really going to come to an end 1 day, this looking down into the calyx of flowers that grow tender and wild up to the edge of the forest, and the eyes of the small blue flowers, how could I ever do without them, Lily writes, is that really going to come to an end, this brings *real tears,* doesn't it, the snow-blind vibration, etc.

A friend asked me to draw something in his favorite book, I say to Blum, but before I started I didn't know what I was going to draw, then I drew the figure of a snail, I was thinking about the EYE OF A HURRICANE, but he told me that what I had just drawn depicted the essence of architecture . . *127 telemorning* and a coughing ape, or apse, swelling on my mortal carcass, I say to Blum, or corona, at my feet swelling carpet like the bristling fur of a wild animal—

Thirst is desire, and what I write down is always somewhat, I mean I keep missing the real center, I keep missing the point around which my thoughts and senses revolve, it can't really be captured in words, they are things I can see and detect, but not capture, hold on to, a taste perhaps, most likely the perception of a physicality or a lucidity that is constantly changing, etc., there are of course any number of additions, I say to Blum, such as, I pressed the REPEAT button of the CD player, the first sequence of "*ich habe genug,*" Johann Sebastian Bach, BWV 82, there is enough of real-world relevance in that, I say to Blum, by the way Thomas Kling is entertaining my flesh, Lily writes, *white cap of obligation, downpour,* thunderstorm in winter, Lily writes, I am decoding Joseph's looks and words, I say to Blum, which means that I still, again and again, although I have rejected, had sworn off everything connected with Joseph, I say, the consequence of all this is that I experience his looks and his words as the embrace of the cosmos or a quivering descent into the visage of the ocean, right, thirst is desire, and then suddenly the fur coat unbuttoned, because winter seems to have come to an end, where it had only begun, isn't that right, I say to Blum, or they are wearing, the CHALK MEN, in winter when everything was covered with snow, *white robes* and I was terrified, they were shrouds, or they appeared to be, they moved around here and there, even on the scaffolding, or was there only a suggestion of movement, in fact these days NOTHING is anything more than allusion it seems, every one of our lives only alluded to, being so short, so fleeting, everything alluded to, and everything made up of some sort of white poles, wooden beams, strips of wood, boards, skis, it was a blurred image, a vague image, almost like a dream, but I knew I wasn't having a dream, it made its way over my line of sight, I was very touched, but didn't know why, it was both an image to be perceived in all its detail as well as *something scattered,* the way images from dreams so often are, and no 1 thing could be distinguished from another : and everything in this whiteness appeared equalized, etc., "the pursuit of his FAVORITE COURSE OF STUDY : poetry, he, if I were a male, did not want to give it up entirely nor pursue it with restraint," I say to Blum, I had put the footbath under my desk, but forgotten to soak my feet, and didn't even know if I had done so or not, *that damned coda,* I say, you shouldn't even be struggling for it, there's something unseemly about it, isn't that right, I say to Blum, better to have everything end worn out, rotten, ragged, each and every sequence simply disintegrating, without an end point, without *remedial icing,* etc.

Less redundance than before in your most recent work, Joseph says, a flake whitish gray in front of my eyes, I say, and lay my hand on his shoulder blade, right shoulder blade and he doesn't jump, thirst is desire, I say, a meteorite on my desk, I say to Joseph, it is as if you had brought this into motion with a gentle hand / GESTURE /, because I imagine that I did not put my hand on your shoulder but that you caused me to do it, and this is how everything starts up all over again, I say to Blum, again and again, how will I *handle* it, this wildness : CURL, brown wildness, wild alluring language and repast, have so *many Hermes outbreaks / Hermes pressures,* don't have to scratch anything together myself, right, my armored face in the mirror, 3 yawning jackets in the window, and everything raw, my insides raw, or as they put it : UNPOLISHED, because I'm a lot like my father, like him I *toss* my knife and fork onto a plate or into a bowl, salt shaker, coffee spoon, empty glass on the floor, *the only time I make any effort to control myself is when I am with decent people!*

Ordered Schreber's memoirs at 3 bookstores, treat inserted notes like dust, sweep them into the furthest corner with a wooden sandal, I say to Blum, my rubber bathtub, my main printed work is hanging on the wall of my room, I say to Blum, in the middle of my palm a dark cross, deep-black felt-tip pen, for the first time heard the phrase FALLEN CATHOLIC from someone I know.

12/6

without a break in the clouds

all of the coats piled 1 on top of the other in the early morning, all the tears down my cheeks in the early morning, all of the envelopes in my typewriter, I say to Blum, thick stuff, and then at this point I discover there were three envelopes, and the keys could not get a clean hold, SEMPER SEMPER, I yell, there's such a beautiful rain, very fine rain, I write to Joseph, I am continuing with my new book, haven't destroyed your letters yet, seems like killing stabbing heads to me, sometimes the feeling, now in my work there is *a quite rigorous style or voice breaking through,* Karla Woisnitza writes to me that, *our little pamphlet* is working along secretly on its own, it was from the small blue bowls I first learned that one (of two) of your dishes was smashed to pieces, and anyway : all of these bowl, shard and Triton stories, the year was full of them, your invention of the word DRAPERY EXISTENCE has stayed with me, before that I knew neither what a drape was nor what steam smoke cloud colors were, I am getting such good things to eat, manna, *don't really know what I am drawing or painting,* a friend gave me reproductions of Leonardo's drawings : sticks and poles flying off to the side, each 1 within a cloud of cloth or a smock : torn open by the wind, torn apart by the wind, a TENT, whose frame was made of wooden poles, etc., I dreamed the 3 couches, I mean I had a dream about 3 couches, from that a deepened sense of how much sliding around there is when you climb a green mountain (grass or pine needles / carnations)?, I delight in looking around strange living rooms at the various possibilities for seating, forms and styles, at least facsimile, or something of the sort.

The many scarves, jackets, turbans, enormous footwear, capes, umbrellas and walking sticks, backpacks, cases and bags, I say to Blum, whenever

I travel, I drag everything along with me, and at home too, I mean I am always *hauling* so much stuff around, as if I were having difficulty gathering all of my thoughts, ideas, contents of my dreams before the jump, I don't know myself just what this jump might be about, these *refugee texts* : first drafts that get away from me the moment I try to fit them into the final draft, fleeting—oh, how fleetingly they withdraw, also because so much fresh material is shooting up, among them, you see, the watermark on the white pages belongs on the lower margin, I say to Blum, *blood, fringes* on the street, these rags of blood, where do they come from, moving my head back and forth as if I did not want to admit it, did not want to believe, the root word is following me, pursuing me, Franz Joseph Stadler writes, just as fashions and customs, actually costumes persist over longer periods of time due to the fact that they are separated by the Alps from the influence of foreigners, your language has also remained true to its early simplicity, etc., TODAY NOLDE, written down on a dirty old slip of paper, I say to Blum, not at all clear to me anymore what it's supposed to mean, DIALECT and BOOK LANGUAGE, what a huge gap there is between these two terms, maybe all of my notes are articulated layers of subconscious, I say to Blum, I mean when I am talking to my reader (to one single reader whom I don't know) and saying I AM WRITING ALL OF THIS TO YOU FROM ANOTHER WORLD, etc., but this, I say to Blum, is all impulsive and arrogant, in any case suffer from being impulsive and arrogant, cardinal flaws of my existence, but can't really be exorcized anymore, I'm afraid, can't really be cast off, probably not even in the event of some unyielding stroke of fate, somewhere in the steam (gauze) of the MORNING ARENA I hear an alarm clock ringing actually it is a crowing, a jarring crow conjuring up an entire wave of childhood memories, etc., so early in the morning hardly 5 o'clock a.m. the opened windows vis-à-vis, everything so unsecluded, in one of the windows a wolfhound in beige, probably Marquise, scrap of paper from the margins of a notepad on my desk so old, amphibiously slick, I could puke, I yell to Blum, as soon as I go back to what I was reading (Alexander Kluge), I start hearing Joseph's voice, I start reading Joseph's style, when I briefly close my eyelids after an early-morning onslaught of artificial light, in shining blue garlands I see something like drawings penciled over : reflex reality, I say to Blum, which still informs of sleep and dreams, nighttime sleep as always short and fitful, or, you might say, *mildly satisfying,* deeper sleep not until early afternoon, I say, but waking up from these segments sleep's remains invariably diffuse stuff : I perceive neither time nor place, can't locate myself, heart and stomach seem to be out of

order, early-afternoon sleep took my senses away, robbed me of my orientation in space, but provided me with the illusive feeling that I would be able to start the day all over again, it also allowed for an entirely new evaluation of my own private circumstances, I say to Blum, and what had shot forth in the early-morning hours after a brief and leaky sleep,—ideas, bold observations, analyses, new words, connotations, promising new directions—was remarkably different from my state of being after this sleep in the early afternoon, this early-afternoon sleep had furnished my conscious being with an aged deliberateness and slowness, which, it seemed, wanted to rethink everything from the very beginning and either discard this all-morning display of ganglia fireworks as mad or at the very least expose it to the rigors of sober inspection . .
at such moments I felt the need to extinguish any sort of enthusiasm or BATTERY OF THE SOUL, retrieve from mailboxes letters I had already sent, rescind promises made by phone . .
Thrushes, word thrusts, washed dirty laundry, I wonder : CHIRPING? I wonder : white poodle maybe silk-coated dog in the sun appearing to glisten, I wonder : all of these packages to the post office, but how? tied up together, *like a sled* over the stairs, and wonder finally, how this literary *output* (what a word!) is ever going to be dealt with, my own included, there just aren't that many readers, I say to Blum, sometimes it seems to me that there are more people writing than there are reading, more furious writers than willing readers, isn't that right . . and lash mane and ankle while taking a knife and scissors to hair and sock, Joseph would add : AND A GRAY SCARF!

12/7

we let ourselves be CHIMPANZEED by crowns of flowers and blue-handed rags billowing in the heavens . .

I mean the crowns crowning blossoms, the weaseling water in the pots raging over the flames, the purple oil on the kitchen floor, as well as thick winding trails of honey dripping from an open honey jar held askew, my household or helping hand is leaving, I say to Blum, no guest is welcome now, I say to Blum, we call each other at the very same second and both telephones are busy, those are precious conjunctions, I say to Blum, garment flakes are falling in my lodgings, I call to Blum, an ACHING CLASSIC ON 1/30/97, I say to Blum, that's what occurred to me while soaking my feet today, *copying from* the open HOPKINS lying in my lap, Matisse's GOLDFISH on my desk, glimmering pink tones in the morning sky, in the evening sky, and then Joseph and I surrender ourselves to the clutches / drizzles of constellations, I say to Blum, *but / we / we don't talk about things like this,* I mean in any case this thing with the MIMESIS has gotten rather suspect, half-asleep and then a deep-red angel leading me into the temptation of getting involved again : all over again, in the ecstasy of *hieroglyphing*—pay close attention to the use of this word my dazed reader—because this is not simply a matter of writing something down, it is feeling for, groping, twirling around, brandishing signs, tones, feelings, kindling, tearing apart, dismantling of ideas, experiences, memories, colors and a reassembly, welding together into new previously nonexistent objects, flaming apparitions, thrushes, word strands, the way they fall in blond streams from the walls of the flower shop, flower arrangements in velvet, tears and blinding glare, blinded by tears, word tears, we are then *enthralled by a waiting ribbon of songbirds,* that is, the moment I dial the number of the Museum of Natural History, all of the birdsong in the background, ah this virtual spring!, I call to Blum, swarming spring, and

Alma was talking about a deer, a virtual deer that darts across the scene and flees into the forest, I mean the trembling *Zeiss rage* or siskin rage or ZEISERL RAGE, see footnote, and those are the images up and down, I say to Blum, the shifting movement of an easy chair in the next room, the way the shifting movement of an easy chair in the next room imitates the growl of a dog, right, and all of this, all of these small and smallest tiniest movements, touches, dawnings, exposures, decipherings and resolutions . .

I am antechambering in my own quarters, I say to Blum, what do you think of a formulation like this, I look up MUMPITZ, this crumpled word, no information in any of my books, MUMPITZ, I change glasses, I want to write down : MUMPITZ : this stinking MUMPITZ : wire beating, in the next room the sun is beating down, winter sun, scratching my view, this SYLLABLENESS, which means : worse than SINGLE SYLLABLENESS, right, in my aching memories of mother, she crawled through the kitchen, the entryway, to the front door, laboriously pulled herself onto her feet to open the door for the medics . .

as I'm waking up, 4 o'clock in the morning, I hear a storm outside : *wailing storm,* immediate thoughts reactions : how many airplanes are going to come crashing down out of the sky today, etc., while my MORNING BLOCKER (Trasicor retard 160 mg) has actually *hidden itself* in the caverns of my mouth before I wash it down with a glass of mineral water, and then I slowly turn over onto my right side and fall back asleep, in a dream someone is removing a long black strand of hair from the smoothly shaven face of a haggard old man, and says THIS STRAND OF HAIR IS 1 OF YOURS, masquerade of course, I say to Blum, this tablet in my mouth is engaging in a masquerade by concealing itself, prolonging the swallow down my throat, after which "write 17 lines for Michael Hamburger and Johann Sebastian Bach," useless, I tell myself, everything totally useless, I say to Blum, curses and expletives aimed at myself, my writing, rattling clothes hangers upon which you go *slithering off* once they have covered the bath tiles, the kitchen tiles, I mean *these days* the SHORT AND SMALL ONES (= the youngest) don't go sledding / ice skating anymore, they slide down park slopes on cardboard or plastic shovels, everything has to be practical, fast and effective, easy and comfortable, etc.

Zeiserl rage, personal idiom, derived from Zeiserl wagon or sinsin wagon, ladder wagon with board seats, party wagon around the turn of the century, drawn by horses and used for COUNTRY CELEBRATIONS "*failing again failing better failing,*" Samuel Beckett, in a truck / January forest, I mean the labels of my being, I say to Blum, this masquerade I am presenting to the outside world, inflicting, this wanton : wild use of human characters in my writing, imputing steps, gestures, movements, facial expressions, even inside my own housing WHILE MY BLOOD BOILS, I mean registering, the way heartbeats surge through the body with an alarming velocity, not to be tamed, steered, restrained. WRENCHED : ranched : rancid (the butter spread, e.g.) . . may be, our hearts overflowing, a brackish brew in the vat, and in this way I kept finding myself ensnared both inside and out, slipping and sliding along my way and the whole world, etc., I mean the people around me could not contain their compassionate smiles, thus only adding to my misery, etc.

Numerous lines notepads filled during the night, could hardly make them out in the morning, which resulted in sentimental reverie and *the yellow tear* . . when the telephone rang I spilled my bathwater, I ran out of the water when it rang, out of the hot bathwater, and Blum on the other end, who said JUST WANTED TO KNOW WHAT YOU'RE UP TO AT THIS EARLY HOUR OF THE MORNING, morning is bunching up, I say to Blum, I am sitting at the typewriter, my feet in water, blood surge, writing urge, can't be stifled any longer, etc., attitude defect, rigid stocking leg filled with plaster, I say, me through the house howling : ICH HABE GENUG (J. S. Bach), am now working without music drive, omit passages from the rough draft that have an all too narrative cast, I say to Blum, passages which have lost their *thunderous thrill* over the chronological distance between the rough draft and the manuscript, *or how we raise our head into the air and speak in viperly ways,* isn't that so.

The time I spent on the train seemed *boundless,* I say to Blum, past white shimmering fields and farms, from time to time masked figures leaning into the snowy winds, snowy guards : WINTER SKIN, I mean the pink tip of skin up in the branches, twigs *glorifying* themselves under their burden of snow, etc., WINTER SKIN : skin fragments of fear, I say, or : while I wintered against those branching fears which could not result in anything but an annihilation of the nervous system, I say. What kind of fears were these, I ask myself, I say to Blum, what was I afraid of when I thought about Joseph and the tensions in our relationship—but Blum just sat there in silence as he always did, and I said to him, YOU SEEM TO HAVE BEEN ASSIGNED A NONSPEAKING ROLE IN THE BOOK I AM CURRENTLY WRITING, FICTIONAL EAR, OR YOU ARE HERE IN ORDER TO HELP ME MAINTAIN : A VERY DEFINITE PERSPECTIVE, etc.

have always worshiped, I mean, I have always worshiped Joseph, but there is also a term *worshipful,* I wonder what it means, to vaguely mirror the wavy form of the soul, perhaps, I say, or *such lovely veiling of the sky* (HOPKINS), WITH HIS PAWS THE POPE WILL, an image coursing through my mind, but don't know how it will be resolved, not even when Elisabeth von Samsonow writes to me : THE TINY LEGS OF YOUR SMALL DESK SHOULD BE SET UPON A BED OF ROSES FOR ALL ETERNITY, FROM WHERE THE SOURCE SPRINGS FORTH . .

am so disoriented in my soul, I say to Blum, but am devoted to his *nerve sight,* and his handwriting like a field of flowers, you see, some sort of postscriptum more or less, or footnote.

Fling the bottle of valerian pearls against the heaplike pages of rough draft because finished it off, 8 or 9 little capsules licked from the palm of my hand, etc.

(Soon won't have any more underwear, *because of nothing but writing* no time to wash the stuff . .)

12/12

the way my mother always said AVOID BOTTLENECKS touches my heart, what did she mean, and the water glass half emptied at the cry (of the cocks) completely inaudible, Brachfeld, Morgentau, 1 listener asks after the reading : how am I supposed to understand all of this, *make sense of it,* had I cheated him and the others of the sense, had I withheld the sense from him and the others, I ask myself after the event, I mean how do I convey to him and the others the sense of : TREMBLING NEW MOON, or : PAIN IMPERIUM, etc., but everything so empirical here, I say to Blum, everything empirical, I say to Blum, now the handle on the door will tear apart, the handle on the door shatter, the way I ignore the melting piles of snow along the streets, gray balls of snow next to the SAMOVAR, where Joseph and I in the deep dusk of the bar, with the Chaliapin voice in the background, spooning down borscht, Russian soup, agnus dei.
The stuffed stockings, I say to Blum, on pillows, blankets and mountains scrunched together, stockings stuffed full of my fissured feet, crazy remains of my feet, I say, Joseph and I in this SAMOVAR, crumpled soul, light source of an eye, he has a gentle eye, I say to Blum, Joseph has a gentle eye, those weren't deep-red drops of flower petals in the outside pocket of a backpack, they were folded table napkins : a soul's anguish folded anguish of a soul, background music, vodka vapor / clouds while he is lighting his cigarette in the flame of a red table candle, whatever you want, I write to Joseph, everything just the way you want, I write to Joseph, but my pen bristles at these words, deep-red table napkins, I say to Blum, folded spillage disbursements of a soul . . whatever may have been in the outside pocket of that backpack they weren't deep-red flower petals, the kind you put inside letters to a person you love, they were folded table napkins, like the ones we took with us

from the SAMOVAR as a souvenir of our time together there, Joseph and I, I say to Blum, admittedly they were deep red, shades of violet, green, blue, a mother's red cries, dripping cries, before she gave up, isn't that right, oh, I write to Joseph, everything is dripping : my voice your voice your eye, it flickered in the light of the candle at our table and I could have screamed, but then the soup came, violet soup, borscht, then the steaming rice, the sticky rice from the POT, right, the sticky greenish rice, the discolored bread, etc., or slices of Easter snow while outside December light, ravaged innards, in this backpack, I say to Blum, fantasy foliation what else, in the outside pocket of a backpack I am always carrying on my back, even when I sleep, always on my back on my shoulders, do you understand, it did me good, as if a hand were there, Joseph's hand, but wasn't actually I mean he avoided touching me. But I'm losing my way here, *I am getting into trouble,* I call to Blum, everything in a pompous overtone, that's not the way it should be, this BRAIN TOP is supposed to be in good working order, no not brain shot, BRAIN TOP!, I shout to Blum, *the Strauß of Bethlehem.* The record I had been playing to myself for hours, I say to Blum, in order to inspire me to work, it kept resounding throughout my room for a long time, even throughout my entire housing, as if something like an echo had been induced and I heard myself *humming,* something that is very unusual for me, entirely counter to my habits that is, and long after I had finished this day's writing work, in my head I could still hear : Johann Sebastian Bach : Cantatas, Aria 1 : "*ich habe genug,*" BWV 82—and on top of that my half face in a mirror or the way I observed it this morning in a bookstore window, in Indian tones and with a foolish smile . . "I took the Savior, the hope of all good men, into my hungry arms . ." that caught my attention, again, and again it made me think of Joseph, this *took into my hungry arms,* and because I was waiting for his call and the telephone had rung several times and I had not been quick enough to pick up the receiver, it seemed to me that it was a sign he would appear, suddenly, without speaking to me, simply appear, as an image . . I ordered a glass of wine in a bar but didn't drink it, well, yes I sipped at it from the edge of the glass, and went home, with my thoughts about Joseph, I mean I was occupied with everything that concerned Joseph, etc. I had bought a book for him, a book he wanted, without saying he wanted it, but I had guessed it because he had spoken about this book with great enthusiasm, with a pen with a fine point I wrote down on the first page in a scrawl : "in a letter 1 September you mentioned KLAUS VON FLÜE, who was considered a saint because he didn't eat." And I woke up with a sense of well-being and 1 dream phrase had seeped away

during the night, I didn't have enough energy to write it down, but it had something to do with : SWIM WORK, BELLBOY, HEAD BURIAL, ENTIRE MICE OF KNIGHTS (?) and : CONTACT PANTS . .
in the bar or rocking room I caught sight of Joseph, I say to Blum, and I'm already burning again. Say to Joseph : there are still some moves to be made : flying desires, thoughts, those gondolas feelings flitting through the night which we don't want to admit to ourselves, etc., then the earth was flowing the earth was running like water the earth was rolling like tiny mad drops of mercury, and I leapt over the encrusted tire tracks, hopped toward strangers passersby who were carefully making their way along the street, I say to Joseph, just imagine! suddenly I've *uncovered : invented the beautiful art of storytelling,* against which I've struggled so often and so long, *weathered* that is . . ah, I say to Joseph, what shall I do with my BOX OF WORKING MATERIAL with my paper with my impulsiveness, it will turn out all the same no matter what I do, *the fine art of storytelling* is a trompe l'oeil, pretense, *and there is a spirit rumbling around in me,* mad spirit that is always and again and over and over again resisting this contrary SEDUCTIVE notion of a systematic / rational writing process, right, I mean I am spitting into a folded sheet of grayish white writing paper, HAVE YOU COUGHED UP ANY BLOOD?, the doctor asks, I bend over my folded and ragged *sackcloth* and writing paper and say : strands of blood, I say, there are these life strands in blood, leave me my life strand of blood, leave me my devastation, my wild curses, the temptation to pitch myself out of the window, my viper's brood, etc.
Wrote down a few notes, that evening, played the piano, saw what was formerly a baptismal church floating on water . . with spotted, no *spattered* pants, I say to Blum, and I am letting my hair fall down over my face, I say to Blum, and running out into the snow without shoes, and the LOVE SCENES from my first draft, I call to Blum, I can't keep them, so distant now, we are sitting in a tavern kitchen, I say to Blum, in this SAMOVAR, but it just isn't coming back to me, these events just grown irrelevant or something like that, I say, red rubber ring on my night table, like the scroll on a violin, I say, such HEAD HOLINESS, when the dogs piss on me, the angels rain down on me, etc., I haven't opened yesterday's mail yet, haven't read the newspaper for days, unopened newspapers scattered across my bed CREASES PRESSED, I am firmly stuck, on the trail of honey, I say to Blum, just being able to write occupies my entire consciousness, Joseph occupies my entire consciousness, my consciousness is occupied with these two temptations, I want my language to keep getting more and more torn, and

at the same time I'm trying to practice intense storytelling, I say to Joseph, how am I supposed to be able to do that, I say, I want my writing to keep getting crazier, and at the same time I want it to be well formed and fiery, I should get more exercise, the doctor says, I shouldn't neglect my swimming, the doctor says, but how can I do all this given my writing temptations, I ask my doctor, the kitchen lighting is inadequate, I say to Blum, we need more light now, the doctor says, now that our eyes are being fitted with sunglass lenses, shadow images are taking over, I say, as I roam : roam and rove around, I say, *the tone of this flight, this flute* coming from wind sweeping through the loose blond hair of a young boy with a baseball cap a little insolent or show-offy or stylish, I say, but what a SIGHT!, I shout, then the wind immediately blew him away, in vain I searched, looking back into the teeming crowd for him. I dreamt : auto-body engineering, tinted swallows, lamp flora, I say to Blum, in the morning my distorted face in the mirror, devastation, I say, of an advanced scene of life, *a didactic piece,* I say, or : ICH HABE GENUG . .

how I screamed inside the uterus, I say to Blum, in our prebirth state we visualize the entire cosmos we will subsequently traverse over the course of our lives, SOMETHING LESS THAT IS ALL WE ARE PLEADING FOR, Samuel Beckett, don't have any teaspoons in my workshop, anyway I'm leading my existence on the floor, I mean all I'm doing is crawling around, swords in my neck, etc.

All that *violet hair,* I say to Joseph, *your violet hair,* and tearful morning, *the 10-day girl,* I write to Joseph, while briskly striding along : while I slide my arm into his, I take his arm, he lets me do it and smiles I believe, a smile permitting me this freedom, perhaps the way you might indulge a child : she made a mistake but you indulge her, but a few hours later, as we were leaving the restaurant, you offered me your arm, of your own accord, and my arm slipped into yours / wings / we flew up and away, our stride so swift, I mean the speed of our march was so UNREAL that I thought I felt us rising into the air, it was the coldest night of the entire winter. The cold is creeping into my joints but I am burning as if there were a fire raging inside me, etc., this description is rather anachronistic : a thousand times and more compellingly put by all the saints of world literature, isn't that so, I say to Blum, then, when we parted everything damped back down again, I cover his face with kisses, his eyes, his forehead, his temples with budding kisses, I lay my left cheek which is cold on his left cheek which is hot, I press my body into his, he presses his body into mine, I look straight into his eyes, *shoulder to shoulder,* cigarette butts in the ashtray, a meal of mussels, the cypress tree in the yard, *I am racing toward the psychiatrist,* I am my own aide-de-camp, the music box has picked up the final cadence, I have swallowed a cigarette butt, Joseph is sitting with his legs crossed, like one of Francis Bacon's figures, I say to Blum, 1 leg under the other, barely visible, where is the leg where is the foot, what is the significance of this his favorite pose, everything masked, everything externalized, etc. Mandarin of pain, I shout, concrete wonder, I write to X (or William or Ferdinand), bubbling water in the washbasin a figure leaning up against its rim, I mean this strudeling bareness, I have how has it come to this a heavy head in my sticky hands, my shattered face resting in my hands, my eye has closed, and now I have carried my fantasy to the grave; after having long ago carried my reality to the grave, now I have also carried my fantasy to the grave, I mean the garden, the UNSCRUPULOUSNESS OF WRITING, might you call it that? before I ever send a letter to Joseph again, I'll tear it to pieces, cardboard my life, Joseph says, his day passes so without moment that it frightens him when twilight suddenly falls, immediately after the break of day, I am mixing up my poets, *sedan chair in the clouds,* the wild foot, I'm so miserable.

A sinking winter sun a dazzling giant balloon in the west over the rooftops, I say to Blum, I can make out the small kitchen garden, I say, the concept of mimesis has served its purpose, I say to Blum, in its place discovery : *now we're going to get right* into the stuff, the landscape, into the real things of this world, the way we get into a piece of clothing, get inside, with our head and upper body and arms, right, completely filling it out with our own spiritual physicality, oh, I say, while my mother was putting on a flowered silk dress in the morning, the silk dress covered with blue and white flowers : blue and white flowers in a yellow field : it gathered her up, so that when she was found lying stretched out on the floor, head and torso and arms all appeared to have been sewn up in the silk fabric, while dark-stockinged legs protruded, *or the way a butterfly slips out of a cocoon,* etc.

In her beautiful flowered dress, I say, then, the NEGATIVE BEACH, *today mother turned 3 revolutions,* Alma said, my body tells me how I have to behave, mother says, did you see the ponds in the middle of the street, a sleeve waved in the wind, not a single person called today, mother says, you start to feel so neglected or forgotten, you see—

my whole day really is occupied with this work I am writing, I say to my mother, I mean this writing of mine has *anchored itself* or it has implanted itself in my thorax, or it is rotating around inside me or I am rotating around inside it, or it is this painful rotation in my head, or Franz Schubert is singing "no I don't know any cheerful music," etc., or Johann Sebastian Bach intones "I am looking forward to my death oh that it might already be . .". Writing points me toward one clue and then another, and I have to follow them down, back and forth, speeding ahead, turning back, and this is how I spin myself into my soul's net, shooting off my threads. TEMESTA 0.1 : cult compound, I say to Blum, bunch of radishes with wilted greens on a ceramic plate, pretty soon I'm going to be in the same state my father was when he was 80 years old, he always took the same walks because he knew he had sufficient energies to complete a given route, but he still found himself stopping at every display window to catch his breath, and from time to time he even felt faint, those times he had gone out without having eaten enough.

The lustier your tears, I say to Joseph, the cleaner your eye, I cry a lot. Our closeness : a beginning both offered and rescinded, isn't that right, and that is how I understand the way you hold your head your movements your eyes; your childlike hands : soft, a little too short, but you only use them for writing, 1 hand is lying on the seat next to me in the car, pale hand, showpiece, this pale hand next to me in the car, but it is speaking, this pale hand of yours has the power of speech, it says DON'T TOUCH ME! it will not allow itself to be touched. I can see from the back of your neck that you are a pragmatist. A phoenix book, a Prague is a phoenix book, the secrets of delay. In any case the world cannot be experienced through any of the solitary disciplines, isn't that right, I say, the tormented monocle, straw blond wig in the flower shop to hang on the wall like the long hair of a woman, etc.

12/16

"lungs wings altar, or a FOREST DISASTER"

this is my CULT COMPOUND, I say to Blum, this medication is my CULT COMPOUND, then I can sit, I say to Blum, stay put, I am *a wart* in my cult works or ward, don't have any *teaspoons* in my cult workshop, oh the *spooning down* every morning, these mountains of medication, pills, tablets, batteries, syrups, capsules, a whole drug dairy, and I can't just thoughtlessly, I mean, I tell myself, not to think about my writing when I take the small spoon, I almost swallowed the teaspoon, because taking the syrup so mechanically, right, I say to Blum, and the swallowing of a teaspoon would exacerbate in the extreme the whole situation I'm in, actually I mean *complicate,* I say to Blum, I mean these devastations in my quarters, the felting, jungle states of mind, etc. oh this fate's GETTING A GOOD BEATING, I shout, dog odor, I'm so miserable!, I shout, panting, gasping for breath, no not only me, I shout, out here in the hallway the *gas meter* : panting, short of breath the way mother was during her afternoon naps, and while I am taking notes worms are crawling all over my towel, all of these tiny dark flowers, 10 empty envelopes crash, Blum in high spirits, shouts : HORSES ASSES!, followed by salvos of laughter, followed by salvos of laughter, spasms of laughter, his, mine, HORSES ASSES!, he repeats, you NIGHT OWL, he calls out to me, you your LETTERNESS!, then from her beach cabana shouts: good God : what made me do that . . her fish's body in steaming bathwater, the thumb of my right hand fits perfectly into this groove, she shouts, she is kneading her feminism, I say to Blum, she doesn't need any man, I say to Blum, you'll have to grant her that, I say, desire, I say to Blum, desires of the body, desires of the word body are to be satisfied every morning, I say to Blum, *or Hegel as a swallow or Hegel as a falcon,* isn't that right, or ratty haired, oh this CAT OF YOUTH!, I shout, I see Joseph

wrapped in his large white bath towel, only his head in view ("bather / tousled hair . .") etc., all I see is his head with its handsome cowlick and the white tow of the towel, while the music plays "*ich habe genug,*" Johann Sebastian Bach, I trudge through snow up to my ankles, I say to Blum, we sit on a corner bench in a coffeehouse, and on the corner bench, I say to Blum, I mean Joseph and I, we have images of our loving touches set out / sketched out so to speak and you'll have to excuse me here, I say to Blum, but I was imagining meadows, AMALFI meadows, white AMALFI blossoms, with Joseph, that is what I was imagining, I sketched out my feelings / laid them out, but sometimes at night I give up on the feelings I have for Joseph, do you understand what I'm saying, it goes in cycles, I have sketched out / laid down / given up on everything, and what's left is a shadow, it seems, a shadow that crosses my own or swallows it, and I no longer have a shadow of my own, the only shadow I have left is Joseph's, he's laid himself over my shadow, he has obliterated my shadow. In the underbrush, and thus I will be subdued.
The influx of misty passages, NEOLOGISMS, I say to Blum, confining set pieces such as "lettership" and "cookie provisions" and "composition silk" and "knapsack" and "writing orgy" are now going to be eliminated once and for all, because lacking purpose and direction, *furthermore soft,* worn out, used up, well, I don't know : a softness like snow blown up against the window, like snow cornices in the park square around City Hall, right—a DIGRESSION, question *what errant needlework like this actually accomplishes, etc.*
Maybe we have simply an urge for ravens, for revenge, I say to Blum, an urge that is to surrender ourselves, a revenge thought, and it thinks : now I am going to surrender myself, etc., comparable to feelings now transmitting themselves to me, I view a painting by Francis Bacon (*Self-Portrait, 1973*), the figure with crossed legs, 1 leg crossed under the other, the way Joseph sits, with one white running shoe, drifting somewhat to the right, drifting that is shifted, sitting on an old kitchen chair, grinding the wasted chair, next to the *fountain (founts),* in this *laundry room* with this miniature sink that looks something like a urinal, and because everything is so cramped in the painting, the water faucet instead of in the middle installed on the left side of the basin, and the image of a sitting figure as a reflection from the adjacent room. The tightly screwed joints, I say, Francis Bacon's figures in their confined pissoirs, the right of a figure resting on the edge of a miniature sink, smell of carbolic acid or wicker chair, stool : SEATED ORGY, or resting back on your own calves, heels,

straw mat, plastic stacking chairs, then sharp as a razor's edge the reality of world precincts, oh, these DEVASTATION TENDENCIES have become almost insufferable, I call to Blum, but maybe they are artificially induced DEVASTATION TENDENCIES, that / so that writing is at all possible, the more DEVASTATION there is the more breathtaking my writing becomes, right, I say to Blum, the more indestructible this COMPOSITION SILK of mine, the muddier the morass of this life is, the more tender, limpid, fluent (but more piercing and harder too) this writing of mine, I say to Blum, oh maybe I am simply *pursuing* these DEVASTATION TENDENCIES, maybe I have become addicted to them, I say, *as when the primary pattern* : Joseph's primary pattern on my skin, etc., I mean engraved itself, and then produces a singular jubilation like the song of the white AMALFI blossoms, producing the sensation in me that it is always in front of my eyes, and always will be, right, *but thousands but fresh as the morning dew* greetings, X (or William or Ferdinand) writes from Provence, the provinces, IF IT WERE ONLY 1 DROP OF DEW, OF ANOTHER WORLD etc.

But the heart, the way it is spilling over, so much water, this child of god out of hairiness, or something like that, when I kiss the envelope before I have opened it, on which Joseph's handwriting, *Harmony in Red,* Henri Matisse, postcard on the inside, the wallpaper merging into the tablecloth, FIGURE IN A ROOM or ROOM AMATEUR dips left hand into the fruit construct, right holding on to the stem of the glass bowl, next to the stage machinery of bread rolls, of cone blossoms, fish antlers, the bellowing (stags) promontory with tiny whitish meadow stars, and a raging storm which turns the leaves, blossoming bushes into beige bubbles, in which the face of fish antlers, etc., is resolved, entirely UNLETTERED.

with Egyptian curtains, I say to Blum, what does that mean, when I got the book back that I had lent Lily, it seems to have lost some of its heft, I don't understand it, how it came about, what happened, I certify myself a failure, from the earliest years of my childhood on, I say to Blum, always shaping everything into inexact forms, awkward, mashed, disjointed, etc., I submerge myself in the painting by R. B. Kitaj "bather (tousled hair)" (1978), that's the way I would always liked to have written, I say to Blum, write the way this picture was painted, *I am working,* my feet, as they are every morning, in hot water, under my desk, I scream, the moment I hear the telephone ringing, it tugs at me, disturbs, dismays, at high volume Johann Sebastian Bach "Clavierbüchlein für Wilhelm Friedemann Bach," and I scream and I scream : WHY THIS BLOCK, I scream to Blum, when I am trying to render Lily's declaration that she prefers to pleasure herself in a hot bath, why this feeling of consternation, destructiveness, as if I had betrayed someone, as if I were watching someone bleed to death, the sharp stones : chips and debris from an icy road in the treads of the extruded soles of my running shoes, rolling into the color of the carpet, felting up red and green and yellow and orange, I say to Blum, what stable stench, milk vomited up on the linoleum floor of the kitchen, the moth I am chasing to no avail over the sink, YOU CAN GO RIGHT AHEAD AND FAIRY TALE ME!, Blum says, breaking into fits of laughter, evaluate the provisional titles of the book I am now writing, each lasts for a few hours, or days, and then I toss out my latest selection, I now find myself at a complete standstill, I say to Blum, I appear to be writing the standstill draft, I say to Blum, but inside everything is one big trembling ERUPTION, I say, and I feel like I want to throw up, that I am tying myself up in awful fits of coughing, fits of laughter, fits of crying, *or measured by revolutions of my heart,* I say, don't want to be interrupted, anguish and elation as well, have caught up with me, what am I to make of that, I say to Blum, and my heart is no longer bleeding, when I think about Joseph, he has become a character made of cardboard, cardboard comrade, I say to Blum, maybe again, over and over again, inadequate my feelings, arrangements, judgments, I tramp through the deep snow in the courtyard of City Hall, looking for the exit, a uniformed official sitting at the information desk raises an arm, points across the snowy expanse and says there! there is the exit, I cross the snowfield, sinking in up to my knees in snow, a fall, decline, face and chest, the decline the fall not to be halted, no Paternoster, Joseph says, stay away, *he's cracking up!,* in the cellar, then swirls back up into the air, and it's dangerous to take this step into the elevator, too high, too low, trapped, torn to pieces, agonizing end. I write to Joseph, you have beguiled me, or : what kind of route region are we traversing on the front of the card Matisse *Interior with Egyptian Curtain,* 1948, 116.2 × 89.2 cm.

It should be FEIGNING DEATH, but this attempt ends in failure, the dull thud of rooftop avalanches on the sidewalk, I say to Blum, I heard Joseph's voice, his tone of voice, his pulsating laugh, from the mouth of someone I didn't know at all, on the street, I was stunned, *because of the entry into the small abyss that each word is,* etc.

It is a drying up, no more ribbons no more whispers, I say to Blum, my pens have laid themselves at odd angles across my desk, blocking the carriage of my machine, I mean A HONING OF FEELINGS, a sea to cry, or as if *puddles of runoff* were forming under my feet, you see. Then the damp compress which had been draped over the back of my chair, I mean in its dampness it had curled itself around the back of the chair, smacked the damp compress across my forehead, this small appliance : small bough work of this icy morning—

some kind of any sign of domesticity, Lily shouts, what do you think, or proceeding from some sort of Bretonian dot : Bohemian dots!, on Nadja's dress, e.g., from some sort of pines and olive trees, I write to Joseph, but you have already noticed how deafening this silence this slaughter of feelings that is, now and then, and I don't know how I can keep on living keep on writing, *no word for it.*

Alma passed me *my lunch in a bag,* it contained a manuscript and I was to read from this text to my audience, it was in the cheese, in the cheese sandwiches, hidden, Alma said in this dream, I was to unwrap the cheese sandwich and consume it right in front of everyone, and then the manuscript would appear, am simply dazed, from the jeers of my listeners, am beginning to move toward the NEGATIVE STRAND, etc.

12/19

meat to eat to kiss / instant meat

the head of a rose, but the painter calls her picture : flowers behind the window, rosy locks down off the left side of her head, stubbly locks, corkscrew locks, bottle locks, maybe my life and my work are about the life and the work of my favorite poet, I say to Blum, what do you think, maybe my life is something like a fax of the life and work of my favorite poet, right, but I'm not going to sit at my machine today, everything is pulling me this way and that, torn to pieces hat paper tissue paper liquid paper, left wing of my lung knotgrass, honeysuckle, billowing and teetering and waving, what do I know, in the knotgrass of my soul misfortune inconsolable grief reign, engraved dentures, etc., those nauseating maxims again : you must, I tell myself, invest everything you believe, everything you believe in what you have to write, what you have to dare, I mean you must uphold a scrupulous sincere : *ardent* belief in what you have to write, nothing can be allowed to distract you from this, racing on, galloping on, your eyes closed like a lunatic, on toward a goal you cannot envision, horns to the fore, on into the most harrowing unexplored WILDERNESS OF THE SOUL, probably a persecution complex, I say to Blum, my madness is pursuing my assumptions, until they are ready to speak, until my tongue is loosed, words drip from my gums, a flood of tears *plunges into brooks* onto the floor onto clothes, etc., roaring like that on the street and passersby rush to me to quiet me down, it's a sad day, I say to Blum, for a friend I draw a *wispy* figure with a halo of tears, fountains of tears showering out of tear ducts in the face of the figure spray all directions, you see, these tears defy earth's gravitational pull, never seen anything like it before, against the law of gravity they fall up, wanting to make their way back into tear clouds, or that's how it seems, the title of the picture is : "as if there are tears in all directions : *broken down clawed up punched out* tears, and how they come bursting out of the center of this face, bursting and bawling, out of the tear ducts that is and out up into the unknown, just like my own plunge into the unknown, oh what this figure has gushed away : how it pours out, spills, scatters its elongated spotted tears, a seed perhaps, insemination perhaps, at which point we are back with Jacques Derrida again, who can say, these tears cannot be quenched : a swirl of sorrow . ." also sacred fields, and quills, isn't that right, I say to Blum, by the way, as far as my readership is concerned, I say to Blum, I am not in the least concerned that they be able to *put everything together,* no no : whatever is not there is simply not there, no more interpretations, no more excavation for words and meaning, no no, whatever the reader cannot find here has not been put in by the writer, etc., woe unto the reader who manages to convince himself that he must be able to COMPREHEND, oh this antiquated term; simply read what you see here, there is nothing more, there is nothing more than that, but it really ought to be enough, it ought to be enough to make the most jaded of men howl, you see.

This *trembling all over* of mine, I say to Blum, only feeling everything and thinking, but not saying anything now, and writing down even less, like my mother when language began to desert her, when she was no longer able to transpose her thinking and feeling into language, I could see in her eyes how alert and aware she still was, I say to Blum, but more and more often she would begin a sentence and not be able to finish it, tears ran down her cheeks, she was mourning her incapacity to make herself understood, oh my head my head has split apart, she would moan and then cover her face with her hands, *but the electric cabinet (to cry) was always there.*

She had air in her bones (like birds do, sparrows, butterflies), air in her bones, there was still air in her head and rump too, and she said PARDON ME! when a wind escaped her, or the long shell of her throat clearing. I had set the cup down, I had set down the cup full of hot tea, I had left the cup full of hot liquid standing, apparently I had forgotten it, and when I found it again the tea was cold, a thought flutter, I say to Blum, an imitation (intonation), when the mailman calls in to me from the hallway : MAIL! MAIL! and I mishear it, I understand CAL! CAL!, a name, of course, a friend's tone of voice, when he answers the phone, phantom, parable, apparition, etc.

The flight of the winter moth is high and I am finding holes in black things, this flying dragon : *a spastic among insects,* while Alma is asking, *the theme is?* : when she inquires about the progress of my work, difficult to

say, I say to Alma, as the crow flies, so indeterminable and on high, I say, it is this *fountain thing,* can't be plumbed, etc., but then I think about Joseph again, and in seconds my face is drowning in tears, such BREATH IMAGES, I say to Blum, I mean the wild envelope, Joseph's wild handwriting on the envelope, the trembling volatility of his writing, which, before I had even opened, no torn open, the letter conveyed the awful news to me, *he had been mistaken in his feelings : it had all been nothing but an ILLUSION . .*
a zipper in the cheek, came to me in my dreams, I say to Blum, a sleeve was waving in the wind, and : the ladies-in-waiting so fodderly day and night. *I mean that I am being so taken up with this,* you see.

12/26

they had been out *ranging around,* see footnote, put on my dead eyeglasses, turned over the critical edition of Jean Paul, simply took the dusty book in my hand, shook the dust out over my head, maybe even *poured out,* the only thing you can do with Jean Paul is *pour him out,* I say to Blum, he is so fluid, so meandering, so intertwined, so forest and field and deep-blue night and wheel tracks and mosquito creatures and granary and foliage and panting, and matte rose observation and king's mantle and moon slit, etc., heard Britten's *A Ceremony of Carols* early this morning, and saw a figure there, moving upright FLY : FLAME : inspiration roller, and I concluded from this that Britten must have gone about his work with a powerful inspiration roller, I mean there is this ROLLER that flattens everything in its path, and after that everything returns to a harmonious state, and something about this phenomenon was like a flickering light, it had slipped into a dream state for a few seconds, *absented itself,* then this whole UPROAR again, this whole SWELLING again, Britten's composition showed me what inspiration really looks like, a figure with a smooth cellophane body or FLY BODY : something that comes trotting after you, constantly following in your steps in your track, and something like a voice calling out to you, appeal, and pulling you, pulling you up : by your name : your name's tail and you start to tremble and you turn around, and you see him standing there this COMPANION, the inspiration incarnate, and it doesn't have a particularly wholesome countenance (appearance), it is very severe and has a scepter, and has a face like a FLY that is a FLY FACE heightened to the nth degree, and frightening, and better just look away and extinguish, extinguish ev-

to range, a family idiom, otherwise : range = mountain, also oven, also to wander around

erything and try to keep breathing calmly, and then IT is walking at your side, IT has caught up with you and IT is silent, IT is walking silently at your side and you come to know the torments of hell . . and IT grabs your heart, IT grabs for your heart and your breathing is no longer measured, and so *fiddling around* with pills for your body temperature which has just shot up at the mere thought of this figurative inspiration, etc.
This is reason for *celebration,* I say to Blum.
Not another word about Joseph, I have encapsulated him, maybe even swallowed him, I am drinking cold coffee, this *image* of inspiration, it pervades wool things wild cats and MIGRAINES, I say to Blum, and there was something so light and bright about it, in the very early morning heard Britten's *A Ceremony of Carols,* actually unprepared for it, my ear opened right up, I find a slip of paper with the words CAN HARDLY GO ANYWHERE WITHOUT *BLEEDING TO DEATH,* ENCOUNTER YOUR BRIGHT SHADOW EVERYWHERE, YOUR GLOWING EYE LOOKING DOWN ON ME EVERYWHERE, etc., not one single word more about Joseph, I say to Blum, you see what a struggle that is, you can come up with a thousand maxims and not follow a single 1, a white tiger-striped knee or the magnetic tail of the taxi driver in front of me, it irritates me, my knee is moving in time to the music coming from the car radio, but I was already blocked, first hallucination, Blum says, early in the morning, I can see you bending over the first cyclamen in the grass in P., many years, many cyclamen, never went there again . . *today the firmament of the Josephstadt clear :* DETERMINING A CONCEPT AND A GARDENER.
1-sided wash, I say to Blum, a shower passing through my hair thinning hair, and covered with markings, like the clumps of yellowed grass in the rundown patch in front of our building seems to be full of scent markings for the stray dog or *dog out on a walk, or cat or boy,* etc., like making our way through our soul's underbrush, I say to Blum, like our soul's underbrush full of markings, I say to Blum, so taciturn because avoiding eyes because hurried meeting in a café, I say to Blum, which, when you got up to go again after some minutes, I write to Joseph, in order to be DOWNTOWN at a particular time, left me behind in a depressed mood, I write to Joseph, I am not really writing this to Joseph, not 1 more word about Joseph, not 1 more word to Joseph, I am writing this down here, I am playing a role reversal, I say to Blum, I can remember when you came back after less than a minute, taking your gray wool scarf from the clothes rack near our table, and saying THIS IS SYMPTOMATIC!, disappearing again, I felt this was also an indication or marking : in this *having to return* of yours,

to a place you had contrived to leave with such haste, but, and this is the way it simply slipped out, by smiling back at you, : *maybe you really didn't want to go!,* which didn't keep you from racing off without saying a word, profuse shivering, I say to Blum, of course that early-morning harp music on the radio was also a marking, and very likely all of our many touches / encounters were nothing but markings of a phenomenon that has caused me incomprehensible, over the course of time undreamt-of, unforeseeable dismay, etc., all too often, in my life and my writing I allow myself to be guided by passions and random events, for which, in a more sober state I could simply have myself STRANGLED, and so I find myself regretting my precipitate reflexes, feelings, *precipitate letters,* and while I am observing, I write to Joseph, how in the background of the bar Chaliapin's voice is cloaking, I mean your face with a veil, *your tongue a veil,* it speaks in riddles, I say, without saying the word : NOW YOUR FACE IS FULL OF MELANCHOLY. I wrote this letter after having fainted, if however our bodies nothing but CARRION and thus exude the STENCH OF CARRION—what then? Fig leaf, Lazarus and the mirror : water as mirror, in my portable tub, I say to Blum, and I am extraordinarily calm and extraordinarily uneasy, I say to Blum, and I am extraordinarily constrained and extraordinarily unfettered, the reflection of the sooty visage in the water in my portable tub, Seneca's green palms, *you with all your woman's business,* I say to Lily, everything gusting up against it, and I do not actually live in this world, I set the receiver down, on the table, while the talking continues on the other end of the line : mother in her last stage, she was too weak and exhausted to hold on to the receiver, she set it down on the scratched-up tabletop of the old farm table while the talking continued on the other end of the line, a gesture of EVERYTHING HOPELESS! EVERYTHING INFIRM! EVERYTHING ILLUSIVE!, lines broken down, all of us lone creatures, I say to Blum, every last one of us loners, we are not made to behave like social beings, and so I am in ONE-SIDED LOVE, you see, the grace of his soul, oh Joseph, *great feast of mussels at the next table.*

12/29
(postscriptum)

well, couldn't get any further, despite full shelves, boxes, baskets (full of all sorts of notes), and an anxious night, I say to Blum, took notes during the night, and things started to flash . . OUR GLITTERING CLOTHES TOUCHED SO THAT . . but didn't get any further than that, something in my thought chambers was starting to hobble, something was rumbling in there, I couldn't figure it out, it was a beginning that could not be pursued, a beginning which was offered and withdrawn at one and the same time, and how could you possibly expand on a sentence that began OUR GLITTERING CLOTHES TOUCHED SO THAT . . I say to Blum, the next time I woke up it was already 1 o'clock in the morning, and I found myself having to write HE TRACES OVER EVERYTHING, and this sentence was also to remain a fragment, it came to me in a roundabout way, it was *a peek,* I say to Blum, torn to pieces these sentences, dreams, whispers, my whole sound box, then back to the machine, 1 last page to Joseph a very old PRESTAMPED POSTCARD that is no longer in circulation, write: this is a PRESTAMPED POSTCARD, this is a public space, nothing to fear, and no salutation only a signature stamp . . and suddenly this opening : CLEARING early in the morning, all my senses rejuvenated, new seeing, new hearing, new feeling, new touching, tasting, smelling, o wondrous renewal, I say to Blum, and although things dirty and dented in the kitchen, everything seems to be quill-feather(ed), which sounds anachronistic, right, I say to Blum, being heaved high on this morning, what a wonder, the first eruptions out of a frayed chest, *word attacks,* parallels with what I have seen, remembered, dreamed, thought, and when I look at the Kleenex scattered throughout the kitchen the image, *the word image* : like seedlings, white, white-veined seedlings, remind me of wet wash spread out to BLEACH IN

THE GRASS, white unfolded Kleenex laid out in a half circle, on top of this a plastic washbasin, orange, turned upside down, and the word memory, originally heard from X (or William or Ferdinand) : "bought half a village in the countryside, a few little huts standing in a half circle that is . ."
somehow postscript, more or less, and trying so hard to *sip* from 1,000 books in pursuit of something : a fragment of knowledge and pleasure I had not as yet perceived, right, I say to Blum. But as for the chasms of thought where Joseph is concerned, I say to Blum, I can hardly go anywhere I have previously been with him, this flickering body, flickering candle, figure with a smooth body made of cellophane, I believe, and lay my head on his shoulder, as I imagine myself doing, I put the receiver down or I take off my horns, I take off my horns it is on the standard table and it *is rumbling* the potted flower in the window : it is getting leggy like the fading green plant sitting on the cabinet in the women's restroom at the Nobel Café, such a *waste!,* I say to Blum, why doesn't anyone set it outside in the December rain, outside in daylight, in the landscape of ruins . . my sooty anger, my charcoal-blackened fingertips what had I been reaching for?
this morning, I say to Blum, something like a final title for the book I am now writing *worked itself out* for me, *bass hungry,* and the way it crackled and snapped inside me this title (*trickster*).

12/31

yes, the now past beating, the dog's eyes!

a shadow poured out behind the garbage can (media mâche), foot reaching if perhaps black fur blanket isn't feigning shadow, see a face in every crumpled piece of paper, pairs of eyes wherever I look, I had intended not to grow old. Francis Bacon's *Self-Portrait, 1973* is slouching over the sink, resting head on his right arm, sleeves rolled up. Under, next to, behind the chair on which he is sitting with *legs crossed,* a soot-colored (steaming) shadow is spreading out across the linoleum floor, most likely necrological abstinence or liquefaction, the broad-faced wristwatch on his left wrist reads 10:30, our : his and my : yoke association, etc.

Slips of paper are being scattered around, I say to Blum, I'm not taking notes anymore, of course I still note things down, but it no longer has any significance, basically everything has already been written down, basically I am sinking into silence, someone, something has sealed my mouth shut, *in villages, dogs, tentacles that is . .* with the POLISHED TEARS OF A BROTHER : OF A BOOK, isn't that right, my writing excesses are in the process of disintegrating, I can hardly even remember the feeling of writing excesses, because of the uneven floor my foot stumbling, gigantic fragment of a pair of pants, speckles of world when I lean my head out the window, as a motto of passivity a word from Novalis, I say to Blum, it reads : a book is nature *set* in lines (like music) and *made complete,* Joseph's tousled locks fading into a terrible distance, Joseph carried off into the distance, no longer even the certainty that he exists.

Suddenly the urge to call my mother, PIECE OF CHALK growing out of my heart and I am revolving around my own axis, in the middle of my study, I howl : I am going to call now! on a scrap of paper the words : CALL MOTHER!

A pass feeling, actually feeling as if crossing a pass : AS IF I WERE LYING OUT IN A FIELD, I say to Blum, feel myself exposed to a deadly passion, or a grain of sand, hourglass feeling : I leave the room to look for something in the hallway, I forget what it is while I am walking through the hallway, under my skin I sense a grain of sand pressure, didn't I want . . what actually?

3 o'clock in the morning, heart-shaped lady, heart-shaped stare, gaping heart-shaped pastries ("puff pastry") in an old candy box wrapped in plain white paper : sacred coffer, child's whitewashed coffin? every year on certain holidays repeated this act of ATTACHMENT on the side of the *Hercules lady,* image of Christmas, corpses, etc. Typewriter carriage stuck though nothing nearby obstructing its path, heartbeat stuck, apparent sticking, then blowing, blustering wind carousel around my ears in my hermetically sealed study, sensed very clearly : draft around my ears and forehead, quickening vibration, etc.

Joseph always sat with his legs crossed like Francis Bacon . . no visitors!, I give a warning over the phone, no visitors today!, want to BE KINDLED : fantasy kindled, I say to Blum, or kindled fantasy generating itself, right . . in any case, kindled, kindling love, the eye's love, see if the sparkler effect still working wonders (blissful) etc. Breakfast cup left out and then the soup bowl and then an evening coffee, and always the same dishes, and everything tastes like everything else, there was a DOVE PICK, I call to Lily, do you remember, because back then our ice skates had three sharp teeth at the front of each blade so we could come to a stop even at high speeds, and mother freezing behind the bars of the ice rink, for hours, she was wearing a turban, she was wearing a scarf . .

the trench coat's downpour, I say to Lily, mother's trench coat, do you remember, I skip down the street, youngsters firing off around me, *downpours over a leather coat,* mother's leather coat, in streams down the back of the coat, the many downpours of her life, down the back, signs of oh so many downpours on the back streams of the coat, such downpours, I say, like night and haze, on the back of the trench coat streams, such TEAR TRACES : LIFE TRACES, I say, and then the coat disappears, gray in gray, it gradually sinks away, coat skin scratched tangled crippled and flaming coat, finally, reptile skin.

Blum is talking to me, but I am thinking about Joseph, I say to Lily, chasing the deer, I say, I am thinking about Joseph while Blum is talking to me, I take Joseph in my arms, as I imagine, she unbuttons and buttons her coat, I say to Joseph, a trench coat's downpours, I say to Joseph, I am being led

by you, I say to Joseph, the bouquet of barberry, I mean the word bouquet of barberry on the cardboard coaster in the kitchen, you are going to court with me, oh Joseph, I say to Joseph, the range of your dominion is simply incomprehensible to me, and I ask myself, is it just, is this all just the way we are dealing with each other, like the rabbit hand on the stick shift, I mean WHILE THIS HAND GOES HUMMING ALONG . . the exercises you are imposing on me are the most severe. That was after all a butterfly, wasn't it, *fluttering* around my room at the beginning of winter, you come with your Batmobile, that may well be a medical term, I say to Joseph, yes, those wings really do flap . . *blunders from the bread cage,* dreamt, dear Joseph, just as : the sharp knife FROST cuts into lateral finger underbrush, just as : raw crazy meat : bleeding runners in the ice, etc.
(Variations on a Feigned Melancholy).

in the morning *fleeing muscles,* might also be MUSIC (sometimes the typos we make), you read one for the other, in the morning fluid music with long flowing hair. And it seemed to me / came to me, it spread out before me, the CONIFER HEAVEN I mean this wide untamed land : the abundance of the night, de Falla's *Nights in the Gardens of Spain,* out of the radio box or whispers of a sewing box, etc., would like to find out about ANGELOLOGY, I write to Elisabeth von Samsonow, do you know of any texts, I write to Elisabeth von Samsonow, *and then sometimes I even wake up with : with my PRACTICAL apron on,* etc. and with the awareness, today I will not be able to receive any whispers, at the break of this dawn / dong / dawn / dong / dawn, no excited knocking ticking horn blowing baton swinging, the metronome, the sight of the metronome hits me in my stomach, the sun stings my eye, and so there are no vibrations at all, no wings fluttering, flinging of arms into the air in moments of delight, floral eminence, etc., everything shredded into odds and ends, and heavy lifting and rumbling and standing my ground, taking a stand on everything, and drawn out of my emptiness a hollow unfounded word jingling for everything squeezed out from between my vocal cords, but so sincere that most everyone seems to feel attended to, understood, comforted, although only routine processing, make tracks as quickly as possible, wanting not to be challenged, wanting to close eyes and ears . .

as such a day breaks : lock the gates, feel yourself stuffed full of impure influences, corruptions, SOUL CALLUS—which is the worst possible thing because of impeded locomotion, right—overnight what wretched riffraff sneaked its way into me, to overwhelm me, and now I can do nothing but TROT around through my quarters my head hanging : also

TOP or DROP or POT or CROP or TEETHING SKULL!, with groping step, tattered brain—instead of, the way I always hope things to be, to fly to flee into the upper realms, and in soaring up and away embrace the awareness which reveals THE MYSTERY!, because after all everything 1 single MYSTERY, as well the bugs and bone bitters and word trampolines and tufts of hair, the entire EYE DELUGE, and the mystery of wafting breath, this breath : Ariel's, etc., which I am eagerly attempting to catch . . letter and shot (instead of Amor's unloosed arrow) with the most tender shotgun of affection, appropriate to a *footnote friend,* and lanterns at midnight.

a cloven hoof in the door, I say to Blum, a disaster, an infatuated disposition, a raging heart on this morning of the first day of the new year, shooting angled (angel buckle?) into things martial while intestines processing their unedifying contracts (contractions), working through, while the flail formerly WING WORKS as if mechanical strike my most sensitive places. Dispirited morning, instead of morning moon diffuse reflection in the window : the floor lamp! NOT SO MUCH ETHER! wild grim and verdigris (adj.) : hanging around in 1 corner of the room, gnawing hunger, psychopharmaceutical under my tongue, *goatee of silence.*

As far as this *sooty* picture is concerned, Baconic megapainting *Self-Portrait, 1973* or *Self-Portrait with Sooty Scissors* or *Self-Portrait with Sooty Bucket,* these renderings are based on concrete experiences, perhaps on the BLACKENED faces when Russian troops marched in, where we, huddling in a corner of the cellar, heard our house breaking to pieces over our heads—sooty blackened visage, sooty blackened insides, "why do you always wear black?," and so on, sooty black forehead : cross in church on Ash Wednesday, then you had to lift your bangs, which was nothing less than total exposure, you see, or : "come on, let's see your forehead!" he brushes my hair back from my forehead, an act of violence, I say, a rape, a SOUL PLOT, etc.

It is sitting across from me, this figure of Francis Bacon, affixed with several clothespins to a frayed piece of cardboard, hands and hour of the day on its left wrist, hollow-eyed hollow-cheeked : monkey simulation, on the elbow of the left arm that is, or mummy with headband, once you have immersed yourself in this picture for some time, the plum joint around the left knee (plum thigh?) crossed under the right, as a base for your pose : Joseph's base—oh Joseph, the Bacon figure has assumed your pose, I write to Joseph, this Bacon figure has appropriated your pose, or you have copied Bacon's pose, because everything between us is (still) just mimicry, a marking of similarities, right, although you are distancing yourself and have conveyed this to

me in no uncertain terms, something which has once again brought me into a TEAR SHOCK etc.
I render, measure, see through, make transparent, but maybe this osmosis is all too cheap, I say to Blum, but Joseph's PLUM FUR COWLICK!, I mean he is UNTOUCHABLE!, Joseph in his pained untouchableness, how will I ever bring that into line with my understanding of SELF-SENSE? Joseph is unapproachable, I say to Blum, please, just picture this : a person in the same city and UNAPPROACHABLE, UNTOUCHABLE, for me, I come to him from everywhere else, from all the most distant realms, and I just keep coming back to Joseph. All of my resolutions, not to think about him anymore, not to talk about him anymore : a farce, not possible. I seek the company of his friends these days, I meet with people who are close to him, so that I can get a REFLECTION, a MARKING, I almost said : maybe, in this way, *something of Joseph will fall my way* . . this nothing but a snowflake, I say, distinct declaration of dependence, I say, but I sense no feeling of shame in me because of it, stand by my onset of winter, etc.
Anything, just no visitors, I shout into the phone, the DOVE NETTLES in my hair in the mirror, in the morning, *hymen in a cardboard box.*

P.S. *snowflaked day and me quietly shivering (Trick of the Day)*

1/6

am silent a dreamer a dud

the 3rd HOLY VIRGIN I've encountered today, in the bus on the train in the street, each was carrying a bunch of dried foliage in her hand, in her handbag, in a paper bag, don't know what I am to make of these apparitions though, feel as if I've been reborn, I say to Blum, feel myself animated, climbing up some tree or flagpole or pinecone, red tongues on the sidewalk, like red cut-out kisses, little tongues, dripping onto the ground oh Joseph, I write to Joseph, our kisses, leafy tongues, little red heart-shaped blossoms poured out onto the sidewalk, in the middle of winter, saw the star singers in the street, I say to Blum, with little white banners (= skirts / ministrant's robes), white cowls and bowls, standing four in a row, and SINGING, larmoyance of the past few weeks as if swept away, liberating times, and was happy, I write to Joseph, and so a guardian angelness, I write to Joseph, an urge to kiss you all the time, I write to Joseph, and then retreat again, and becoming sensible, and staying passionate, you see, I act so cyclically.

so, 3 LITTLE WOMEN these 3 madonnas of the morning on the street in the bus on the train, carrying shriveled-up twigs around with them, like autumn leaves, in the middle of winter, and I couldn't get at the meaning, isn't it strange : this green grave inside me, and I am thinking to myself, I write to Joseph, that you have stopped raging at me because of my excesses (arrogance), we are laughing again, a page has fallen out of the dictionary, and the center of the earth in my room sucked it up, it was the page from RESIDE to RETARDATION, my logorrhea caught up with me, the SLUMBER effect of electronic devices, Joseph says, something quite unpredictable, occasionally they behave in a very human way, a speaking unit, a breathing unit but completely colorless, I say to Blum, the contents of the mineral water bottle have thrown up, flooding the floor, the white plastic container full of powder is suffering from a CROOK IN THE NECK, took out the celestial chart, looking for Venus, the Big Bear, the Wolf, the titanic stars!, I say, spheroid shapes over our heads, actually unimaginable, I say, wild swan, which aura gave me that, announced it to me? and the heavenly flashes of light (the solitary water) disguised as stars, Blum says, as he is looking over the chart with me. In Giordano Bruno, I say, there is : "thus something wondrous happened in Nepal to a certain noble woman of great beauty, whose hair had been singed by lightning but only (singly) around her vulva, and so it is said that when it singed a wine cask, it left the wine solid or set without the cask," etc., oh, the way mother ran with her umbrella the moment a storm threatened, the first thunder was heard, the heavens grew dark, the first lightning bolt the first celestial flash, and the PUNISHING HAND, she said, now the PUNISHING HAND will come down upon us, let's get ourselves home before the storm breaks, then she would run with her bright-colored umbrella as fast as she could, arriving at home out of breath and exhausted, it had already begun to patter, her eye red and fearful and agitated, kneaded stuff, a small sack full of murmurs, the dying subsiding storm, and then from behind my back I hear something like YOUNG MAN YOUNG MAN as if someone were speaking to me, or as if these bitter temperatures did not suit my organs, not my heart these icy temperatures, so that instead of murmuring along in its streambed it sits up or tips over and beats all around like a wild saint, who is not really a saint, because he is constantly adjusting the halo rotating around on his head, etc., like a wild swan, and to such a degree, I say to Blum, when I am determined to leave my machine, the wild growth the brain power becoming more and more compelling, etc., the meow of that voice that might be peculiar to a tiger cat as well as a . . . . I note down : TIGER DISEASE, and Joseph says, that is when your face is covered with red stripes, and then I feel as if I have been reborn born anew like the voice of fishes and foxes and I also have the red eyes of a tiger cat and buy 3 copies of the same newspaper so that I could write down my notes on the broad white margins, and VIENNESE PRIEST TAKES CONFESSION OVER THE COMPUTER, on the forehead side of the page in large letters ("Lead Article"), I rush along streets empty of others, the wave-shaped, curled edge of a white turn-of-the-century lamp made of porcelain in the display window of an antique store startles me, I imitate the curled edge with my own intestines, giddy torture. The eye of a politician poked out on an election poster hurts, I shut my left eye, and I believe that the

bandage over the eye is slipping, etc. Henri Matisse : *Harmony in Red,* 1908, 180 × 122 cm. The wallpaper flows into the tablecloth, while the FIGURE IN THE ROOM or the HOSTESS IN THE ROOM is dipping her left hand into a composition of fruit, her right hand grasping the stem of a glass bowl, next to stage machinery of bread rolls, coneflowers, fish horns, bellowing (stag) vista with tiny white wildflowers and leek-leaved trees and a raging storm which charms the blossoming bouquets into beige bubbles, in which the fish horns face etc. disintegrate—
and read in connection with this : "in the morning swallows fly up off the naked plate, a flock of birds from my breakfast table, then a shutter breaks, I think to myself, I am afraid that the next time we meet, touch, we will see how distant we have become from one another, or that we each say to ourselves, not 1 single POESIE MOMENT while we were together, etc., with my *contemporary glasses,* then looked at each and every thing through the lens of my contemporary glasses . . *where you are after all such a house speaker : such a cosmic brother!*"

I/7

table bag scene

then saw DALÍ figure : one of the seven holy virgins, rubber tree in her arm, at the elbow, its foliage fanned : waved fanned at her breast, over her head, in time with her stride, that is, in front of me down the street, the cactuses : the captives, I say to Blum, dubious combinatory tactic, obfuscation tactic : POOR READER!, I say to Blum, the role reversal, the narrowness the expanse of Joseph's person : not to be captured not to be grasped not to be understood, I say to Blum, not to be fathomed probably HERMES, hermetic . . am born old, born anew, born from time immemorial and bound to / born from the earth cranial network TIME HAMMER : kneaded brain, especially after midday nap, not knowing where you are, not knowing whether day or night, the sun's rays? the ceiling lights? the reading lamp : forehead light after the fashion of miner's, HNO = medical specialists, angel of the annunciation, buckled on, etc., oracle : Joseph as the patriarch of all oracles! his palate will grow jaded, Blum says, whoever simply *devours* beauty without seeking the truth in it behind it, isn't that right, removed the *table papers : table drawings,* I say, had predominated in my writing space, it was an abyss a robe this café in B., what was it called, I say, with Joseph back then in B., but his thoughts wandered although I was drinking him in with my eyes, drawing him into me, etc.
Am very encouraged, the gas was flaking outside, flaming and flaking the kitchen gas, in front of me in the window the bare morning, wonderful bareness of the morning, and stretching, *roaming,* stomping too, what do I know, stomping through the snowfield, picking through it with ski pole and runners, glow and deafness : I mean when you *gaze* into this snow long enough, you go deaf, eyes go deaf, the view, the murmur in your aural passageways, laborious breathing while striding rapidly through the

snowfield, OUT OF CONDITION! the doctor says, I say to Blum, I dream of a typewriter I can buckle on, typewriter as belly payload and the like, so that even WHEN AWAY FROM HOME, I mean, *what should I do with these bloody bolts of light* from above, *those flickering promises : biting tales* flashing down on my skull . . he was with me, I say to Blum, but his thoughts were wandering, while we were sitting so close together at the small marble table in the café, so close that all I saw was the gleam of his pupils, and he said WE ARE NOT LOVERS, etc., *so wobbly day and night,* and me in socks in MOSES and moss, in swim skins : tears. Drug melts on the tongue, his drug on my tongue, he does not accept my gifts, and when he does, then reluctantly, as if accepting them and at the same time wanting to turn them down, I am stunned, plummet into myself, my fall is deep, the depth incalculable, I mean the dismay, the plunge into my own emptiness, you see, deep into my own emptiness, into the abyss, into the devastation, that is : *fell completely out of my senses, cut so small,* saw a bird fly into the air and disappear behind some flowers, in the middle of winter, constantly vibrating and fear panic STORYSCAPES in my mane, my breast exposed, felted tufted torn wool hair, I scream for help, page from right to left when I write in my notebook, instead of the other way around, I say to Blum, just as I did when I was a child, back then, needlework sewn, stitched, stitches from right to left, instead of the other way around, the photo, I say to Joseph, the one you took of me shows a silhouette with a Napoleon hat, casts a shadow, that is, against the grid of an autumn field, backlit, from behind, with a large fur hat, sweeping cape, and the fur cap, the slight protrusion out and away from my ears, right, like a washcloth mitten ("Madonna was in fresh leaf, etc."), the sales clerk tells me the price of the merchandise, says : 153 schillings, no, she corrects herself, no, she says, 135 schillings, prime angle, non-angle, fore-angle, I say to Joseph, a sign that you might wish for from a lover, but it doesn't come, never comes, at least that's how it seems to you (*"the entire blossom business," etc.*), you have waited all too long for this sign, waited for this call, it was always in vain, I say, we haven't seen each other for a long time, I say to Joseph, my hands (halfway) are covering my face and eyes, am smiling out from behind them, to him, the same height, I say, we are the same height, noticed this today for the first time, I say, the repetition loop, FOREVER, I say to Joseph, just think, CD player, I say to Joseph, you don't even touch a button and it starts playing on its own!— : SLUMBER EFFECT, I say to Joseph, I risk a thought an *allusion,* SLUMBER Joseph says, maybe set on SLUMBER, slumber position, or POISON, I think, it seems to me that we are storming each other, a not always amicable storming up against one another, one storm rages gently : harshly up against the other, hot sandstorm, *each telling the other about the other,* I know your most intimate emotions from your writings, Joseph says, I feel the desire to write something crazy, I say to Joseph, inside my eardrum catching wind of caught wind of something, irritating noises coming from the kitchen, *I find myself inside a mirage,* I say to Joseph, or, as accustomed turn to my reader : just imagine that, dear reader, do you see deception in any of this at all?

I breathe with great difficulty, is this imaginary breathing? the entire horizon has spread out inside me, expanding brain and skin, Blum says it's a drug, Joseph made me swallow this drug, the drug on his tongue, we exchange this drug, I say, I have hardened into a comma, I say, I am living on kiwi fruit and yogurt, from lip to lip, like the DROPS I used to take when I was a child, on the wall of a building in an *old rundown neighborhood* in spray paint : "ALL POWER TO MACHINES! DOWN WITH HUMANS!" . . I am frozen in JOYOUS DELIGHT, I am frozen in a pale COMPLEXION, taking down notes while I walk along the street : my breakfast cup stays where it is, and then it's my soup bowl, and the soup bowl stays put, and then it's the glass mug on a cracked tabletop, and on it no in it Matisse's *Goldfish,* and then it's night and I turn back the covers and crawl into bed, and then it's morning, and I turn back the covers while 1 pang shock, I mean 12 pangs, halo-crowned pangs, and I howl and I curse and I stomp around, but sometimes, I say to Blum, just imagine this, sometimes all I see is 1 strand of the hair on his head or the cowlick at the back of his head, I say to Blum, his delicate feet, he takes off his soaking-wet shoes, I stuff them with wads of newspaper in order to soak up the wetness, they are small, I say to Joseph, small feet, I say to Joseph, without saying a word he slips into the slippers (travel slippers) set out for him, we go way back, I mean RAGING LANTERNS, I mean how are we supposed to feel when someone is preoccupied with the DETAILS OF OUR LIFE? We get some sense of pleasure, and then we sink into a morass of *self-exaggeration*?, then we cut ourselves off, keep to ourselves, keep to ourselves and remain an enigma to others? including an amorous retard, I say to Blum, or our repetition, REPETITION ADDICTION, of images recalled, signs recalled during hours of intense reading, who or what is responsible, who or what has chased these images and shadows in between the pages of the book we are reading, what interrupts our reading revelations for a fraction of a second *like a flash of lightning?* what is happening inside our head at that moment? age-related porousness, distractions, detours, digressions into a past life? presumed basis for sexual relations, profoundly intimate impulse perceptions of early childhood and adolescence, experiences, emotions, I say, the predominance (emergence) of pictures as opposed to logical thought, thought combinations, thought problems? illuminated remembering : momentary images inside the head which force their way in, intrude on, thwart the intensity of reading, break it off, make it run dry, throw it off course, then back to the page of the book . . LOOK OUT!, the next memory image is about to light up, distract us from our reading, disturb us—what is the purpose of the interference factor? why do we allow it to distract us from a most voracious consumption of text? never appears to have any evident connection with what has just been read—

always the same slender book, poems by Sarah Kirsch, falls down on the floor, *because the mantilla I mean billowing* of an apron, and situated on the edge of the counter the way it is, whatever happens, happens, and it falls onto the floor again when I brush past. Mantilla, obsessive falling, *my flirtatious bathwater,* I screw a lightbulb into the socket of the ceiling fixture, note down : 1 pants murmur, glow (shine) from the book, feel rat-headed, I had intended not to grow older but the temple bell . . such a WORK MAKER!

Dalí to Gala : the fantasies of our delirious characters collide with such intensity that we might easily imagine ourselves taking part in the combat of furious roosters in which the normal object comes out plucked clean, in the background newspaper objects, a woman's shoe drenched in fresh milk . .

1/10

and he has this flower in his cowlick, sulfur blossom, sulfur-skinned heavens, I say to Blum, and I had this REMBRANDT DARKNESS inside my head when I looked at his photograph, Polaroid camera . . felt a strong desire, to plunge into hot water right along with my socks and my shoes, this morning I wrote 2 friends, a man and a woman, text of the letters almost identical, including a *transplanted* felt-pen sketch : "eagerly awaiting your new book . ." and "in curls of thought, spirals I feel myself *wired* to you, etc." Often don't know, shall I just stay put right where I am : soaking my feet, or the edge of my hand, take care of the wound from the razor-sharp edge of a piece of typing paper, or listen to the noises below, dog packs, street howls, automobile din, or let out a howl myself, or reel around in texts hidden : believed lost : staggering like this from one temple guardian friend to another.

Light burning since 3:30 this morning, stiff-necked deep-cushioned reading fervor, like my mother, already bedridden, in spite of pillows piled high 1 on top of the other she held her head up straight, stiffly, without support, yellowish winter day, I say to Blum, strange parallels in our WORK FANTASIES, I write to Joseph, my being so attached to this new book of mine, it's keeping me alive, tell myself I've never experienced anything like this before, this high-heeled grace and most profound tearing apart : smashing to pieces my ecstatic spirit blown out of its groove, *and all of a sudden a wave of sobs swept over my whole body,* I write to Joseph, had already half gotten over what had happened to me, I write to Joseph, why was the long gray scarf *symptomatic?,* basically every letter I write to my friends, both men and women, is meant only for you, I write to Joseph, basically all of the letters I write to these friends are letters I wish you had written to me, but you are silent . . *Theorem of Terrier Reading Scent,* I say to Blum, my throat stuffed full of weary old SLOGANS, I say to Blum, a mutual friend mentioned his name, I say to Blum, said she saw Joseph at this event or another and momentarily HE LEFT ME, I mean LEFT ME SO PAINFULLY that it wasn't until this very moment that I realized how much I had MISSED him all these days and weeks, and suddenly I was imprinted with the image of a strange object which radiated cold, in the closest possible proximity to me penetrating right through me, the cold growing more and more intense, and in order to protect myself I actually began to transform myself into this same object of cold. *The stadium blanket the travel plaid* spread out over the EXTREMITIES, head buried in my pillow, and I lay there like that, for hours, for days.

Maybe it would be enough, I say to the *pharmacist,* if you imagine an *artificial* blue sky on the walls of the pharmacy : *föhn* skies, when it rains day after day, why don't you just conjure up a *föhn* sky on the front side of the shop, I say to the pharmacist—she liked the idea of an artificial sky on the front side of the shop, it had simply been trotting along, I say to Blum, do you know this expression, the weather just kept trotting right along in its path and there had been almost no daylight, I loved it, and I say to the pharmacist, I am wishing for half a year of bad weather, half a year of humidity along with the highest possible temperatures, a wall of water, a sultriness of June, a fluttering bird, a visionary locale, a temple benefactor, a quantity of thought pills, etc.

Scribbled down a barred gate while talking on the telephone with Joseph, I say to Blum, am excited, impatient, happy. The object of our affections looks at us like a defendant wrongly charged, I say to Blum, he cannot return our love, and his eyes say : how can I help it if you love me and I cannot return your love : to a person who cannot return the love he is given these feelings being offered to him are a burden, a torment, an intrusion, an act of violence, violation of a profound taboo, a convulsion and he retreats in disgust (suffering as well) . . Variation on Cold, or the tiniest TWIST OF LIGHT hits you in the eye, and smashing.

I/13

then when the invisible insides of the soul like a YOUNG GIRL *naked . .*

in such a way that the prophecy of a higher tone, or a higher water temperature, of a higher frequency of observation makes me uncertain and I begin to vacillate between writing (composing) a letter to Joseph and its refined REFLECTION : continuing to write this book, and for a long time I didn't even know what I had decided to do, even though I continued writing this book, and everywhere minor instances of unevenness finding their way into the fictitious form of address, aimed at Joseph, so perhaps I was writing both at the same time, this letter of mine to Joseph and the continuation of this book (including stolen goods!), *almost swallowed or sobbed away,* with arabesque strands of hair intertwined or damned, and I didn't know which alternative was the more honest more truthful more brilliant, now, in the background, I say to Blum, again this muffled voice on the radio, the telephone, announcing the weather and politics, almost unbearable—as if coming out of a telephone receiver someone in an indifferent (subdued) speaking voice, male child (curlyhead etc.)—while uptake mechanism of my conscience (sense of hearing) is winging its way or *darting around!* through the substance of a piece by Schubert (Fantasy for Piano and Four Hands in F Minor, opus 103) in rapt (heightened) ALERTNESS : 4:45 in the morning, have never heard music this clearly before, I say to Blum, never sensed the transparency of music like this, I say to Blum, truly saw right into the workings of tone intervals head parts raglans blossoms sensations, and in this way an acoustic phenomenon was suddenly transformed into a visual phenomenon, this *eye (augury) obsessiveness* of mine, which constantly with wavy-haired head has hold of me I mean day and night or agile LITTLE WEAVER SHIP, and everything is everywhere at the same time and in this *bulk of notes,* etc., the end of the book, which I must now consider,

the way I think about the end of life, might be arranged in such a way that in the end the lines gradually disappear, this faded handwriting in old notes I mean, pinned up on Styrofoam panels, but no longer of any use, simply artifacts, relics, pale frayed signs, lines, strings of lines which give out, dissolve, wash away, and then I see so much spilled blue when I close my eyes, which when reading at night must suffer this flood of light, switched on all of the lamps, also when taking notes in bed, and I had grown rather tired and folded myself folded myself up on my side like a carved wooden figure, in my bed, *later I wake up on my tongue,* I say to Blum, as a tiny person in my damp shirt, on the trampoline of my language and I hear myself shouting and sliding . . ("minimal artist me! oh what a shame . ." etc.).
In the morning there is perspiration in the wash (throat?), I say to Blum, in the final analysis when this is all over WE are the ones who will be left, who will be left with each other, etc., or *tamped down* : trash heap transformed into the furor of tablets, sensory tools unreliable, etc., simply without inserting any paper : typed right onto the platen : dreadful thought, just as : no longer in evidence the folder you brought to me, and the PHOTOGRAPH OF AN EAGLE, the last time you were here, I write to Joseph, nonetheless unclear whether or not this really is a letter to Joseph, I mean celibate contemplation, I mean everything fictitious, I say to Blum, the agony begins in the legs and rises up into the heart, the foil card empty of pills, threw it into the wastebasket while eating breakfast, it's glistening and crackling, or I write another letter to Joseph and begin with the rather impassioned words : *I am writing this into the palm of your left hand,* etc., presumably as a delayed reply to his potential to sanction : (". . and write these lines to you as if cast in my hand . .")—
I ask myself, I say to Blum, is all of this so untenable because arbitrary MIXTURE of intimate style of letter writing and the making of exact poetic text or SEDUCTION of an ESCHER VISION of converging stairway constructs and black-and-white optical illusions? (whose backgrounds are meant to put us in touch with zones we have repressed : kept secret, *which basically appeals to my charlatanesque nature, you see*).
A student actress writes to me, I wish you a butterfly spring, my fountain pen trembles with excitement, body should have enjoyed some 26 hours of peace, relaxing *in gardens or other recreations . . ,* while my own body lies stretched out flat like a pink terry cloth sheet or corpse on the rug at the foot of my small writing desk, among compromised feelings, aphrodisiac images, like the strand of hair laid on Joseph's vest the first time he was here.

1/19

until comes roaring up, something like ANTI-MOTHER

a red-white-red string the splits : a neck artery (salamander) in arabesques on my writing desk, to some extent or tangled or weighed down with hopes and desires, the belatedly trumpeted sign to the friends of a friend, I say to Blum, you see your reflection in the glasses lying next to your pencils and pens, your face in 1 of the lenses. A reflection like this in all household objects, right, have been longing have yearned to be writing the segment I am writing today have been waiting full of ardent desire in the early hours of the dawn for this new segment to get down to work, missed for so long, no not only Joseph but even more than that this blood dripping out of my head hemisphere, I say to Blum, powerfully spoken, perhaps all too dramatically formulated, well worn accelerated time keeps running, 96 is winding down, I am writing to these friends of a friend in my much-delayed letter in my much-delayed response to a letter regarding their recollections as this year reaches an end, 96 is already winding down, gingerly still, but still we are headed toward summer, which is always the beginning of the end of the year for me, etc., my best wishes to you, this is what my wishes are saying to you, may you think of me from time to time, I write to the friends of a friend—perhaps, I write, in association with some sort of pleasant color, tones, word, etc., enmeshed in such a beautiful piece of work, I write to the friends of a friend, *quandary wrinkles* under my eyes, foothills of the day's events appearing to be as large as they are small, insignificant and at the same time critically important, at one and the same time *desperate* and *devoted,* or dripping with joy or tied up in misery and ill will, or you are drowning in shame in the early morning because of letters you regret having sent off the day before, you just have to *do without some things,* Blum says, you still haven't learned, Blum says, you still don't get it, Blum says, you act like a child. My skull, my throat, I mean strangling, strangled, I say, the sight of this red-white-red cord lying across those glasses, in which your face is being reflected, obsessed with the feeling that I am being asphyxiated by this piece of string or ROPE, or that I'm just going to have to swallow this piece of coiling stage-prop hemp, this earwig made of wool, these secretions from eye and ear and armpit : field blood or absinthe, sitting with my knees pressed squeezed together, in imitation of a small display table, right, too little space, too little level support, what we're really concerned with here is level support, tabletops, open cupboards, secretaries. In my calendar, Blum says, I see that I am supposed to be going to a funeral, but don't know who died, where I'm supposed to be going, and then I couldn't find or didn't see the telephone although it was where it was supposed to be, *a grown boy and he's still wearing diapers : jodhpurs or training pants,* Joseph says, *on the cover of this paperback,* Joseph says, a design by R. B. Kitaj, inner constriction, Joseph says, when you tell me you saw a double image on the train. He was sitting on her lap, I say, caressing her cheek, no, in the background a woman who was holding her chin in her hand, the 2 images *running* together into 1 single image, I say to Joseph, a phenomenon, I say to Joseph, some sort of psychotic state (inner constriction), I say to Joseph, I love to repeat what you say, I say to Joseph, I love my own murmuring echo.

X (or William or Ferdinand)—first has to be informed—recently sent me an excerpt from Nathalie Sarraute's most recent book *ici,* I say to Joseph, he translated a few lines for me from the text of the French original (by hand, in uppercase letters like calligraphy), I will type them out and then I will know that I have them in printed form, not long ago Blum surprised me, I write to X (or William or Ferdinand) with an enthusiastic report on a television program he had seen about Portugal, now he really wants to go there, I write to X (or William or Ferdinand), now, this coming September we just might be going to Portugal instead of Andalusia?

Giordano Bruno talks about the WONDER OF LOVE, I say to Joseph, a fanciful concept, isn't it, in 1 of my dreams Giordano Bruno was dragging his shadow behind him like the train of a gown, I say to Joseph, *or in obedience to the music,* or the annoying image in my letter to you, the 1 I just mailed a few minutes ago, is now going to *have to wait on the corner* for a few hours (in a metal box) before it gets picked up, etc., the ROARING OF ETHERs (HEAVENLY SPHEREs) I hear, as soon as I pick up the receiver and bring it to my ear, MAGPIES chirping. Just how have I been using the time I've been given, I say to Blum, now at the beginning of my life, in the early morning hours I feel as if I'm at the beginning of my life, late in the evening at the end of my life, the shadow of my heart accompanies you, X (or William or Ferdinand) writes in his most recent letter, in this REALM OF ALPHABETS anything is possible, I answer, or quoting Paul Klee "a genius serves a modest breakfast, angels bring what's desired," I put this wafer between the pages of the DALÍ book as a bookmark, I say to Joseph, *wandering around like a lost soul,* but I am *always diligently and solely* wandering around in these books I mean EXCLUSIVELY, and all at the same time, I believe we are now entering an ERA OF HUMAN SUFFERING, I say to Joseph, sighs and laments from all sides, and making yourself dependent upon all sorts of ORACLE FIGURES, right, perhaps an esoteric element on the advance, something I am not at all comfortable with, etc., *at the hour of nectar / how early you wake,* Elisabeth von Samsonow writes, enclosing the feather of a vulture as an insignia . . at the end of her letter : I will never forget you, as if she were planning to leave but wanted to send me this 1 last greeting, a situation which I found terribly unsettling.

1/30

am I at ease / am I ill at ease / who could possibly know, always a little heated hot and bothered *forgetting* (this and that, and everything straight to the middle of my forehead), heading for a forehead wonder, straight to the third eye, what do I know, it's in need of light, not getting any, nothing but dark strands in my sight, wasted molded into the jagged tin crown of a floundering HALO, I mean the general *ruminations,* precisely at sunrise, *with my serpentine lungs,* and no one is in any shape to spell out anything, I say to Blum, had I forgotten Blum, I ask myself, had I *engraved* the damp compresses onto the iridescent skin of my face, I mean what was it like at sunrise or then out on the streets in icy gusts of snow, all these flakes melt on my lips, cold and wet but still like kisses, hot kisses, I say to Blum, just imagine, I say to Blum, I believe I actually forgot you for a few hours for a few days, a person fading out, a presence fading out, etc., how much pain will we have to suffer before we die, Blum phones to me, *banging around with a soul,* I say to Blum, he is after all as YOUNG AS MY PAPA, I say to Blum, so extraordinary, I say to Blum, so melancholy, in the gusts of his heart, I say to Blum, how do you like that, always SWITCHING OVER TO HANDYMAN* OR FACSIMILE, right, a sleeve waving on the street in the wind, I say to Blum, a shopping bag on the edge of the street slightly inflated like silhouette of a mouse, small mouse, fluttering around in the winds, I *banged* the telephone books down in front of your doors, I telephone to Blum, your news was so wonderful and so direct, Elisabeth von Samsonow writes to me, I can see how life is chasing around inside you and that you are in extraordinarily good spirits, and then I see your

*"*a warmer upper*"

wakeful eyes, I assume *in the interest of pursuing truth you are not sleeping,* Elisabeth von Samsonow writes to me, twisted an acupuncture needle into my third eye because my goal fled, Elisabeth von Samsonow writes to me, this DANCE MASTER, presumably I am sitting at my machine, I write to Elisabeth von Samsonow, presumably my feet in a hot bath, so that the most feverish desires I mean the marbleized fundus of the cooking pot steams up vaporizes its roiling bathwaters, etc., please know how grateful I am for your so wonderful letter, which around my neck like a locked seal, I mean do you know this Picasso portrait of a boy with brown hair, who with smock, I mean this sealed envelope around his neck, perched at his desk or pianino, his pen scratches or splashes or thrashes across the REPAIR PAPER, in, indignant facial expression, the unusual interment of the feet I don't know if you know what I mean, knob or cord on each tattered toe, half a towel on my fetish (table) fazzoletto on my knees, in this way LAMPEDUSE, a scrap of paper flutters into the footbath under my desk, on it the words "ROTUNDA" : "day flowed, days flowed away, days dissolved," he, the Picasso boy, had an envelope on his chest, or it was a BIB, this BIB or a smock, I mean he was a CROP CHILD, a sealed extinct BUTTON CHILD, a sealed envelope on his chest actually on his sweater, and at a piano writing or drawing a letter or *epistle of colors,* not to be defined, but the sealed envelope may be guarding a secret, a small dog on wheels in the background (a cupboard) in a brunette DIGEST or plush, the pale face, the left hand clenched into a fist, feet in *red wads of turban,* right, fetish of morning slippers, red scarlet beret cloud against a gray wall, pale thighs tightly pressed together, the CROP-SHAPED FIGURE, left ear with ear clip, etc. Presumably I am sitting at my machine, presumably geyser gushing and hyacinth, I write to Elisabeth von Samsonow, presumably wrapped up in a winter blanket that otherwise hangs over the window to keep out the cold, your wonderful letter in a handwriting ROTUNDA I am always so moved by it and / *no matter how tender it may feel* / hardly dare TOUCH it with my own eyes not wanting to scare it, the INFATUATION this INFATUATION of mine marches on, I write to Elisabeth von Samsonow, this JOYFUL RUINATION of mine, I like reading what you send me, sense mysterious sources (in) there, everything sounds a little nostalgic, right, blue washcloth mitten is standing / upright moving around like a miter in the bluish bathwater, absolutely minimal locomotion, almost floating, *with bent distorted blossom,* I say, segment of rainbow appears on the edge of the tub. As soon as I open the drain to let out the water the washcloth, surrendering itself to the current, arches back toward the opening, in the manner of an armchair of the 30s, finally flattens out, but with a slight bulge near the waist, if you remember or not, I say to Blum, a few relatives : the oldest of my relatives; when they write words with a double "m" or "n" they used to draw in a small horizontal bar over the letters "m" and "n" and not double them, they abbreviated their script, for reasons of ease or frugality, it was titillating, it was libidinous, I didn't understand it, it revealed something like an embarrassing lack of education on the part of the writer, you see. A scene of baseness, a jewel, a silver fish as paper clip, or something like that, I say to Blum, you know what I mean, BRETON READS LIKE A WOMAN'S SHOE MINCING THROUGH THE SNOW, or like a pair of gloves, black, that has been assembled from 2 unlike pieces, I dreamt I saw an onrushing electric train with a gigantic smokestack scattering a spray of sparks, heading through a dark tunnel, I dreamt that both attendants, who were behaving : interwoven in the same colorations of voice (apostle maidens, assistants in dental setting) in their discourse : off-to-one-side discourse like whispering children, which I liked, liked a lot, were wearing storm ponchos, surgical caps, one possessed the other's *echo form,* etc. There was also some talk of CANDLE CHIPS, just cutting through a little *ice migraine,* the way I was sitting in the dentist's chair, daydreaming, half sleeping, *since 1919 (lachrymose).*

I never even attempted it, *NOT* TO UNDERTAKE EVERYTHING IN COLORFUL MESS, Joseph writes, *only the geniuses do it!*—I wanted to send you 1 or 2 greeting cards, Joseph says, but when I got your letter, it made me lose interest, you shouldn't be preempting me all of the time, still must have moments of surprise between us, I mean and then I got your letter and threw all of it (them) in the water, I heard 2 paper clips *jangling* up against one another in the washbasin when I emptied it I hadn't felt them while I was soaking my feet, heavy wrapped-up Sunday, that is an EAGLE CAP, I say to Joseph, you have a whole collection of winter hats at home, including GYMNASTIC WORK.

2/2

the giants the ladies-in-waiting that is are planning / performing / passionate body searches

up to my neck in divinity that is : matted, brushed, ranted in bath and bed, only HEAD PART and smoking works (= flaming strands) still unclean, unenraptured, unshorn, that's the way things are on this 2nd day of February, Candlemas, Maria, Maria Candlemas, Candle Day, to have gone up in flames the rug made by my mother's own hands, once long ago, today transported it home on my back, spread out under the WRITING DESK, *scrunched up* : because it is too large for these cramped quarters : corners folded over, fringes trimmed, tangled bright-colored pelt under the Thonet chair / throne chair folded, and now even my water bucket on nonskid surface, etc. Ambivalent : the dusty parchments *pyro-ceremonious and pomp!*

Was the left orthopedic shoe or shawl an ankle boot stiletto a sandal or something like that, I am wondering. Because one leg of the Thonet chair was standing on it, I thought, the rug had rolled up, sulked, its *bulging lips* undone and causing the chair to stand at an angle just like a child's chair or a wicker chair does when it is rocked back and forth when you rock in it the way you did as a child, back and forth so vigorously that (tipping) the poor thing almost broke its KINGDOM I mean its bones. I mentioned I had been imputed to have affluence : a fervent element (a fever), or the fever cascades had descended on me because I was alternately shivering and burning up, a fiery creature sitting on my shoulder, or so it seemed, but in the end I escaped Candlemas day without even the slightest affliction, while guttering candlelight, *blustering,* saw it guttering / heard it blustering, in my brain, *and in this way it is a workshop of tongues.*

Glittering passage : the terrier belonging to my *cleaning lady* I mean, in my memory's sigh,—no not : eye, SIGH!—this terrier with the rectangular snout, a dog more dearly loved than any of her kin, she always gave him the most delectable pieces although all around BLOOD RELATIVES : blood brother / blood sister / *destitute* and forced to sit by and watch while the dog was better fed than they were themselves, etc.,

oh sweet panic, I write to Joseph, and so I know you are warm and nested down with the study of your writings although no sign of life from you to me, had grim goat's milk : grimacing goat on the label of the milk bottle : shoveled it in just like that I mean beforehand in a state of distraction swept it off the counter, like hot porridge being spilled onto the tiled floor and kitchen cabinets but I still *missed* your voice, I write to Joseph, I mean : longed for yearned for your voice, and every time the telephone rang, I sat down next to it and told myself IT'S GOING TO BE JOSEPH, PULL YOURSELF TOGETHER!, etc., but it wasn't you it was some one of many other NUMINOSA, incidentally, to get back to the terrier's rectangular and gluttonous snout : there was something else entirely different going on here, when I play back the details in my mind, it was something quite different, it probably wasn't a fox terrier but a poodle, it was the poodle cap the poodle's cap, she, the *meandering maid,* probably had a predatory poodle, sometimes your mind just plays tricks on you, right. I also discern past aspects and future aspects over the course of any given day : an aspect of the past late at night that lays me out lays me out flat on my bed with the desire NOT TO HEAR A THING NOT TO SEE A THING JUST LIE THERE AND SLEEP!—an aspect of the future early in the morning : projects!, rejoicing!, illumination!, glorious powers!, sparkling optimism!, etc.

On 1/30 there actually might have been a postscript, I say to Blum, but came too late : it was already night and I didn't even have enough energy to get the baggy pants I mean the sheet I mean the laundry junk up on the hangers but instead rolled everything up in a bundle and half dazed set it down on my most recent pages. The next morning everything crumpled paper and pants, zenith and rough draft, etc., but Blum had said, I HAVE ALL THE TIME I NEED, that's what Blum had said when I was talking about having too little. I clearly have too little time, I had said to Blum, he lay sprawled out across the sofa and looked at me with a sad smile on his face, he had grown very wise, even more wise than he had always been before, that's what I told him and he answered with silence. Then, after a while, he said I HOPE IT COMES QUICKLY AND I DON'T HAVE TO SUFFER—

I had accumulated stores of *joint supplies* I mean knots of neck scarves or muffs, woolen shawls, mammoth ties to stave off maladies of the throat, coughing fits, optical extravagances, because, I write to X (or William or Ferdinand), you must know that I start reading at 4 o'clock in the morning, my chambers are cold and vibrating, my hands numb from obsessively tight grip on pens and pencils, even at times when I have nothing to write, my notebook between bare knees, I was freezing. It is a matter of discourse it is a matter of reflection it is a matter of overview it is a matter of argumentation, THE PUPILS OF YOUR EYES, their glow has begun to grow weaker, I write to X (or William or Ferdinand), their glow has already grown weaker, *hair curled up and eyes,* it is a plea for support, right. The sequence you are planning to use as the motto of the book, Elisabeth von Samsonow tells me on the phone this morning, is indeed from Ariost, from his ORLANDO FURIOSO, Giordano Bruno has often quoted from it, today painted my little rider, Elisabeth von Samsonow tells me on the phone, the 1 I had carved from elm wood, a very brave rider, because while he is galloping off on his tiny horse his feet are dragging along behind him : in kindergarten I had this kind of relationship with the pony I loved so dearly . . when I look at this small horse in this light, I feel as if I have reclaimed something I had long ago lost, Elisabeth von Samsonow phones to me, I call : actually that's always the way it is when you are finally able to finish a SMALL WORK, and you wonder where it came from how it ever got to you fell into your lap, who can it be the person who gave you this sacred gift, and perhaps you have *again been given* something you had once possessed long ago but believed you had lost, right . . contemplating the end and also full of good cheer, this balancing around in grammar and that this can be read both as CREATING SENSE and CREATING SENSES, which sounds epoch making, *spacious goat*—

2/8–2/10

Picasso's childlike world of the senses

I am not oriental in the morning, I say to Blum, when I turn this music box on, *plop it on* like hat shit, to find out what day what time of day it is, I say to Blum, I am not oriental (veiled) in any way whatsoever, much too *extroverted!* I say, while everything I write looks completely *introverted!* as you say, I say to Blum, imagine that, what kind of tension this produces, constantly switching back and forth between an Extroverted Disposition and an Introverted Disposition—I mean I hardly recognize myself, whenever I spend a number of hours in outside company : straight out of AUNTY HATTEDNESS into AUDACITY, right, or to be more precise, out of the pursuit of inner signs and scents, very gentle and contemplative, and full of tears, wistful, etc., into the awfully brash witty *well-practiced routine* of my dealings with the outside world, a grim routine, because in retrospect I always find myself wanting to take back everything, feel ashamed for things I said, things I promised, all those things so forested over all those things so concealed : shaved clean, aired out, stripped bare, what a pathetic metamorphosis, right. I mean this panic / no, much more to the point this Prussian transcription, notation, writing down, had in fact made myself a note : STRETCH SHOES, STUFF SHOES WITH OLD NEWSPAPER, when Joseph comes in out of the cold, out of the ice and snow, if he shows up at my door, freezing, hungry, a little curly / with curls like that cover photo of Kitaj, right, or the Picasso boy, he had something of each of them in him, so, when he arrived, had very Prussianly made a note to myself, I say to Blum, had written everything down, or as mother used to say, *I'll remember that!, I won't forget!,* whenever I gently suggested, shall I write that down for you?, and then she did not remember, did not recall but forgot, simply forgot, because after all much too focused on that one blackish spot, etc., so back to what I was saying, I had noted everything down, a whole list, beginning with STUFF wet shoes, mouse registry, cake replica etc., details unnecessary here, I say to Blum, had Prussianly noted everything down, I say, but then came the *celestial* I mean the unimaginable joy that Joseph actually showed up at my door, he was like a vision, came in, took his shoes off, slipped into the house slippers I had set out next to the doormat, slowly turned around in the study, put his briefcase down next to the armchair, smiled at me, this is more or less the way it all happened, you never knew if there might not be some variation or other, but most of the time this is the course things took, I was charmed, and reality simply swept away, I mean *he* swept it away, or it swept itself away inside my brain, a game of marbles presumably, the small orbs got lost in the swirling sands, and in this way it became a syndrome of happiness. I mean these small orbs got lost in the desert sands when you threw them threw them off in the direction of the dunes they would keep *swirling back* on themselves and producing hollows of their own, I kept silent, while at the same time being in a great surge, I mean I simply found myself in a *supernatural* surge, which brought about nothing more, contained nothing more, intended nothing more, was not capable of effecting anything more in any logical way, etc. And although I had written myself such beautiful lists, I refer to them as REGISTRIES and sometimes CATAFALQUES, although they have absolutely nothing in common with my lists, there are also times in my KINGDOM (= SEAT OF MY BRAIN) when I come across the word CATASTERISM, which means that after their death both man and animal are transformed into stars, which is of course unlikely, etc., so, although I had written everything down in my lists, what I should do (and not do), as soon as Joseph appeared, all of it was suspended in imponderability, invisibility, inarticulation, yes there were even times when we avoided each other's eyes and instead looked directly out at the two windows located some distance away, behind which the sun was beginning to set and Joseph made the following observation, there is a shadow in the pane, no an incision, a crack, a break, I say, been there for a long time, perhaps for decades, I avoided having the pane replaced, do you understand, I say to Joseph, I mean, they will remove the window and I don't know if I will ever get it back again, and then everything will be taken apart, cut apart, I mean this sunset in winter I'm not going to let them take that away from me, the setting sun caused Joseph some pain, his eyes closed halfway, and he held a shielding hand to his forehead, I pulled the curtains shut and he said, there are shutters, too. And I was silent, while at the same time being seized by a great surge, and although I had recorded everything just the way things are recorded in a REGISTRY, nothing but chaos ensued, even the room in swirling and rotating disarray, actually DISINTEGRATION, nothing left but smoke, *whatever could be puffed.* So, although I had prepared everything, shoe tree, newspaper pages and doormat, so that the newspaper, the pages of newspaper could be stuffed into his toe, I mean stuffed into the leather etuis enclosing his toe, into the toe of his shoe that is, the toe of his leather shoe, which, as Joseph remarked almost disinterestedly, soaked up water like a sponge, and I was astonished that this was the simile he used, I became aware of the *entirety* of my failure only once Joseph had left, after he had slipped into his still damp shoes and waved back at me as he was running down the steps, there was no way I could make up for my failure, I say to Blum, Joseph would rush to the train in his wet shoes angry with me because of inattentiveness, my negligence, I say.

A wild and desolate phenomenon or panorama, I say to Blum, rolling everything up again from the beginning, rolling it up again, doing it all over again, I say to Blum, who had, while I was reporting all this to him, as it seemed, developed the hint of a beard, I mean this extensive contact with feelings and words had given him, as I see it, something like the hint of a beard, no : that isn't really the right word, hint is not the right word, it is something much more comprehensive enclosing the entire face in a BEARD WEB and stretching out over his cheeks and chin and around his lips, I mean it had grown into a shooting and sprouting out, presumably my remarks had gone on for hours, you see, I can't explain it any other way, and BEARD GROWTH had actually taken place, THORN STYLE, your THORN STYLE, I say to Blum, how is something like this to be understood, feet wrapped in white bandages, I say to Blum, the loafers. Wild and desolate phenomenon or panorama, I say to Blum, imagine that, you have been corresponding with someone for years without ever having met this person—over all these years you try to *imagine* a shape a character for this person, the way I did in the case of Helen Stark-Towlson, then 1 day she is standing right before your eyes, you are astonished, irritated, your *capacities* had endowed her quite differently, tall, slender, perhaps even somewhat plain, fastidious, careful, very friendly (kind). She is short, sturdy, an ever-present smile on her face, is urbane, perhaps somewhat too smooth : having just barely escaped the guillotine of history, that's how I read her face, her eyes. While I am writing these lines, I say to Blum, my left hand my left arm is getting tired. An afghan spread over my knees and thighs, love of pain or edifying texts, everything with "philo," when I was a child I was a philhumenist, which means that I collected empty matchboxes and saved clippings of my parents' fingernails and toenails, but back to Helen Stark-Towlson, I accepted her appearance, and after some time a letter comes from her and now a kind of misdirection takes place : as I am reading her letter I try to see her the way she actually looked when we met, but the image I stored in my memory does not return, what comes back to me is *the previously imagined the invented figure,* before we had met, only gradually, after many hours, as if approaching it from a great distance, does the image of how she actually appeared resurface, making me tremble, how could this have happened, what had I let myself in for, had my actual encounter with her simply passed me by leaving no impression at all, had I really registered everything so superficially, had nothing sunk in, no word, no real acquisition of any sort? nothing but this constant respectful unchanging smile on her round well-formed face and *necktie hair,* I mean swept back like a necktie or swept away her NATURAL WAVE, you could shake it and it would fall right back into place her NATURAL WAVE, Tristano, I say to Blum, *Picasso's childlike world of the senses,* occurs to me, the reproduction, and I *blindly* : swept it backwards under the shelf where I keep important pictures and photographs, *a pool,* is the technical term, by return mail, I say, alchemy by return mail or something like that, I no longer write to Joseph because my silently being with him holds us together more closely than ever before, I say to Blum, have a paper banner with SPLOTCHES (red / black) on this millimeter paper, which because of its graph lines no longer looks white but somewhat greenish instead, attached it to the tiny plastic basket, I mean the insignias on this flag I mean a *dead certain little sheet,* do you understand, and I can see another one very similar, when born, when crashed, I ask myself : rosette (red ballpoint pen), and next to it an illegible note in every color there is, I say, where I am so monosyllabic when it comes to using colors, right, I can feel them *coursing down* my back! these colors! and *rattling* too like an agglomeration of metal tools, and every movement I make it clanks and jingles and *slogs away,* I mean my spinal diaspora reacts to every tiniest impulse, etc. So much impetus early in the morning, I leap out of bed, first to the machine on trembling knees, fired away, breakfasted, typed, everything in the early morning hours, at 4 drawing first breath, which inflates my lungs to such a degree that I see them opening up before me, puffing up, like a balloon, yes and what are your lungs telling you, Joseph says, he is in a good mood, or what other branches of the organism are taking part in your EXERTIONS (writing!), or the way you tuck a sleeping child in after it has *thrashed around* and kicked off its blanket, feet nervous and cold, little face crossed out, I mean what do we really know about the convulsions inside our heads, the ACCOMPANYING PROCESSION of our lunatic feelings, right, I say to Joseph, I have been doing sketches of some special hearts but they disappear whenever I try to recall them, I am following in your footsteps, I say to Joseph, although what you have been drawing for me is an incredibly wild and overgrown *territorium,* I am making progress, but it is only a pseudoglorification, you have nothing to fear, and the mimosas in the next room have already rolled themselves up into tiny balls, I say, which indicates that they are preparing to enter a state of having to wither and wilt, I say. Is it possible that you might be allergic to flowers, I say to Joseph, he opens the PENITENTIAL MIRROR, his right leg drawn under his left and asks for his part WAS I REALLY THE ONLY ONE YOU SAW?, can that be? I answer, yes you are the only person I saw among all the many people there I saw only you, I mean I only had eyes for you, his question is like poison, a bright red heart in sandalwood fragrance, I am infected, it is an intimacy : his question is the most profound (sweetest) intimacy, it is more intimate than the look in his eyes and his kisses, his question transports me into a state of ecstasy into the vehemence of my reawakening senses, I mean the way I am sitting here in my retreat, I am being devoured by my own metaphors, I say to Joseph, actually *brought down,* I must constantly open up new pathways in my language, you see, or I have become an *incense eater an incense swallower* I mean I am being taken in by visions of Saint Catherine, Saint Anne, Saint Cecelia, Saint Aquilea.

Completely lucid bouquet in my study at 4 o'clock in the morning, entire bunches bundles of light, entire light grapes, feeder lights, permanence lights, pneumatic lights, while outside in front of my windows *leisurely flaking,* etc. *incense choirs,* I say, whole quarter puffing away, for my birthday, I say to Joseph, I would like when asked my name not always (still) to being coming across so many uninitiated for whom I must spell it out MARTHA ADAM YPSILON RICHARD ÖSTERREICH CÄSAR KARL EMIL RICHARD. X (or William or Ferdinand) calls me SWEET YOUTH, which I like, I say to Blum, the map, as brightly colored rag rug, included with the mailings from the Nobel bar : the dappled RAYON, as portrait, not to be missed, I say to X (or William or Ferdinand), on a scrap of paper the black wing of a bird at great heights : an eagle, I say, means time to book my flight, *completely overgrazed,* on another sheet of paper the words SMALL PANTS, don't know what that means, layer upon layer, of my consciousness, everything dust-covered, yellowed, but this morning : worked like mad, worked furiously, I say to Blum, which might be 1 edge of PARADIGM which itself might be 1 edge of PARASOL, etc., shield and screen or small hat, Joseph writes to me that GIORDANO BRUNO HAS TREMBLED RIGHT THROUGH THE 20TH CENTURY, Elisabeth von Samsonow sends me a photographed grave plate at a memorial site, with an engraving, in Antiqua (in large format) : *Maria once stood here.* And this is how the circle closes, I say, I mean the way I am sitting here in my retreat, my machine feels warm, for a moment my study is filled with the fragrance of evergreen and mimosa, a young girl, *made fit,* with rucksack, brass watering can dangling off to one side, portable radio (POWER MACHINE) and a folding chair, stumbling along in front of me, possibly treasures from the flea market, this glowing brain, I say, this THOUGHT CYCLE (Hölderlin), as if falling under a spell, I say to Blum, like Saint Vitus' dance, and you really are *a clown,* you throw yourself down on the ground gesturing wildly and making everyone feel like crying and laughing.

2/12

an essay in art appreciation, I will now undress this Picasso boy and it will make me cry, and my tears are a honeycomb, I say to Blum, do you understand what I am saying, I am undressing the Picasso boy with the red tasseled shoes, and it is an art form a honeycomb, I say to Blum, do you follow me, a honeycomb art, it is metamorphosis per se, I say to Blum, it is these fiery red slippers these woolen, I mean I cannot write down anything other than PUDGY, slippers, it is these plump woolen (pudgy) house slippers, you can feel their warmth, he is keeping them between the stalks of the table, the pianino, the altar of this house, his left fist is performing a transplantation, I mean a cubed planting, up the left arm, no : nudging its way up the left arm, the art of the metaphor on his left sleeve blue / gray / blackish pattern, unfathomable, the right hand is drawing, diving, who knows where to, flap on top, flap below, the knee pants, the steeply sloping knees, tiny chair with arms, knees *kneading* the steles of the table or piano or desk, I don't know, the face is *distressed,* distraught I mean withdrawn, the latch at the neck, the closed envelope on his chest, the polonaise of the Polaroid mystery, I am already beginning to have problems with the alphabetical organization in the dictionary of foreign words, I say to Blum, I am peeling the clothes off this boy he has *a combed head,* I say, a head that has just been combed with a wet comb, in his left ear a jewel, a clip, the petulant fold of his eye, the sweet sullen mouth, the hatpin between his thighs, how did it get there, a catalog of pain, I say, mouth, lips, thighs, lap, I am undressing the boy, I am removing the hatpin between his thighs, I know he's resisting, the thinning smock I am pulling the smock off his body, his lower torso is completely naked, only the red slippers are left, the pattern of blue / gray / black / cubes on his shirt, with breast

pocket, portfolio, or letter envelope, the cubist letters on his face, this boy in the small armchair, I am peeling his clothes off, I am now undressing his upper body too while inside the red woolen balls (turbulently) his feet are scrunching up tightly and pushing, as if they were operating both of the PEDALS under the table or the pianino, what do I know, it is a miracle, I say, an ingenious miracle not a one of us can explain, I mean this white Picasso boy is now completely unclothed, his *shoot* hanging limply between his legs, calves wedged in between the hermaphroditic legs of the pianino, the red felt shoes on the pedals, I hear music making its way into his ears, I hear it droning and rumbling, the pencil in his right hand on the dotted paper, I mean the nakedness of his bent knee is a scandal, and a sacrament too, I don't know if you understand what I am saying, I am down on my knees, I am moving my lips to his sex, he is closing his eyes, he surrenders himself, his closeness arouses me, maybe a pair of steel-rimmed glasses on the TRIM AROUND THE ROOM, the room has trim around the top very high like an old wardrobe, I say, musically American, there are two holes in his ears, a brownish strand of hair spilling down over his left ear, and now I am also undressing his feet, I am sliding the slippers off his small feet I am perspiring I am taking his shoot between my index finger and thumb I am sitting at his shoot, it is gushing, I see brownish shadows on the sheet of paper, iron pajamas, the boy says, a secret code Joseph says, a small field a field. Everything completely masturbated, I masturbated him, everything spilling out, I say to Blum, skin damp, feet standing in wetness, I compared Innerhofer's towels, which were as stiff as a board and *stank,* with the selection of towels I had on offer when guests came, I mean I compared them with the condition of my own fountains of clothing—

and then let myself be buried and then let myself be buried with the beautiful boy, the elastic stocking engraving my calfs, small crocheted patterns, I say to Blum, it is a heresy, when Joseph came I gave him the cleanest towel I had, when Joseph came to stay, I set out two clean towels for him, sometimes, as soon as he washed his hands I handed him a towel to wipe them dry, *I sacrificed a compress to him,* or the time X (or William or Ferdinand) the way he was walking out of the bathroom toward me dressed only in Christus linen, etc. it was a Mass cloth, no not book, but CLOTH, a work cloth a prayer linen, no not bed linen : prayer linen, there was something sacred about it, I mean the way I offering Joseph a clean towel, there was an aspect of a sacred segment secret sacrament, I say to Blum, I was his minister his ministrant, which means servant, oh the anachronistic (sweat out) stage props of my mind, I say to Blum, if I take a closer look at it, I say, *half dog half feeblemindedness,* I say to Joseph, this strange capacity I have for memorizing (MEMOIRS) telephone numbers, e.g., signs of a certain sort of infantilism (of the whole being), etc. *And isn't he a well turned out little boy,* and I ask myself in what sense do we mean well turned out, anachronistic props, I say to Blum, like HAIRPIN, e.g., never used one, never had anything like a braid, make up, made up : hairy PURSUITS, etc., in my childhood, FOX TALKING NEWSREELS, do you remember, I say to Blum, when you walked into the theater it was already dark, all you saw were these words flickering on the screen, FOX TALKING NEWSREELS, and a twinkling tune passed the aural organs, FOX TALKING NEWSREELS and I reached for my mother's hand, the poodle hair, the talking picture, all these frivolities perversities, we asked the neighbors for SALT : "Mother sent us to borrow some SALT," we were 2 young girls, barely 5 or 6 years old, she, the older one, Lore, with her embroidered collar, white smock, pleated skirt, but she was bad, I didn't know it, she practiced her powers of seduction on me, I succumbed to her lying ways, she drew ever tightening circles around my soul, we posed for a picture in a wicker chair, squeezed tightly together, my father took the photograph, she was a beauty, later I lost sight of her, I was naive, of a bewildered nature, I had black hair (brunetteness) I learned to lie. Cracked my right ankle, sandals on my feet, torn dresses (kiosks) in my fractured fantasy, blindly living through childhood, *robes of the jackal, eagle in my ASSIGNMENT BOOK,* maxims of geography, my mother's talent for drawing earned me good grades, with my tongue I licked the brightly colored plumage on the paper, sensed the resistance of the eagle's feathered wing, my own soul's longing for immortality as yet undiscovered, during the summer in the village I jumped into the open sewage ditch, sole of my foot cut open, splinters of glass not visible to the naked eye, I say to Blum, to pick them out, cut them out, pull them out is an excruciating procedure, or washing them out, I say, which means you must SOAK the sole of your foot for hours, for days in a water bath until the splinter until the splinters come free, and then suddenly the fir tree is standing *upside down* in the bucket or the KEYBOARD being pulled down off, etc., but as far as LANDSCAPE-like aspects are concerned, I say to Blum, wasn't it also a matter of . .

while I am writing this sentence down, the idea breaks off, I mean while I was writing down the first part of this sentence, I lost the connecting link of the image (*the imitated*), it had been standing right in front of my inner eye, I had seen it in all its individual parts, but in the matter of a 10th of a second it had dissolved into NOTHING, I ask myself where it could possibly have gone now that I have lost every trace of it, where had it fled, leaving me unable to proceed any further in any direction any that had seemed so promising, will have to involve myself in other onrushing images, Joseph says, here in Nathalie Sarraute's newest book there are a lot of points between the lines, in Nathalie Sarraute's case there are 3 points, while in your work there are only 2, I say to Blum, maybe it was the lopped-off image of the irises in the front garden of the cottage that had appeared and then disappeared from view, the sight of the irises that is on a stretch of grass in front of the museum, Blum appears to want to interrupt me, the sight of the irises in front of the museum, I continue with my expository remarks without allowing Blum a single word, I mean that we circled around / the mighty old oak which I had in my PRESERVATION : in the beams in the strands in the underbrush and thorny limbs *of a spring's onslaught,* etc.

Parasite angel : perspiration angel I believe, I say to Blum, which transforms the entire housing into a field : small field of mimosas I mean *just more yellow than fragrance,* and a RIOT IS IN FRAGRANT COLOR, I say, and deafening arrangements, etc. a dedication, an orgy broken loose, I say, mimosa orgy or dedication, and I had to open the altar window I mean the cross of the altar window, a phantom of course, an aesthetic force of will.

Joseph, I say to Blum, is something like a *virginal man,* he is so chaste that you might say he's a prude. That only makes him all the more attractive for me, you see, I say to Blum, what a breathtaking sensation it must be, I say to Blum, to be loved by such a prudish man . .

2/16

on my mother's team

quiet in the afternoons of a MAY and goldfinch. It was not clematis (= apron strings)—but what flower was it then, I ask my mother, blue violet petals tiny but nonetheless arresting bowing to even the gentlest breeze, then being buffeted off into tall lancet green, scattered to the wind, fragrant and tumbling earthward onto the ground at the iron gate, where SHE was standing, the owner of the house, frail. And attaching herself to the cast-iron gate, letting pass her by : stroll by the deities of tennis balls and sidewalk, retirees of the landscape, who had just coursed through half-uprooted stands of birchwood forest : scrub of birchwood forest, from time to time grabbing hold of trunks lopped off to half height, etc., perhaps to catch their breath, the way my father used to do when he stopped at the display window of an expensive shop, as if he had been especially attracted to something there, where unnoticed by passersby he could rest, when like a warning bell the beat of his heart began to disconcert him I mean. He walked (gave evidence of full stride) along the main street, straight and flat, first the clearing halfway, then the old housekeeper at the iron gate, and the sundial on the front side of an old foursquare, behind it a *miscalculated* ruin of grime, a rundown chicken yard, that is, where the creatures scratched around in the rubbish, and the old building out of which *wound,* as if it were about to be delivered : just having been delivered out of a bloody uterus, under development a new structure with raw brick walls, as far as the forested area which rose like a stairway, on whose lowest stair there was an unfinished wooden bench, a FOREST SANCTUARY as it were, which as soon as you approached in your exhaustion was always occupied by ranks of *leisure makers* tightly squeezed up against one another, or you sensed it at least a few hundred meters in advance, even before the bend in the

road opened up an unobstructed view, the appearance once again of a fully occupied bench, thus no foot station, no seating or platform support, no expectation of any sort of refuge delights, which put us in the position of having to decide whether to settle down into the terrain of an uneven damp moss-covered embankment BEHIND THE BENCH, or to set out on our retreat, setting down 1 foot after the other, more dragging and shuffling than striding, completely spent, apathetic, weak from hunger, and on top of all that an impudent sun now sintering down the regions of my back. Silence and white paper, my mother always at my side, and our reciprocal question, what would we do if our bench were in fact occupied, whether we should immediately turn around and head home or simply drop down into the damp moss behind it, which would induce a rather awkward sensation in us, I mean, sitting at the back of these 5 or 6 people : LIKE A COMMANDO UNIT! A PAIR OF SPIES!, we shout to each other in unison, in just the same concealed stooped camouflaged position, us at the back of these beings at rest, who from time to time turned around and looked our way, seeming to feel themselves OBSERVED, EAVESDROPPED UPON, THREATENED, you see, and now and then one or the other of them stood up and offered his place with an ostensibly courteous gesture, while actually wanting to escape because he could no longer stand being observed from behind, or to be more precise : the feeling he was being observed from behind. From here, in the *unruly* underbrush, assuming you had sufficient energies, you might easily scale the wooded summit, rising directly behind the bench, it rose like a stairway, and over the course of a few short minutes you arrive at a clearing, immersed in the whitish greenish shimmer of beech leaves breathing, beholding the heavens beyond, filled with a sense of well-being and good cheer.
I was lying on a branch : the skeleton of a beechnut which was cutting into my flesh, listening to a roaring forest storm raging relentlessly over this rise and drawing my gaze up into cloud formations racing past at great speed, and at the sight of this deep-blue sky and the clouds flying past I knew these were unmistakable signs of storm-filled days and swept blue skies and sun flashes (fatalities) to come. In cold mornings the stinging flame of the sun, in my rucksack I mean, made it bulge or swell like a malignant tumor, *stoutly flaming,* sun in my rucksack, which as soon as I swung it onto my shoulders endeavored to pull me down to the bottom of the earth. *In the shirt of a MAY,* I say to my mother, the prickly collar, TURNED OVER the damp earth with a spade, charming grave, the way it once was in the expansive garden next to the foursquare, delightful strip of land. The

complete opposite of NATURE here, I say to my mother, such a desolate phantom! furious storm movements in the bare stripped POLES of trees at the edge of the forest, and harbingers of an evil to come, of a collapse, of a RAINFALL, which lasted for days.

And into my boot, the open left boot under a small table, then into the JAWS OF A SHOE, tossed the crumpled wads of paper which bore the trembling annotation *finished* or abbreviated : *fin,* which led to the a chain of association : fins, fini, finland, fintail, finger, fingering, while the composite flowers of the evening climb into the rosy flesh of the village sky like antennas of smoke, *then the infinite reading matter / much-loved reading matter swelled* me up head bloatingly, at which point a small garçon appeared before us, it (no, not he : it!) : tiny shorthand symbol : little mouth, tiny aperçu, tiny tongue, codicil, appendix, twisted point of a beard, mustache, ringed viper : grass snake unjustly hunted down trampled slaughtered BY THE BOYS!, you see, after it had directed 1 last flicker of its tongue our way a gesture of tender self-defense, etc.

It was this small garçon we were concerned with, as I was walking along with my mother, searching : searching all through the countryside, it was this small garçon we were concerned with, led on by, or as we were led onto the asphalt street, mother always at my side, most of the time we were silent or *exchanged a few tiresome walnuts,* fragments of sentences, because we had long ago lost all our energies, and so we wandered along on the edge of the street past swampy meadows, overgrown with reeds, and the constantly recurring realization that it would be unwise to settle on such unstable ground, *blubbering Christmas.*

2/17–2/19

there are dream images that can define an entire life

—C.K.

Ship or script gardens, I say, or as Socrates says, a decent soul. Found paper clip / crack / sewing thread / strand of hair sticking to a water glass, presumably trace of CANDIED WRITER, I mean PEN, etc., like the size of the balloon sailing over my heads (: yes, heads : plural), pretending to be a cloud.

This writing ruination, I say to Blum, this crumpled-up poppy in a mug with no handle, these household utensils *locked out of* use, household tools, only because they're dusty, having gone unused for years, and my own arm not fluent enough to wipe the dust off them, right, and so they have been assured a neither-here-nor-there existence, they stand papering around, get shoved this way and that, are put away, are heartened simply because they have gathered dust, white paper banners in a winter tub, say, my feet in a winter tub, and on top of it all this writing despair, I say to Blum, a word usage which stigmatizes me, etc., this REALM BETWEEN LIGHT AND SHADOW, hermetic realm, tiger gradients, tiger attacks, green migraines, *and plunging the small spoon into winter bag brim full,* which in translation might read : small spoon fell from the counter into the open garbage bag, right, this writing ruination or desperation making you fear the ring of the telephone, because then a word in the process of welling up, thoughts welling up get lost because voice on the other end cuts and snows and fiddles around mills around and drenches and stares, right, and what really matters is collecting, I mean collecting the rainwater, the semen, the tears, the thoughts, the words; the way rainwater was once collected in small village gardens in gutters, storm rains, precious water, in tubs, for a bath in the evening etc., or to water the flowers. On the surface water bugs, petals of *storm blossoms* swimming on the surface of the water, strewn across the

surface of the water in the tub and looking like a garland, a heart bouquet, etc., or willow branches in city streets, end of winter, roofs bare of snow vis-à-vis, but meanwhile I am able to *whisper* my person and my prose into this THOMKINS segment, I write to Joseph, dear Joseph, I write to Joseph, this word EXORBITANT, e.g., that you used in your latest letter, is swimming toward me like a buoy on the sea, I mean it *appears* to be swimming toward me, it's really only rocking back and forth, which to a certain extent I find unsettling, because, I write to Joseph, how can a word mimic (assume) the form of a BUOY, I write to Joseph, not only its form, no, but its nature and forbearance too : stage prop chugging along here and away and choking with emotion, but don't forget, the site of conception and the moment of conception for a writing product can be of an absolutely arbitrary nature, entirely out of proportion to the result, right, 2 times stone or star in the room, I write to Joseph, sometimes when we talk to each other on the telephone and I call : I am just reading your letter!, and you call : I just got your letter, it is as if our speaking to one another on the telephone has *precluded* the possibility of a written response, I mean a deep-rooted *rapport pleasure,* an addiction, actually, etc., a need for rapport, to write to one another, repeat things already said, recurring patterns on wallpaper, rug and stacks, constantly recurring motif on paper, fabric, skin, places.
As a child I confuse stones with stars, I pour water into myself. I say, this bubbling no *swarming* stacks (see all meanings of this word!) have completely cut me off from any sort of practical responsiveness, from any sort of practical understanding of life, *baci* was the word at the end of your most recent letter, which came from Italy, I write to Joseph, *baci,* dear Joseph, I write to Joseph, how is it that depending on the time of day I either love you or do not love you, long for you to be near : am happy to be at a distance, etc., our moods, pitch, replies are so changeable, our states of mind, communication, agreements. ("And I will write to you again tomorrow . ." etc.), 5 sesame seeds on the inside of my hand 5 sesame seeds are sticking to my hand, a breath of Swiss pine replaced the fragrance of mimosa, arrogant this thought complex, witch complex of an *oral insatiability,* of an ingestion, I say to Blum, a sexual insatiability, tiptoeing up to the machine this way early in the morning like secret love play, a kind of insatiability, too, the way I incorporate you, Joseph, the book, language, the world, things and animals, right, an oral savagery, I am always wanting to get something between my lips, between my teeth, my tongue always wanting to feast itself on something, my desires reside in my throat . . there is a whole bundle ("bunch"—no : delete : too orphic here!) of LILY NOTES

held together with a plastic clamp, I say, may all be rather off-color stuff, I say to Blum, that part about sitting over the rear axle of the bus, rocking back and forth in the upholstered seats on an extended train trip : all of it glorification (trophies?) of carnal pleasures, etc.,—here is where the letter breaks off, I say to Blum, the short-leggedness the invalid leg the balloon / like a sandbag / on the doorframe of the room : bulging with pill supplies, I mean a small blue pill somersaults, 1 blue wheel, rolls off the edge of the table, falls onto the carpet, oh, I say to Blum, there is this TABLET PERSPECTIVE of mine, the empty silver foil sheets, ruptured foil sheets (folios) on the floor in the morning, empty eye sockets, right, and GROWING WOODEN over time, the days of this life dwindling, crumbs of time everywhere, time no longer bundled into hours, days, weeks, months, years parceled (in hindsight) but all that is left bundled pieces : BACK THEN and BACK THEN and BACK THEN, and THE DONAU AGAIN AND THE DONAU AGAIN AND THE DONAU AGAIN THE DONAU, and now, such chunks, monoliths, no longer to be differentiated, no longer anything specific, measurable, impressions only. And we too, from one hour to the other we are completely different people, no longer understand ourselves, throw out what we've written, charge ourselves with some sort of fickleness some sort of make-work, etc., go out with a shoulder bag and shop and a frosty relationship with the world, with people. And that is why you must not praise (hold in high regard, laud) what I have written all too highly, I say to Joseph, otherwise I will be afraid that compared to what I have most recently written, I will be unable to do justice to what I have yet to write, etc., it would be better if you tempered your remarks, I say to Joseph, although I yearn for even a single word from you : *an analysis, slapping* (onomatopoeic for the sound of two nonviscous masses hitting up against one another), straightening out my writerliness—*figures* : because just as heads can stand for head, so can figures for figure : sketch : rough draft : scribbles! or what do you think, I say to Joseph, what do you think, all of this is really nothing more than some PROVINCIAL ARGOT spilling out over its edges : this writerliness of mine, isn't that right, can't be classified! into meadowland (Mahagoni), I remember meadow vistas like that : meadow splendor in soft and humid summers when like green like seed like sap the wafting, wafting away I mean glittering MEADOW SPACES in the air gusting back and forth, a breath of wind, a wind harp, an exchange, that is, between heaven and earth, between heaven breathed—enraptured green such celebrations of earth, expanses of billowing Pentecostal meridians, and the way feet immersing, immersing into : dew covered early in the morning, and late in the day returning in *deeply rutted* wagon tracks (coach and horses), and with sand and dust on hands and feet, and the way my mother crossed the small forest (which she called the PRATER!), and strode off and bent over here and there to mushroom and berry, flame and beech tree, salamander face and solar reflex, pale yellow under the glow of a cloud her flowery evergreen eye, full of HELIOS, I say, and being a HELIOS herself, etc., there in her countrified dress, deep in thought, or even cheerful now and then, content, looking down at the ground while walking, in some sort of lingering way lingering in the blessings of memory or someplace like that, and she rarely spoke about these things. And it never occurred to me to think about it, unless, in a small leather bag on my back, pulling it up and out of the small leather bag, etc., you know what I mean.

2/21

from head to toe washed and dreamt

strangely enough, I say to Blum, I sling *my morning motto* I mean my morning pills down my maw, my maw snaps at them the way a dog snaps at things falling off the table, *the sinewy things,* I say, shot right into my oral cavity, under my tongue, into my left cheek making it inflate : inflate like a balloon, ridiculous, I say, if I happen to be looking into the mirror, truly ridiculous, *absurd,* I say, and dial everything back 100 years or more. I sling my pill feed into my oral cavity precisely under the tongue : intimate locale or opening, because I keep my mouth open or wine, wining mouth, but today we feel more like playing around, I say to Blum, I call Blum on the phone and say, it's a long time since we've been as happy as we are today, but I don't know why I am so happy, it's a high-spirited happiness, a kind of happiness I seldom experience, I say, and I sling my pills down, pour them into me, I say, have a friend who takes 9 pills at once that she is supposed to be taking over the course of the day, pours them into herself and washes them down with red wine, may be an addiction, am addicted to buying books, left ankle slightly *sprained,* I say to Blum, do you remember, I say to Blum, my father always said DID YOU SPRAIN YOUR ANKLE? or BROUGHT YOU SOME RABBIT BREAD FROM SCHOOL, etc., oh dear god, I call to Blum, I call Blum on the phone, what a wonderful day, oh dear god, I say to Blum, I am the image of my father, dear god, of my mother, that is not a trivial accounting NOT AT ALL or NOTHING I am providing here, but most of all I must say I resemble my grandmother on my mother's side of the family and that I feel her presence in me as if I were carrying her around with me, in my body, my limbs, as if I were peering out at the world through her eyes, which were very blue, into a sky which was blue as well, in order to find something that I would not otherwise be

able to find anywhere, that's the way she always seemed to me, she seemed like a figure who was always looking up into the sky, and back then I couldn't imagine what she was looking for, in broad daylight, she couldn't have been on the lookout for constellations, etc., now she would be at least 100 years old or older, but she died when she was 47, so I have already survived her, I already have the guarantee of surviving her . .
such a *worm-eaten style,* I say to Blum, permanently on the brink of madness, MOZART FOR 4 HANDS, Blum says, MOZART FOR 4 HANDS, I interrupt him, no, I say, REQUIEM, the only thing that will make an impression on me, Blum says, nose snaps and cracks and rattles and crashes down on the floor, I mean, Blum says, something just fell on the floor and looks up at the metal brace on the easy chair, and look there the *black wooden skis* from my childhood, imagine that, Blum says, talks to me on the phone, several hours in the morning, *black wooden skis from chess set,* Blum says, in the middle of the armchair under the armchair, *while the spoon in the chair,* in the column, I interrupt him, worm-eaten days, language bag *language turkey,* now we have to get ready to go to the Language Turkey or to Bozen / Bonn . .
and that's just the beginning : this GAGGLE GOSSIP of playing things down, dunes, dunces : bare back of Picasso boy (*Paul Drawing,* 1923), the way he cuts off the sock at the bottom, the sock quotient, so that only the heel, even though full of holes, is covered, but not the front of the foot or the toe feed, it is just this delicate : digital toe plexus of a boy brilliant in its substance, coherence, beauty, while the rustling : like silk rustling artificial stuff : dirty laundry in a bag in a corner of the entryway and the repetitions in my head grow into : "My Dear Butlers Ladies and Gentlemen Butlers,"—how do I accommodate the English plural-s without detracting from the originality, better : the rhythm of the originality in this form of address, I ask my reader, no I won't ask him, this is old hat, I will certainly not ask my reader, this is passé, I will ask Blum and Joseph or some other character in my book, I shout "My Dear Butlers Ladies and Gentlemen Butlers," everything comes to an end with my NEARLY A NEIGHBOR (2 floors down), lively 80-year-old, as ravaging of the subject matter, you see, or as my father used to say, SQUANDERING HEIGHTS, whenever I threw whole and hale (holy) left-overs into the garbage bucket and which was meant to mark me as an artist of extravagance of effusiveness, etc., split lip, dog of decay, etc.
I write to Joseph : lots of implications / observations / connections lead to a center, but may also vehemently resist any attempt at classification, I have been sensing this for days, throughout my entire housing the pages of letters, scraps of paper, the jumbled flaking and tearing of my soul, I am unable to

steer this onto 1 specific track it's beginning to look a lot more like costuming, trickling from nose and mouth, dripping from the eye . . the perspective is missing from which a point of view, an overview might be established, your letter, I write to Joseph, with strangely wondrous Christmas stamp : Christ child half-naked (immediately associate Picasso boy), left shoulder and arm hidden behind dotted peacock brilliantly beautiful gloriole, surrounded by snow-covered Christmas tree milieu pilgrimage church (Mariazell?), child standing in charming pose on a green bolster : pedestal. Coming into possession of those days, dear Joseph, I write to Joseph, on which individual segments came into being, is a questionable enterprise, how can we possibly *come into possession* of a thing, a constellation of circumstances, a phase of our life, a person (doesn't even come into question!) : an expression of such obsessiveness, or an expression of seizing possession, such a monomaniacal concept!, the 2nd paragraph of your letter, I write to Joseph, puzzles me, it contains the expression IRREVOCABILITY, and not IRRETRIEVABILITY but IRREVOCABILITY—and I can't seem to get it out of my mind, still can't find a good answer, unless I respond with melancholy. You have a passionate craving for the images behind thought, you write, I ask myself, are there images in front of thought, I mean before thinking begins to take place : first a concentration of the brain then the pressing : expressing of the brain . . or does the INGENIUM, if we are to put it this way, reside somewhere else in the body? in the breast (heart?), in nerve endings, in the fingers, the feet, the forehead, *the body shell?* after all, we write with our skin, our hair, our eyes, our teeth, our sense of smell and taste, and our pupils too, our earlobes, the motion of our blood, vortices of water etc., see Giordano Bruno.

And then painted underpants, *oh thinking in motifs,* or the way bunched mistletoe looks in the bare crowns of elm trees the way a single veined leaf, landscape flowered over and entwined . . I graze the spaces in your soul the landscape of your soul, I say to Joseph, pastureland close to the water's edge, or put another way : the green, that is, landscapes of the soul : seascapes : landscapes of a soul's suffering here in this pasture a miracle of touch wonder, close to the water's edge, etc. I have no patience with infantilism though I am myself more *childlike* than almost anyone else I know of my age, the spheres of booklinesses darting around, I write to Joseph, the fox-trot shanks of an open scissors on my pillow, the urgency (ESSENTIAL) of a countermovement inside me, where on the floor and once and for all *Johann Paul Friedrich Richter* is covering a cut-out stamp portraying the Queen of England—haven't I been telling you : THERE ARE SOME THINGS THE TEXT DOES ON ITS OWN!

2/29

have vibrating addendum to most recent entry : the rolled-up (cleaning) apron, figuratively speaking in brightly colored paperlike stiffness, cleaning apron Christianity, or something like that, rolled up and stored on top of the refrigerator, etc., then a thought occurred to me, that I don't like to be THUNDEROUSLY showered with gifts : *constantly* showered with gifts from people who are not particularly close to me, it's embarrassing, you see, I say to Blum, some distance much wished for, please keep your distance, and still, I say to Joseph, once asked you an embarrassing question, which really should not have been embarrassing at all, if I had structured the question differently, but as it was, the whole thing came out rather distorted as it was being uttered by me, but maybe it was also a game of hide-and-seek, I mean maybe I was afraid to ask you a question like that and that's why its form changed of its own accord on the way from my head to my tongue, right, I mean this pitch into my mouth (out of my mouth) I mean from my head into my mouth onto my tongue, I believe it was the moment between utterance and swallowing actually I wanted to swallow my question in its inception, I wanted to leave it unuttered, but it forced its way out, literally forced its way out from between my teeth, was distorted, no longer had any shape, no longer any *similarity* with what I had intended to say . .
then I think up a music of walking for myself, a few *meadow celebrations* or *interments,* a procession with shoes abandoned, that is a procession in bare feet, I mean wilted promenade on my part, I say to Joseph, undulating procession on yours, and I am then no longer able to see you, because you have gotten so far ahead that I cannot catch up even with my eyes, I will simply lose sight of you, and then I would be left sitting in the wingbeat of this early spring early morning in a dirty old fur coat on the steps

of the cathedral, and plunk myself down there in my fur coat plush stuff chopping board and florestan, and twirling the small red bead between my fingers, red bead SIMILARITY I do not know what to do with in my mind, and along the ebbing course my foot treads while my eyes take me places my feet will not, where hilltops in the landscape would oppress me and you would call me by my name and I wouldn't be able to answer the way it happens in dreams where your voice fails you and your foot drags through mud and mire, simply a marching-in-place.

Always a lantern on the front of the train roaring into the station, a TONGUE OF FIRE, I say to Blum, there actually was a lantern on the front of the car, between the running board and the edge of the platform, too, which to me seemed something of an intimation of hell, enchanted vision, magical manifestation, and this was not the first time I had seen it, either, I say to Blum, it would have captivated you, too, or when I look at the cerebral fields of André Thomkins, *the milk in my head breasts stops flowing* : "5 to 7, announcing itself, wish to visit the ALPINE GARDEN again, after so many years, the garden with the unusual orangery flowers (organisms), herbal faces, flexible skin color of luxuriant roses in Alpine valleys and always rondeaux too, WILD WREATHS in vertical, hanging ovally from bee-covered trees, which *taste* better, you see, . ."—would like to go inside and around mazily and not have to think about what's outside ("THE BELVEDERE IN VIENNA") etc., *and the way I go down the church / down the church /* in my rash and reckless way actually unreflecting and soaring exhilaration in my ears, I say to Blum, experience most-exalted sparkler : this stomping exhilaration green, the way I find it in a picture by André Thomkins, and thereupon find myself *in naked stature* floating over steps and loge to an arched window, overpowering the soles of my shoes : abandoned long before, as were such things as standards counsel warnings, smoke a half pipe, trample some of my notes, alternate between retch cuisine and heraldry—formulation may be too crude, better to say spittoon cuisine, but getting back to impulsive and unreflective, the way I think of my mother's EXTREME CAUTIOUSNESS I mean the way she was extremely cautious *and* fearless at one and the same time, she plunged into the depths without knowing how to swim, while, on the other hand, giving wide berth to any puddle in her way, etc., when I turn the radio on in the morning, the RABBIT FOOD is already blaring my way, meaning : *always pizzicato,* but this morning around 5 I hear a nocturnal voice, somewhat sleepy and she gave the name of the composer of the piece to come, but my pen couldn't keep up, the voice of the announcer faint and weak, on and off wave, as if you were walking barefoot on the beach in warm sand as the first waves came in, lapping around the soles of your feet, enough to make you cry, isn't it, I say to Blum, and I did have all those letters spread out over my honey table, everywhere intending 1 word, a few sentences burning in my chest, I mean the burning had engraved itself onto the sheets of my response before I had even composed them, it seemed as if I had prepared, planned, a distinct and different burn mark for each letter writer, imprinted like a seal at the top of each piece of paper, this house with its outspread wings / side wings, I say to Blum, formerly the War Ministry, I say, what's walking the halls these days, I'd like to know, but back to the letters, then there is this something glittering in my pen in my pencil in my machine SPARKLING, must be captured, by the writer : by the recipient. And then the letter after that, from the recipient back to me, me back to the writer and back to me and again and over and over again so many times, and so it goes back and forth and is really only a game of affectation : mirror of affectation, decorated with a dramatic tear, etc., these chirping *quietly racing* intimations of an excitation of the senses and the mind, which are the prerequisite of a sparkling : perfected letter-writing style, and how it twinkles! An experience of the zephyrs, I say to Blum, I sit there like my father, holding the arm of the chair in my grip, gaze out into the blue of the window, just the way he did, sitting there now the man who has been moldering for 18 years, and out of the bag . . (FROM THE MEN'S JOHN)

sometimes I am accompanied by an ambulant feeling, a feeling always coming and going the way I do myself, always in motion the way I am myself, the mountains are alive and they lay themselves down and stretch their arms, they love unconstrained activity, they love inactivity, it is such a wonderful thing, up the mountain and through the clouds, the mists, I steer, I smoke mountain air, mother had tied a white cloth around her head in my dream : *wrapped,* which is a drastic way to be treating the skin of her joints and braids hanging down the side, she was holding bouquets of anemones in front of her beautiful face, sitting on the sidecar machine, bunches of green and white before the melting oval of her head, she was of shy nature and knowledge, her dark curls fell to her shoulders, I am reading a paragraph by Roland Barthes which REVEALS ME, I mean IT REVEALS ME TO MYSELF : it reveals a place in me that I had not known, and now it was illuminated for me, and I believe the experience made me smile, because it was so beautiful, but it disappeared immediately, dissolved, you see, by the next day there was nothing left of it that I could fathom, it was lost, covered, and just as it had previously been discovered it had now regressed back into an earlier state, it had of course assumed a shape, but it was a shape which did not endure, a water had flowed over it, leaving its outlines barely visible, I write to Reinhold Posch, what magical handwriting you have, as if you were constantly attempting to tell of the GNOME NOSE, or as if *an archaic swan* had taken wing, above the village pond in P., and was now stroking its gentle wing writing over me . . putting new life into my brain with ornamental fish, there's something fluttering around here!, I say to Blum, it's been a long time since I experienced anything SACRED, but yesterday, when I opened things up, a thing fluttered past the back of my neck, and I turned around, I was afraid : something, someone had come very close to me in a way I had never known before, maybe it was the touch of a shadow, as my mother used to say, she could not only hike over the mountains but also inside, she often hiked through the mountains, it was in preparation for heaven. She had cyan-blue eyes which in later years grew paler, but my writing has taken on a temper I could only have dreamt of even a few years ago, I say to Blum—oh, let's forget Joseph, even if it pains me to forget what I want to forget, what I should forget, etc., all around the entire literature of music on tiptoes, turning in circles, walking on tiptoes I'll be ruined if I stop and listen, such a roselike mezzo-soprano, such a trembling countertenor, such floating organs and piano pieces!, I feasted on certain phrasings, etc., or poetry as a fetish object, in the kitchen, out of the kitchen a burning smell, besieged by a salmon-skinned figure, flames and beech tree, *salamander face,* I write to Joseph, who has gone away somewhere : perching on the limb of a leafless tree, I cannot reach him, etc., I write to Joseph : *a stage kiss is a stage kiss* usually nothing behind it, I write to Joseph, *your kiss is a stage kiss nothing behind it* . . various aggregate conditions have me on tenterhooks!, I am writing to you on my knees, *these mostly glacier ideas* and have my ear to my dwelling place in the forest—in this glittering interplay of relationships, a fire has been fanned inside me and it is devastating, one exaltation after the other that is, but at the same time I am capable of walking right over it in crude wooden clogs and crushing everything, *the text flank to be precise,* on the road the fresh glittering tar, *and it smells like vinegar and shit.*

3/2

letters, wagtails speedster / razor

when we are dealing with compartmentalized / combed-over languages, I say to Joseph, at the same time trying to focus on the top row of his teeth, when we are dealing with languages embodied, I say to Joseph, these CLAIMS TO GRACE—you know who I mean, Breton, Derrida, Roland Barthes, the related relatives, Beckett, Jean Paul and the others, over whom our plain and bare-toed foot flies and floats, just what is it floating? it is floating something in, it is letting something flow in which is unavailable anywhere, I mean we cannot find these things anywhere else, or perhaps in BRUNO, Giordano, Filippo Lippi, Dalí, the enchanting boy at the desk, by Picasso, the new (young) the new (agile) the new postulates, the sacred images . . I was concentrating on your upper row of teeth, what a sweet abyss, but couldn't see, somehow the upper row of your teeth had disappeared I mean they had set, I mean in which profile? or we hardly even touched one another, and when you kissed my cheek, you aimed for my cheek the left one or the right one, unknowingly, no, *in passing* grazed my lips which seemed more humiliating than loving, etc., I consider what you said about SIMILARITY, but you have no similarity with anyone else, it is a state of confusion, dear Joseph, I say to Joseph, a soul shepherding soul sorrow soul supplying, when you look at me, when you are explaining something to me, and I take notice. Again the synesthetic wound : the synesthetic stigma, I take notice, I take notice of the sun, I mean I look to see if it is shining, what a peculiar expression THE SUN IS SHINING, I look I catch sight of the wind, take notice of the wind, but not in the usual way that we mean when we say : now I am listening to hear whether or not it is blowing, but instead : I look at the wind, looking and listening at the same time, the way I did that time we were in the subway station and you kissed me,

completely uninhibited, right in front of everyone, I was looking and listening, listening to you, which can be developed into two different meanings, but it was not a case of looking at the wind, I don't mean : I am now looking to see if a leaf is stirring, a twig is moving, no it is much more like *a tearing open of the breast,* yes, that's it, a painful tearing open of the breast A REAL SENSATION or something like that, it is no mystery : far from it, it is something entirely flesh and blood, it is an obsessive tearing open, losing blood bleeding to death, something like that while at the same time experiencing a sense of joy, sublime sense of joy that hardly any other can even approach, a whole sea away while the SEA HERRING : that sounds mortally inappropriate, doesn't it, I say to Joseph, but the SEA HERRING is related to the SEA SNAKE, and that, after all, is what we're concerned with here, right, *and I am breaking open,* and this in a sense other than I am bringing things to an end off in this direction or that, THINGS ARE BREAKING OPEN IN ME, everything in me has already broken open, my chest and my heart and the other organs too (soul) what do I know, I am breaking open and the storm and the wind and the sea are breaking in into my gaping chest and I can hear the way the wind and the storm are speaking, something seductive, of course, we are only interested in hearing seductive things, you and I, and we are playing an old game, although you aren't really playing, I mean you are more of an observer of this game, and while I begin to cry, I ask myself, what SIMILARITIES, what kind of SIMILARITY, which *mountains mountain sisters of similarity* you are talking about, what rage of similarity, which wavy-haired Picasso boy, about whose description in my text you will not express your thoughts, presumably you think it is an obscene piece, etc. I roam around in my bony scaffolding in my wretched mental scaffolding, and then a small spoon starts growing out of my bottle of MELATONIN, as if it had been forgotten there, and it is so small that you *must* believe you should gulp it down, etc.
Oh, I say to Joseph, maybe all of this is nothing but an illustration of the *stimulation music* I am incessantly playing, Placido Domingo, SONGBOOK, while the yellow wildflowers in his hand, I say to Blum, like Saint Benedict, or the *approaching* birds I mean : cars while they are braking, the chirping sounds, *and can't find an end and can't find an end and can't find an end . .*

everything screwed up and cursed and inhibited and yet what *alfalfa extracts* I mean our naked feet on the tiles on the wooden floor of the stone structure, and I am shivering and the rabid red bull and I am caught up in this rapture and hooked on this rapture, and have SMOKE in me, it comes smoking out of me, comes steaming out of me, I have the smoker and the discoloration and the stylistic means, and I am a defender of my stylistic means and feel HORRIFIED UNHINGED and am the speeding train that leaps the tracks and am smoking mountain air, am rage incarnate, and I take care of Joseph's clothes by hanging them up in the closet, and while I am hanging his jacket and coat in the closet I touch the seams of collar and the shoulder to my lips, SPECIFIC SPIRIT, I call, smile invitingly, and see myself in profile the way I am smiling at him, but I am only pretending to seduce him and I am both cheerful and sad, like having a permanent erection, I say to Blum, can you understand that, to the point of being disgusted with myself, oh Socratic stage setting . . *through a door slightly ajar my parents—*

in the MUSTACHE LIGHT, I say to Joseph, and find no end and find no end and find no end and would like to begin with you and end with you and stay with you and see in you and hear in you and out through your eyes and out through your tears, out through your ears, out through the tips of your fingers, out through the tips of your toes, and slipped into my shoes and my curls (shock of hair) I mean the rage and the futility and the plight my mind and my emotions are in regarding my environment, and then a bush blooms : a bosket from *navel wall,* no, not : fog wall : NAVEL WALL under the lamp by my bed, next to it Matisse decor and woolen clothing, but back to the bouquet sprouting out of the wallpaper, no, not Matisse wallpaper miracle but dark luxuriant bunched-up bundles of flowers panicles blue and gray that is and pushing their way out of silk collars without ever being visible to the hand holding the art object, etc., what has happened to all the grand themes, I ask myself, I say to Blum, earthshaking themes, a packet of pills falls to the floor, providing me with my answer, my life is lying in front of me on the floor, no matter how narrow-minded the perspective may be.

Agitated eyes, I say to Joseph, unstressed motion speaking, contemplation and exhaling, the silence of elation, an absoluteness of writing, sitting still, hermetic hysterical plagiarism (Roland Barthes?), I mean the fox-trot shanks : frog's legs of the scissors tossed aside and now on my bed pillow as tragic manifestation, etc., I am the scriptwriter who has returned, practice showing : taking back, revealing : covering up again, *until my head takes off and flies away* . . eyes on a kiosk turning inside out and dripping, bloody with tears, wild torrent of curls hanging from temple, terribly beautiful visage, Ukrainian mime.

3/8

the Tuesday group is approaching, don't find any more napkins, no more deflection shirts, no small marble tablets (which from a distance on Greek island might be taken for wet laundry hung out to dry), insect in my bed, I say to my mother, maybe I have just leapt over a few tree rings : rituals of uncontrolled rage, I mean since I have come so close to you, or happened upon you under circumstances not of my own making, I call you at home but no one answers, I call your sister, and she speaks like you, a voice full of caresses . . in the morning *am still a human being or a shirt,* but as the hours progress completely lost : a blur in front of my own eyes I mean the shape in front of me starts to blur in front of my own eyes, the Chinese chimes Hubert A. sent me : a blood-red greeting card and when you open it a wonderfully seductive sound unfurls, as if half-prone in a cradle the morning at my honey table utterly lost in a sensation of wavelike motion lulled and enveloped in inaudible (arrested) peals of laughter, I say to my mother, I have a fantasy of your sister from that shimmering rainbow-colored dress she wore that time in W., maybe Nadja, my mother says, I remember the silken powder the silken rubbish on her cheeks. After my reading in Bonn, someone asks me to write in one of my books : UNDERSTAND IF YOU CAN, and when I gave him a questioning look, he said, this statement was an expression of his *usual mood,* this sentence might also convey consolation and renewal, etc., also on the occasion of his approaching birthday JUST LIKE A PROCESSION he had need of reading this sentence over and over again, but I am not up to all of this crush anymore, I say to Blum, completely disoriented in the afternoon, keep hearing my mother's voice in my head more and more often, I say, then I *burn with enthusiasm* but only in the morning, I have an idea regarding the character of ECHO, my mother's garlands of myrtle pulled down over my forehead, back then, in that wedding portrait, in a flowing white crepe de chine dress, it made me think of a crown of thorns . . the term SIMILARITY can't get it out of my mind, I write to Joseph, today and tomorrow, preparations for trip to Bonn, etc., can't find yesterday's *flesh wound,* I know there was a *flesh wound* on my instep, maybe we should actually call it a *flesh wonder,* I can easily imagine how Noah must have been feeling : all around his tightly closed hut nothing to be seen but the white caps of waves, perhaps through 1 or 2 tiny hatches, and so he looks out through these hatches of his and all he sees is small and large caps of waves : just as he had imagined it, he did imagine all of it, because, presumably, he was not able to see much of anything, even when he felt he must look out of the hatches to see the enormous ALL AROUND, he must have been curious after all, and in the background the teeming mass of animals, 1 pair of each kind, and strangely enough, even here, the whole misery of propagation's machinery, right, I ask myself, what did he put over the hatches to keep all of the water out, fish skin, human skin, mouse fur, some sort of prehistoric substance we no longer can even imagine, I just cut my finger, into bloody pieces I mean, am eruptive in the morning, rocked by eruptions, left and right the carriage of my typewriter keeps crashing into stacks of books and writing paper, bright-red blood, and Marguerite Duras died today, I fall into fits of uncontrollable rage, sit naked at my machine, I drew a blue heart in the lower right-hand corner of a page of letter paper, quite sparing, as Georg Kierdorf-Traut asked of me, the small blue heart on an empty piece of letter paper, he would be as happy with that as with the small yellow corner of a wall in the painting *View of Delft* by Vermeer Marcel Proust was so happy with shortly before his death, Georg Kierdorf-Traut writes, the fragrance of the violet ink in his letter would, he hopes, last all the way to Vienna, and traces at least would reach me, etc., *for example for a letterhead,* I say to Blum, have been a juggler all my life, Georg Kierdorf-Traut writes, that is a rubbing of your heart, I write to Georg Kierdorf-Traut, because I mislaid lost the beautiful little white cards, yes they really have disappeared, I drew the blue heart with a colored pencil, on my honey table, which already has grooves and furrows, as do I, I write to Georg Kierdorf-Traut, so now you not only have a blue heart from me but also an *effigy,* and the writing frenzy on top of all this, I say to Blum, tomorrow Bonn, and this is how the day glistens, I kiss death, the fact of death is an injustice an outrage a scandal, it is not, presumably, just a STATE OF SUSPENSION IN NATURE, etc., I saw *Signer's Suitcase,* by Peter Liechti, saw it with Blum, and I believe he put his arm around my shoulders in the movie theater, and caressed my left cheek, I believe that's how it was, that's how it must have been. *Ham-fisted, that's the way I am every evening so tired,* as if I were already dead, I write to Joseph, saw the (lilac) film *Signer's Suitcase,* we will probably all mourn ourselves when we die, or what do you think, but not even you are clever enough to tell what that's going to be like, full of rage and untamed I am, when faced with the inevitability of my own death, would like to write something *purple-colored* like that, I say to Blum, now these orange-colored days have begun, I don't know if I should welcome them or not, maybe a little curious about them, I say to Blum, I liked the long winter it did me good, etc., in this thundering air, etc., I mean in the evening I feel as if I've got a built-in restraining mechanism, it collects in all of my limbs and starts moving very slowly slow-motion slowly, while my head is proceeding in a countermovement, my head is agile, my body lying down, my head with its endeavors, passions, which can take on almost any form and color, while leaning on these persons, figures, ideas, images, already miles away, right, and I, with a ravenous hunger for the phenomena taking place in this head of mine turn and look back at me lying there, with wilted body, longing to be ignited by my head, but my head just leaves it : my body lying where it is, my head has nothing to do with my body, doesn't want to have anything to do with it anymore, with this body of mine lying resting on the bed, it, my body can't keep up anymore, it my body is too tired, it observes my head the urgency with which it is pursuing its thoughts its revelations, and it envies my head all of its leaping fluttering magic accomplishing desires, ornamentations and fantasies, etc., envies my head all of its passions and agility and begs for a little energy a little madness, calculus, a little lunacy : *lunatic heath,* pleasant head objects, etc.— : no arrangements possible, my body in its shadow chamber, I say to Blum, damn it! no more pleasure for my body, no more physical intelligence and wit . .

imagination's course does not describe a circle but a spiral, Jean Paul says, I say to Blum, the PULP WRITERS, I say to Blum, are the HUMUS on which fine art flourishes, isn't that right, that which we refer to as the results of the most extreme exaltation, *the pellicle of an aria.*

That at some point we will have to part, leave each other, you and I, I write to X (or William or Ferdinand) leave (give up) everyone, is certainly the most horrible mistake, the worst mockery, the cruelest flaw in the so-called history of creation, *especially the tents in my memory,* or cowering on a park bench, she was staring at the verdigris-colored mush next to her which she had just thrown up : a young well-dressed woman with a red face. Statuette of a leg whispering, card with umbilical cord, bundle of notes in the morning found on my bed, hunting socks, suddenly pants, rain trumpets—dillydallying around in my image recall, I say to Joseph, has, it seems, paid off, a phenomenon : *a celestial disaster* that I didn't sense your presence and you were sitting right there next to me in the darkened auditorium, when I came late.

the open : book hungrily opened wide, pages 190/191 : Pasolini's PETROLIO for example as stimulus to write, escalated myself with DOMINGO'S SONGBOOK for example, am delirious, chased myself away with dreams, been daydreaming, sleeping through the day, a slip of the pen, on paper, am devoting myself to Joseph, am devoted, am an eccentric, what a word, actually only used in reference to old women, strangely enough. Words called up, back, forth, I say to Blum, quickly noted down before nodding off, otherwise gone, lost, and like a grain of sand in my shoe it irritates me, a word (along the way) lost, *and there ladies-in-waiting will be ladies-in-waiting and ladies-in-waiting (will be) and ladies-in-waiting, etc.*, and so on forever, I say, and now I am preparing myself for another 100 years, I say to Blum, until my face loses its epidermis, and this face of mine horribly exposed, can only show itself with its subcutis, grotesque like skinned game, rabbit skin, in the butcher shop . .

. . that it would come to this, I say to Joseph, who now really does not *show up* = appear anymore, is no longer talking, still : Joseph, because he is the one person who would most likely understand my chess moves, manipulations, aberrations, appeals, nerve endings, the sense of my associations, my breakdowns, etc., and it really did happen this way, that I found my way back to this book THE POSTCARD, by Derrida, taking numerous detours, I had bought it about 15 years ago, and fell for it then, the way I fell for Joseph, and I carried it with me everywhere I went : in my rucksack, briefcase, sleeping bag. On walks, trips, rotundas, visits, but then one day it disappeared among others of my favorite books booklover's books and never turned up again, it never surfaced again, maybe I lent it to someone, I say to Joseph, I took a detour and a very long detour to find my way back to this book that I was now acquiring for a 2nd time, at just the right moment I believe, because if I had had it when I began writing this work it would have been too great an influence, and so there was a detour through any number of other books Bashō, Hopkins, Giordano Bruno, Breton, Duras and Issa, and Alexander Kluge, Roland Barthes and Ajgi, Michaux, and I read each 1, not completely, most just partially, or the same sequences over and over, but I was always left with a feeling of INSUFFICIENCY : something skinned, something peeled, the peeled face of the aged painter M. W. for example, and so I fled into my own writing, into what I had already written, into a searching rereading of what I had written, what I had written myself, you see, and, since I returned to my reading, and could not bear it for very long, could not bear reading for very long, that is, or when reading inspired me, and then released me just as quickly, right, and so with my eyes closed, as it were, I returned to my own writing, the way we exchange kisses : with our eyes closed, sometimes when kissing I've opened my eyes, and looked into the eyes of the other, sometimes when we kissed, Joseph and I, I opened my eyes for a second to see IF HE WERE REALLY THERE, or I contained my desire to look and see if he were really there, because I was afraid I might discover that he wasn't, etc., but this time, in this book : THE POSTCARD, by Derrida, which I have just obtained for a 2nd time, by the time I reached page 5 or 6 I was convinced the ONLY ONE, the ONLY RIGHT ONE, that it was the REAL ONE, the MOST IMPORTANT book, and that I would be able to read it from the first to the last page . . while I am listening in the *da gamba, gable garden of Bach,* while the *da gamba, gable garden* rouses me, etc. And I considered how great the risk might be of reading this book again because it would draw me in, I mean ensnare me, even though my observations were already approaching an end, isn't that right. Maybe it would be better if I just set it aside so that I won't become infected, because I would have to trace its glow, I had no other option, I say to Joseph, I put a white napkin between pages 10 and 11 so as not to become completely spellbound by the seductive voice of this poet, and maybe then I would be able to continue writing in the knowledge that I was in possession of a treasure without touching it, without having to make improper use of it, I say a prayer, and everything that happened up until this point was only a journey taken to reach this book, here 1 end had been arrived at, everything I had read on my way to this book had become interwoven, bound up into 1 whole, seemed intertwined, and it led me here, to the *real true one* book, which might be compared to MESSENGER PEOPLE when they encounter me on the street, and delude me into believing I am seeing a person I once loved, still love, who make me wince, because they conjure up those people I have loved, positioning, maybe even doubling for them. HERALDS so to speak of those people we carry inside ourselves, and have for such a long time!, essence, gradual progression of similarity, transformation in orders of magnitude which finally present us with the ORIGINAL PERSON, after 5 or 6 copies have appeared, that is, a game perhaps, but one which exhausts us. Exhausted by the excitement these HERALDS have aroused in us, so that we are hardly even able to recognize the REAL person, that it is almost impossible for us to rejoice in them, maybe because they too, we think, are only an illusion, we put our arms around them, kiss them, spent as we are, on the cheek and the mouth, or say : "come, I will think you and you will speak?" (Oswald Egger).

In front of the window a *dense* (thick, gloomy) snowflake curtain its strands wafting here and there : roaming : swirling, so there must be a storm out there, food supply limited, mostly liquids, I say to Blum, then a voice on the telephone, woman's voice (Lily), and : *cuddling head of her voice* I mean her voice as a cuddling head, in this case CUDDLING not negatively charged, I say to Blum, I lie flat on my back, across from me the twilight of the dancers' white tutus : *élèves* by Degas on the wall, I say to Blum, but in actuality they were white holes in the sky between the trees, the white child underneath, that was you back then, I say, *early-headed,* I say. Turbulence of a cataract of the eyes, cataract of that abundance of snowflakes and it plunges down in front of our eyes, pours down, floods and sprays . .

3/17

not into the arm of the housecoat the hand the arm slips into the small breast pocket story pocket story cup on the upper left—Memo : and this is how we find our way!

voice PRAGUE VOICE coming from the radio, I write to Franz Wurm, so similar to yours that I immediately to the machine to write (this) to you : this letter that I have owed you for so long, and this is how I have come to send this long-promised letter to you, a handwritten one, several small scraps of paper, in the transcription : typed version, brash, and am then cast in the form of a drop of water, present in the form of a drop of water, etc., I write to Franz Wurm, rubbish heap.

The roller pants there aren't any roller pants anymore, the rapturous green or whatever they say, a higher order : monkey green : mandarin with rum—when I turn the radio on in the morning, *there is always a pizzicato,* I write to Franz Wurm, does this happen to you too, various masses of water around my footbath, cascades cataracts everything in a juggling disposition, counselor's bath, and over and over again a torch keeps showing up in front of my eyes on the front end of a car roaring into the subway station, that is, the fire tongue, there really was a torch on the front end of the approaching train, magical sight, of course this is not the 1st time I've seen it, it would have intrigued you too, am smoking a half pipe, trampling on some of my notes, change in laundry room now, am entitled to a little social preening, rough draft notebook sketch or spot that is, *I am writing to you on my knees and that can mean two different things.*

Wrapped pink turban around toe parts again, stopgap packing, a WOMAN'S TRIP; I am *completely lost,* Blum says, but he means, he's not aware of the day the time, he gives me a signal in the presence of others, he doesn't say, give me a glass of red wine, he utters an extended ROUGE!, that's what he says : ROUGE!, got ROUGE?—

oh dear Joseph, I write to Joseph, how have all our omens gone wrong . . so nothing will help, *dejection a mood* : I read (read again and again) in your latest letter dear Joseph, oh dear Joseph all of these puzzles, I think I'm afraid to call, I'm even afraid to call you, I think of INNOCENT'S LINGERIE, better INNOCENCE LINGERIE, I believe it was tender blackmail, I blackmailed you when I asked you to finish writing that letter you had begun, and begun to talk about, and send it to me, maybe we might say that you rid yourself of me by finishing the letter you had begun writing to me you rid yourself of me in this letter of yours which I wrung out of you, or I had extorted a promise from you to finish writing this letter to me, that's what it was, wasn't it, that's no way to do things . . the drink tastes flat, I say to Joseph, or the drink had a *bland* taste, we exaggerate by making everything visual, how thorough we are, I mean I look through everything in my monkey case *monk's case* everything that has found a place there and I don't immediately understand, I keep on looking through my monk's case, but slowly I begin to see my way, this hopping around in my head, I have been suffering from a gradual loss of memory for a long time, I say to Blum, I have decided not to write to Joseph anymore, I say to Blum, I have decided not to write to you anymore, I write to Joseph, the end is near, I have decided not to write to you anymore : the results you are holding in your hand, an amateur, photo automat snapshot of how stranded I am, or sophisticated : the pine forest on the tabletop, etc. The decision grew inside me, not only after I had read the letter I had coerced from you the letter I had wrung out of you for the hundredth time, but also while I was reading this book by Derrida, the 1 I acquired more than 10 years ago : THE POSTCARD—I don't know if you have ever read it, you should *you must read it*: he is a clairvoyant, he foretold everything that has been happening to me recently, etc.
Still remember it WRITING ON THE TABLET and SCRIBBLING ON THE TABLET, I say to Joseph, and the way you inserted 1 word in open spacing in your computer text in order to prove me wrong, to prove to me, that is, *that there is after all something between the lines* (which I had denied) : that moved me really moved me, but also SCARED SOMETHING INTO ME, like a laugh, a compulsion to laugh, in the sense of BURST OUT LAUGHING / BURST FREE, etc. As far as the get-together with the GROUP is concerned, I say to Blum, I was hardly able to relax, I mean as far as the arrangement of those present was concerned, in any case you could tell by how they were dressed (their outfits) whether they were attending as *goats (factotum)* or as something of higher rank, I didn't know

if I should genuflect curtsey or bow as I took my leave from the affair, perhaps just a subtle nod of the head, or a sullen affectation *because of the drinks, which were served too cold,* smiled stupidly down at my plate, which was and remained empty because I didn't dare help myself at the lavishly set table, so, you see, I was not to partake of the JOYS OF THE TABLE or what else can I say, stones in my brain and belly, etc., everything covered . . sat there and kept up a constant stream of YES YES to everything the person across from me was offering, fluency and hot air, and so I kept on saying YES YES unvoiced only a shake of the head : YES YES even though a shaking head is more often associated with no, but I avoided saying no because my table companion might expectantly demand : *reasons why saying no!,* etc., and so nothing but YES YES, however it might be interpreted, lips pressed together, *sometimes smiling,* simply tossed in like rational conversation, not really talking only MOOING!, sometimes saying "hm," as if intensely involved in what the person sitting across from me was saying and thinking, uninterruptedly thinking : CATASTROPHIC! SUCH A RECEPTION : CATASTROPHIC! and thinking : NEVER AGAIN!, full of dismay thinking of departure imminent departure : who to greet, take my leave from? 120 hands to shake or simply a polite nod of the head, smile, wave in all directions?—too jovial!, etc., awkwardly abstruse conduct : prior to exit sweeping every full glass from the table, inundate the table, screaming ooohhh! : slapstick scenario, with my handkerchief trying to *sponge up what is steaming up off the floor,* peals of laughter from all sides, with a corner of the second handkerchief so sacrificed, and while, because deeply bent over, feeling a red blush shoot to my head and about to faint, and in reverse slowly : cautiously : out of the hall . . and then taking flight, on the street WINTER EXCESS, wonderful WINTER EXCESS and a heavy snowfall which blanketed fogged neutralized everything, and back home : reaching for my book and thinking, perhaps his letter Joseph's letter tomorrow, but all of this without emotion, simply so, looking into the book, reading, reading over again until eyes tired, head falling sideways and OUT—

melody in my sleeping bag, the open shanks of the curling iron / making curls? / gauze veil of the republic / survived celebration of the republic, shaving cup on top, I say, *trampling on letter belly,* I say to Blum, if you know what I mean by that, in a fury put the machine back where it belongs the machine slips around on the tabletop when I write, keeps slipping around until left and right it bumps into books, notes, manuscript pages, on top story cup shaving cup paper cup or something like that, translucent, right through each and every instance, the world in the morning—

successive drops of honey the head of state, *it has a moonbeam the upholstery,* or caprice! fleeting perspiration on my nightgown, bed rolling, how much honey, I say to Blum, already flowed down my throat in all the years the decades, how many images raced past our eyes how many whirlwinds through our soul, fleeting shadowy apparitions behind windows, facades, fleeting shadowy apparition behind the bicycle in the hallway as if someone had just darted past, actually a man, dark in felt cover, only saw his back last of all a sign a mark on his back, then on the street another figure darting past, *means water sensation?*—these all mysteries I cannot solve, or I won't succeed in solving a single one, the spark not only has to jump, I say to Blum, but it must also JUMP ACROSS, to the recipient, that is the whole secret, these are not literary structures in popular use around here, I say to Blum, but something completely different that I am not able to describe : half a jacket presumably tongue workshop, trivial partitur stood on its head, etc.
(And reported the weather to one another : mother and I. Reported the weather to one another : invented for one another weather of delicate constitution, you see.)

3/29, 3/30, 3/31

things are going the same way things are going for the statue in the fountain, I say to Blum, that's how things are going for me I mean things are pouring out of me I am throwing up I am spitting up and screaming aversion nausea and the scream of the unconverted and blond-headedness when I hear D's voice on the telephone, it's as if I've doused myself in blond-headedness or blondness but also in lunar ecstasy and I flow into the deep pool and I am inundated with an overpowering wave of cheap associations and me (bang!) a supporting character in a supporting role poke around and stomp and thrash, and the way I sit here in my retreat unable to breathe everything overgrown with rowanberry branches behind which the bird eyes of the blackbird pair I mean are *peeping out* or piercing through the way we stick holes in cardboard, or whatever, or are grabbing at me with their small claws and consuming me, and stands of horsetail have long since engulfed me, and the message of the bonsai twig, completely covered with dust from the street, just a few steps away from the Japanese counsel coax tears and screams from me and the shadow of Joseph's wings I mean the sweetness of its beats and strokes send me wandering out into a naked almost spring day, like my eyebrows, as if he were directing me with icy baton and papyrus, etc., with reading glasses, carried on playful platonic correspondence with a few young men, I say to Blum, or I had such a platonic correspondence with S. many years ago but then a time came and he said where he said that's enough of this! and he tore the clothes from my body and sank into me, etc.,

all this from *bird beating, a good bird beating,* I say to Blum, also wing beating, I mean I was sitting behind him and off to 1 side in the café, he didn't know I was there, but I imbibed everything, the beat of his wings, as if he, Joseph, had been sitting right across from me, he was talking with a friend, it seemed, like drops of water, it was a background voice and I could understand almost everything he said, although the general noise level, I mean this wonderful smoky bell of subdued voices and vibrations in the room, cloaked a lot, have the sweetness (the strokes) of the impulse to write (scraps of writing) in front of me, sit there as if I were sitting at a keyboard, strike the highest keys, *just tinkling* a little, also whistling tones, swinging hierarchies, my own blackbird claws, the way I am sitting in my sanctuary, that is, feeling like a fountain statue, to the right / to the left dripping and trickling from the corners of my mouth and into the bowl (coffee) full of intention and *the last dance,* I say to Joseph, until my housecoat is stained, the tray of my housecoat, neckbreaking hem : like silken arrangement : moldy monitors, feels to the touch, I say to Joseph, just think, 10 minutes before leaving on a trip, taxi, in order to go to Zell am See, I mean I sense MOUSE START, also MOUSE STEP, can you make any sense of this, and for a while I think, where is the shadow on this sheet of paper coming from, the paper on which I am writing to you, this shadow I believe I have just discovered, and which I at first thought was a long-stemmed flower with a bowed head, but then discovered it was *the frame* (Heidegger) of my typewriter glasses, and a strand of hair falling in the same *astronomical direction,* and I ask myself how I can be writing about astronomical directions in this context, on the train very inspired by Roland Barthes's *Critical Essays III* and I took a lot of notes, which I can hardly use now, because the FIRE does not remain the same, etc., I should have, would have to have made use of them then, in any case, I won't be, am not able to decipher much of what I wrote, shorthand here and there, FLOWERS WAVERING, came to me in a dream, I mean, dear Joseph, I write to Joseph, I don't know what significance WAVERING FLOWERS might have, I can't explain it to you, can't even explain it to myself, but there is this *flower red calyx cuff* and I can't get it out of my mind, I pull my feet out of my rocky bath, I mean, all the particles of soap gone solidified on the bottom of the pool, and I am confused by the spelling of cough, English, and Blum says to me, you pronounce it coff, more like coff, diphthong, not really cuff but coff. I mean this detail of me from a photograph keeps coming up again and again, showing me with blurred head of hair and versified bib on a wooden chest, used up critique stuff etc., while I am emptying the basin, my gaze falls on a bottle wrapped in Christmas paper, the gift giver's business card with flickering candles still attached, next to it pieces of a cup just broken, favorite pink cup, fingertips immerse deep inside, no cabinet no table,

I say to Blum, and everything smells of fish just like James Joyce's place, even the lemon, *a tear came courting,* I looked through my correspondence with Joseph, I lay a sheet of my thinnest writing paper down as a napkin, it immediately crinkled up in the spilled glass pieces of the mug, and the pressed juice flooded everything, manuscripts books shelves DOG'S PAWS and DOG PAWS, reeds, spring was already crashing up against the window : weather vane grapevine votive candle blind man's cane, I shout, still it's the end of March, beginning of April, Christ's nails, I shout, these little clouds of sloth, strokes of the brush, we drank a lot last night, Blum says, we incorporate something that is a drink, presumably we are dealing with a supernatural substance which brings us tidings of something which would otherwise not reach our consciousness, the HONEY ASSORTMENT, HONEY RESERVES, e.g., I shout, which are supposed to be making my voice strong, while drinking (vocalisms?) collect in the CREEL OF THE MOUTH, in front of the teeth that is, the orange seeds and lemon seeds, the o's and a's and the i's and e's, and all the blessings of the sun and moon and sacred times and signs, and basket for catching fish : CREEL, also related to frill, to canework, beehive, reverence, I am spooning down honey and candied sugar, carbon paper, 3, 4 layers 1 on top of another, in a fanlike array, I shout, writing paper instead of napkins, thin-skinned delicate, quivering scraps of paper under a mug with hot liquid, etc., oh, I say, the way Monika Böhmert trembled, how she trembled, her hands, her arms, her lips trembled when she handed me the galley proofs, and her trembling made me start trembling too, my voice began to tremble, my heart, too, everything began to tremble, I say to Blum, do you remember, the limousine, Monika Böhmert writes, gliding along over the land, proofs in hand and erecting a reading zone for letters of the alphabet, Monika Böhmert says, she writes me a long letter, women's writing flights into infinity, I say, the day must last longer, be extendable : periscope with curving barrel. Joseph says, I will go with you to the train station, Joseph writes, I like this poem, wavy curved paper instead of napkin, poked around and embossed with rings from saucer and mug, and X (or William or Ferdinand) writes "I am now living a love story; my last. It is not all joy, of course, there is also a sense of dismay at how happy or unhappy I can be at one and the same time . ." oh dear Joseph, I write to Joseph, I wish I had a WRITING TELEPHONE, and don't know myself what that might be, and I wish you could read along with me as I write, I believe the individual flakes. Oh this long soulful winter what a gift from heaven, I am sitting at the window, in 1 specific corner : castrated corner : the satellite dish on the rooftop across

the way looks like a small frozen banner, French colors, the French flag, Joseph shouts, as he discovers the book which I have bundled together with red, blue and white rubber bands, I use it so often it shares my bed with me, the pages have all come loose, I always carry it around with me, "*the postcard,*" by Jacques Derrida, I am pointing to the emblem on the first page of the book, daylight rural lamplight, while I am sitting reading the galley proofs of the book I am writing (the first part has already been set), the introduction, the wish, I say to Blum, the possible fulfillment of my wish to look him up, Joseph, where he lives, is shooting together with the image of a certain lakeside resort in the Salzkammergut, late at night, when the abundance the surface of the water is barely rippling, profoundly seductive emanations, and I rush out to the shore while satellites and their reflected glow flow into me and make me silent with joy . .
hadn't I glitteringly surrounded myself : made friends with all sorts of FETISHES : feather hats, until I found their source again in his, Joseph's, eyes, I say to Blum : he sat in front of me and his body soul glowed out of his eyes and into mine, I mean it was truly a graft an ATTACHING OF EYES, etc., like a TIGER speaking with a person, and of its own accord, utterly apparent, I mean the ABYSS filled and our steps took us across, let's read that as wittily suppressed : 1 DAY, to understand this unshakable fidelity in us that lies somewhere between a profound sense of justice and fantasy, isn't that so, and naturally the *flank is a wing,* I mean Joseph's flank is a wing, he had a pale complexion, I say to Blum, and I believe we both cried it was an astonishing wafting of flakes in the window, it was the end of March, first the encyclopedia lay in his and then in my lap, open, parted, I say, when was it you last (the last time) spilled a tear, we cried together and I believe we were then reflected in the next room where a large mirror hung on the wall, there was a deep silence, then he stood up and said I will go now, the ABYSS opened up again . .
TANGERINE, the conductor on the platform shouted, but meant THE TRAIN IS LEAVING, I felt as if I had been electrified and I also had a fever, I say to Blum, if you are going to memorize a telephone number, it must have a rhythm, it must be a rhythm, I say to Blum, intimate banalities, I say to Blum, I work with intimate banalities, right, constructions of a situation, GALA OF A KNIFE on the bedspread, the wrinkled and tattered spread, Blum says, the everyday antipodes, you won't get anywhere if you go on like this, Blum says, everything too short too small too constricted, which makes you yourself too short too limited, short of breath, prone to panic, gullible, Blum says. *I sewed all my papers together,* I say, cut piece

at the bottom, once my father's letterhead, with name address telephone number, *needling mail,* etc.

The train arrived, and I saw, I would not be able to open the door, it was too high for me, had I been telescoped shut, shrunken, had I condensed myself? began to cry, because I wanted to board the train, and then the conductor tilted the train toward me along its entire length, and I was able to reach the door handle, strange as this may seem, everything magical, there were strands of hair in the scissors, or I dreamt I had not yet written anything, never written anything, not a single memory of ever having written a thing, I couldn't recall ever having written anything down, still, when a diffuse sense did arise that there must be some notes somewhere, books written ("*genius writings*") I couldn't picture what the individual pieces looked like, how far back had I gone, what, what had I written about back then, in front of my eyes, on the page of a book were things that could not be interpreted, I had not written most of it, instead it had been written by a poet I know very well, pieces of cloth interleaved, and this morning I had also spent a long time looking at the mysterious poster over my bed, a print of the little white pony by Dominguez, and fell in love with it again, the way it is trotting through the old bicycle frame, a woman's mare—yellowish glass wool distastefully stuffed into the skylight of a toilet cell, next to it a muffled DOG THUD, when at the table Blum was unwilling to talk for a very long time, because something or other had frightened him, or confused him, something seemed to be occupying his mind and he couldn't shake it off, I began to talk to him, ABOUT SOMETHING ENTIRELY DIFFERENT, this, IT, *pitied him,* which basically means : IT EMPATHIZED WITH HIM, a bark in the stillness of the night, *gallantry of the pupil of an eye,* I say to Blum, small crocodiles, toads, cow bells, *a laugh as bouquet of carnations, carnation mood in the back of the throat,* etc., I'm swimming away from myself here, I say to Blum, no longer really attached to this book I am writing, I say to Blum, a NEW RAISON has already made its appearance, a new paper lantern is glowing, the book I am writing and have been writing for so long has already been forgotten, has already freed itself from its purpose and turbulence, I receive a letter from an old friend, and these words are enclosed : YOU WONDERFUL HONEY WOMAN, which leads me to say to myself, IT'S ALWAYS THE *WRONG* MAN WRITING ME THINGS LIKE THAT. The spare life I am leading, almost suffocating in paper wrappers and paper *ducks,* the disarray in my head corresponds to the disarray in the *family of my clothes and turbans and sandals,* I say to Joseph, arbitrarily spontaneously the way I deal with words, the way I deal with the choice of my clothing, supra fat of the land life, can no longer keep things under control, reliquary : closet for props in my head in my housing everything driven by chance, by chance I come across a word or a braid, randomly rotate my boots, undershirts all jumbled up together, (knotted) perception of context, horizon lines, shadowing of objects, accidental my cantos, my unscrupulous balloon, etc., you talk about *a rapture of similarities,* I say to Joseph, the voice holds a very high note : like a lark a soprano : "the Youth and the Bee" by Hugo Wolf, this voice this card, I say to Joseph, contains something—maybe that veil of quiet and beauty, of earthly happiness and cryptic fear (see the blurred cloud of letters soot smoke above on the right), which will be aired out on the morning of the new year of life, I think you will be able to decipher the smoke signal . .

4/4, 4/5

and would simply need a woman to help and to bring me a packet of valerian or saffron or sage or confessional catechism from the vestry (apothecary) . .

o how wrinkled the packet moves along the table, this open box of pills skids along the oval tabletop, how the plastic bag crackles next to the typewriter when the carriage touches it, the packets skitter back and forth, the wobbling table the wobbling tabletop, moving without any mechanical means of propulsion, you might almost believe there is some magic behind it, absolute bewilderment, I say to Blum, should take my temperature, or when sometimes I don't know which day which hour which BAR or with which words Joseph closed his most recent letter, etc., maybe I'll work in a poem a few verses, am maneuvering into the bilge water this is the prose of the Easter garland, I say, I maneuver the packet into the middle of the tabletop it maneuvers along the table, the small oval table wobbles, there is the SWOLLEN CAGE of this heavy heart, I say to Blum, I have been paging through the Matisse catalogs, he's drawn these *enchanting* women's hands / fists, he drew these women's hands that suggest devastation, which merge into the bulging chains these women wear around their necks, women's hands as claws, ruffles, chains, while wings of parakeets like half-opened slanting eyes near expanse of foliage . .
the pink paws of the women among pink boxes, isn't that right, I say to Blum, the small pink boxes which are sliding around on the tabletop, young woman in 3/4 view, 3/4 time, to discover my portrait on a naked female figure, pierrot tassel on the instep of my right foot which is taking stride, paper tassel like a nightingale, the dissolute eye, hung the wet stockings over the door handle. Everything is compressing my breath, saw a coach with two horses whose manes were decorated with brightly colored garlands of paper, as is the custom on the Monday before Lent, when they parade through the streets in celebration, I mean the horses are celebrating

with their eyes, they don't wear blinders then, you see you hear the horses celebrating and snorting, I mean the coach with the paper curls turned out to be a truck in the sleet, or a water truck that inundated everything and snorted and billed and cooed in the unalterable wetness and making a waterfall in the city, I saw the shadow behind me, closing in on me, following me, so I was prepared for the worst, I saw a small leather strap, a strip of leather on a well worn hat or cap, leather cap of a motorcycle rider, with a strap and clasp, there really was something of that sort, a banner behind me, a leather banner, a skirt, watermark, rain hat made of leather, right, I saw it behind, snapping up next to my right eye, didn't know what it was, then the figure of a man in leather pushed its way out in front of me, laughed, grinned, ridiculed me, towered over me by more than a foot, saw something like a butterfly in my room : tear on cheek, I say to Blum, sometimes I feel uprooted, completely uprooted, pulled up out of my earth, root and stem, tarsus and flesh, and I not knowing where headed and where to settle, all this terror and world of shadows, and unable to place the nature of my vision and my own place, my own rootedness and the oil perspectives of a painter, and from above the way tormented waves of carpet on the walls : like a Matisse, I say to Blum, you have to see wallpaper beauty which pours down onto the tablecloth, the floor, the woman with a set of antlers, and everything in POWDER RED, I say, you have to see the sets of antlers on the walls and how they pour down over the table making it appear to bend and curve, and the sets of antlers, the way sets of antlers in the wallpaper bury themselves in the hair of the woman at the table with a set of antlers, etc.

I have been negotiating with this book for a long time, dealing with this book, been tempted to identify it as one of my favorite books : Balthasar Gracian Palm Reader and the Art of Earthly Wisdom, German by Arthur Schopenhauer, but then, after a few pages it no longer charmed, I am no longer able to reconstruct the exact sequence of events, at first I was very attracted to it, especially the title, but after a while it really was too *high-flown,* and too *imprecise, or I simply didn't strike gold,* couldn't find my way into it, or IT couldn't find a way into my desires, you see, it only worked for a short while and then the spell it had cast was broken, maybe it just wasn't adequately blended (or well-balanced), not quite a blend of rigor *and* grace *and* mystery *and* THE SORROW OF ROSES—

in any case these days so full of sorrow because no response : thoughts : feelings from Joseph, I say to Blum, and I've had enough of calling him, spelling out : J = O = S = E = P = H, and on his part, I mean, not 1 sign, right. A small spoon is lying among the envelopes, books, still-life objects, martyred angels, chimpanzees, chopped lynx ears even pages of books . . *cudgels and tree,* well you know how everything swirls around in my head, how this restlessness manifests itself in alphabetical sign language, I mean imagine a face with 2 dark blinking eyes staring out at you : picture in a movie magazine, and then a script appears under the eyes, vertical, Japanese characters, nothing but tiny addition problems or alphabet tracks : the left eye shows signs of a scratch, almost all the way down to the middle of the nose, dried blood most likely, there is a band-aid on the mouth, a captivating sight . . the way you, angel on wheels, I am speaking to the face in the film magazine, shall I let my book find its end, I have already written out beyond the boundaries, I mean the contingent has been used up or the contingency, *o cudgels and tree,* or charm—a charm has been spoken over me and it is this : up to this point and no further!, I have been writing out past the edges of this paper this book the page of this book, the neutral zone for a very long time, out past the edge of the page and right onto the bed sheets, and bedding, pillows and bolsters, making it impossible for the readers of my book to read what I have written beyond the borders, written out past the boundaries, they will not be able to decipher my bed sheet script, they will not be able to read what I have written on the sheets and the pillows, in the end a shrunken poem or stump of a poem, I say to Blum, imagine that, fragment, torso, that could be the end of the book, a page full of dots for example. Context no longer intelligible, a small milk-encrusted spoon as a paperweight on my art-deco table, if it starts raining, I say to Blum, maybe Joseph will find enough time to write to me, late at night as if I'm hearing a rotating tone, vibration of 1 single tone, which afflicts my eardrum more severely than the blast of a trumpet or a howl, it is my innermost skin tearing apart, I say to Blum, I am bleeding to death, it is the scratch effect the excruciating effect of the scratch on my innermost skin bringing me down, almost every night, the way the canals rage in a continuous downpour, the tenderness of the *letter photos,* I sit in front of them and am utterly charmed, *as well as in silence,* for example, when I say IN UNFORTHINKABLE DAYS : TIMES : YEARS, I am presumably referring to the days of my childhood which may be considered UNTHINKABLE UNFORTHINKABLE UNIMAGINABLE, because they are so distant, so remote, cut off, right, and the colors they carry are so faded, like rushing torrents of letters. My mother's black silk belt, for example, I say to Blum, is in the same way a small piece of a clothbound book which in adhesive strips holds the pages of a notebook together, and although nothing but

her tablets calendars notebooks have survived, I am constantly preoccupied by the image of her ashes which are resting in a closed vessel (in cardboard box) on a stool between my study and the bathroom, *ciphers and notes,* and I am preoccupied with a sense of the omnipresence of her ashes, as if her ashes were lying here next to me, in a cardboard box, for example, between the two rooms. Easy to decipher certain unstressed signs, silent intimations, ciphers and notes, votive images, picture puzzles, addresses, visualized confessions, tacit understandings, etc., my father's signet ring let's say (*a command*) in the open drawer of his desk, back then, as silent declaration, he slipped it off before he was taken to the hospital, while I was away, or my mother's anguished gaze in the direction of the filing cabinet, 2 or 3 weeks before her death, where she had deposited her valuables. Her gaze said TAKE EVERYTHING OUT IN TIME PUT EVERYTHING IN SAFE KEEPING!, her gaze lasted for no more than a quarter of a second, but I had understood her, I didn't say a word, her mute gaze, her no longer being able to speak had resulted in silence on my part, I was dumb, simply nodded once with my head, she seemed full of despair, seemed to feel completely forsaken, I say to Blum, *caught in a fall . .*
(these SHARP WINTER EYES like blackbirds when their sharp eyes flash through the bare thorns of the bushes).

4/7

growing dark a (doubtful) AFFAIR OF THE HEART *right on through the beechwood grove, etc.*

and I see the flowers : egg-yolk blossoms, lizard blossoms which transform seem to transforming themselves over and over again into young swans (duck feathers) on the algae green pond on lotus blossom waters whose *mists rising up* into the castle warden's cottage : housing like a moated castle where playmates wrapped in tendrils of ivy air in and air out and jumping, leaping and looking (watch), and shouts audible as well children shouting, and then the rowboats the pier and into pond, and what seems (as I observe) to be taking on dimensions of acute-angled ecstasy, which in the degree of its restriction was unlike any I had ever been able to measure in any other place : the reduction : so tiny that anyone would be amazed if more than 2 boats were ever be able to cruise its meandering waters and the resonance of lapping elements rose up into my heart . . *these morsels of foot,* I say to Blum, in BLOCK SHOE the (half) duck raising its rump banner high into the air, dipping its bill deep under water, hoods and eddies of lesser waves like Botticelli hair, long tresses, *trespassing.* (Re)counting curls, the water : wintery element pouring down over my body, I say to Blum, or suddenly, all at once, 1 small feather, brightly colored, right in the middle of the text, I mean 1 small feather, brightly colored, you are showing, I say to Lily right in the middle of your PLUMAGE, in the PLUMAGE of your soul, I say to Lily, 1 small brightly colored feather in *his* color, the color of the one you loved dearly for so many years, 1 small feather of *his,* clearly showing how your souls once embraced, you see, suddenly a poem right in the middle of a prose text, in the texture of prose a verse, etc., danger of madness coming closer, I say to Blum, *bodices enormously on the sidewalk,* imprints of some sort of wetness : rain or slender rivulets of piss, horns branched and windblown curls banners = small dresses—there was something like this, a flag : watermark : *rain* hat or skin, that's what we used to say when I was a child : TAKE YOUR RAINSKIN!, it was actually a cape, gray or salmon pink : cape and a hood, too, you see, but very stiff and when the wind blew into it the thing inflated and provided very little protection, etc., *the wing of an eye,* that's how you did your tracing of me, your study, your transparency, your phosphorized image, I say to Blum, *and I am unable to thank you for it,* because my eyes / thoughts still / again and again to Joseph, although he forgot me long ago, he left me somewhere, left me behind, like an object you leave, leave behind, the thing, you leave it, you leave it behind, your handbag your umbrella, it wasn't really all that important, left it, left it behind, forgot it, at some insignificant point, find a pair of scissors in the pot, arsenal of writing instruments, cushion on the back of my armchair a Matisse motif, first noticed it today, I say to Blum, yes, *my dearly embraced reader!,* it is about time, that you, even if you are a patient reader : the most patient reader in the world : to slam the book shut in rage, thinking THIS HAS GONE TOO FAR!, *and it has gone too far*—the word "too" doesn't really belong here—and while I am writing this down, I am thinking of RATTLE SHOE I mean the translator's tongue : RATTLE SNAKE TONGUE : the translator's delicate tongue, translator's flickering tongue, delicately flickering translation, a translator residing in the chair of Pythia, in the sacred green place, in the place of *language* and *speaking,* isn't that right, such a sense of nostalgia, i.e. such a profound *affection,* and suddenly I recall how many years ago Margaret B. told me she had entered all of my poems into her COMPOSER : typed them into her COMPOSER, and from one moment to the next, *everything was clear to her,* she was able to understand everything, as if someone had translated them from a foreign language into her own, and then everything which had been so blurred had now taken shape, and she had come to love them all and felt so attracted to them, etc., the photographer's cap : 2 or 3 spattered drops of blood on the photographer's yellow cap, he was here for a few hours and he said to me as I was typing around on my machine, NOW YOU HAVE COMPLETELY FORGOTTEN MY PRESENCE, and : THAT'S HOW THINGS ARE WITH POETS!, and I answered, no, I didn't forget you, but I was enveloped by something like a WALKING IN THE MISTS, in a way that is otherwise unfamiliar to me, when someone I don't know is here for a time, in my housing, spends time here, perhaps a side-effect of the pills I am taking, I say to him, it is something very different! when I am *really* working, then it is a mystery, I mean, then everything is *mysterious* : an awful mysterious process, and no one else may be present!, it is the most secret thing you ever do alone, it is *the essence of intimacy with yourself,* it is not anything

I can explain to anyone else, I say to him, he moved back 1 step with his tripod and we were both silent for a long time. There was something extraordinary about this silence we shared, the fact that I was so silent in the presence of a person I didn't know, yes, there was something obscene about this silence between us, and the way I let myself be posed, let myself be winterly posed. The chronicler with the Hasselblad camera says : the gods! he says, but maybe you have some piece of clothing or other which will show your neck, a bit of skin would lighten the whole thing up, the exposure, says the chronicler with the Hasselblad camera : a sublime thing, skin as background color indicates a distant light, etc., (MOTIF SPRING).

4/14

a 3-layered coat around my hips, if you actually suppose suspect, I say to Blum, the reader will not be able to penetrate this heap of words—foreign texts included—to the general mood of the person writing, you're BARKING UP THE WRONG TREE! (where do you suppose this expression comes from, the BARK and the TREES, and bushes : lithe and towering high up into the sky, etc.), you feel the breath of the person writing, even if the writer is masking himself with foreign material, disguising his voice, etc., a sensitive ear can distill the true CANTO out of it all, don't you think, as I understand it, how X (or William or Ferdinand) is getting along these days, when he writes from the south of Italy, "and it is indescribable completely incomprehensible what the eye registers here, the house hangs on the steep Amalfi coast and is surrounded by a wild garden. Gorse and mallow, peach trees, lemon and orange trees are full of ripe fruit, I don't know where to look, and the sea spreads out a hundred meters below—it is the most extreme place I have ever found, on the whole : EXTREME, while in detail it is quite gentle and idyllic . . and isn't it absurd that right here (in this very place) I stop and embrace you . ."

drank the clear February drank it all down, drunk on a clear February, the way you must be drunk while writing, calculation alone is not enough, otherwise it is a sacrilege; that you break off in the middle of your letter, I write to X (or William or Ferdinand), corresponds completely with the situation in which we all find ourselves at this time, I am breaking off, too, again and again, right in the middle, of thoughts, actions, reflection, ventures, feelings, that my writing paper is making waves the way the sea does where you are, lying on a red-hot table top, on which a pot with boiling water (for inhaling) had stood, have 2 amateur speech therapists who are always at hand to help cure the hoarseness in my voice, etc., have now fixed your name as "X (or William or Ferdinand)" because of the rhythm, and as Flaubert says, it is important to give prose the gravity of poetry : "like a good verse," Flaubert writes, "a good prose sentence must be IMMUTABLE, just as rhythmical, just as sonorous, the sentences in my book must quiver like the leaves in the forest, which all differ from one another in their similarity, etc." Otherwise, the situation is unruly-layered, complex-banal, and still quite M E R C I F U L, have wrapped my feet in my travel blanket again, it is wet and stormy, almost mid April, or May, what do I know, *cauliflower relics* in the sink, egg hand grenades next to the dishcloth, which all sounds very militant, right, but that's just how I saw it, on my right cheek in bed a slumber, after a satisfying (spare) meal, the narrow cup (fare), I mean a cup of soup, smelling of damp wood, cattle and garden, although securely locked up in my room and kitchen, pouring hot water over my head to cure myself, I enjoy spare meals, spread them out over the day as several smallest possible courses, abundance doesn't agree with me as you know, 1 drop of water is enough to sate body and stomach, etc., and then the pillow position favors this CAP and paraphrase . . in my region certainly more *rabbits and fruit* than in any other I know, on the emaciated day, dear X (or William or Ferdinand), *cauliflower gurgling away,* and in the next room, the CORPSE OF THE MEAL, if you know what I mean . . have only hallucinated all of this, surround myself with melancholy friends because it encourages me to work, and you can't blame me for always coming back to it, it is keeping me alive, so I have to keep talking about it, coarsen it by talking about it and writing about it, etc., and the INTOXICATION OF NOTES : all over my housing small *crumpled up* cards and pages covered with red green and pale violet scribblings, blue pencils, cylindrical stencils, sugar loaves and lunar postponements, as if it, the moon were losing its normal shape and elongating itself, transforming itself into an oval, which may be explained by my ever increasing shortsightedness, the *eccentricity* of my whole person, I mean, *its tendency to fall* . . . . (continuation of this letter illegible) and back again after such a long time, were where?—and again breast tearing open, or crying out, or tearing out, a SENSATION, put the camel away, had been galloping around on a doily on top of the CD player, I mean its, the camel's, position changed in order to play the Bach disc, organ, I open a book, I say to Blum, find a scrap of paper with these words from Job : "back then, when I washed my feet in butter . ." etc., then looked up the word CONTEMPLATIVE, couldn't find the word CONTEMPLATIVE, also many other words I couldn't find, only thoughts of Joseph, I say to Blum, with him alone, and my shoulder, and the way my shoulder touches Joseph's shoulder, and with my head touching Joseph's shoulder, rested my head on Joseph's shoulder I mean—how often I had wanted to do it, never managed to because he wouldn't have wanted it, then a somersault a leap *splits,* with both legs across the bare *bed bolsters* rolled up in one corner of the room as well as the Kelim and the Persian, over the wet rags laid out on the floor to dry, as if out on the grass, or rolled up like mats or carpets, isn't that right, I say to Joseph, and throw my arms around his neck : don't do that! Joseph says, and peeled the apples, spread them out on the bare table top, later heard your voice on the telephone, I say to Joseph, and you in front of my eyes in your wild tenderness and resolute and self-possessed and in your glow, I say, glowing eyes etc., and then to the café and being hungry *into the café with hungry eyes : service* and ordered something to eat and was served bread and butter and a drink, and butter scraped off the bread with a spoon, no knives there, and smeared butter all over the plate, fingers too, and then dipped into it with my teaspoon and said, WITH MY TEASPOON BECAUSE NO KNIVES HERE, and scratched out eyes the eyes of the café and the waiter scratched out, standing there as if they hadn't

understood and nothing, empty bar and forlorn, no one in the bar, lethal stand, isn't it, broad daylight, etc., and with the back of my knife scraped the shit off my pants, that's how I cleaned out the zipper, Blum says, and a salamander (gecko) on a stone in the street, and *contemplative,* I mean Maria Lassnig's self-portrait with small rodent, 1982, on the pavement, open melon as moon, in a side-street, and filtered the rays of the sun falling at an acute angle into the side-street, and the euphoria of writing lines, I say to Joseph, and as far as Hiroshima, rice, *relais,* Rabelais, or mango are concerned, I say to Joseph, it is all a mind trauma, drama, or let's keep right on associating : a dream, daydream or trauma, until all I can do is flee back into this housing of mine, forest hut, hay mow, *polishing of woods and ink,* the way a thought is allowed to wilt, I say to Joseph, on delicate white paper, *just something sniffed out,* I say to Blum, and at times feel overcome by a longing a desire, apprehension, greed, the part of me on a pilgrimage, or a table on a pilgrimage with wedges of apple, apple peelings, apple core, in the realm of the kitchen, on a pilgrimage I mean, me, through this book, standing in front of the oval table, half naked, leaning over the book, resting on my elbows, read a few pages, in the book that's bringing Joseph to me, I say to Blum, has brought me, devotedly passionately reading, on the trail, such an erotic glow, a hammering in my chest, reading around in the book which is giving me answers to questions I have been asking, always have been asking, as no other book, rapidity of spirals, I hear it coursing through my head : an uncontrollable clanging and banging around in my head, this the stigmatized idiom of my imagination is bringing me to the brink of insanity, I say to Joseph, and sail off across the kitchen floor on scattered kernels of rice as if over freshly fallen snow, *smashed fly* : fly with bell around its neck, etc., heavenly weather, ironed the pages of my favorite book because during the night I lay, because I slept on it, I slept on the pages of my favorite book, I say to Joseph, now it is all crumpled up, mangled, scribbled notes down on the back of an obituary, just look at this, I say to Blum, just look at X (or William or Ferdinand) and you are a better person, isn't that right, 6-person bed, through forest and field in a sailor suit in my childhood, I shout, the MISS TAKEN : the mistake, the MISS TAKEN WORDS, *the whole glandular node, etc.*
The speckled pear looks like a trout, the coloration of a trout, I say to Joseph, pear disguised as a trout, pear whose skin is like the skin of a trout, the way it darts through the murkiest of village streams, across the whole place, and like crumbs of words, I mean I also see these covered with specks, later coffee moustache on the inner rim of the cup, the violet

fronds of evergreen trees by the light of the snow, Psalms at the seashore in the evening sun, no, not palms : Psalms, I say to Joseph, soaked paper, *and incessant bleeding all around myself like Alma.*
The colors : Hiroshima : shepherd blossom, and how the final draft moves voluptuously on along its way, I say to Blum, *rolls out long,* like honey, drawn out like a sex act, isn't that right, desire up to the point of orgasm, almost to the point of orgasm, this breeze in my head, I say to Blum, oh wilderness in my head, she, Alma, didn't have any hands (on the street, messing around right in front of us), holding her hands like a young child, etc., but neither of us knows who Alma is after all, what Alma looks like, she wasn't introduced, she is only a name, isn't that right, the reader, but we too, has only a vague image of Alma, and whenever I am *unfaithful,* I say to Blum, I mean when I think disparagingly, speak, about motherhood : childhood, about the grizzling of very young beings, something quite bad happens, some sort of misfortune, most of the time I am run over, a car, a baby carriage, the mark of Cain, a kind of glowing effect, and I pray, cry, say to myself : oh, escaped again, oh my mother saving me again from on high, or wherever she might be these days, if at all, but so much evidence already, after her death, so much corroboration that she does guide me along my way, that she is protecting me from the agonies of death and slaughter, and her REPRIMANDS : above all her REPRIMANDS! : please don't do this, or that, even more strongly than before, while she was still among the living, etc., she never forbid anything, just showered me with her advice, her suggestions, her dearest concerns, requests, hopes for the future, etc., and every time, I say to Blum, when he, Joseph, when Joseph sat down quickly or stood up : this obvious bulge low on his torso, which gave me away, of course, I mean my eyes my eyes registering this phenomenon, I mean I gave myself away with my shameless glances, isn't that right, and my wondrous dreams during the night, I see him standing on the top floor, waiting for me, a palace guard and a strapping young squire, or slender, or again his image through the frosted glass window of the elevator door before I step out, no profile nor robes for him, basically speaking. As far as Alma is concerned, Blum says, let's leave it with the name, eyes, augury, 1 ear hanging down, cherry hearted ear, Blum says, the vibrancy of your memories, Blum says, the photographs from your childhood, the yellowish brown silhouettes with ragged edges, etc., the paranoia, the psychiatric of your childhood, isn't that right, in a time that came and went yesterday, in a time coming and going today, I took my hair down, I say to Joseph, spread it out on a chopping board, cut the ends off straight with a knife,

they had been frizzy, very dark, perhaps somewhat negroid, then put my hair back on, put it back on, although, it had not been styled as a wig, but the hair could be taken off and put back on like a cap, ironed the hair on the sides : pressed flat, cut : styled, etc., and I saw that this hair had been cut too short, was very curly, back to the beginning again and again back to the beginning again and out to the kitchen with the cutting board and completely disoriented, out and back and very distraught, as if interrupted, as if intercourse interrupted, the small splinters of glass in the sole of my foot, and books started to read and then stopped reading and started reading other books and then others, and no longer knew what I was reading, not even the title, the author of the book, and every time FOREST NAKEDNESS when I was called upon to explain, isn't that right, so better keep quiet, always preferring silence to speech, or spouted forth like a fountain heartless stuff, empty words, incomprehensibly drippy, most excruciatingly. Rummaging around the whole of world literature this way, never really capturing anything, only touching on it, putting it back down, reading around and setting down, bending corners of pages everywhere, scraps of paper as bookmarks, pencils, clothes pins, slipping one text in between the pages of another, markers here and there, wedging old letters in, and then stormily reading on, having forgotten the context long ago, starting all over again, from the beginning, nothing but fragments, pieces, palm of my hand, foot, shattered course of my life, and in my rucksack *so many* of my several FAVORITE BOOKS, of which I can at least say : yes! this place and that place, yes! this and that formulation, this and that word!, these and those colors, atmosphere, practices, vanguards, shadows of people, but *so many* carried with me carried around wherever I went, even if it were only as far as the supermarket across the way : a rucksack with my favorite books on my back, another on my chest with vitally necessary medication necessary for survival, like MOUNTAIN CLIMBERS sometimes, I mean you can see them, carrying 2 rucksacks on their journey, etc.
Lined up in front of the door like CARDBOARD COMRADES, the pet dogs large and small, yapping forlorn and to such creatures I usually tip my beret in order to console them, and while I am offering them consolation encouraging them to persevere and inside the pearly wares of the Turkish dealers like draperies (star visors) or flower's son : flower's salon, chest of jewels or journal, etc., actually, to tell the truth, I say to Blum, most of the time Joseph and I talk about death, my death, and what will have to happen, what Joseph might do to undo my sudden death, then I will be sitting in a turquoise colored Turkish ice cream parlor, or a house painted with

every color there is, with a small work area that has been prepared for me actually built especially for me, incredible home altar, but just above, next to, in among the boxes of candy, above, next to, in among the cookies, cans of milk, coffee cups, on a sideboard that is, in among, next to, over closed jars of honey, dirty soup spoons, *biscotti cannula,* or as Edit K. whispered to me, *it is so extraordinary* : small hands are : *biscotti* in Hungarian. A cozy voluptuous milieu for my writing hysteria, even over there, in the great beyond, because everywhere in this future housing of mine there will be pens pencils and sheets of paper waiting for me, so that in all heavenly haste I will be able to *scrape* something together, because everything will be the way it is here, I think, chalk and pens, pencils and knives, units of stored blood, pin cushions, clothes pins, scandal.

And everything is all worked in together like playing cards (shuffled), I say to Joseph, what do you think about that, the images of my past, the way I taste them, smell, see, hear : tones and color, agonies of voices, *fields in front of my eyes* reproducing themselves, my EYE'S FIELDS with lids closing and opening again, fields of forget-me-nots, violets, enzian . . traces of spilt drink on the plank floor, carpets, straw mats, spilt red blood, pools of red colored water, *prognoses of stuttering, whispering, swarms,* and I say to Joseph : in your writing so much intimate, substance, isn't that right, Joseph doesn't seem to want to understand what I am saying, he says THE CHILDREN'S PHONE : YOUR PERFECT (PICANTE) TACTIC OF ENCIRCLEMENT! isn't that right, all of it probably nothing but an infatuation with the phenomenon of letter writing, I ask Joseph, no matter whom the letters are directed to, *of course most of the letters are directed to lovers of a certain artificiality,* fountain blood which shoots up in great sprays into the treetop blue (of delights), soaring iridescent force which manifests itself as the page of a letter, tablet, sheet of paper in the machine (upper case / caisson), conjuring up a smile on my face, *a temple sleep,* which is not actually sleep but on the contrary represents extreme anticipation and attentiveness and the capacity to see through all things, or when you speak about the *book of moments,* then *I feel tongues flickering passionately inside me again, etc.,* while the rivulet of my chaps : catwalk of my tears : along my cheeks, seeping into creases and hollows, the corners of my mouth and chin, of my dripping head and into the neck of my shirt deeper the steps 2 stories deeper between my breasts, into the middle of my body, and growing more and more *menstrual* this congealing flow, the anger that is *tapestries of a decline,* or, as is often said : impetuousness (frenzy) in your breast, in your pupils the sighing gardens of exhaustion . .

in the weeks of midsummer on some kiosk or other an archaic Christmas card appeared, with deer and a garden of clichés, everything full of balls of snow, and sleds, and dusting of gold, and a banner reading MERRY CHRISTMAS, and then a half year later these spurious greetings launched on course to friends, strangely enough, I say to Blum, do you remember, and then I start talking to MYSELF in the second person, familiar, resurrection implausible, notes fleeting because I can't keep up with my note taking despite stenographic abbreviation, *despite small black boxer shorts, or paw,* and anchorings, when in the morning, writing down on my knees, some letter or other to friends, because mountain of papers not yet cleared off machine, so scribbling, and written glorious things, in all directions, acknowledging my friends with cursory tributes, greetings, affection, small mysteries, breathless confessions, etc., as if mother were on the ASCENT in an unimaginable RESURRECTION and continuing to speak, although I had long since left the room, was in the entry, but as if I were still sitting next to her, she kept on talking and talking, and I was not able to understand what she had said, maybe she hadn't noticed that I was no longer there, she kept speaking, even though no one was there to listen, it seemed that she simply wasn't aware, this morning the radio announcer, I say to Blum, early in the morning as if he were picking each syllable up off the floor with a delicate hand : *touch!,* like a *piece of sack cloth just ensnared* and holding it up in the air, DISGUSTING, its effect I mean, and I had to keep telling myself that *you are losing weight auspiciously,* I say to Blum, and in my head, I say, all the letters I've begun, letters never finished, letters never sent, a number of case studies on desolation, right, I say to Blum, thinking, that our arteries : our circulatory systems cannot take care of everything all at once, all at 1 time, and it is such a relief when 1 OBLIGATION or another is satisfied, but as we grow older it seems that we are more determined than ever to unburden ourselves of every 1 of our OBLIGATIONS actually, pay the ransom, I mean, until in the end there is nothing left but JUDGMENT DAY, and another metaphor : a small stream which finally frees itself of its banks and pours out into open waters, or the way reddish rivers flow into the sea, but it's like hemorrhaging, it is the end of an existence, it is an ecstasy of pain : the image of an infinite hemorrhaging over yourself while holding yourself in your arms, like Alma.

As far as Alma is concerned, Blum says, we don't know who Alma is, when she began, or even if she were ever a presence in your work or not, but there was a figure, from the very beginning, I say, whom I have forgotten whom I was mad about, that is, Alma, that is, with whom I have been exchanging texts and pictures since the 28th of July last year, now, since the book I am writing, still writing, have almost finished writing, I remember that I wrote letters to Alma, at irregular intervals, she wrote me picture letters and I answered her picture letters with text letters, and things went on this way, and although she was never mentioned in my work, she did play a significant role in it—so that all our correspondence might be / best be / summed up, on the other hand I would like to / prefer to / forgo it given the RUBBER BANDINGS of life with which we must be provided day in and day out, and given my DRAPERY EXISTENCE the legitimacy of which exists only from today until tomorrow, etc., and then my RUBBER HANDS, garishly yellow RUBBER HANDS are hanging around everywhere on lines and zippers, these my garishly yellow stray RUBBER HANDS, and in every niche, border, mutilations, to such an extent, that when I am forced to spend a whole day with someone, by evening I feel used up, gutted, exhausted : *like vinegar gardens.*

I mean the nature of this small nail brush, corsage, heart cherry, as far as the nature of the heart cherry, of *all* heart cherries is concerned, they first appeared to me, it first appeared to me downtrodden, cowering, covered, obscure, concealed in a brownish paper bag, later opened with a passionate stroke of the hand, torn open, *revealed,* on the table top, in the kitchen housings, and, *dropping* onto a stoneware plate, the entire contents of the bag out onto a stoneware plate, dropping into a stoneware bowl, etc., or emptied where in its purple color : color of cheeks, like *the hangings of an entire cherry tree,* etc., and then I paint the wing of a swallow onto my eye, I mean because these pearl strands, curtains of pearl strands : STUTTERING from 1 knuckle to another knuckle, the way you string them together, pearl on pearl, and they chatter, incessantly, while Alma haltingly passes her voice to me I mean like a bouquet of flowers, or something like that. Only then started working again, I say to Joseph, once the glaring light of this July day had softened, so that without being blinded I, at the machine, and not taking a bath for weeks, because always hung full of wet undershirts jackets slips, I say to Joseph, everything *afflicted* I mean everything impeded by these all-enveloping afflictions, forced as it were even in these assimilations, into ourselves the concerns, affairs, circumstances of others, virtual head visualizing, etc., or the nuts cracking in your last name, the teeth gnashing, oh dear Alma, the way I speak to you, hardly know you, teeth gnashing, Alma's nut cracking, and while I crush Alma's last name such a granite colored last name between my incisors and my molars / jaws, oh dear Alma, would like to tell you, no confess : that I intend to write *permanently provocative books,* forever, in all eternity, imagine that, *in all eternity and forever more!,* but on a scrap of paper in my bed, I mean some sort of angel raises a fluttering banner on which can be read : someone else wrote my books, not me! of course there is some truth to it!, maybe I should call the book I am still working on "A Woodland Rapture" or "Pilgrim / Flamingo in a crumbling, in a Wood by whirling specters defined : defiled" or "Convalescent's Repast and Sitting Schiwei Cheira Book Nagykaniza, 18th Century" or "with Quarter of Cemeteries. ." but, according to Libgart Schwarz, though nothing is happening it is exciting, and, according to Libgart Schwarz : the phenomenon is, you must THINK! THINK! when you THINK, according to Libgart Schwarz, it must be done with absolute precision in order to set up a *differential current,* etc.

Glued to the edge of my chair, my notebook on my knees, I contemplate : what does it mean to reach old age, to have reached—you live from year to year and have lived almost unconsciously, because everything always so perfectly natural and following its usual course, all you did was wake up, when from time to time in a sharp curve the CARRIAGE *hurled* us out of our equilibrium, right, and although the number of years lived alarming, we are, everything considered, much the same people we were 50 years ago, *but not quite!,* still we would like to keep right on going unswervingly, and keep right on going and not be TIED DOWN absolutely not.

In any case nothing but grand exploits, I say to Blum, cut my lips open so badly that I almost bleed to death, and am losing my eyes again because I am tired I mean, and they are falling out of my head, *a delusion,* right, *a garden of rogues,* : out with colored pens bunches of pendulous heads of poppy blossom, out of a three-cornered forest full of DARK ROSES, etc., in between 2 telephone calls I say to myself : LET'S NOT START PRODUCING ANYTHING AMORPHOUS HERE! oh—on Ara on Alma's shoulder, in the café, and echoed what she was saying, and Ara bit into my flesh when I attempted to pet her on the head, and bit right into my lower lip and I bled so much and was so afraid that I didn't know whether or not I had relieved myself, I see Alma and Ara before my eyes : opaque objects! I see Alma with a black net in her hair or is it the sunglasses she has pushed (set) back into her full head of hair the way young women often do : a slight gesture of smart (stylish) gallantry, isn't that right, but it worked so well with her COMPLEXION, etc.

And so charming, her Lady's Rubber Glove script on the envelope, like a convict I mean or a ridge (home range) presents itself, and prepares : in the summer with fragrant pine forest and gentle (calming) flowered carpets on its slopes so that the leathery sun and summer sandal too slid backwards in the ascent (scurrying) up a slippery forest floor covered with the needles of fir trees, on whose floor was a layer of old pine needles, etc., and me tipping forward : ANCHORING possibility of crawling along on hands and knees *as if like ants* up toward the escarpment and along the way always slipping back : backwards, while Alma is telling me about her latest trip to Rome and how Roman women are running around with *bare legs and fur coats,* in May and April, and drink slightly buffaloed milk and wearing fezzes and antlers or with decorated hats, *and the way the flowers glowed in the airplane,* straw flowers between newspaper pages and knees, a strand or a bird in the bushes, etc., but in the middle of June or July already signs of winter again, isn't that so, I say to Blum, *already half wintered in snowed in mid-June, July,* right, when the days so wet and cool that we imagine, oh the things we imagine, a descending glide over the sloping roofs of the city, emerging out of the brew of dark clouds, down, and equipped with winter gear, with roller skates, skis, silken roller skates, in the wet wailing storm, and soon jackets, undershirts and down, soon we'll be slipping back into our jackets, undershirts and down, the warm and cozy way Alma had painted them, and picture the quilts I had *chauffeured over* to Alma when 1 night she arrived at her flat without luggage and it was empty and cold, etc.

The silken lip, that is, swallow swallow up my own blood and ask myself in vain how it tastes, get a FILING CABINET from Alma and seems more of an annoyance than a gift, because of how cramped things are, get a FILING CABINET from Alma, I say to Blum, and instead of making me happy it upsets me, weighs me down, plunges me into despondency, into a quandary, as if a bird were hovering over its nest in fear while a vulture circles in the distance, *lame comparison!* or as Giordano Bruno writes : "In regard to the sympathy between a human being and a lion I will remain silent here, I will pass over what I know of the wonders of a relationship between a dragon and a boy . ."

Window thrown open, drapes shoved back, light caught in wide open arms, swift lured this way, swift flew in, wrote to Alma : whenever I eat from the soup bowl you decorated for me, on which a lioness, long and willowy, is sneaking up on me, I mean the watery portrait of a lioness on the prowl, I think, this time she's going to get me, and I'm not going to be able to get away, the collage fish on the oval plate with the *petri : parsley stem* in its wide open mouth has gotten terribly thin, nothing but bony whitish scaffolding, etc.

Oh this BEHEADING AND STUFFING I mean HYENAS SCREAMING *amidst the ringing of the moon's bells,* and downy air, and must be *touched* if I'm going to start writing, I mean if I haven't been *touched,* nothing will come of it! I say to Joseph, at least at the beginning, when I start writing I have to be *touched* the way we like to linger over a book stop at a tree a butterfly a cliff a spring, just like *some childhoods in the mountains,* and because of the trace of something RELATED : this is the way in which I have loved being with you, have loved all too much being with you, etc., *the one who sleeps late into the morning, Wednesday in the envelope,* footprints of avian past, I say to Joseph, tell me how TRANSPLANTED I already am, whatever that means, and green plants grew in the middle of a flaming oak forest, no they exploded on the edge of a southerly slope, and I thought, I cry : pollen : streaks painted on my glasses, I cry if they are actually tears in all darknesses, in all directions *crushed tears* : don't actually know if the tears being spilled by this figure are real, who can say, the tears cannot be stilled, a thousand tempests, I contemplate, I cry, how will I structure the end of the book I am still working on, what will I exclude, what will I lure my way, what will I encounter, how will I assemble the individual pieces, I say to Joseph, *the troll foot*: the shuffling foot, this bird of the great beyond, I say to Joseph, the way he's resting his feet on my bowed back, the white beast, its lingering eye (Breton), plucking my feathers : exhuming me out of my melancholy, etc., so orchestration of the melancholy which drives me to my machine in the early morning hours, the bird which descends on me every night in my dreams, etc., and mother dies every day every year, mother will keep dying, she dies every day every year at the same hour, *forever and crumpling all around herself* ("MAMA IS NO LONGER HERE / PAPA IS NO LONGER HERE / AND FOLD : PLI OR PLEATS, etc. . .")—

my heart is spinning : a windmill, the shielded protected eye, X (or William or Ferdinand) writes, and in the wilderness in one of his most recent letters he writes : "apparently I am afraid of the emptiness waiting for me when MY LAST LOVE is gone, and so I am taking on a lot of work, knowing that I won't be able to finish it, you write, this summer is fascinating, and do I know what one must do in order to *stay alive stay alive forever,* still what Horace said of himself also pertains to you :

> Not on wings exhausted and grown thin will I allow myself to be transported through the shimmering ethers, a singer in two forms and I will no longer remain on this earth and removed from envy

I will leave cities below me
(. .)
I, I will not die
and the stygic river will not have me.

(Shortly before falling asleep the word space : I, the shudder of my birth on the milk shovel . .)

as far as *the art of walking* is concerned, all in all, this life has left *no tracks,* in hindsight that is, a life in devastation misunderstanding a darkening of the soul, with *brain scraper* in constant operation, isn't that right, I say to Blum, how is it, e.g., that the bottle looked so large in the display window and so tiny when I picked it up in my hands? this and other Leverkusen wonders and woodlands have come to me on the wing, and while I dip into a steaming footbath, it is as if in the icy cold, a complexity, annihilation of the senses, that's how it seems, I mean a fluttering scattered LORD'S PRAYER, because trading under some other name, because bunched together in other language bundles—when for week upon week I am not able to work, helplessness and rage grown almost unbearable, I say to Blum, feeling of being on a streak of bad luck, broken tongue, forlorn, this celebrated passerby, I say to Blum, as if her hips were *anchored* in the haze of the streets, and then it occurred to me : "her croup moved itself gently through the crowds," etc., like FALLING SNOW in a store window, *but they were photographs,* just imagine, I say to Blum, while her *mug* and double eye . .
I mean here I am sitting in a broken chair, half cradled position, *table curls* coiling all around me, the illusory nature of our existence, a lament a defenselessness in the face of a world equipped with the sharpest of blades, keep sinking deeper and deeper into howls and sorrow, and completely *small souled or accompanied,* no this isn't linguistic conceit and it's not nonsensical (stammering) emotion, either, it is actually more like a given FINGERING, when I can effortlessly remember 9 or 10 dozen phone numbers, but English, I say to Blum, it's beginning to get me down, I say to Blum, over the past few years it seems to have become (German) vernacular, I'll have to think about it, be careful about what I use, one critic writes, I say

to Blum, and it makes me angry, I say to Blum, these *incessant images* are a problem for him, the author seems to jump from one image to another without really tying them together in any way, etc., for several days now *a feeling of insufficiency* in my consciousness I mean there is something unfinished, lacking in the corpus of this work, something is still bleeding, showing stigmata, still not completely healed. Everything has to be completely healed, only then does a text possess validity only then can it be considered finished, isn't that right. Today is a strange day, with a full trough under my work chair, my feet inside or out reddened by steaming hot water, stubs of thought scattered across the parquet, cookie crumbs, etc.

That we might plant a few more points in the COMMON MEADOW, this talk, imposition, idea from Alma, I say to Blum, really got me worked up, there was, I felt the beginning of a stumble in my innards, I staggered and reeled, sensed a clawing, cawing, stinging and scorn in my chest, something which got me angry and fascinated both, it immediately inspired me to *paint in* all the pictures in my mind, the way children do with cardboard patterns, that we might plant a few more points in the COMMON MEADOW, as Alma said, rosettes, arbors, garlands of flowers, enormous oak trees, birds meandering through the air, garden snakes beauties (chimpanzees), and she said we might add a few touches of color, it would transfigure the COMMON MEADOW, she said, my intestines and my heart were torn to shreds, I disappeared into an alley and vomited.

To stand on your own 2 feet, I say to Blum, the clay under your soles, what expectations I have, and of course there was something of a NARCOTIC in it, it was part calculation, I say to Blum, because I knew that K. would be here in a few hours to take pictures, so I left everything scattered around, on the floor, on tables and cabinets, meant to show off a little, with this Phoenix book original book, this jungle, to show off my jungle, I say to Blum, then later I say to K. "a photo in mirror-image is a counterfeit photo, think about that," tears and human being is our good fortune, Elisabeth von Samsonow writes, feelings are probably a luxury.

These are various kinds of *stimuli to investigation* communicating themselves to me, I say to Blum, we are sitting in the Tomaselli, Bizet caps on, I say to Blum, the rectangular clothing having gone slack, grown loose, columnar torso, I say, part of a sentence out of my awareness broken, entire sentence useless, fragrance of WELLA shampoo in the entryway, plump passerby stops in, spreading her arms, calls through the open window on the ground floor, where head appears : "real CARMINA weather we're having today, CHARISMA weather . . "

so I listened to organ music for hour after hour without knowing who the composer was : without wanting to know, always my masked eyes in every life situation, and therefore closed, when I was asked for information about everyday occurrences, while the stuffed stockings, I say to Blum, these stockings stuffed *with my infatuated feet* wrapped themselves up in seating spaces and bed, the rags in my ear produced a *damned* sensation of fainting : a SWALLOW ORIENTATION, that is, and I ask myself what it means what it can possibly mean, this flood of images from an inner world, an outer world, and how they, the images, are marching into my consciousness into this my gasping consciousness, which no longer seems able to free itself of so much profound hurt / wondrous ROSA FLORIBUNDA, while HUNTING CLOTHES, I say to Blum, my mind feasts its eyes on Joseph's HUNTING CLOTHES again and again, because the separation process is not yet complete / thwarted by painful relapses on my part the moment we accidentally cross paths again . .

as far as the Bizet cap is concerned, we are sitting with one such cap in the Tomaselli, I write to Joseph, already started with letters to him again (which he never answers), I write to him : first impulse to call you to thank you for letter and page with PRINCE OF WALES; BORN INTO MODEST CIRCUMSTANCES triggering trembles. Get drunk, breathe Tipp-Ex, inhale seductive CD music, I write to Joseph, think about this detached hand : BORN INTO HUMBLE CIRCUMSTANCES (Alexander Kluge), have a torrent of thought and in this way glittering down the entire river.

My *borderless* friends encourage me in this, I say to Blum, to try IT again, to DIRECT the contents of my dreams, that is, the way I always did when I was a child, back then I could conjure up whatever I wanted, my subconscious followed my instructions, scribble full gray pages that appeared to me, but I would like to have been able to figure out what was going on with ABRAHAM AND ARIES, and RENO IN A HOUSECOAT. Oh, all the time this bawling : bellowing, I say to Blum, the WAY we keep hoping it will continue! it must continue! : if we only sit at the machine long enough, something will have to come of this wretched hiccup of words sentences sequences and intellectual figure skating, the penetration I mean into the small gap that each word represents. Because, I ask myself, how else are we to transform undefined (unsituated) emotions if not into language, we can't just go *head raging : raging around* without steering this passion of ours into conclusive ENORMOUS pathways, but it apparently has something to do with grottoness, I say to Blum, our whole existence just one single grottoness, grievous dejection, an orange blossom in Alma's hair,

everything in this famous wet and soggy balance, I say to Blum, everything is this enchanting hauntingly lilac color, right, and then the way the hand suddenly appeared and crawled along in front of the open window : mother's hand, and me, half naked, nothing but notes and commentary on the edge of the day, only my legs covered, everything else naked : in a broken white, etc. Today found entire baskets boxes with material for the end of this work, I write to Joseph, always carrying your letters around with me, through any number of seasons, and the double cap in my field pack, along with the *woolen sirens* climbed into the footbath, bordeaux red here books lying scattered around as if on exhibit, like mock-ups of books, they will never be read, because there are too many of them, maybe I'm only trying to prove to myself that I still belong to that small number of people who hold on to books, persist, right, without reading them all, in any case not from beginning to end, every single book a guarantor that we are still alive, that we are still writing, that we are still reading.
I got something out of this : delicate subject, I say to Blum, I want to report to you, I GOT SOMETHING OUT OF THIS : she whom I do not know, to see her crouching down in this degrading position lower parts split, head raised to the stateroom door, which was not locked, deeply shocked that I had surprised her. Not because I am in the habit of amusing myself with things of this genre but because like almost no other it seemed to me to reflect a straightforward and genuine expression (shorthand) of the human profession as animal—exquisitely that is the more minor nuances of woman's nature, etc.
THE FEMININE THE VIOLET . . reading faces everywhere, pairs of eyes, in the walls, on a dirty floor, in scraps of paper, in the torn wallpaper, in a crumpled paper napkin, everything so emblematic, I say to Blum, everything so imminently close to madness, everything in sighs, I say to Blum, on the street corner the rumor monger, for example, chasing off the first leaves of autumn fluttering down in front of his feet as if he were chasing off a swarm of flies. Absurd, I say, that we are not able to SEE what constitutes a glow from the great beyond, threadlike handwriting of Nikolaus B. in today's mail, hinting at something like this, some sort of mystery which cannot be solved. At 4 o'clock in the morning the growl of a motor that refuses to start, my heart goes wild, Dürer's bouquet of violets, suddenly SWALLOWED THE FRILLS of an actress's dress, see her right before my eyes on the silver screen : wrapped in *foaming* robes, all in pink, but I have no idea which FILM STAR it might have been : extremely overacted, some kind of curly blond head, only this one scene (Spree) of

the play with neither beginning nor end, and every morning the feeling I have finally reached the end of this work, not able to add anything more, should not, but not able to leave this ROUTINE, always going back to this raging place, not being able to let go, have to add words, paragraphs, closing sequences again and again, somewhat like the obsessive need to return to a beloved person from whom you have parted so many times before, and then being inconsolable when you find that it really is over (*of an electrical nature, etc.*).

Memory is a sin—no not burden : sin, says Blum, BWV 1043 : what a horrible transgression, I say to Blum, the Swingle Singers, in the morning, infuriates me, sit trembling at the breakfast table, my bundled nerves, am going to throw up.

People *want* what's popular, Blum says, they *want* to hear AIDA in the amphitheater in Verona, they *want* AIDA, and only AIDA!

Debussy and Mussorgsky are lying up against each other, I say, I am in a good mood again, forget to tear open the package that came in the mail, so many presents, where is this all going to lead. Elisabeth von Samsonow writes, she wishes me an alphabet delirium, a state of illumination, that is, : the coming of white light . .

("The two of you said something about a dog or did the cat bite you—I am starting to confuse everything," I write to Alma, "the sick old Dalmatian and he's going to die, the two of you phoned and told me or was it Fanny and Herbert in a letter, and the cat clawed or bit because you so clumsy putting it into the basket when you moved, isn't that right . .")

(And winding its way out from under the blanket the blue undershirt, the apparent multiplication of blue lilac pelts, at the foot of the bed, with long meandering arms, ribbed structure, and soaking wet), then read several final chapters in my favorite books in order to transplant them into mine, a hysteria, I say to Blum, parroted stuff, *Bashō above all* (Odem).

Because if you are not mad, rabid, nothing will work, a rabid dog if you want to write, right, I yell to Blum, tearful tumult, terrible frenzy, yes, and that is probably everything, this is probably the end, because you see, as Paul Valéry says, a true writer is a person who cannot find his words.

Avant-Garde & Modernism Studies

General Editors
Marjorie Perloff
Rainer Rumold

Consulting Editors
Peter Fenves
Stephen Foster
Christine Froula
Françoise Lionnet
Robert von Hallberg

Avant-Garde & Modernism Collection

General Editors
Rainer Rumold
Marjorie Perloff